THE SPIRIT RING

LOIS McMASTER BUJOLD

BAEN

THE SPIRIT RING

A Baen Books Original

Baen Publishing Enterprises
P.O. Box 1403
Riverdale, NY 10471
www.baen.com

ISBN: 0-671-57870-7

Cover art by Bob Eggleton

First paperback printing, October 1993
Third printing, May 2000

Distributed by Simon & Schuster
1230 Avenue of the Americas
New York, NY 10020

Library of Congress Catalog Number: 92-21733

Printed in the United States of America

FOR JIM AND TRUDIE

Chapter One

Fiametta turned the lump of warm reddish clay in her hand. "Do you think it's done yet, Papa?" she asked anxiously. "Can I break it open now?"

Her father closed his hand over hers, testing the heat. "Not yet. Set it down, it won't cool the faster for being juggled."

She sighed impatiently, and laid the clay ball back down on the workbench in the patch of morning sunlight falling through the window's iron grille. "Can't you put a cooling spell on it?"

He chuckled. "I'll put a cooling spell on you, girl. You have too much of the element of fire in you. Even your mother used to say so." Reflexively, Master Beneforte crossed himself and bowed his head, when naming the dead. The laugh faded a little in his eyes. "Don't burn so fast. It's the banked coals that last the night."

"But you stumble in their dark," Fiametta parried.

1

"What burns fast, burns bright." She leaned her elbows on the bench and scuffed her slipper across the floor tiles, and regarded her work. Clay, with a golden heart. In his Sunday sermons, Bishop Monreale often said Man was clay. She felt a melting sense of union with the object on the table, brown and lumpy on the outside—she sighed again—but full of secret promise, if only it could be broken open.

"Maybe it's marred," she said nervously. "An air pocket ... dirt...." Could he not sense it? A pure, high hum, like a tiny heartbeat?

"Then you can melt it down and do it over till you get it right," her father shrugged. "It will be your own fault, and just what you deserve, for rushing ahead and pouring before I came to watch you. The metal will not be lost, or it shouldn't be—I'll beat you like a real apprentice if you manage such an apprentice's trick as that." He frowned ferociously but, Fiametta sensed, not altogether seriously.

It wasn't the metal she was worried about losing. But she had no intention of confiding her secret, and risking disapproval or derision. When she'd heard her father's step in the hallway she had hastily rubbed away the chalk diagram with spit and her sleeve, and swept the recipe sheet, carefully copied in her best hand, and the set of symbolic objects—salt, dried flowers, a bit of unworked gold, wheat seeds—from the workbench. The apron into which she'd bundled them sat on the end of the table looking dreadfully conspicuous. Papa had, after all, only given her permission to cast *gold*. She hitched her hip over a tall stool, rubbed at the leather apron over her gray wool outer dress, and sniffed at the chill spring air slipping through the workroom's unglazed window. *But it worked! My first investment worked. Or at least ... it didn't back-blow.*

A pounding penetrated from the house's heavy oak outer door, and a man's voice. "Master Beneforte!

Hallo the house! Prospero Beneforte, are you awake in there?"

Fiametta scrambled up to the table, to mash her face against the grille and try to see around the corner of the window frame into the street. "Two men—it's the Duke's steward, Messer Quistelli, Papa. And," she brightened, "the Swiss captain."

"Ha!" Master Beneforte hastily pulled off his own leather apron, and straightened the skirts of his tunic. "Perhaps he brings my bronze, at last! It's about time. Has no one unbarred the door this morning?" He stuck his head through the workroom's other window, that opened onto his house's inner court, and bellowed, "Teseo! Unbar the door!" His graying beard pointed, left and right. "Where is the useless boy? Run and unbar the door, Fiametta. Tuck your hair under your cap first, you're all awry like a washerwoman."

Fiametta hopped down, untied the strings of her plain white linen cap, and with her fingers pushed and combed back strands of her crinkly black hair, which had escaped unnoticed in her absorption with her morning's work. She tightened her cap smoothly over her head again, though in the back a wild cushion of ringlets defied order, cascading over her nape and a third of the way to her waist. She now wished she'd taken the time to braid it at dawn, before racing off to lay the fire in the little cupellation furnace in the corner of the workroom before Papa woke and came down. Better still if she'd put on the real lace cap from Bruges, that Papa had given her last spring for her fifteenth birthday.

The pounding resumed. "Hallo the house!"

Fiametta danced into the stone-paved hallway and slid back the bar of the main door, opened it, and swept a curtsey. "Good morning, Messer Quistelli." And, a breath more shyly, "Captain Ochs."

"Ah, Fiametta." Messer Quistelli gave her a nod. "I'm here to see the Master."

Messer Quistelli wore long dark robes, like a scholar. The guardsman, Uri Ochs, wore the Duke's livery, a short black tunic with sleeves striped red and gold, and black hose. He bore no metal breastplate nor pike nor helmet this peaceful morning, only the sword at his hip and a black velvet cap with the Duke of Montefoglia's badge on it, perched on his brown hair. The flower-and-bee badge was Master Beneforte's own work, copper-gilt, appearing solid gold, keeping the secret of the captain's relative poverty. The Swiss sent half his pay home to his mother, Master Beneforte had whispered, shaking his head, whether in admiration for this filial piety or dismay at his financial fecklessness, Fiametta had not been sure. Captain Ochs's legs filled his hose neatly, though, no sad drooping bags to them like the leggings of skinny young apprentices or dried old men.

"From the Duke?" Fiametta asked hopefully. The leather purse hanging at Messer Quistelli's waist next to his glasses bulged in a most promising manner. But then, the Duke was always promising, Papa said. Fiametta ushered the men inside and led them into the front workroom, where Master Beneforte advanced on them, rubbing his hands in greeting.

"Good morning, gentlemen! I trust you bring good news about the bronze Duke Sandrino promised me for my great work? Sixteen pigs of copper, mind you, no less. Are the arrangements made yet?"

Messer Quistelli shrugged against this importunity. "Not yet. Though I'm sure by the time you're ready, Master, so will the metal be." His raised brow had a faint ironic tilt, and Master Beneforte frowned. Her father had a nose like a hunting dog for the faintest slight or insult; Fiametta held her breath. But Messer Quistelli went on, touching the purse at his belt. "I do bring you my lord's allowance for your wood and wax and workmen."

"Even I am not so great a conjurer as to be able to make bronze from wax and wood," growled Master Beneforte. But he reached for the purse anyway.

Messer Quistelli turned slightly away. "Your skill is unquestioned, Master. It is your speed my lord has come to doubt. Perhaps you try to take on too many commissions, to the detriment of all?"

"I must use my time efficiently, if my household is to eat," Master Beneforte said stiffly. "If my lord Duke wishes his wife to stop ordering jewelry, he should take it up with her, not me."

"About that saltcellar," said Messer Quistelli firmly.

"I have pressed it forward with incessant industry. As I have said."

"Yes, but is it finished?"

"It lacks only the enamelling."

"And, perhaps, the functionary spells?" Messer Quistelli suggested. "Have you laid them on yet?"

"*Not* laid on," said Master Beneforte in a tone of injured dignity. "This is no hedge-magician's spell of seeming your lord requires of me. The spell is integral, built-in, worked along with each stroke of my chisel."

"Duke Sandrino requires me to observe its progress," said Messer Quistelli a shade more diffidently. "The news is not general yet, but I am to tell you in confidence, his daughter's betrothal is being negotiated. He wants to be sure the saltcellar is finished in time for the betrothal banquet."

"Ah." Master Beneforte's face lightened. "A worthy debut for my art. When is it planned?"

"The end of this month."

"So soon! And who is the fortunate bridegroom to be?"

"Uberto Ferrante, Lord of Losimo."

There was a distinct pause. "I see my lord Duke's urgency," said Master Beneforte.

Messer Quistelli made a hands-down gesture, blocking further comment.

"Fiametta." Master Beneforte turned to her, taking a ring of keys from his girdle. "Run and fetch the golden saltcellar from the chest in my room. Mind you lock both chest and door again behind you."

Fiametta took the keys and exited at a ladylike walk, no childish skipping under the eyes of the Swiss captain, until she reached the stairs in the courtyard to the upper gallery, which she took two at a time.

The big iron-bound chest at the foot of her father's bed contained a dozen leather-bound books, several stacks of notes and papers tied with ribbons—anxiously, she tried to remember if she had indeed replaced them last time identically to their previous arrangement—and a polished walnut box. The chest was redolent with the aromas of paper, leather, ink, and magic. She lifted out the heavy box and relocked both chest and room with the complex filigreed iron keys. She could feel the spells of warding slide into place along with the bolts, a tiny jolt up the nerves of her hand. Most potent, to be sensed at all, given Papa's incessant drive for subtlety in his art. She returned to the downstairs workroom. Her light leather slippers padded almost silently across the flagstones as she approached. A chance word in the captain's voice caught her ear; she stiffened and listened outside the workroom door.

"—your daughter's mother Moorish, then, or Blackamoor?"

"Ethiope, surely," Messer Quistelli opined. "Was she a slave of yours?"

"No, she was a Christian woman," replied Fiametta's father. "From Brindisi." There was a certain dryness in his voice, whether with respect to Christian women or Brindisi Fiametta could not tell.

"She must have been very beautiful," said the Swiss politely.

"That she was. And I was not always so dried up and battered as you see me today, either, before my nose was broken and my hair grew gray."

Captain Ochs made an apologetic noise, implying no slur intended on his host's face. Messer Quistelli, also aging, laughed appreciatively.

"Has she inherited your talent in your art, Master Beneforte, while avoiding your nose?" asked Messer Quistelli.

"She's certainly better than that ham-handed apprentice of mine, who's fit only for hauling wood. Her drawings and models are very fine. I don't tell her so, of course; there's nothing more obnoxious than a proud woman. I have let her work in silver, and I've just started letting her work in gold."

Messer Quistelli vented a suitably impressed *Hmm.* "But I was thinking of your *other* art."

"Ah." Master Beneforte's voice slid away without actually anwering the question. "It's a great waste, to train a daughter, who will only take your efforts and secrets off to some other man when she marries. Although if certain noble parties remain in arrears on the payments an artist of my stature is properly owed, her knowledge may be the only dowry I can afford her." He heaved a large and pointed sigh in Messer Quistelli's direction. "Did I ever tell you about the time the Pope was so overwhelmed by the beautiful gold medallion I crafted for his cope, he doubled my pay?"

"Yes, several times," said Messer Quistelli quickly, to no avail.

"He was going to make me Master of the Mint, too, till my enemies' whispers got up that false charge of necromancy against me, and I rotted in the dungeons of Castel Sain' Angelo for a year—"

Fiametta had heard that one too. She backed up a few paces, shuffled her slippers noisily on the tiles, and entered the workroom. She set the walnut box carefully before her father, and handed him back his keys. He smiled, and rubbed his hands on his tunic, and with a word under his breath unlocked and opened the box. He folded back the silk wrappings, lifted the object within, and set it in the middle of the grid of sunlight falling on the table.

The golden saltcellar blazed and sparked in the light, and both visitors caught their breaths. The sculpture rested on an oval base of ebony, richly decorated. Upon it two palm-high golden figures, a beautiful nude woman and a strong bearded man holding a triton, sat with their legs interlaced. "As we see in firths and promontories." Master Beneforte enthusiastically explained the symbolism. A ship—Fiametta thought it more of a rowboat—of delicate workmanship near the hand of the sea-king was to hold the salt; a little Greek temple beneath the earth-queen's gracefully draped hand was meant for the pepper. Around the man sea horses, fish, and strange crustaceans sported; around the woman, a happy riot of beautiful creatures of the earth.

The Swiss captain's mouth hung open, and Messer Quistelli pulled the spectacles from his belt, balanced them on his nose, and peered hungrily at the fine work. Master Beneforte swelled visibly, pointing out meaningful details and enjoying the men's astonishment.

Messer Quistelli recovered first. "But does it *work*?" he demanded doggedly.

Master Beneforte snapped his finger. "Fiametta! Fetch me two wineglasses, a bottle of wine—the sour wine Ruberta uses for cooking, not the good Chianti—

and that white powder she uses to destroy rats in the pantry. Quickly now!"

Fiametta scampered, glowing with her secret. *I designed the dolphins. And the little rabbits, too.* Behind her she could hear Master Beneforte bellowing again for Teseo the apprentice. She flung across the courtyard and into the kitchen, meeting Ruberta's protests at her flurry with a breathless "Papa wants!"

"Yes, girl, but I wager he'll want his dinner as well, and the fire's gone out in the stove." Ruberta pointed with her wooden spoon at the blue-tiled firebox.

"Oh, is that all?" Fiametta bent over, unlatched the iron door, and turned her face to look inside the dark square. She ordered her thoughts to an instant of calm. "*Piro,*" she breathed. Brilliant blue and yellow flames flared up like dancers on the dead coals. "That should do it." She tasted the heat of the spell on her tongue with satisfaction. At least she could do one thing well. Even Papa said so. And if one, why not another?

"Thank you, dear," said Ruberta, turning to fetch her iron pot. By the aromatic evidence on the cutting board she was about to do splendid things with onions, garlic, rosemary, and spring lamb.

"You're welcome." Quickly, Fiametta assembled the items needed for the demonstration upon a tray, including the last two clear Venetian wineglasses from the set the carters had broken in their move here to Montefoglia, almost five years ago. Papa had forgotten to mention the salt or the pepper; she snatched their jars from the high shelf and added them to the array as well, and marched it all to the workroom, her back straight.

Smiling to himself, Master Beneforte tapped a little salt into the bowl-hull of the ship. For a moment, his face took on an inward look; he whispered under his breath and crossed himself. Fiametta touched Messer Quistelli's arm as he started to speak, to keep him from interrupting what she knew to be a critical step. The hum from the saltcellar that answered Master Beneforte's whisper was deep and rich, but very, very faint, musical and fine. A year or so ago she could not have sensed it at all; Messer Quistelli clearly did not.

"The pepper, Papa?" Fiametta offered it.

"We shall not use the pepper today." He shook his head. He then placed a generous spoonful of the rat powder into one of the wineglasses, and tied a string around its stem to mark it. Then he poured the wine into both glasses. The powder dissolved slowly, with a faint fizz.

"Where *is* the boy?" Master Beneforte muttered after a few more minutes of waiting. Fortunately, before his master could work up to true irritation, Teseo slammed through the front door and appeared in the workroom, his cap askew on his head and one hose sagging with points half-tied, and a towel bundled in his nervous hands.

"I could only catch one in the midden, Master," Teseo apologized. "The other bit me and ran off."

"Huh! Perhaps I'll use you for a substitute, then." Master Beneforte frowned. Teseo paled.

He took up the towel, which proved to imprison a large and wild-looking rat, its teeth yellow and broken and its fur mangy. Teseo sucked on his bleeding thumb. The rat snapped, hissed, writhed, and squeaked. Holding the beast firmly by the scruff of its neck, Master Beneforte took a fine glass tube, drew up some now-chalky-pink wine from the glass with the string, and forced the liquid down the rat's throat. After another moment he released the animal onto the tiles. It snapped again, started to run, and began whirling in circles, biting at its sides. Then it convulsed and died.

"Now observe, gentlemen," Master Beneforte said. His two guests leaned closer as he took a sprinkle of salt between his fingers and dropped it into the plain wineglass. Nothing happened. He took a second, more generous pinch, and dropped it into the poisoned wine. The salt flared, grains sparkling orange; a blue flame, like ignited brandy, breathed up from the surface of the liquid and burned for fully a minute. Master Beneforte stirred the mixture slowly with the pipette. The contents were now as clear and ruby-bright as the other. He lifted the stringed glass. "Now . . ." his eye fell on Teseo, who squeaked rather like the rat, and apprehensively stepped back. "Ha. Unworthy boy," Master Beneforte said scornfully. He glanced at Fiametta, and a strange inspired smile curved his lips. "Fiametta. Drink this."

Messer Quistelli drew in his breath with a gasp, and the captain clenched his hand in shocked protest, but Fiametta straightened, gave them a proud and confident smile, and took the wineglass from her father's hand. She raised it to her lips and quaffed it all down in a single draught. Captain Ochs started up again as she grimaced, and just the faintest alarm flared for a moment in Master Beneforte's eyes, but she raised a hand in reassurance. "Salty sour wine." She scraped her tongue over her teeth, and smothered a small belch. "For breakfast."

Master Beneforte smiled triumph at the Duke's steward. "Does it work? Apparently so. And so you may bear witness to your lord."

Messer Quistelli clapped his hands. "Wonderful!" Though his eyes shifted now and then to recheck Fiametta.

Regretfully, Fiametta stifled a malicious urge to clutch her belly, drop to the floor, and scream. The fleeting opportunity might be beautiful, but Master Beneforte's sense of humor did not extend to jokes played upon himself, nor did his respect for revenge include justice for insults he laid upon others. *It's a great waste, to train a daughter. . . .* Fiametta sighed.

Messer Quistelli touched the beautiful goldwork. "And how long will it last?"

"The saltcellar, forever, for that is the incorruptible nature of gold. The spell of purification—perhaps twenty years, if the piece is undamaged, and it is not used without need. The prayer of activation will be engraved upon the bottom, for I fully expect it to outlast me."

Messer Quistelli raised impressed brows. "That long!"

"I give full value in my work," said Master Beneforte.

Taking the hint, Messer Quistelli counted out the Duke's monthly allowance onto the workbench, and Fiametta was sent again to lock both the saltcellar and the purse away in the strong chest.

When she returned, Messer Quistelli had gone, but Captain Ochs lingered with her father, as he often did. "Come, Uri, into the courtyard," Master Beneforte was saying, "and see your martial twin before I clothe him in his clay tunic. I finished laying on the wax but two days ago. The clay has been seasoning for months."

"Finished! I'd no idea you were so far along," said Captain Ochs. "Will you invite the Duke to inspect this new soldier of his, then?"

Master Beneforte smiled sourly, and held one finger to his lips. "I wouldn't even be telling you, if I didn't want to check a few last details. I mean to mold and cast it in secret, and surprise my impatient Lord of Montefoglia with the finished bronze. Let my enemies dare try to insult my diligence then!"

"You *have* been at this for over three years," said Uri doubtfully. "Still, 'tis always better to promise less, and do more, than the other way around."

"Aye." Master Beneforte led the younger man into the open courtyard. The pavement was still in morning shadow, though a line of light was almost visibly creeping down the wall as the sun rode higher. Fiametta tagged along very quietly, lest by drawing her father's attention she win an unwelcome chore that would send her out of earshot.

Beneath a canvas canopy a lumpy linen-shrouded figure stood, a man-and-a-half high, ghostly in the grayness. Master Beneforte stood on a stool, and carefully unwound the protective wrappings. A man's strong hand, raised high, emerged first, holding a fantastical snake-haired severed head grimacing in a death mask. Then the calm, heroic face beneath a winged helmet, then the rest of the figure's smooth nude shape. Its right hand held a fine curving sword. The supple muscles seemed to hold the whole body poised, live as a spring, beneath the grisly trophy brandished in triumph. Its translucent surface was all made of golden-brown wax, exhaling the faintest aroma of honey.

"Truly," breathed Uri, moving closer, "it's magical, Master Prospero! He almost seems ready to step off his plinth. Better even than the plaster model!"

Master Beneforte smiled, pleased. "No magic to it, boy. This is pure art. When this is cast, it will glorify my name forever. Prospero Beneforte, Master Sculptor. Those ignorant fools who call me a mere goldsmith and tinker will be utterly routed and confounded the day this is unveiled in the square. 'The Duke's Decorator,' hah!"

Uri stared, fascinated, into the hero's wax face. "Do I really look like that? I fear you flatter me exceedingly, Master Beneforte."

Master Beneforte shrugged. "The face is idealized. Perseus was a Greek, not a Swiss, nor pocked like a cheese. It was your body that was so invaluable to me as a model. Well-knit, strong without that lumpiness that some strong men have."

Uri mimed a shiver. "Glorious or no, you won't again talk me into modeling naked in the winter while you sit swaddled in fur."

"I kept the brazier full of coals. I thought you mountain goats were impervious to cold."

"When we can move around. Our winters keep us hard-working. It was the standing still, all twisted up like a rope, that did me in. I had a head cold for a month, after."

Master Beneforte waved a dismissive hand. "It was worth it. Now, while I have you here, take off your right boot. I have a little worry about this statue's foot. When the statue is cast, I must force the metal down nearly five cubits. The heads will do famously, for fire ascends. But he is to be Perseus, not Achilles, eh?"

The Swiss captain dutifully removed his boot, and wriggled his toes for the sculptor's inspection. Master Beneforte compared flesh and wax, and at last grunted satisfaction. "Well, I shall be able to mend what is lacking, if need be."

"You can see the very veins of this waxy fellow's flesh," said Uri, leaning close. "I'm almost surprised you didn't put in my hangnails and calluses, he's so lively. Will it come out of the clay so fine like that, in bronze? The flesh is so delicate." He hopped, pulling his boot back on.

"Ha! Of that, I can give you an immediate demonstration. We have just cast a fine little conceit in gold—I'll knock off the clay before your eyes, and you can see for yourself if my statue's hangnails will survive."

"Oh, Papa," Fiametta interrupted urgently, "can I undo it myself? I did all the other steps by myself." Surely he must sense her new-cast spell, if he handled it so fresh.

"What, you're still moping around? Have you no chores? Or were you just hoping for another glance at a naked man?" Master Beneforte jerked his chin toward his waxen Perseus.

"You're going to put it in the town square, Papa. All the maidens will see it." Fiametta defended herself. Had he caught her peeking, at those modeling sessions?

The live Perseus, Uri, looked like this was a new and unsettling thought. He glanced again at the statue, as if inspired to ask for a bronze loincloth.

"Well," Master Beneforte chuckled indulgently at her flusterment, "you're a brave good girl, Fiametta, and deserve some reward for drinking sour wine for breakfast to confound that doubter Quistelli for me. Come along." He herded them both back toward the front workroom. "You'll see, Captain. The lost wax process is so easy, a child can do it."

"I'm not a child any more, Papa," Fiametta put in.

His smile went bland. "So it would seem."

The clay lump lay on the worktable where she'd left it. Fiametta gathered up the tiniest chisels from the rack on the wall, held the ball in her hands for a moment, and recited an inward prayer. The spell's inaudible hum became almost a silent purr. Her father and the captain leaned on their elbows to either side and watched. She chinked away with the chisel, and clay flew off in chips. Gold gleamed from its matrix.

"Ah! 'Tis a ring," said Uri, leaning closer. Fiametta smiled at him.

"A little lion mask," the captain went on, interested, as her fingers worked a needle to clean away the last of the clay. "Oh! Look at the tiny teeth! How he roars!" He laughed.

"The teeth are meant to hold a ruby," Fiametta explained.

"Garnet," Master Beneforte corrected.

"A ruby would be brighter."

"And more costly."

"It would look well on a lord's hand, I'd think," said Uri. "You could recover the price of a ruby."

"It's to be my own ring," said Fiametta.

"Oh? Surely it's sized for a man, maiden."

"A thumb ring," Fiametta explained.

"A design that's cost me twice the gold of a finger ring," Master Beneforte put in. "I shall hedge my promises more carefully, next time."

"And is it a magic ring, Madonna?"

Master Beneforte stroked his beard, and answered for her. "No."

Fiametta glanced up at him, from under the protective fringe of her eyelashes. He neither smiled nor frowned, yet she sensed a sharp observance beneath his bland demeanor. She jerked around, put the ring in the captain's palm, and held her breath.

He turned it over, stroking the tiny waves of the lion's mane with one finger. He did not attempt to slide it on. A puzzled look came into his eyes.

"You know, Master Beneforte, how bitterly you have complained of your lazy and clumsy workmen? A thought just came to me—how if I write to my brother Thur in Bruinwald? He's only seventeen, but he's worked all sorts of jobs at the mines and forges there since he was a boy. He's very quick, and he's assisted Master Kunz at the furnace. It wouldn't be like breaking in a young and ignorant apprentice. He already knows much of metal, particularly copper. And he must be much bigger and stronger now than when I last saw him. Just what you need for your Perseus Gloriosus."

"Do you write your brother often?" asked Master Beneforte, watching him turn the ring in his hand.

"No . . . heavens! I haven't been home for four years. A miner's life is hard and spare. The memory of those dark close tunnels gives me the shivering fits even yet. I've twice offered to get Thur a position in the Duke's guard, but he says he's loathe to be a soldier. I say he doesn't know what's good for him. But if the Duke's glory in arms won't lure him out of that hole in the ground, perhaps your glory in the arts might." His hand closed again around the ring; he handed it back to Fiametta, and rubbed absently at his palm.

"Worked at copper smelting, has he?" said Master Beneforte. "Well. Yes. Do write him. Let's see what happens."

The captain smiled. "I'll go and do it now." He made a pretty leg of a bow to Fiametta, bade Master Beneforte good morning, and hurried out.

Fiametta sat down on the stool, the ring in her hands, and heaved a huge sigh of disappointment. "You're right, Papa. It's useless. I just can't do magic."

"You think not?" said Master Beneforte mildly.

"The spell didn't work! I put my heart and soul into it, and nothing happened! He didn't even put the ring on for a moment." She looked up, realizing she'd just given away her secret, but Master Beneforte looked more thoughtful than angry. "I didn't exactly disobey, Papa. You didn't tell me I mustn't try to work magic in the ring."

"You didn't ask," he said shortly. "You know very well I've never encouraged you. Metal magic is too dangerous for a woman to work. Or so I've always thought. Now I begin to wonder if it might be more dangerous to leave you untrained."

"I was very careful to use nothing but holy spells in the ring, Papa!"

"Yes, I know—do you think you are transparent, Fiametta?" he added at her unsettled look. "I am a master, child. Even another master could not use my books and tools without my knowing it."

She slumped. "But my magic failed."

He took up the ring and turned it in the light. "I

should beat you for your slyness and sneaking. . . ." He flipped open the folded apron on the end of the bench, examined its contents, and pursed his lips. "You used the true-love spell of the Master of Cluny, right?"

She nodded miserably.

"That spell does not create true love, child. That would be a contradiction in terms, for magically compelled feelings are not true. It only reveals true love."

"Oh."

"Your ring may have worked, though the Master of Cluny's magic is no exercise for an apprentice. It truly revealed that the handsome, if pock-marked, Captain Ochs is not your true love."

"But . . . I like him. He's kind, and courteous. A gentleman, not like the usual rough soldiers."

"He's simply the first man you've seen, or at any rate, noticed. And you have certainly seem all of him."

"Well, that's not my fault," she said grumpily.

"It's all your giggling girlfriends, who've inspired you to this unbecoming forwardness."

"I'll be sixteen in a few weeks, Papa. You know my gossip Maddalena was betrothed last month. She's already getting fitted in her wedding clothes. And here, the news this morning—the Duke's daughter Julia is only twelve!"

"*That* is pure politics," said Master Beneforte. "And of an odor not of roses, at that. See you hold your tongue on that news, or I'll know where the rumor came from. Lord Ferrante of Losimo is fully thirty-five, and has a dubious reputation. His second wife was not yet sixteen—the same age as you, and think on that!—when she died in childbirth not two months ago. I shouldn't think you'd find her fate so attractive as all that."

"No, of course not! And yet . . . all of a sudden, everyone seems to be getting married. Except me. All the good men will be taken, and you'll sit on me till

I'm old and fat, just to keep me handy for your spells. 'Bleed you a little into this new greenwood bowl, love, just a drop'—till *I* drop. Virgin's blood. Virgin's hair. Virgin's spit. Virgin's piss. Some days I feel like a magic cow."

"Your metaphor is terribly scrambled, Fia-mia."

"You know what I mean! And then you'll betroth me to some old rooster with skinny legs and a head as bald as an egg."

Master Beneforte suppressed a grin. "Well, rich widows don't lead so bad a life."

"Ha! It's not funny, Papa." She paused, and said more lowly, "Unless you've tried already, and found none to take me because I am too black-complexioned. Or too poor-dowered."

"No daughter of mine shall be called poor-dowered," he snapped back, stung enough to finally drop his irritating air of amusement. He composed himself again, and added, "Bank your burning soul in patience, Fiametta, until my great Perseus is cast, and the Duke rewards me as I deserve. And it won't be some poor soldier I'll buy you for a husband, either. Your chattering girlfriends' jaws will stop—most unaccustomedly—and hang open with envy at the wedding procession of Prospero Beneforte's daughter!" He handed her back her ring. "So keep this golden bauble as a lesson to yourself to trust your father before your own ignorance. This little lion will roar at your wedding yet."

I drank your poisoned wine. How much more trust do you require? Fiametta hid her ring deep in a pocket of her gown, and went to get a whisk broom to clean up the clay from the workbench.

Chapter Two

Snow slid beneath Thur Ochs's boots as he climbed from the little valley village of Bruinwald toward the lift shed at the mine's mouth. He kicked reflectively at a gray-white mound beside the trail; it flew in sad lumps, not the fine cold powder of a few weeks back, nor yet spring slush. He would have welcomed slush, any hint of the coming warmth. The leaden dawn promised another leaden gray day of a winter that seemed to linger forever. Not that he was going to see much of this daylight. He repositioned his pick over his shoulder, and stuck his free hand into his armpit in a futile attempt to conserve body heat.

A shout halloed from above, and he glanced up and hastily moved to the side of the trail, prudently behind a tree. On a wooden sledge, a boy sitting atop a heavy pigskin sack of ore and whooping like a Tartary horseman skidded past Thur, followed shortly by another, racing each other to the valley floor. There would be broken bones at the bottom if they didn't drag their feet before the next curve. Somehow, they made it around, out of sight, and Thur grinned. Sledding the ore down to the stream had been one of his favorite winter jobs a couple years back, before he'd grown to his present size and everyone spontaneously began assigning the heaviest tasks to him.

He reached the wooden shack sheltering the lift machinery and ventilation bellows, and stepped gratefully out of the chill dawn breeze hissing down from the rocky wastes above. The mine foreman was there before him, measuring the day's oil into their lamps. Thur's workmate Henzi was unblocking the lift pulley and checking the teeth and rundles of the gears. Perhaps next year they could afford to have the machine enlarged, and a hitch of horses or oxen to turn the axle. In the meantime, ore must be raised, so two big men trod a wheel that turned beneath their straining legs. Heavy work, but at least they could see daylight.

"Good morning, Master Entlebuch," Thur said politely to the foreman, rather hoping to be assigned to the wheel today. But Master Entlebuch grunted to his feet and handed him a lamp. Farel the pickman entered, stamping the snow from his boots, and also received an oil-charged lamp, and the baskets and wooden trays for the black copper ore.

"Master Entlebuch, has the priest come to fumigate for the kobold infestation yet?" Farel asked anxiously.

"No," said Master Entlebuch shortly.

"They're getting awfully forward down there. They knocked over two lamps, yesterday. And that broken water-pump chain—that wasn't just rust."

"It was rust," said the foreman grumpily. "From the slapdash job somebody did of oiling it, most likely. And as for the lamps, 'kobold' is but another word for 'clumsy,' in my belief. So get yourselves down there and find some decent ore today, before we all starve. You two start on the upper face."

Thur and Farel packed their tools in the ore lift bucket, and started down the wooden ladder into the mine.

"*He's* in a foul mood this morning," Farel whispered, above Thur in the plank-lined shaft, as soon as they were out of earshot of the lift shed. "I bet he just won't pay for the priest's incense."

"Can't, more like," sighed Thur. The few veins they were presently working had been growing poorer all year. There was no longer enough washed ore to keep Master Kunz's smelting furnace working more than twice in the month. Or Thur would have been down helping at the forge this very day, cleaning the spent furnaces, stoking the roaring fires, and watching Master Kunz's marvellous transformations of black dirt into pure shimmering liquid metals. He would have been warm as toast, working for Master Kunz. Perhaps he ought to try hiring himself out to the charcoal burners, though with the smeltery at enforced rest there was little market for charcoal, either. The Bergmeister threatened to shut this mine down soon, if its profits did not improve. It was this specter of dearth that made the foreman so short-tempered and jumpy, Thur's uncle had said. As for Thur, well . . . he must just keep a careful eye out for kobolds.

They reached the bottom of the vertical shaft, and Henzi lowered their tools. Thur hitched his hood up over his head, to keep the rock dust out of his blond hair and off the back of his neck. The slow silence of the stone pressed on Thur's ears as they made their way down the sloping tunnel by the flickering orange glow of the oil lamps. Some men found the quiet eerie, but Thur had always found it rather comforting, patient and unvarying, enduring as a mother. It was noise, the sudden groan of shifting rock, that terrified.

Some forty paces into the mountain the way split into two crooked forks, each following what had once been a rich vein of copper ore. One sloped steeply downward, and Thur was mildly grateful not to be hauling baskets of ore up it today. Other dark holes led off, veins played out and abandoned and robbed of their supporting timbers. They followed an upper, more level branch till it dead-ended at last in a raw rock wall.

Farel set his lamp down carefully out of the range of flying chips, and hoisted his pick. "Have at it, boy."

Thur positioned himself where his backswing wouldn't strike the other man, and they both began whaling away at the dim discoloration in the rock that was the fading stringer of ore. A half hour's work left them both gasping. "Hasn't that idiot Entlebuch started the bellows yet?" Farel wiped sweat from his brow.

"Go yell up," suggested Thur. He shovelled their half-basketful of ore for Farel to take with him, as long as he was going. In the pause, Thur could hear distant echoes of the pounding now going on at the lower tunnel's working face. The rock was hard, the ore was thin, and they'd extended the tunnel barely fifteen feet in the last three months. Thur adjusted the leather knee pads his mother had fashioned, knelt, and attacked the face lower down. He hacked till he was winded and aching from his crouched position, then stood and leaned to rest a moment on his pick.

Farel was not back yet. Thur glanced around, then stepped up to the rock face and leaned against its chipped and scarred surface. He spread his fingers against the discoloration and closed his eyes. The babble of his thoughts faded into an inarticulate silence, at one with the silence of the stone. He *was* the stone. He could feel the stringer of ore, like a tendon running through his body. Thinning ten feet in, dwindling . . . and yet, a few feet farther on, like a swordstroke slanting down: a rich vein, native copper glorying along like a bright frozen river, crying for the light that it might shine. . . . "The metal calls me," Thur whispered to himself. "I can feel it. I can."

But who would believe him? And how did these visions come? Or were they devil-dreams, false lures? Stussi the tanner had babbled of visions in a fever once, then a long worm had slithered out of his nose, and he'd died. Thur's vision throbbed with a pulse of danger, maddeningly vague, melting away the moment his emptiness was clouded with the very question, What . . . ? His hands clenched, on the stone.

A flicker in the corner of his eye—lamp going out? Or Farel returning? He sprang away from the rock, flushing. But there was no tramp of boots, and the lamp burned no more badly than usual.

There. A shadow in the wavering shadows—that funny-shaped rock *moved.* Thur stood still, barely breathing.

The rock stood up. It was a gnarled brown mannikin, some two feet tall, with what seemed to be a leather apron like a miner's about its loins. It giggled, and jumped to one side. Its black eyes glinted in the lamp glow like polished stones. It skipped over to Thur's basket, and made to put in a lump of ore.

Thur made no sudden moves. In all his time in the mines, he'd never seen a gnome so close and clear, only movements in the corners of his eyes that seemed to vanish into the walls when he made to approach them. The mannikin giggled again, and tilted its narrow chin aside in an attitude of comical inquiry.

"Good morrow, little man," Thur whispered, fascinated, hoping his voice would not startle it away again.

"Good morrow, metal-master," the kobold returned in a tinny voice. It hopped into the basket, peered over the top at Thur, and hopped out again, in quick jerky motions. Its arms and legs were thin, its toes and fingers long and splayed, with joints like the knobs of roots.

"I'm no master." Thur smiled. He hunkered down, so as to loom less threateningly, and fumbled at his belt for the leather flask his mother had filled with goat's milk before dawn. Carefully, he reached for the bateau, the wide wooden dish used for carrying out the best ore, tapped it upside down to knock out the dirt, and poured some milk into it. He shoved it invitingly toward the little creature. "You can drink. If you wish."

It giggled again, and hopped to the rim. It did not lift the vessel, but put its head down and lapped like a cat, pointed tongue flicking rapidly in and out. Its bright eyes never wavered from Thur as it drank. The milk vanished quickly. The kobold sat up, emitted a tiny but quite distinct belch, and wiped its lips with the back of one twiggy wrist. "Good!"

"My mother fixes it, in case I thirst before dinner," Thur responded automatically, then felt a little idiotic. Surely he should be trying to catch the creature, not conversing with it. Squeeze it to get it to tell him where gold or silver lay, or something. Yet its wrinkled countenance, like a dried apple, made it seem venerable, not evil or menacing.

It sidled toward Thur. He tensed. Slowly, one cool knobby finger reached out and touched Thur's wrist. *I should seize it now.* But he couldn't, didn't want, to move. The kobold jittered across the stones, and rubbed up against the discolored vein in the rock. It oozed, seeming to melt—*It's getting away!*

"Master Kobold," Thur croaked desperately, "tell me, where shall I find my treasure?"

The kobold paused. Its half-lidded eyes stared directly at Thur. Its answer was a creaky chant, like the overstrained wood of a windlass lifting a heavy load. "Air and fire, metal-master, air and fire. You are earth and water. Go to the fire. Ice water will put you out. Cold earth will stop your mouth. Cold earth is good for kobolds, not for metal-masters. Grave digger, grave digger, go to the fire, and live."

It melted into the vein, leaving only a fading giggle behind. Riddles. Ask a blasted gnome a straight and simple question, and get riddles. He should have known. The cadence of its speech had infused its words with doubled meaning. *Grave digger.* The solemn miner, or the man who chipped out his own tomb? Meaning himself, Thur? The sweat drying on his body had chilled him to the bone. He sank shivering to his knees. His heart was laboring, and there was a roaring in his ears like Master Kunz's furnace when the bellows played. His eyes were darkening . . . no, it was the lamp flame dwindling, low and weak . . . but there was plenty of oil. . . .

Farel's voice rang painfully in his ears. "By Our Lady, the air stinks in this pocket!" And then, "Hey, boy, hey . . . !"

A strong hand closed around Thur's arm, and hauled him roughly to his feet. Thur swayed dizzily. Farel swore, and pulled Thur's arm across his own neck, and began to guide him up the tunnel.

"Bad air," said Farel. "The ventilation bellows are pumping all right now. There must be a blockage somewhere in the pipe. Damn! Maybe the kobolds did it."

"I saw a kobold," said Thur. His heart was still pounding, but his vision was beginning to clear, in so far as anyone had vision in these staring shadows in the heart of the mountain.

"I hope you shied a rock at it!" said Farel.

"I fed it some milk. It seemed to like it."

"Idiot boy! For God's sake! We're trying to get rid of the vermin, not attract more! Feed it, and it'll be back with all its brethren. No wonder we're infested!"

"It was the first time I ever saw one. It seemed nice."

"Agh." Farel shook his head. "Bad air, all right, and bad dreams from it."

They reached the fork of the tunnel. The air was fresh enough here. Farel sat Thur down beside the hollow wooden tube that piped the forced air into the lower reaches of the mine. "Stay there, while I get Master Entlebuch. Are you going to be all right?"

Thur nodded. Farel hurried away. Thur could hear him shouting up the lift shaft over the creaks and groans of the wooden machinery. Thur was still chilled, and he wrapped his arms around his torso and drew up his long legs. Farel had taken the lamp. The blackness closed in.

In time Farel returned with Master Entlebuch, who held his lamp up to Thur's face and stared at him in worry. He questioned Thur about his symptoms and went back down the tunnel with Farel, tapping the wooden air pipe with a stick as he went. At length, Farel came back, carrying Thur's abandoned lamp and tools.

"A piece of pipe was crushed in a rockfall. Master Entlebuch says, forget the upper tunnel today. As soon as you feel able, go join the crew on the lower face, and haul baskets for a while."

Thur nodded and rose. Farel shared flame from his lamp to rekindle Thur's. *Air and fire*, thought Thur. *Life.* He did not feel so shaky now, and he started down the lower tunnel in search of the other work crew. He was careful on the steep descending track, so as not to spill or splash his oil, and even more careful on the ladder in the vertical shaft that drove downward another thirty feet. This bottom tunnel had followed a corkscrew-twisting vein, going down, then up again. At the end he found four men, taking turns in pairs chopping at the hard rock face or sorting over the chips while catching their wind. They greeted him in tones ranging from Niklaus's habitual good cheer to Birs's melancholy grunt.

Thur loaded a basket with good chips, heaved it to his shoulder, and carried it down and up the lower tunnel to the shaft. He emptied it into a leather bucket, climbed the ladder with the basket slung over his arm, turned the windlass and raised the bucket on its rope, refilled the basket, carted it to the upper lift shaft, dumped it in the big wooden bucket, and shouted for Henzi, who raised the load out of sight. Then Thur went back for the next load, and the next, and the next, until he lost count. He was weary with work and hunger when Henzi at last lowered a bucket packed with bread, cheese, ale, and barley water, which the men at the lower face greeted with much more animation than they'd greeted Thur.

After dinner-break Farel joined them. "Master Entlebuch and I sawed out the broken pipe, and he's gone to get another length made to fit." Farel was taken into the work gang with the usual acknowledging grunts. Thur did a stint with hammer and pick on the hardest part of the tunnel face, making the rock ring and the chips fly, till his arms and back and neck ached. The smell of the mine seemed to fill his head: cold dry dust, scraped metal, hot oil, the smoke-stink of burning fat (for it was not the best oil), sweat in wool, the cheese-and-onion breath of the men.

When they finally got enough good ore to make up a heavy basket, Thur and Farel took it together. They were halfway to the ladder when the orange oil light glinted off a small gnarled shape, moving by the side of the tunnel.

"Pesky little demon!" Farel shouted. "Begone!" He dropped his half of the basket, snatched up his pick, and flung it forcefully at the kobold. The shape melted into the rock with a tiny cry.

"Ha! I think I winged it," said Farel, going to retrieve his pick, which had stuck in the stone.

"I wish you hadn't done that," said Thur, perforce letting his side of the basket down also. He balanced their lamp atop it. "They're gentle creatures. They don't do any harm that I can see, they just get blamed if anything goes wrong."

"No harm, my eye," growled Farel. He tugged at his pick, which had stuck fast. He yanked, then put his foot to the wall and heaved. The pick jerked free, taking a big chunk of the wall with it, and Farel fell over backwards, cracking his head on a bracing timber. "No harm!" he yelped, rubbing his scalp. "You call this no harm?" He scrambled back to his feet.

A crack was propagating from the new hole in the side of the tunnel, darkening strangely even as Thur stared. Water began to seep from the crack.

"Uh, oh," said Farel in a choked voice, peering around Thur's shoulder.

The mountain groaned, a deep vibration that Thur heard somehow not with his ears, but with his belly. The trickle became a spurt, then a spew, then a hard stream that shot straight out to splash and splatter against the far wall. From down the tunnel came a crash, yells, and an agonized scream.

"The roof's coming down!" Farel cried, his voice stretched high with terror. "Run for it!" He flung his pick aside and galloped up the tunnel. Thur, horrified, ran hard on his heels, his hands held up to keep from clobbering his head on a timber in the dark.

At the foot of the ladder, fumbled for in blackness, they paused. "Nothing else has fallen," Thur spoke into Farel's hesitation.

"Yet," said Farel. His hand came out of nowhere, feeling for Thur; Thur grasped it. It was cold with sweat.

"It sounded like someone was hurt back there," said Thur.

He could hear Farel swallow. "I'll run for Master Entlebuch, and get help," Farel said after a moment. "You go back and see what happened."

"All right." Thur turned, and felt his way back down the tunnel. He could sense the whole weight of the mountain pressing overhead. The great support timbers could splinter like kindling if the mountain shifted further. *Cold earth will stop your mouth, grave digger.* . . . He could not hear shouts or cries up ahead any more, only the snaky hiss of the water.

The tilted basket of ore, the lamp still burning atop it, came in sight. The water gushing from the wall flowed away down the tunnel. Thur took up the lamp and slipped and slid down the now-muddy tunnel floor. Near the bottom of the dug-out vein's curve, a sheet of water roiled. It stretched from Thur's feet across to where the roof of the tunnel dipped to meet it. No wonder he'd heard nothing. The men at the work face were cut off in an air pocket, the water seal blanketing their cries. Until the cunning water, pushing up through whatever fissures it could find, squeezed the pocket smaller and smaller. . . .

A wet head broke the opaque shimmering surface, spat, and gulped air in a huge hooting gasp. A second head came up beside him. Anxiously, Thur reached out and helped the figures heave out of the water, the second clinging to the first.

The second man had a dazed look and a cut across his forehead that, mixing with the streaming water, seemed to be bleeding buckets. The first man's eyes were rolling white with fear.

"Are the others coming behind you?" Thur asked.

"I don't know," Matt, the first man, panted. "I think Niklaus was pinned in the rockfall."

"And Birs stayed with him?" Brave Birs. Braver than

Thur, that was certain. If Thur's father had had such a brave workmate six years ago, he might be alive today.

Matt shook his head. "I thought he was coming with us. But he has the horrors about water. A hedge-witch once prophesied he was safe from all deaths but drowning. He won't even drink water, just ale."

The rising flood lapped at Thur's toes, and he stepped back. They all watched avidly, but no more heads popped up. The bleeding man swayed woozily.

"Best you walk him out before we have to carry him," Thur observed. "Help should be coming. I'll . . . stand watch, here. Tell them up above to keep the ventilation bellows pumping. Maybe it will help hold the water back in there or something."

Matt nodded and, supporting the injured man, staggered up the tunnel. Thur stood and watched the dark water rising. The longer they waited, the worse it would get, deeper and more difficult. *Ice water will put you out.* No other heads appeared. The water licked Thur's toes again, and again he stepped back. He muffled a tiny wail of dismay in the back of his throat, a squeak like the injured kobold's. He set the lamp down on the floor several feet back up the tunnel, turned, and waded into the water.

The icy shock when it came up over his boots and hit his crotch took his breath away, but he pushed on till his feet left the floor. He breathed deeply, held it, turned, and began to shove himself along the inundated tunnel roof. Down, down . . . he could feel the pressure growing in his ears, even as they began to numb. Then up, thank God! It was all uphill from here. He pulled himself along faster. Unless there was no air pocket on the other side, in which case he—

His hand splashed through to unresisting air, then his head. He gasped as wildly as Matt had done. There was a little light; someone's oil lamp had stayed upright. His feet found solid ground, and he sloshed up onto dry stone. His *eyes* were cold, his scalp tingled, and his fingers were crooked numb claws. The orange-tinged air, chill as it was, seemed like a steamhouse in contrast.

Birs was standing by the water's edge, sobbing. A struggling shape in the shadows on the floor near the rock face was Niklaus, swearing at him. The swearing paused. "Thur? Is that you?"

Thur knelt in the dimness beside Niklaus and felt for damages. The edge of a tilted slab pinned Niklaus's leg to the floor. The bone was shattered, the flesh pulpy and swelling beneath Thur's fingers. The slab was so damned *big*. Thur grabbed for a pick, scrabbled its point under the slab, and heaved. The rock barely shifted.

"Birs, help me!" Thur demanded, but Birs wept on as though he neither saw nor heard, so lost in his own imagined damnation he was missing the real one going on behind his back. Thur went round and shook him by the shoulders, at first gently, then hard. "Witless, wake up!" he shouted into Birs's face.

Birs didn't stop crying, but he did start moving. With pick, shovel, a bar, and stones shoved in to hold each heave's grunting progress, they raised the slab. Niklaus screamed as the blood rushed back into his leg, but still managed to jerk free and roll away.

"The water's still rising," said Thur.

"It was foretold!" wailed Birs.

Thur's hands clenched, and he loomed over the man. "The hedge-witch told truth. Your fate *is* drowning. I'll hold your head under myself if you don't help me!"

"You tell him, Thur," gasped Niklaus from the floor.

Birs cringed away, his terror dwindling to a suppressed whine.

"Take Niklaus's other arm. There's naught to do but

hold your breath and push yourself along. The other two both made it."

They dragged Nicklaus into the water and waded out. Thur pushed off with his feet, and started under. Flailing, with a panicked cry, Birs retreated.

No help for it. Tugging Niklaus, who at least had sense to claw the wall with his free arm and help push, Thur kept going. The heat sucked faster this time from his aching flesh and bones. When they broke the surface again, Niklaus's eyes had rolled back in shock.

But Master Entlebuch and Farel were waiting, with two other men. The team of three quickly laid Niklaus on a blanket and started away with him.

"Anyone left?" Master Entlebuch asked.

"Birs," Thur wheezed, his body racked with shudders.

"Is he hurt?"

"No. But he's all in a twist through terror of the water because of some fool fortune-telling."

"Can you swim back and get him out?"

"He could get himself out, if he would." Thur's woolen hood, tunic, and leggings were saturated, sagging and leaden with their burden of water, a dead weight on his body. Irked to distraction by it, he pulled the dripping hood off over his head like a horse collar, and let it fall with a sodden splat.

The mountain groaned again. The thick support timbers skirled like bagpipes, followed by a hail of tiny popping noises from within the wood.

"It's going to go." Master Entlebuch's voice rose taut. "We've got to clear this tunnel *now.*"

Muting his own inner wail, Thur turned and waded in for the third time. His growing numbness almost mitigated the cold. His head was pounding and strange red lace swirled before his tight-shut eyes before he felt his way to air again. When he fought up out of the water this time, the stony beach in the air pocket had shrunk to a mere yard. Birs was crouched there, praying, or at any rate crying, "God, God, God, God. . . ." He reminded Thur of a sheep bleating.

"Come on!" yelled Thur. "We'll be buried here!"

"I'll drown!" shrieked Birs.

"Not today, you won't," snarled Thur, and clipped him hard across the jaw with his bunched fist. Rather to Thur's surprise, Birs bounced off the wall and fell dazed at the single blow. It was the first time Thur had hit anyone with his new man's strength, not in a boys' scrambling puppyfight. Birs's jaw looked strangely off-centered. No help for it now. Thur clamped Birs's head under his arm and dragged him into the freezing water.

Even dazed, Birs struggled against Thur's grip as their heads went under. Thur clamped it tighter, heaved and pushed. His lungs labored and pulsed against the seal of his mouth. He let a little air out, he couldn't help it. *Ice water will put you out . . .* but not today, not today, not today. *God save me for hanging.*

He surfaced to air and confusion. The black was pitch-absolute. Master Entlebuch was gone. And he'd taken the lamp with him. Thur's free arm waved, disoriented, seeking wall or floor or roof or any guide. He thumped at last into the wall, stoving his reaching fingers. His feet found the sloping floor. He was cramped, bent like a bow from the cold and with knots in his legs and arms that felt like walnuts. Out of the water with his burden. Birs was choking and sputtering, therefore alive and undrowned. Thur was afraid to let go of him in the dark, even when Birs rolled over and vomited about a quart of swallowed water into Thur's lap. Thur struggled to his feet and began march-dragging Birs up the tunnel.

The ladder at the lower shaft proved a nightmarish barrier as Thur tried to shove his dizzied workmate up it. He shouted threats and encouragement up at Birs.

"Move! Move! Move your hands! Move your feet!" His own fingers were numb to the point of paralysis, crippled claws. Then from the tunnel below them, came an almost rhythmic series of splintering cracks, and a thunderous rending crash. Birs's boots vanished from before Thur's nose—*He's fallen,* was Thur's first panicked thought. Then pebbles pattered down on his head from Birs's mad scramble out the top of the shaft. *No, he's recovered.* Thur scrambled too, and ran like a crouching rabbit after he heaved himself into the upper tunnel.

He added his hollering to Birs's muffled screams when they reached the lift shaft. It seemed to take forever before the ore bucket descended. Thur stuffed Birs into it and took to the ladder. He almost blacked out, halfway up, but the gray light overhead drew him up like the silver promise of heaven. Henzi was unloading Birs when Thur arrived. Thur stood in the lift shed, his hands braced on his knees, lungs pumping like bellows.

"Didn't you bring out any of the tools?" Master Entlebuch asked him anxiously.

Thur stared at him like a dumb ox, stupefied. Birs, once on his feet, mumbled something unintelligible but distinctly hostile in tone, swung a punch at Thur, missed, and fell over. Outside the lift shed door, spring sleet was hissing slantwise down the wind.

"I want to go home," Thur said.

Incoherent from the cold, he reached his cottage at last. His mother took one horrified look, stripped him of his freezing garments, stuffed him into her own bed between two feather mattresses with hot stones, plied him with steaming barley water sweetened with honey, and never asked after tools or even his missing hood. Even so it took him two full hours to stop shivering, racking shudders like an ague. He gave her a jerky and truncated account of his day that nevertheless left her face drawn and lips compressed. She never left him till his teeth stopped chattering.

When his steadying voice at last reassured her of his probable survival, she went across the room to the mantle over the fireplace and came back with a piece of paper that crackled as she unfolded it. "Here, Thur. This came this morning from your brother Uri. He has found you a fine opportunity."

Uri, still after him to take up the mercenary's pike? The letter's red wax seal was already broken by their apprehensive mother, who greeted every rare communication with suppressed terror, of news of disease, inflamed wounds, amputation, loss of money at play, or disastrous betrothal to some whorish camp follower, all the hazards of a soldier's life.

It wasn't exactly the risks of a soldier's trade that repelled Thur. All life was a hazard. And he'd be willing enough to make swords. He'd seen Milanese armorers' work that had taken his breath away. But to then take that work of art and stick it into a live man . . . no. He vented a long-suffering sigh, and took the paper.

A curious shock ran up his arm. His fingers warmed. As he read, his weariness dropped away, and he sat up. Not soldiering after all. His eyes raced faster over the phrases. . . . *apprentice to the Duke's goldsmith and master mage . . . marvellous bronze underway for my lord Duke . . . needs a strong smart lad . . . opportunity. . . .*

Thur stroked the paper. The sun would be warm now on the southern slopes of the pass into Montefoglia. In the summer the sun would blaze like a furnace mouth. He licked his lips. "What do you think?" he asked his mother.

She took a brave breath. "I think you should go.

Before that devilish mountain eats you as it ate your father."

"You'd be alone."

"Your uncle will look after me. I'd rather have you safe in Montefoglia than up in that vile mine every day. If Uri wanted you for a soldier, it would be different. You know how I hated it when he went for a mercenary. So often the boys come back, if they come back at all, either broken and sick, or turned strange and hard and cruel. But this, now . . ."

Thur turned the letter over. "Does the master mage realize I have no turn for sorcery?"

His mother pursed her lips. "I confess, that's a part I do not like. This Master Beneforte is a Florentine. He may be a dabbler in the black arts, or worse perversions, as dangerous to boys as to maidens. Still, he works for the Duke of Montefoglia, who by Uri's account is honorable, for a nobleman."

"Montefoglia." He had never noticed before how the very name sounded warm.

"You can read and write in two tongues, and have a little Latin, too. When Brother Glarus was teaching you he once told me you might go to Padua and study to be a doctor. I often dreamed of it, but then your father was killed, and things got harder."

"I did not love Latin," Thur confessed warily, suddenly realizing there could be worse fates than soldiering. But his mother did not pursue that subject. She rose to tend to the pease porridge bubbling over the fire, made with extra ham in honor of Thur's narrow escape from the mine.

He burrowed back into the feather mattress and clutched the letter to his chest. His flesh was still cold as lard, but the paper seemed to radiate warmth. *Grave digger, grave digger, go to the fire. . . .* He laughed, and muffled the laugh as his mother glanced over and smiled though not knowing the

joke. Montefoglia. *By God and the kobold, I think
I'll do it*. He lay back and watched the firelight
flicker like reflections off water on the whitewash
between the dark roof beams, and dreamed of incandescent summer.

Chapter Three

Ruberta the housekeeper helped Fiametta lift and slide the heavy red velvet gown over her head, and smooth it down over her fine linen underdress. Fiametta brushed at the folds of its wide-cut skirt, so profligate of cloth, and sighed pure satisfaction. The dress was far finer than anything she'd dared hope for. Master Beneforte had produced it, quite unexpectedly, from an old chest when Fiametta had complained of the sad figure she would cut at the Duke's banquet in plain gray wool. The dress had once belonged to Fiametta's mother; Fiametta and Ruberta had spent a week cutting it down and resewing it. Judging from the measurements, Fiametta was now nearly as tall as her mother had been, though more slender. Strange. She remembered her mother as tall, not short: tall and dark and warm.

Fiametta held out her arms, and Ruberta pulled on the sleeves and tied them to the dress at the shoulders, and fluffed out puffs of the underdress for contrast at the elbows. The red velvet sleeves were embroidered with silver thread, echoed by a silver band running all around that wonderful hem.

"Don't bounce so, girl," Ruberta complained mildly, and pinched her lower lip with her teeth in concentration as she knotted the bows just so. She stepped back and regarded Fiametta with judicious pride. "Now for your hair."

"Oh, yes, please." Fiametta plunked down obediently on the stool. No little girl's cap today, nor hair in a mere simple braid down her back. The dress had come with a matching hair net of silver thread and pearls, magically untarnished with age. Ruberta parted Fiametta's hair in neat, if wavy, wings, wound it up on the back of her head, and fastened the net over the mass of it, except for two dark ringlets she made to bounce artfully in front of Fiametta's ears. Fiametta stared greedily into her little mirror, delighted, turning her head back and forth to make the ringlets jump. "Thank you, Ruberta!" She flung her arms around the housekeeper's aproned waist and hugged her. "You're so clever."

"Oh, your slippers—they're still in the kitchen. I'll go get them." Ruberta hurried out. Fiametta tried the mirror at various angles, and ran her hands again over the soft sumptuous cloth. She sucked on her lower lip and, on impulse, rose and went to the chest at the end of her bed.

She pushed aside linens and found a flat oaken casket. She opened it to reveal her mother's death mask. Many people kept death masks of wax; Prospero Beneforte had recast Fiametta's mother's in bronze, darkened by his art to a rich brown close to her original skin tones. The alert dark eyes were closed, now, like sleep, but a strangely sad sleep, above the soft curves of her nose and wide mouth. Fiametta held the mask up to her dress and peeked over it into her mirror, held out at arm's length. She squinted, in an effort to weld face and dress in the blur. Then she lowered the mask to her chin, and compared the two faces. How much of the paler one was Prospero Beneforte, how much this lost woman? Fiametta's nose had a definite bridge, and her jaw was more sharp cut than this dark visage, but otherwise . . . *Who am I? And whose am I? Where do I belong, Mother?*

Ruberta's step sounded on the gallery, and Fiametta hastily replaced the mask in its casket and locked it away again. Ruberta handed the polished shoes in through the door. "Hurry, now. Your Papa's waiting downstairs."

Fiametta jammed her feet into the shoes, and skipped out of her bedroom and around the upper gallery overlooking the courtyard. She took up her skirts to descend the stairs, then shook them out and walked more sedately, as befit her lady's hairstyle. No slave's gown, this, nor mere servant's, but obvious proof that her mother had been the true Christian wife of a great artisan. Fiametta held her chin up firmly.

Master Beneforte was standing in the stone-paved hallway. He looked splendid too, Fiametta decided. He wore a cloak of black velvet that swung to his knees, and a big hat of the same fabric, wound round like a turban with a jaunty fall of cloth to the side. His tunic was of honey-brown cut velvet, high to his neck where a bright white line of linen showed, with a pleated skirt to his knees and black hose. Despite his graying hairs Master Beneforte still resisted the long gowns of the aged, though the sober colors he'd chosen suggested a suitably powerful maturity. He'd set off the tunic with a gold chain of his own workmanship, displaying his art.

He turned at Fiametta's step. "Ah, there you are." He looked her up and down, eyes going strangely distant, muttered "*Huh,*" and shook his head as if to clear his vision.

"Do I look well, Papa?" asked Fiametta, alarmed.

"You look well. Here." He thrust out his hand to her.

Draped over his palm was a silver belt of cunning workmanship. Fiametta took it up, surprised. It was in the form of a silver snake, round and flexible as a rope. The gleaming scales were as fine as a real snake's, their overlapping plates concealing whatever linked its skeleton. Its head was solid silver, modeled as in life, with green chips—emerald? glass?—glittering for eyes.

"Put it on," said Master Beneforte.

"How? I see no clasp."

"Just loop it. It will stay."

"It's enchanted, isn't it?"

"Just a little spell for your protection."

"Thank you, Papa." She fitted it around her waist, curling the tail around behind the head, and indeed it held fast. Only then did she think to ask, "Does it come off?"

"Whenever you wish."

She tried it, and looped it back on. "Did you just make this?" She thought he'd been working night and day to finish the saltcellar.

"No, I've had it for some time. I just cleaned it and renewed the spell."

"Was it Mama's?"

"Yes."

Fiametta stroked it, her fingers sliding over the scales. They emitted a faint musical vibration, almost too thin to hear.

The Duke's saltcellar sat waiting on a bench against the wall. Its new box was satin-lined, ebony to match the base, with gold clasps and gold handles on the ends. Fiametta had helped assemble and polish it. She would not have guessed her father to be nervous, but he opened the box and checked its contents one last time, and rechecked the seating and security of the clasps, then wandered into the workroom and peered out the window.

"Ah. At last." His voice drifted back to her, and he returned to the hall to unbar the door for the Swiss captain and two guards. The guards' breastplates gleamed like mirrors, and Captain Ochs was dressed in his best and cleanest livery, with a new doublet with gold buttons issued in honor of the betrothal.

"All ready, Master Prospero?" the captain smiled He nodded to the ebony casket. "Shall I have my men carry it?"

"I'll carry it myself, I think," said Master Beneforte, lifting the box. "Have them walk one ahead and one behind."

"Very well." And they started off so ordered, the captain and Fiametta flanking the goldsmith.

"Keep the door barred till my return, Teseo," Master Beneforte called back, and the apprentice bowed awkwardly and closed it behind them. Master Beneforte paused till he heard the bar slide into place, nodded, and marched down the cobbled street.

It was a bright day two weeks after the holy feast of Easter, just barely cool enough for velvets to be comfortable. Trees had budded into new leaf in the weeks since Fiametta had cast her ring. She clutched the lion mask on her left thumb, and let the—sigh— garnet catch and wink back the midday sun. That light glowed, too, off the yellow brick and stones and red tile roofs. Sad dun in winter, Montefoglia almost looked like a city of gold on long summer afternoons. They passed from the street of big houses flanking her father's home and workshop down into older, more crowded construction.

Crossing a side alley leading down to the water, Fia- metta glimpsed boats and the docks. A few lazy lake gulls swooped and squawked. Pehaps when Papa took her fishing again this summer, he'd finally teach her the secret spell he used for baiting his hook. The narrow lake extended eleven miles north from Montefoglia, toward the foothills of the Alps beyond which lay Captain Ochs's home. The first pack train of the season had come down over Montefoglia Pass a week ago, Fiametta had heard. Higher and more difficult than the great Brenner to the east, the route yet served the needs of the little duchy. Montefoglia was hard hill country, and would have been poor indeed without the trickle of trade and the fishing of the lake.

On the east shore, north of town, the monastery of St. Jerome kept grape vines, spring wheat in terraces, orchards and sheep. The main road ran up the east side of the lake past its stone walls, the west side being too sheer, rocky, and wild for any but goat paths. Fiametta could see a few figures on horses and a slow ox cart moving on the dusty white ribbon. St. Jerome's scriptorium also supplied illuminated books for the Duke's library, pride of the castle that dominated the bluff at the far end of town. It was the Duke's boast that his library held none of that cheap modern printed matter, but only proper calligraphed manuscripts bound in rich decorated leather—over a hundred volumes. It seemed a constrictive stipulation to Fiametta's mind, but perhaps it was because Duke Sandrino could read but not write himself that calligraphy seemed to significant to him. Old people were ridiculously conservative about the oddest things.

"And how go the betrothal celebrations?" Master Beneforte inquired of the captain. Fiametta, lagging, quickened her step and closed the gap to listen.

"Well, the Duchess had an illumination in the garden last night, with a tableau and madrigals. The singers sounded very pretty."

"I'd have been doing the costuming for that set

piece, but for the Duke's insistence upon this." Master Beneforte lifted the ebony box. "I'm surprised that dolt di Rimini didn't botch the effects. The man couldn't design a doorknob."

The captain smiled dryly at this aspersion upon Master Beneforte's most notable local rival in the decorative arts. "He did all right. For your consolation, there was a bad moment when the candles set fire to a headdress, but we doused the lady and got it out, with no injury but to her feathers. I knew I was right to insist on having those buckets ready, backstage."

"Ha. I understand the future bridegroom rode in on time this morning, at least."

"Yes." The captain frowned. "I must say, I don't like the retinue he rode in with. A hard-bitten bunch. And fifty men-at-arms seems excessive, for the occasion. I don't know what Duke Sandrino was thinking of, to allow my lord of Losimo to bring so many. The honor due his future son-in-law, he says."

"Well, Uberto Ferrante was a condottiere, before he fell heir to Losimo two years ago," said Master Beneforte judiciously. "He hasn't really been there long enough to establish local loyalty. Presumably these are men he trusts."

"Fell heir, my eye. He bribed the Papal Curia to overturn the other cousin's claim, and again for dispensation to marry the heiress. I suppose Cardinal Borgia wanted to be sure of a Guelf in Losimo, to oppose the ambitions of Venice and the Ghibbellines."

"From my experience of the Curia, I'd say you guess exactly right." Master Beneforte smiled sourly. "I do wonder where Ferrante got the money, though."

"The ambitions of Milan seem a nearer threat, to me. Poor Montefoglia, sitting like an almond between two such pincers."

"Now, Milan's an example of how a soldier may rise. I trust Lord Ferrante has not been studying the life of the late Francesco Sforza too closely. Marry the daughter, then make yourself master of the State.... Take note, Uri."

The captain sighed. "I don't know any heiresses, alas." He paused thoughtfully. "Actually, that's exactly what Ferrante did, in Losimo. I trust he does not seek to duplicate the ploy in Montefoglia."

"Our Duke and his son are both healthy enough to prevent that, I think," said Master Beneforte. He patted the ebony box. "And perhaps I can do my little part to help keep them so."

The captain stared down at his boots, pacing over the stones. "I don't know. I do know Duke Sandrino is not altogether happy with this betrothal, and Duchess Letitia even less so. I cannot see what pressure Ferrante can be putting, yet I sense ... there was hard bargaining, for the dowry."

"Too bad Lord Ferrante is not a younger man, or Lady Julia older."

"Or both. I know the Duchess insisted it be put in the contract that the wedding not take place for at least another year."

"Perhaps Lord Ferrante's horse will dump him on his head and break his neck, betimes."

"I will add that to my prayers," smiled the captain. It almost wasn't a joke.

The conversation lagged as they reserved breath for the final climb to the castle. They passed through a gate flanked by two sturdy square towers of cut stone topped by the same yellow brick common in most of Montefoglia's newer construction. The soldiers escorted them across a stone-paved courtyard and up the new grand staircase the present Duke had installed in hopes of softening the austere and awkward architecture of his ancestors. Master Beneforte sniffed at the stonework in passing, and muttered his habitual judgment. "Should have hired a real sculptor, not a country stonecutter. . . ." They passed through two dark halls and out another door to the walled garden. Here among the flowers and fruit trees the tables were set for the betrothal banquet.

The throng was being seated, just the timing Master Beneforte had hoped for his grand presentation. The ducal family, together with Lord Ferrante and the Abbot of Saint Jerome and Bishop of Montefoglia (two offices, one man) occupied a long table raised on a platform. They were shaded by awnings made of tapestries. Four other tables were arranged at right angles, below and beyond, for the lesser guests.

Duke Sandrino, a pleasantly bulky man of fifty with nose and ears of noble proportions, was washing his hands in a silver basin with rose petals floating in the steaming water, held by his steward Messer Quistelli. His son and heir, the ten-year-old Lord Ascanio, sat on his right. One of Lord Ferrante's liveried retainers was adjusting a footstool with a padded leather top beneath his master's boots, in the shape of a chest carved with Losimo's arms. The portable furniture was evidently for some idiosyncratic comfort, for Lord Ferrante's legs were of normal shape and length. Maybe his silk hose concealed an old war wound that still pained him. Fiametta schooled herself not to gawk, while trying to memorize as many details as possible of the overwhelming display of velvets, silks, hats, badges, arms, jewels, and hairstyles before her.

The Lady Julia, seated between her mother and her bridegroom-to-be, wore spring-green velvet with gold embroidery and—ha!—a girl's cap. Though indeed, the green cap was embroidered with more gold thread and studded with tiny pearls. Her hair was braided with green ribbons in a blonde rope down her back. Did Duchess Letitia deliberately seek to emphasize her daughter's youth? Julia's slight flusterment made a vivid contrast with the Lord of Losimo on her other hand. Dark, mature, powerful, clearly a disciple of Mars: Lord Ferrante's lips smiled without showing his teeth. Perhaps his teeth were bad.

The abbot-and-bishop was seated to Lord Ferrante's left, no doubt both for the honor and to give Ferrante an equal to talk to if Julia's girl chatter or bashful silence grew thin. Abbot Monreale had been a flamboyant knight in his youth, when he'd been severely wounded, and made a deathbed promise to dedicate his life to the Church if God would spare him. He'd kept his promise with flair; gray-haired now, he had a reputation as a scholar and a bit of a mystic. He was dressed today as bishop, not abbot, in the splendid flowing white gown and gold-edged red robe of his office, with a white silk brocade cap over his tonsure. Monreale was also the man who yearly inspected both the workshop and the soul of Prospero Beneforte, and renewed his ecclesiastical license to practice white magic. Master Beneforte, after making his leg to the Duke, his family, and Lord Ferrante, bowed to the abbot with immense and unfeigned deference.

As they'd practiced, Master Beneforte knelt and opened the ebony box, and had Fiametta present the saltcellar to the Duke with a pretty curtsey. The snowy linen of the table set the gleaming gold and brilliant colored enamels off to perfection. Master Beneforte beamed when the occupants of the table broke into spontaneous applause. Duke Sandrino smiled in obvious satisfaction, and asked the abbot himself to bless the first salt, which the steward hurried to pour into the glowing boat-bowl.

Master Beneforte watched in breathless suspense. Now was the time, he'd confided to Fiametta in their private rehersal, when he'd hoped the Duke would fill his hands with ducats in a magnificent gesture of generosity before the assembled guests. He'd hung a large purse, empty, beneath his cloak in anticipation of the golden moment. But the Duke merely, if kindly, waved them to places prepared for them at a lower table. "Well, he has a lot on his mind. Later," Master Beneforte muttered in his beard, concealing his chagrin as they settled themselves.

A servant brought them the silver basin to wash their hands—one of Master Beneforte's own pieces, Fiametta noticed—and the banquet commenced with wine and dishes of fried ravioli stuffed with chopped pork, herbs, and cream cheese rolled in powdered sugar. Baskets of bread made entirely from white flour appeared, and platters of veal, chicken, ham, sausages, and beef. And more wine. Master Beneforte watched the upper table with sharp attention. No blue flames flashed up from anyone's plate, though. Fiametta made polite conversation with the castellan's wife, a plump woman named Lady Pia, on her other side.

When the castellan's wife rose for a moment, beckoned by her husband, Master Beneforte leaned close to his daughter and lowered his voice. Fiametta braced herself for more grumbling about the Duke's ducats, but instead he said, unexpectedly, "Did you notice the little silver ring Lord Ferrante wore on his right hand, child? You stood closer to him than I."

Fiametta blinked. "Yes, now that you mention it."

"What did you think of it?"

"Well . . ." She tried to call it up in her mind's eye. "I thought it extremely ugly."

"What form had it?"

"A mask. An infant, or putti's face, I think. Not ugly, exactly, but . . . I just didn't like it." She laughed a little. "He should commission you, Papa, to make him something prettier."

To her surprise, he crossed himself in a tiny warding gesture. "Say not so. Yet . . . how dare he wear it openly in front of the abbot? Perchance it came to him secondhand, and he doesn't know what it is. Or he's muted it, somehow."

"It was new work, I thought," said Fiametta. "Papa, what bothers you?" He looked disturbed.

"I'm almost certain it's a spirit ring. Yet, if it's active, where can he have put the ..." He trailed off, lips thinned, staring covertly at the upper table.

"Black magic?" Fiametta whispered, shocked.

"Not ... not necessarily. I once, er ... saw such a thing that was no grave sin. And Ferrante is a lord. Such a man should be easy and conversant with forms of power not so appropriate in lesser men, yet proper to a ruler. Like the great Lord Lorenzo in Florence."

"I thought all magic was either white or black."

"When you've grown as old as I have, child, you will learn that nothing in this world is either all white or black."

"Would Abbot Monreale agree with that?" she asked suspiciously.

"Oh, yes," he sighed. His brows rose in a sort of eyebrow-shrug. "Well, Lord Ferrante has a year yet, to reveal his character." His fingers curled, suppressing the topic as Lady Pia returned.

The meats, what little was left of them, were taken away by the servants, and platters of dates, figs, early strawberries, and pastry confections were set before the guests. Fiametta and Lady Pia collaborated on selections and did great damage to the dried cherry tarts. Musicians at the far end of the garden began to play above the chatter and clink of cutlery and plates. The Duke's butler and his assistants poured out sweet wines, in anticipation of closing toasts.

Messer Quistelli hurried out of the castle and stepped under the tapestries shading the high table. He bent his head to whisper in the Duke's ear. Duke Sandrino frowned, and made some query; Messer Quistelli shrugged. The Duke shook his head as if annoyed, but leaned over, spoke to the Duchess, and rose to follow his steward back inside.

The castellan's wife entered into a negotiation, across Fiametta, with Master Beneforte to mend a little silver ewer of hers that had a broken handle. Fiametta could see her father was not flattered to be bothered by such a domestic trifle, apprentice's work, till his eye fell on her.

He smiled slightly. "Fiametta will mend it. It can be your first independent commission, child."

"Oh. Can you do it?" Lady Pia looked at her, both doubtful and impressed.

"I . . . suppose I'd better see it first," Fiametta said cautiously, but inwardly delighted.

Lady Pia glanced at the high table. "They won't start the toasts till the Duke returns. What can be keeping him away so long? Come to my rooms, Fiametta, and you can see it right now."

"Certainly, Lady Pia." As they rose, Messer Quistelli returned, to speak this time to Lord Ferrante. Ferrante grimaced puzzled irritation, but evidently compelled by his host's command got up to follow the steward. With a jerk of his hand Lord Ferrante motioned two of his men to fall in behind him. If she'd seen them on the street, Fiametta would not have hesitated to dub them bravos. The senior of them, a tough-looking bearded fellow missing several front teeth, had been presented as Ferrante's principal lieutenant. Captain Ochs, leaning over to chat with some lady at one of the lower tables, looked up, frowned to himself, and followed. He had to lengthen his stride to catch up.

The two women waited for the men to clear the doorway, then the castellan's wife led Fiametta within. Fiametta glanced aside curiously as they crossed the chamber. Through a door at the far end into a cabinet or study she could see the Duke standing at his desk, with two travel-stained men, one a grave-faced priest, the other a choleric nobleman. Lord Ferrante and the rest of the retinue then blocked her view, and she followed Lady Pia.

The castellan had rooms in one of the square towers. Lady Pia took the ewer from a shelf in her tiny, thick-walled bedroom, crowded with her bit of furniture—a bed and chests—and waited anxiously while Fiametta carried it to a window slit to look it over. Fiametta was secretly pleased to find it not a mere soldering job, but one requiring more expertise; the handle, cast in the form of a sinuous mermaid, was not only loose but cracked. Fiametta assured the castellan's wife of a swift repair, and they wrapped the piece in a bit of old linen and returned with it to the garden.

Passing again through the large chamber, Fiametta was startled by Duke Sandrino's angry shouting, coming from the cabinet. He was leaning across his desk on his clenched hands. Lord Ferrante stood facing him with his arms tightly folded, his jaw set and features darkening to a burnt brick red. His voice rumbled in reply in short jerky sentences, pitched too low to be clear to Fiametta's ear. The two dusty strangers looked on. The noble's face was lit with malicious glee. The priest's was white. Captain Ochs leaned with his back to the doorframe, apparently casual, but with his hand resting on the hilt of his sword. Lady Pia's hand tightened on Fiametta's shoulder in alarm.

Duke Sandrino's voice rose and fell. ". . . lies and murder . . . black necromancy! Sure proof . . . no child of mine . . . insult to my house! Get you gone at once, or prepare for a war to spin your vile head, condottiere bastard!" Spluttering with fury, Duke Sandrino bit his thumb and shook it in Lord Ferrante's face.

"I need no preparation!" Lord Ferrante raged back, leaning toward him. "Your war can begin right now!" As Fiametta watched open-mouthed, Lord Ferrante snatched his dagger out left-handed. In the same continuing upward arc he slashed it across Duke San-drino's throat, so powerful a blow it half-severed the neck and bounced off bone. Ferrante struck so hard he unbalanced himself, and he and his victim fell into each other across the desk as if embracing, smeared sudden scarlet.

With a shocked cry that was almost a wail, Captain Ochs ripped his sword from its scabbard and started forward. In the confined space of the cabinet a sword was little more effective than a dagger, though, and both bravos had their daggers out. The gap-toothed lieutenant took the choleric nobleman through the heart with a blow almost as sudden and powerful as his master's first stroke had been. Aged Messer Quistelli, unarmed, ducked, but not fast enough; the second bravo's knife blow knocked him to the floor. Uri, lunging forward, deflected a follow-up blow, then found himself wrestling the man.

As the priest raised his hand, Lord Ferrante gestured toward him with his bunched right fist; the silver ring glared and the priest clutched his eyes and screamed. Lord Ferrante stabbed him through his unguarded chest.

"I must get my husband!" The castellan's wife dropped her ewer, picked up her skirts, and ran for the garden. The lieutenant looked up at the noise, frowned, and started toward Fiametta. His eyes were very cold. Dizzied with shock, her heart hammering, Fiametta whirled and sprinted after Lady Pia.

She was almost blinded by the sunlight. Halfway across the garden, the castellan's wife was hanging on her husband's arm and screaming warnings; he was shaking his head as if he found incoherent the cries that made perfect sense to Fiametta. She looked around frantically in the white afternoon for her father's big black hat. *There*, nodding to some man. The lieutenant turned his head in the doorway, and plunged back inside. Fiametta flung herself onto Master Beneforte's chest, her fingers clutching his tunic.

"Papa," she gasped out, "Lord Ferrante just murdered the Duke!"

Uri Ochs spun backwards through the door. There was blood on his sword. "Treachery!" he shouted. Blood sprayed from his mouth with the words. "Murder and treachery! Montefoglia, to arms!"

Ferrante's men, as surprised as Montefoglia's, began to gather together in knots. Ferrante's lieutenant, pursuing Captain Ochs through the door, cried his comrades to his aid.

"The devil," hissed Master Beneforte through his teeth. "There goes my commission." His hand clamped on her arm, and he wheeled around, staring. "This garden is a death trap. We have to get out of here *now*."

Men were beginning to draw swords and daggers, and the unarmed to snatch up table knives. Women were screaming.

Master Beneforte started, not for the door, but toward the high table. Captain Ochs and Ferrante's lieutenant were also heading that way at a pell-mell run. Ferrante's lieutenant leaped and aimed a sword swing across the linen at little Lord Ascanio that would have taken off the boy's head if Captain Ochs had not knocked the blade aside with his own. Abbot Monreale started up and dumped the table over on the gap-toothed Losimon as he stumbled and turned for another strike.

With a wild lunge, Master Beneforte caught his salt-cellar as it arced glittering through the air, and bundled his cloak about it. "Now, Fiametta! For the door!"

Fiametta yanked convulsively at her skirt, pinned under the edge of the heavy table. "Papa, help!"

Duchess Letitia clutched her daughter and half-jumped, half-fell over the back of the platform into the tapestries. Uri, leaping up, grabbed Ascanio and shoved him toward Abbot Monreale. "Get the boy out!" he gasped. The abbot swirled his red robe around the terrified child, and parried a bravo's sword thrust with his crozier, followed up quite automatically with a powerful and well-aimed kick to the man's crotch.

"Saint Jerome! To me!" Monreale bellowed. His prior and brawny secretary sped to his aid. Another bravo's descent on Ascanio was met with an odd motion of the abbot's staff; the man's face grew abruptly blank, and he wandered off over the side of the dais, sword drooping. He was struck down by one of Montefoglia's guards joining the fray. Master Beneforte, halfway to the door, heard Fiametta's cries and started back.

Uri, guarding the group now growing about the abbot and Ascanio, locked in murderous swordplay with Ferrante's gap-toothed lieutenant. Uri's breath bubbled strangely. In a thrust-and-parry, Uri kicked aside Lord Ferrante's footstool-chest over the edge of the dais. It bounced on its side and spilled open. It was packed with rock salt, which cascaded across Fiametta's feet.

Pickled in the salt curled the shrivelled corpse of a newborn infant. Fiametta screamed, and ripped her caught skirt out from under the table in her recoil. Uri glanced aside, his eyes widening; Ferrante's lieutenant lunged and thrust his sword through Uri's new doublet. Fiametta could see five inches of blade sliding out of the captain's back. The gap-toothed man turned the blade, put his foot to Uri's torso, and yanked it back out with a dreadful sucking sound. Blood gushed from both wounds, front and back. The captain fell. Fiametta wailed, stooped, and flung a heavy platter at the Losimon lieutenant with all her strength. Master

Beneforte grabbed Fiametta's arm and dragged her toward the exit.

The doorway was clotted with struggling men. Master Beneforte fell back, dismayed. He shoved the bundled cloak containing the saltcellar into Fiametta's shaking hands and snarled, "Don't drop it! And stay on my heels this time, damn it!" He snatched up a bottle from one of the tables, and drew his own showy dagger with its jewelled hilt. The mirror-polished blade, never yet used, flashed in the sun.

Master Beneforte tried again to force his way through the garden's only exit. A knot of men exploded outward as more of Montefoglia's guards charged through. Master Beneforte darted forward into the brief breach. Just inside, one of Ferrante's men cut at him. Yelling, he parried, and splashed the contents of the little jug into the man's face. The Losimon yowled and swiped at his eyes with his free hand, Master Beneforte knocked his sword aside, and they were through.

"Magic?" gulped Fiametta.

"Vinegar," snapped Master Beneforte.

There was another vicious struggle going on at the despised marble staircase. Master Beneforte practically tossed Fiametta over the balustrade, and vaulted after her. They pelted across the courtyard toward the tower-flanked gate, now being hotly contested by Ferrante's men and Montefoglia's.

Lord Ferrante was there in person, gesturing with a sword and shouting encouragement. "Hold the gate, and we'll have the rest at our will! Hold!" Almost casually, his sword licked out and tore open the throat of an attacking soldier in Montefoglia's livery. The man had ribbons in Ferrante's colors tied to the flower-and-bee badge of his cap in honor of the day's festivities, and they bounced wildly as he fell.

"Christ Jesus, it's going to be a massacre," Master Beneforte groaned.

Lord Ferrante turned and saw Master Beneforte. He stepped back a pace, his eyes narrowing, then raised his right fist with the silver ring face-out. Master Beneforte growled "Stupid!" in his throat, and raised his own hand in a peculiar rapid wave, fingers moving very precisely. Fiametta's belly wrenched with the tilted gut-feel of clashing magics. There was no subtlety in this. The silver ring began to glow, then suddenly emitted a brilliant flash and an earsplitting crack.

Lord Ferrante, not Master Beneforte, screamed, dropped his sword, and clutched his right hand with his left. A distinct odor of burnt meat wafted beneath another sharp tang Fiametta could not identify.

"Kill them!" Lord Ferrante roared, stamping his boots in agony, but the soldier facing Master Beneforte gave way in confused panic. Master Beneforte skipped backward a few paces, dagger brandished, as Fiametta picked up speed, then they both ran from the castle gate as hard as they could.

At the bottom of the hill Fiametta glanced back. Lord Ferrante was pointing her way, holding up a purse, and yelling something; a pair of bravos sped out the gate. As the houses grew more crowded, Master Beneforte darted between two shops and into an alley, then dodged into another alley. They fought through someone's laundry hung out to dry, and vaulted a sleeping dog. Fiametta was gasping for air; it felt like someone had stuck a dagger into her side, so sharp was the pain of her laboring lungs and banquet-laden stomach.

"Stop, Fiametta. . . ."

They had come to the edge of the buildings, by the shoreline of the lake. Master Beneforte sagged against a wall of dun brick. He, too, was gasping, his head bent to one side. His right hand kneaded his belly, just below his chest, as if to push back pain. When he looked up his face was not flushed, as Fiametta's was, but of a gray pallor, sheened with sweat. "I should not . . . have gorged so well," he blurted. "Even at the Duke's expense." And, after another moment, in a strange, small voice, "I can't run any more." His knees buckled.

Chapter Four

"Papa!" She wouldn't dare let him fall. She might not be able to get him up again. She twisted up under his armpit, and pulled his arm across her shoulders one-handed, juggling the bundled cloak under her other elbow. He was incredibly heavy, draped over her. "We have to keep going. We have to get back to the house." Her throat clotted in panic, more frightened by the weird gray color of his face than by the bravos seeking them through the alleys like a pair of hunting dogs.

"If Ferrante . . . takes the castle . . . he will take the town. And if he . . . takes the town . . . our old oak door won't stop his soldiers. Not if they think there's treasure inside. And if he takes . . . the town . . . he'll take the duchy. No place to run."

"With fifty men?" said Fiametta.

"Fifty men . . . and the moment." He paused. "No. He'll take the town at most. Then he'll wait for reinforcements. Then the rest." His face was furrowed with pain. He hugged his torso and stood bent over, swaying. "You run, Fia-mia. God, don't let them catch you. The blood lust will make them crazy for days. I've seen men . . . get like that."

A stone quay served several wooden docks built out into the water. A little fishing boat was just bumping up to the pilings. Its sole, sun-burned occupant tossed a rope around a post to secure his craft, then turned back to his lateen-rigged sail of coarse brown hemp, which he'd half-lowered as he'd coasted in. He straightened its folds and lowered it fully. He climbed out onto the dock and took up the rope to lead his boat around the end to its proper mooring on the lee side.

"The boat," breathed Fiametta. "Come on!"

He squinted at it, beard pointing. "Maybe . . ." They stumbled forward.

"Master Boatman," Fiametta called as they came near, "would you please hire us your boat?" She suddenly realized she was carrying no coins. And neither was Master Beneforte.

"Eh?" The peasant stood, and pushed back his straw hat, and stared dully at them.

"My father has taken ill. As you see. I wish . . . to take him gently across to Saint Jerome's, and see Brother Mario the healer." She glanced back over her shoulder. "At once."

"Well, I have to unload my fish, Madonna. Maybe then."

"No. At once." At his offended frown, she tore the silver net from her hair and held it out to him. "Here. There are as many pearls in my net as you have fish in yours. I'll trade you even, but *don't argue with me.*"

The astonished boatman took the hairnet. "Well . . . ! Never before have I pulled pearls from Lake Montefoglia!"

Fiametta moaned in her throat, and coaxed Master Beneforte to sit on the edge of the dock. From there he dropped heavily into the open boat, and motioned urgently to his bundled cloak. She shoved it into his hands and he clutched it to his chest. He looked worse, his mouth open with pain and legs drawing up. She jumped in after him, fighting her velvet skirts. The boat rocked wildly. Bemusedly, the boatman standing on the dock tossed in the bow rope, and then, after another glance at his handful of pearls, his straw hat as well. It spiraled down into the bottom of the boat. Fiametta squatted and grabbed an oar, heavy in her hands, and used it to shove them hard away from the dock.

A man in Ferrante's livery emerged from the alleys, spotted them, and shouted over his shoulder. He started for the dock. He had a drawn sword in his hand.

Fiametta pointed back toward the shore. "Watch out, Boatman! Those two men who are coming will steal your pearls." And beat out his life as well, she feared, in their frustration, as casually brutal as wolves.

"What?" The peasant wheeled, and stared in panic at the two bravos, who had nearly reached the dock. His hand tightened on his new treasure.

She found the rope to raise the sail, and hung on it, hand-over-hand. The warm afternoon breeze was faint, but steady, and more importantly, from the south, blowing them away from the shore even while she struggled with the sail and had no hand free for the steering oar. They had drifted a good forty feet away from the dock by the time the two shouting bravos reached the end of it.

They shook their swords at Fiametta and cried obscene and violent threats. They were just turning back to wreak lethal vengeance on the poor man who had helped her, when the peasant, who had fallen back and picked up a long oar, charged forward with it like a knight at joust. It struck one sword-waving bravo square in his steel breastplate; with a yell, the man fell backwards into the water and sank. Swinging the oar around like a quarterstaff, the peasant took the second bravo in the chin with a crack that echoed across the lake. He staggered back, unbalanced, and splashed after his comrade.

By the time the two men had saved themselves from drowning, at the cost of abandoning their heavy metal weapons and armor to the lake bottom, and splashed soddenly back onto the beach, the boatman had thoroughly disappeared. The light spring air filled the little boat's brown sail. The angry figures on the beach shaking their fists and impotently biting their thumbs seemed as tiny and feckless as gnomes.

Master Beneforte, who had been watching over the side with great anxiety, loosened his white-knuckled grip on the gunwale and sighed, sinking back into the bottom of the boat. His face was still very pale, though his breathing seemed a shade less labored. He must be sick and in pain indeed, not to be even offering criticism of her handling of the boat. She almost wished for a scathing remark, just for reassurance. Was it heart-sickness, or Lord Ferrante's evil magic that had laid him so low? Or some pernicious combination of both?

"The pearls in that hairnet were worth more than this entire leaky boat," he said after a moment. But it sounded more of an observation than a complaint. "Let alone the day's catch." The fish in question lay covered in water in a wooden tub in the bow, the drying nets piled beside it.

"Not at that moment," Fiametta pointed out sturdily.

"True," he breathed. "Very true." Wearily, he leaned his head back, adjusting his hat for a pillow.

Fiametta, sitting in the stern with the steering oar,

loosened the rope and let the boom swing out a little more squarely to the following breeze. It seemed miraculously calm and peaceful, with only the creak of the ropes, the slap of little wavelets, and the bubbling of the wake astern. It was a day for a picnic, not a ghastly massacre.

It wasn't a very big sail. Nor a fast boat. Nor a strong breeze. A determined horseman or two, paralleling them on the white road along the eastern shore, could outpace them. They had water in abundance, and certainly needed no food—her stomach was still stretched and leaden with the betrothal banquet—but sooner or later they must come to shore. Where hard-faced men would be waiting. . . . The green shoreline blurred as tears filled her eyes and spilled down her cheeks, wet annoying tracks. She ducked her head and rubbed the tracks with her sleeve. There were dots of darkening stain on the red velvet. Blood splashes. Captain Ochs's blood. She couldn't help it; she began to cry in earnest. Despite her weeping she kept the steering oar straight, guiding them between the two shores. Unusually, Master Beneforte did not demand she stop her blubbering or he'd beat her, but just lay and watched her, till she gulped her way back to coherence.

"What did you see happen in the castle, Fiametta?" he asked after a time, still supine. His voice was tired, unhurried now; despite the question, the tone steadied her. As best she could remember, she stammered out an account of the men, words, and blows she'd witnessed.

"Hm." He pursed his lips in thought. "I first guessed it was some long-laid treachery, Lord Ferrante assassinating his host. Take the daughter and the dukedom. . . . But stupid, for he already had the daughter, and could do murder in secret at his leisure, if that was his mind. But if, as you guess, those strangers brought some slander sufficient to break the betrothal, then Lord Ferrante was hurried into his treachery. And will prove his wit—or lack of it—in the aftermath. He must carry it all the way through, now." He sighed. "Poor Montefoglia." Fiametta wasn't sure if he meant the Duke, or the dukedom.

"What do we do next, Papa? How do we get home?"

His face screwed up in distress, compounded with disgust. "My work in progress—the jewels, the money— all forfeit! My great Perseus! What a woeful day. If in my foolish pride I had not insisted on presenting the saltcellar at that banquet, we might have lain low, let the affairs of princes blow by overhead. Plow under one duke, raise another, as Fortune spins her deadly wheel. Maybe, if Ferrante had secured himself as tyrant of Montefoglia, he would have continued my commissions. Now—now he knows me. I hurt him. I fear that was a grave mistake."

"Maybe," Fiametta floated a cautious hope, "maybe Lord Ferrante will lose the fight. He could be already slain."

"Mm. Or perhaps Monreale really will get little Lord Ascanio out. I would not underestimate Monreale. In that case it's civil war, though. Oh, God save me from the affairs of princes! Yet only the patronage of princes can support great works. My poor Perseus! My life's crown!"

"What about Ruberta and Teseo?"

"*They* can run away. My statue cannot." He brooded.

"Perhaps—if the soldiers come to our house—they won't notice the Perseus," Fiametta offered, frightened by this agitation, worsening his obvious illness.

"He's seven feet tall, Fiametta! He's a little hard to miss."

"Not so. He's all clothed in his clay, now, and he just looks like a big lump in the courtyard. And he's much too big to carry away. Surely the soldiers will look for gold and jewels, that they can hide in their clothes." But would they take—say—a bronze death mask? That was certainly small and portable.

"And then look for wine," groaned Master Beneforte. "And then get drunk. And then start smashing things. Clay, and my genius, so fragile!" He looked like he was about to cry himself.

"You saved the saltcellar."

"Accursed thing. I've half a mind to pitch it in the lake. Let it bring bad luck to the fish." He didn't move to do so, though, but hugged the bundled cloth tighter to himself.

Fiametta drew up some cold lake water for them both in the fisherman's tin cup she found under the rear seat. Master Beneforte drank, and squinted in the afternoon glare, and scrubbed his wrinkled brow with hooked fingers.

"The sun is troubling you, Papa. Why don't you put on that straw hat, and keep it from your eyes?"

He plucked it up, turned it over, and snorted. "Stinks." But he put it on. It did shade his jutting nose. He rubbed his chest. There was still pain there, a deep ache, Fiametta judged by his awkward movements as he turned on his side, then back again, in a futile quest for ease.

"Why didn't you use magic, to escape the castle, Papa?" She remembered Lord Ferrante raising his fist, and the glaring putti ring. "Or . . . or did you? *If I had been a trained mage, I would have done something to save the brave captain.* Would she have? The confusion and terror of that moment had overwhelmed her. She'd barely been able to save herself from her own skirts.

"Magic in the service of violence is a very perilous thing," Master Beneforte sighed. "I have done magic, and God save me I have done violence, even to murder—I've told you of the time I took vengeance upon a corporal of the Bargello for the death of my poor brother. I was twenty and hot and stupid, then. It was a great sin, though the Pope gave me a pardon for it. But I have never done violence *with* magic. Even at twenty I wasn't that stupid. I used a poniard."

"But Lord Ferrante's spirit ring—twice I saw him use it to do violence."

"Once, it bit him for his pains." Master Beneforte smiled in his beard, but his smile fell away. "That ring was more evil than I'd feared."

"What is a spirit ring, Papa? You said you'd seen one before, in possession of the lord of Florence, and it wasn't a sin."

"I *made* the spirit ring now on the hand of Lorenzo d'Medici, child," Master Beneforte confessed with a low sigh. He glanced uneasily at her, from the shadow of the straw brim. "The Church forbids them, and with reason, but I thought, the way we had this one set up, I might cast such a powerful work and yet not be tainted. I don't know. . . . You see, if a corpse is preserved unshriven and unburied (which is against holy law), the new-riven spirit tends to linger by the body. And with proper preparations that ghost can be harnessed to the will of a master."

"Enslaved?" Fiametta frowned. The word had the distaste of iron on her tongue.

"Yes, or . . . or bonded. How it came about in Florence was, Lord Lorenzo had a friend, who was dying in great debt. He struck a pact with the man. In exchange for his soul's service to the ring upon his natural death, Lorenzo would care for and look after this man's family. Which oath Lord Lorenzo has kept to this day, as far as I know. Lorenzo also swore to release the spirit if he feels his own death approaching. Ghost magic is immensely powerful. I feel there was no sin in what we did. But if some more narrow-minded inquisitor ruled otherwise, Lorenzo and I could burn at the stake back-to-back. So keep this story to yourself, child." Master Beneforte added reflectively, "We hid the body in an old dry well, beneath some new construction of the d'Medici in the heart of Florence. The ring's power diminishes, when it is taken too great a distance from its old bodily home."

Fiametta shivered. "Did you see the dead baby, when the casket of salt burst open?"

Master Beneforte blew out his breath. "Yes. I saw it."

"That cannot have been . . . some little sin."

"No." Master Beneforte's lips compressed. "You saw it closer—was it a girl-child?"

"Yes."

"I greatly fear . . . that may have been Lord Ferrante's own still-born daughter. Unnatural. . . ."

"Still-born? Or murdered?" Surely it was only the poor who secretly strangled unwanted daughters.

Master Beneforte bowed his head. "That's the trick of it, you see. A murdered spirit has . . . special powers. Special rage. A murdered, unbaptized, unburied infant . . ." He shuddered, despite the heat.

"Do you still think nothing in the world could be all black?"

"Mm." He huddled down in the boat. "I confess," he whispered, "I begin to have grave doubts of the hue of Uberto Ferrante's heart."

"An infant could not have chosen to bond its spirit. She must be enslaved," said Fiametta, frowning deeply. "Compelled, without knowing why."

One corner of Master Beneforte's mouth curved up. "Not any more. I released it from the ring. It sprang away in that great flash you saw."

Fiametta sat up. "Oh, good Papa! Oh, thank you!"

He raised his brows, bemused by her eager approval, warmed in spite of himself. "Well . . . I'm not so sure how good it will prove. Lord Ferrante must have gone to great lengths, to bind those powers to his will. His rage will be unbounded, to so lose all his trouble in an instant. The burn on his hand will be as nothing, compared to the loss of such a potency. But the burn will remind him. Oh, dear, yes. He will remember me."

"You've always wanted to be remembered."

"Aye," he sighed. "But I fear this fame could be too final."

The afternoon wore on. The southerly breeze pushed the crude boat along at little more than a walking pace, but unfailingly. The shoreline crept through its changes, farms and vines and patches of forest to the right, rubble and scrub and sheer rock faces growing higher and wilder to the left. To Fiametta's relief, Master Beneforte slept for a time; she prayed he would feel better when he woke. And indeed, when his eyes blinked open again in the slanting light of late afternoon, he sat upright for the first time.

"How go we?"

"I think we're going to run out of lake and light at about the same time." She almost wished the lake would run north forever. But when the shifting hills had parted around that last curve, they'd revealed not another stretch of lake, but the capping shoreline, with the tiny village of Cecchino huddled on its edge.

"As long as we don't run out of wind."

"It's grown more erratic, the last little while," Fiametta admitted. She made another adjustment to the sail.

He stared at the cloudless turquoise bowl of sky, arcing between the hills. "I trust there will be no storm tonight. For becalming, we have oars."

She glanced at the oars with unease. There went her last hope of avoiding the dreaded shore, even if the wind failed, which it seemed inclined to do. Over the next half-hour their progress slowed to a crawl.

The surface of the water grew silken, and the little slap of wind waves against the hull muted to pure silence. The village was still a mile off. She gave up at last, and lowered the sail.

She jiggled the heavy oars into the oar locks, and made to sit on the center bench.

"Give over," Master Beneforte snorted. "Your puny little girl arms won't get us there before nightfall." He evicted her from her place with a wave of his hands, and took it over. With a grunt, he started them forward with powerful sloshing strokes that made whirlpools spiral away from the oar blades into the smooth water. But after two minutes he stopped, his face grown gray again even against the orange glow of sunset. He gave up the oars to her without even arguing, and was very quiet for a time.

It was dusk when Fiametta's last aching pull nosed the bow onto the pebbled beach. Stiff-legged, they stumbled out of the boat and pulled it another foot up onto shore. Master Beneforte let the bow rope drop to the gravel crunching underfoot.

"Will we stay here the night?" Fiametta asked anxiously.

"Not if I can get horses," said Master Beneforte. "This place is too small to hide in. I won't begin to be easy till we're over the border. Hole up somewhere beyond Lord Ferrante's reach, till things sort themselves out."

"Will we . . . ever get to go home again?"

He gazed south, over the darkening lake. "My heart stands in my courtyard in Montefoglia, covered with clay. By God and all the saints, I will not be sundered from my heart for long."

Over the course of the next hour, they discovered that fisher-folk were not notable horsemen. Boats, after all, did not require expensive hay and grain. They were handed from one head-shaking peasant to another, less and less hospitably as the night grew darker. At last Fiametta found herself standing with her father in a shed at the end of the village, looking at a fat white nag that was over-at-the-knees, gray-headed, bewhiskered, and venerable.

"Are you sure you don't mean us two to carry him?" Master Beneforte, dismayed, asked the gelding's owner. Fiametta petted its wide velvety nose and listened. She'd never had a horse before.

The villager launched into a lengthy list of the beast's great strengths and manifold virtues, ending with a declaration that the horse was practically one of his family.

"Yes, your grandfather," muttered Master Beneforte in his beard. But after further negotiation, the deal was struck: a jewel and the boat for a horse. Master Beneforte prised a jewel from the hilt of his dagger under the man's suspicious eyes. He drew the line in outrage at the villager's request for a second jewel for a saddle. The subsequent crescendo of argument almost broke the deal again.

Still, the horse trader offered them bread, cheese, and wine. Master Beneforte denied being hungry, though both he and Fiametta drank a little wine. They packed the bread and cheese along.

The rising moon had just cleared the eastern hills when the peasant helped boost Fiametta up behind her father on the horse's warm, wide back. The bare-back's downward curve was practically a saddle in itself. The night was clear, and the moon still near-full, its light sufficient for them to make out the road in front of them. At the speed they were going to be traveling, it would be quite safe. Master Beneforte clucked, and beat the horse's fat sides with his heels, and they ambled off. As they left the environs of the village the horse seemed to perk up at this break from its usual routine, and stepped out . . . well, vigorously was too strong a term. Normally, perhaps.

The heavy red wine, combined with the gruesome day just past, made Fiametta's eyelids droop. She laid her head against her father's back and dozed, lulled by the horse's steady rocking *clop-a-clop*. The horse trader had earnestly warned them of demons abroad in the dark. After today demons seemed homey to Fiametta, compared to men. She didn't fear the dark at all, as long as there were no men in it. . . .

Her blood was beating raggedly in her ears as she jerked awake at a sudden jounce of the white horse, under her. Her father was slapping the beast into a trot, hissing. And no, the thrumming noise wasn't inside her head, but outside. Hoofbeats on the road behind them. Jostled and sliding, she clutched Master Beneforte around the waist, and cranked her aching head around to stare over her shoulder.

"How many?" Master Beneforte demanded in a strained voice.

"I . . . I'm not sure." Horsemen, yes, dark shapes on the road behind them, cold light glinting off metal. "More than two. Four."

"I should have bought a black horse. This cursed beast shines like the moon," Master Beneforte groaned. "And this country has no cover worth a whore's spit." Nevertheless, he yanked the horse off the road and headed them across a silver-misted meadow toward a coppice of spindly trees.

It was too late. A shout went up behind them, cat-calls and hooting as their pursuers, seeing them, belabored their horses into full gallop.

Three-quarters of the way across the meadow, Master Beneforte pulled the white horse's head back around. He drew his dagger.

"Get down and run for the trees, Fiametta."

"Papa, no!"

"You're more a hindrance than a help. This needs my undivided attention. Run, damn it!"

Fiametta huffed out her breath in protest, but she was half-sliding off the horse's slick back anyway. She fell to her feet and skipped backwards. The four dark horsemen were turning in to the meadow and spreading out in a frontal charge. Actually, not quite a charge; their horses bounced in a hesitant, reined-in canter, as if the idea of attacking a master mage in the dark was beginning to lose its appeal with proximity. *They do not know how sick he is,* Fiametta thought.

The leader pointed at Fiametta, and shouted to one of his men, who peeled off from the rest and started forward at a much more convincing pace. Fiametta picked up her skirts and sprinted for the trees. The coppice was close-grown; if she reached it first, he would not be able to force his mount in among the lashing branches. If she didn't . . . A panicked glance over her shoulder showed the other three closing in on Master Beneforte, who waited for them, dagger raised, the drama of the tableau slightly spoiled by the fat white horse fighting to put its head down and eat grass.

"Pigs!" Master Beneforte's shout echoed in her ears. "Scum! Come and be slaughtered like the vile herd of swine that you are!" Master Beneforte had often maintained that the best defense was a good offense, most men being cowards at heart. But his labored breathing drained much of the threat from his tones.

The man detailed to pursue Fiametta was clearly not in the least frightened of her, however. She crashed into the coppice just ahead of him; he made his horse rear to a stop, and dismounted to follow. He didn't even draw his sword. His boots were heavy and his legs were long. She dodged around the tree boles, the ragged ground catching at her light slippers. He loomed closer—with a lunge, he caught her flying skirt, and yanked it up, dumping her on her face. The ground came up like a blow, knocking her teeth painfully. She spat dirt. He landed on top of her, and pressed her to the ground. She twisted around to claw at his eyes. He was winded, but laughing, teeth and eyes gleaming in his shadowed face. He pinioned both her wrists in one hand. Her lungs burned, too breathless to scream. She tried to bite his nose. He jerked his head back barely in time, and cursed.

Methodically, one-handed, he began to pull off her jewelry. Her silver earrings and necklace, of no great value except for their delicate design, he stuffed into his doublet. Luckily the wires gave way before her earlobes tore; her ears stung where they'd twisted free. He had to lie across her chest and use both hands to pry up her thumb and strip it of the lion ring, while her legs kicked, unable to reach a target. He held the ring up to the moonlight, and uttered a "Ha!" of satisfaction at its weight, but then rather absently laid it on the ground. He pushed up on his hands, and looked down her body. The faceted green eyes of the silver snake glinted in the leaf-dappled moonlight.

"Oh, ho!" he said, laid his free hand on the belt, and jerked. The belt held fast. He jerked again, harder, lifting her hips from the ground. Intrigued, his hand left the belt and closed over her crotch, and he pinched her hard through the thick velvet.

The snake's eyes glowed red. The silver head rose, waved once from side to side, curved around, gaped its mouth wide, and sank silver fangs deep into his groping hand.

He screamed like a man damned, a ridiculously high-pitched shriek to come from that big throat. He clutched his hand to his chest and rolled off her, folded into a ball, and kept screaming. The howls became words—"Oh God, I burn, I burn! Black witch! Oh God I burn!"

Fiametta sat bolt upright in the dirt and leaf litter. He was rolling from side to side like a man possessed; his back arched convulsively. She patted the ground all around, groped up her lion ring, stuffed it back on her thumb, scrambled to her feet, and clawed her way through the spring vegetation.

Surely they would expect her to run away. She circled back toward the meadow instead. An opening slashed through the branches of the coppice proved to be from a large old beech tree, fallen slantwise, with its roots ripped up. She burrowed under its shadow into a leaf-filled depression, and went as still and quiet as her heaving chest and raw whistling breath would permit.

She could hear the men shouting to each other, but not Master Beneforte's bellow. The snakebite victim, still howling, finally found his way back to his fellows, and the hideous din dimished. Their hoarse, coarse voices blundered no nearer to her, anyway.

Her command of her own breath returned slowly. Finally, multiple hoofbeats faded into the distance. But had they all departed, or just some of them? She waited, her ears straining, but heard only the whisper of branches, a few insects, and the call of a nightingale. Leaf-shadows wove a brocade with the moon, now at zenith.

With her eyes wide, she picked her way quietly back to the edge of the meadow. No bravo jumped from ambush. Only the white horse was visible, halfway across, its head down in the milky mist. She could hear its teeth ripping up and grinding the juicy meadow grasses. She crept out into the cold, dew-soaked clumps.

She found her father's body not far from the horse. He lay tumbled, silvered beard pointing upward, open eyes blearing in the moonlight. The Losimon bravos had stripped him of the saltcellar, cloak, gold chain, jeweled poniard and scabbard, and his rings, as she'd expected. They'd also taken his tunic, hat, and shoes, leaving him only his ripped linen shirt and black hose, points half-untied. It was terribly undignified. He looked like an old man overtaken by death on the way to the garderobe.

Fearfully, she patted him for sword wounds, but found none. She laid her ear to his dew-dampened chest. What could you hear, if a heart had burst? Who would hear hers, if it burst now?

He must have been felled by his own illness before he'd even had a chance to defend himself. Perhaps the efforts had been the final blow. She'd thought the day had drained her of every possible reaction, but apparently she still had tears left. Her face cried on almost without her, as if she were split in two. Her other part methodically dragged his body to the lip of a small gully that drained the meadow. She recaptured the horse—the Losimons had apparently scorned to steal the old nag—led it down and positioned it in the low spot, and dragged Master Beneforte across its swayed back. The abandoned husk of Master Beneforte. Wherever he was, her father certainly was no longer in there.

The horse's fuzzy white ears flicked back and forth, confused by its odd burden. Her father's arms dangled down, and his hair hung lank and strange. She chose to lead the horse from the other side, holding the husk's foot to keep it steadily balanced. Still crying, strangely calm, she coaxed the horse back onto the road and began walking north.

Chapter Five

From winter to summer was but a two-day walk, Thur noted to himself with contentment. He patted the shoulder of the big brown mule he led for Packmaster Pico. Yesterday morning the pack train had crested the snowy heights of Montefoglia Pass, all barren rocks and treacherous ice and biting, clawing wind. This evening they strolled along a poplar-lined avenue, grateful for the green shade against the glare of the westering sun arcing down into the soft rolling hills. He wriggled his toes in his dusty boots. His feet were warm.

The mule's long furry ears, aflop to each side, rose to attention, and its tired plod quickened. Up ahead, Pico had paused to let down the bars to a pasture gate. He led his pack train within. Judging by their pulling, the eight mules were familiar with this stop, though it was all new to Thur.

"Keep them moving to the grove," Pico, pointing to

76

the stand of trees shading one end of the pasture, shouted over his shoulder to his two sons and Thur. "That's where we'll camp. We'll take their packs off first and then turn them loose."

The mule tried to nudge Thur toward the green grass and the little stream, but Thur dutifully dragged it to the grove and tied it to a tree. "You'll be happier to have your pack off first," he told it. "Then you can roll." It waggled its absurd ears at him in disagreement, and snorted through its cream-colored nose, and Thur grinned.

He pulled off its heavy pack, loaded with copper ingots and hides, and the pack of its work mate who followed on a rope, and turned both beasts loose. They thudded away toward the stream, squealing happily. The pasture's only other occupant, a sway-backed, old white horse, regarded the invasion with both interest and suspicion. The look on its long gray face made Thur think of the old scholar, Brother Glarus, presented with a troop of rowdy new students. Thur turned to help Pico's younger boy, Zilio, with his mules' heavy packs, which threatened to crush the lad. Zilio smiled gratefully and sprang about rather like the released mules.

Pico, his sons, and Thur lined up the packs and set the bright striped saddle pads atop upside down to dry and air. The boys began to unload their meager camp gear, and Pico started to build a fire in a charred circle from a handy stack of wood. Thur stared around with interest. On the other side of the road rambled a big two-story stucco house, white-washed a pastel pink, with outbuildings in a yard behind. The whole was surrounded by a high pink stucco wall with broken glass and rusty nails set in its top frosting of cement, but a wide double wooden gate stood invitingly open to the road.

"You could take a room at the inn, if you liked,"

said Pico; seeing Thur's gaze, he nodded across the
road. "If you're tired of sleeping on the ground.
Innkeeper Catti's beds are good. But I warn you, he's
a great greedy-guts, and charges plenty for his linen.
He really prefers prelates to muleteers for custom-
ers, when he can get them."

"Will you sleep there?"

"No, I always stay with my beasts and my load,
unless it's pouring rain or snowing. He charges me
enough for the pasture and the firewood. 'Tis a good
stop, though, and good fodder, and the beasts like
it. And with an early start, I can usually push all the
way home to Montefoglia by dark, in the summer.
Catti's wife sets a good table, on the nights when the
rain makes my fire too miserable. She smokes the
most excellent hams. Which reminds me, I promised
to bring one home to my neighbor who watches my
place when I'm away. Don't let me forget, when I
go over there to settle my charges."

Thur nodded, dug out his bit of tallow soap, and
went to wash his hands and face upstream. The brook
was icy, but refreshing, and the evening air so warm
he was lured into washing his hair and upper torso,
and then, much more quickly, his lower half. Pico's
older boy Tich, a gawky fifteen-year-old, came over
to watch. Intrigued, he shuffled off his boot and stuck
an experimental foot into the brook, then yelled with
the cold.

"It's not that bad," Thur said mildly.

Tich hopped in a circle, shaking the drops off.
"Mad mountain man!" He stuffed his foot back into
his boot.

"The water in the mines is much colder."

"God save me from the mines, then," said Tich
fervently. "I'm for open road. Isn't this the life?" He
waved a possessive arm at the encroaching spring
evening, as if he owned it all to the horizons. "You

should join us, Thur, not shut yourself up in some nasty little dark shop."

Thur shook his head, smiling. "It's the metal, Tich. Hundreds of men labor to get metal like the copper we're carrying into the hands of some fancy smith, and who gets the credit? The artisan, that's who. Besides . . . ," Thur paused, hesitating to confide his heart's hope to a possibly unsympathetic ear. *I want to learn to make splendid and beautiful things.* "Besides, it can't be any darker or more nasty than the mines."

"It's all in what you're used to, I guess," Tich allowed, too amiable to argue.

Pico strolled over to redirect Tich's energy. "Come on, boy, you've got mules to curry."

Thur shrugged his dusty wool tunic and leggings back on. Those must last till he reached Montefoglia, and found a washerwoman. Perhaps he could strike a deal, split firewood or something in exchange. Working his way with Packmaster Pico, Thur had not yet had to tap his little store of coins, and he hoped to make them last as long as possible, so as not to be wholly dependent on the charity of his brother Uri.

He shared his soap with Pico, while Tich attempted to dragoon the ten-year-old Zilio into helping with his assigned chore, and Zilio protested. Their squabbling faded in the distance as Thur and Pico walked across the road to the inn. The men's shadows lay long in front of them, as the sun reached for the rim of the hills to their backs. Thur's stride lengthened. The pink inn seemed poignant with some undefined promise, drawing him on. Thur decided it must be his thirst.

He shouldered through the front door after Pico, who called cheerily for Catti. The whitewashed front room was set up with tables on trestles and benches. A few coals glowed in the banked fireplace, ready to ignite a neat stack of wood waiting to be piled on later as the evening cooled. Several promising kegs with taps sat on more trestles against one wall.

Master Catti emerged from the back of the building, wiping his hands on a grimy linen towel. He was a graying man, his waist thickened more with age than good living, and he stumped along quickly on short legs.

"Ah, Pico," he greeted the packmaster eagerly. "I saw you come in. Have you heard the news from Montefoglia?" His smile was welcoming, but his eyes looked strained.

Pico, arrested by the hushed tones, dragged his gaze from the kegs to his host. "No, what?"

"Duke Sandrino was assassinated, four days ago!"

"What! How did it come about?" Pico's mouth gaped. Thur's happy warmth washed from his belly in an instant, to be replaced with a cold knot of ice.

Catti rocked on his heels, grimly satisfied with the effect of his gossip. "They say he had some sort of quarrel with the Lord of Losimo at the betrothal banquet for his daughter Julia. Daggers were drawn, and . . . the usual followed. A terrible mess, by the accounts I've heard so far from people coming up the road. Lord Ferrante's troops have captured Montefoglia, at least for the moment."

"My God. Have they sacked the town?" asked Pico.

"Not much. They still have their hands full with—"

"My brother is in the Duke's guard," Thur interrupted urgently.

"Ah?" Catti raised his eyebrows. "He's just botched himself out of a job, I'd say." And, a little less tartly, "I hear some of the guards fled with little Lord Ascanio and their wounded behind the walls of Saint Jerome, with the Abbot Monreale."

And some of the guards, presumably, had not. Yet Thur could picture Uri, defending the boy-lord, getting him safe behind the monastery's stones. Being last through the gate, no doubt.

"Ferrante's troops march about and glare at the walls," Catti went on, "but they don't quite dare attack the Brethren. Yet. Ferrante has the Duchess and Lady Julia as hostage, and has sent to Losimo for more troops at the quick-march."

Pico the packman whistled through his teeth. "Bad . . . ! Well, my place lies outside the town, and there's little enough to steal there. Thank the Virgin I brought Zilio with me this trip. I often leave him with my neighbor. I think I'd better lay over a day or two with you, Catti, if I can have your pasture, till we get some hint of how things fall out."

"I should think you'd get a good price down there right now for your metals, from one side or t'other," said Catti. "They'll be wanting armor, weapons, bronze for cannon. . . ."

"I'm more likely to have it stolen from me, by one side or the other," said Pico gloomily. "No. 'Twould be better to cut over the hills and go west to Milan. My mules will eat most of my profits in the travel, though." He glanced at Thur. "You're free to go on to Montefoglia if you wish, Thur. To seek news of your brother. Though I'd be sorry to lose your strong back."

"I don't know. . . ." Thur stood stiff with doubt and worry.

"Stay the night," suggested Catti. "Decide in the morning."

"Yes, that would be best," Pico agreed. "There may be better news by then, who knows?" He clapped Thur consolingly on the shoulder, in awkward sympathy.

Thur nodded thanks and reluctant agreement. "Do you still want your ham?" he remembered.

"Not now. . . . I tell you, though, Catti, if your wife has any of those big smoked sausages, I'll take one.

We can toast slices over the fire, tonight and on our way to Milan."

"I think she has a few left from the last pig, hanging in the smokehouse. But—"

"Good. Thur, go pick out one for us, will you? I had better go tell my boys the bad news." Frowning, Pico went back out the door and recrossed the road.

Catti shrugged and led Thur through the inn and across the back yard. Thur readily identified the small shack that was the smokehouse by the aromatic gray haze that seeped out under its eaves and hung promisingly in the still evening air. Thur ducked into the smoky dimness after Catti. Catti bent down and inserted a couple more water-soaked sticks of apple wood into the coals of the fire pit in the center of the dirt floor. The aromatic cloud thus released tickled Thur's nostrils, and he sneezed.

"There's four left," Catti reached up and tapped one of a row of brown, gauze-wrapped cylinders hanging from the blackened rafters, and made it swing. "Take your choice."

Thur glanced up, then his gaze was riveted by what lay in the shadows *above* the rafters. A board crossed them at right angles. Balanced on the board was the nude body of a gray-bearded man, close-wrapped in the same sort of gauze as the sausages, like a thin swaddling shroud. His skin was shrivelled and tanning in the smoke.

"Pico was right," Thur observed after a moment's stunned silence. "Your wife *does* smoke the most unusual hams."

Catti glanced up after him. "Oh, *that*," he said in disgust. "I was just going to tell Pico the story. He's a refugee from Montefoglia who didn't quite make it. Penniless, it turned out—after the bill was run up."

"Do you do this often, to guests who don't pay?"

asked Thur in a fascinated voice. "I'll tell Pico to settle our bill promptly."

"No, no, he was dead when he got here," Catti exclaimed impatiently. "Three days ago. But the priest was gone and there's none to shrive him, and none of my neighbors will allow an unshriven dead sorcerer to be buried on their property, and frankly, neither will I. And the hellcat girl won't pay. We had to do something with him, so I thought of the smokehouse. So there he lies, and there he can stay, till his bill is settled. And so I told my wife. She can flounce off to her sister's in a fury if she wants, but I *won't* be cheated by a dead Florentine's servant." Catti crossed his arms, to emphasize his resolve.

"I think he eats and drinks but little, Master Innkeeper. How much are you charging him for the smoke?" Thur inquired, still craning his neck upward.

"Yes, but you should see how the horse he rode in on gorges," groaned Catti. "As a last resort, I'll confiscate the horse. But I'd rather have the ring, for surety. The ring won't drop dead suddenly, as the nag looks to do." He waved an impatient hand against the rising smoke, pulled a sausage down off its hook, and motioned Thur out of the smokehouse ahead of him.

"You see," Catti went on, after drawing a lungful of clear air, "three mornings ago this half-Ethiope girl dressed in filthy velvet came dragging him up the road, slung across that white nag now in my pasture. She said they'd fled the massacre in Montefoglia, and been robbed, and him murdered, by Lord Ferrante's men, who pursued them past Cecchino. Except he hadn't been murdered—there isn't a wound on him—and she hadn't been robbed, for she wears a big gold ring on her thumb a blind bandit couldn't have overlooked.

"I had my suspicions, but she seemed in distress, and my wife has a soft head, and she let her in and got her cleaned up and calmed down. The more I thought it over, the more suspicious I became. You have to get up early in the morning to make a fool of old Catti. She claimed the old man was a Florentine mage, and her father. The Florentine part I'll grant. I think she was his slave. He died of apoplexy on the road, or maybe black magic. She robbed his body and hid his things, and rolled in the dirt and made her hair wild, and came in telling this tale, meaning to be rid of him at my expense and circle back later for his treasure. The proof of it is, that gold ring is a man's ring. She probably stole it off her master's finger. Well! I saw through her ploy, and charged her with it."

"And then what happened?" said Thur.

"She had a screaming fit, and refused to give up her stolen ring. She said if her father were alive, he'd turn me into one of my own bedbugs. I don't think *she* could turn beer into piss. She's barricaded herself in my best room, and screams curses at me through the door, and threatens to set fire to my inn, and won't come out. Now I ask you! Isn't it suspicious? Is she not a madwoman?"

"You would almost think she fears being robbed again," Thur murmured.

"Quite demented." Catti frowned, then his gloomy gaze traveled up Thur. A dim light animated his eye. "Say. You're a big, strong lad. There's a pot of ale in it for you if you can pull her from my best bedroom without breaking any of my furniture. How about it?"

Thur's blond brows rose. "Why don't you evict her yourself?"

Catti mumbled something about "aging bones" and "hellcat." Thur wondered if Catti were seeing himself as a bedbug. Could a mage even turn a man into an insect, and if so, would it be a man-sized insect, or tiny? Well, he'd been thinking about dipping into his coins and buying some ale to go with that toasted sausage tonight. The tap room had breathed a delicious aroma, from the vicinity of those kegs.

"I could try, I suppose," Thur offered cautiously.

"Good!" The innkeeper reached up and clapped him on the shoulder. "Come this way, I'll show you where." He led Thur back inside.

On the second floor of the inn, Catti pointed to a closed door, and whispered, "In there!"

"How is it barricaded?"

"There's a bar, though not a very stout one. And she's wedged it with something. I think she dragged the bed against it."

Thur studied the wooden door. From downstairs came a man's voice calling, "Catti! Hey Catti! Are you asleep up there? Get your fat self down here and pour me a mug, or I'll help myself."

Catti wrung his hands in frustration. "Do your best," he urged Thur, and hurried downstairs.

Thur watched the door a moment longer. The strange, inarticulate longing that he had identified as thirst, outside, was much stronger now, knotting and coiling in his stomach. His mouth was dry. He shrugged, and went up and put his shoulder to the oak. He wedged his foot to the floor and tensed. The door resisted; he pushed a little harder. An unfortunate splintering sound came from the other side. Thur paused, worried. Had he just lost his pot of ale? He pushed again against a skreeling of wood across wood that reminded him of the windlass in the mine. The gap widened a bit more. He stuck his head through, and blinked.

Some black iron bolts holding the bracket for the door bar had torn out of the doorframe, and the bar swung loose. A bed with four posts holding up a canopy had been shoved a little way back by the inward-moving door. Standing not three feet from him was a brown-skinned girl in a red dress with long linen undersleeves, holding a heavy flower-painted ceramic chamber pot high in both hands. Its contents sloshed ominously under its ceramic lid.

Thur's breath stopped. He had never seen anyone so extraordinary. Midnight-black hair tumbled like a stormcloud. Skin like toast, breathing the heat of a Mediterranean noon. A petite, alert, yet well-padded body that reminded him of the walnut-wood carvings of angels around the altar of the parish church in Bruinwald. Brilliant eyes, the warm brown color of his mother's precious cinnamon sticks. She looked . . . she looked warm all over, in fact. She shrank back, glaring at him.

That wouldn't do. He squeezed the rest of himself through the door, shifting the bed across the floor with another shattering *skreek*, and clasped his hands together in what he hoped was a nonthreatening manner. His hands felt as big as cheese paddles, and as clumsy. He swallowed, and remembered to exhale. "Hello." He ducked his head politely at her, and cleared his throat.

She backed another step. Her arms bearing up the chamber pot sank a little.

"You really can't stay in here. Not forever, anyway," Thur said. Her arms were shaking. "Does that greedy innkeeper bring you any food?"

"Not . . . not since yesterday, when his wife left," she stammered out, not taking her wary gaze from him. "I had a bottle of wine that I was making last, but it's gone now."

She was staring at him as if he was some sort of monster. Really, he wasn't that big. He bent his knees a little, and slumped his shoulders, and tried futilely to shrink. It was the little room that set him off to such disadvantage. He needed a bigger room, or the outdoors.

The gold ring on her pot-clutching thumb riveted

his eye. A lion mask with a red gem in its mouth seemed to glow with a Saharan heat, drawing him like a fire. He nodded to it. "Is that the ring Catti wants to steal?"

She smiled bitterly. "He wants to, but he can't. He's tried twice, but he can't keep hold of it. Only one man can wear this ring. I'll prove it." She tossed her mane of wildly curling hair, and set the chamber pot down on the floor. "I was planning to break this over Catti's head, but on you I can't reach that high." She grimaced, and shoved it away with her foot. She pulled the ring from her thumb, and, sourly smug, held it out to him. "Just try to put it on. You'll find you can't."

It glowed, in his palm. When he closed his hand over it, it felt alive, like a beating heart. Automatically, he slipped it over the ring finger of his left hand, and held it up to the last sunbeam, a golden slice of light that penetrated the room's shutters and made a bright line on the wall. The tiny lion's mane shimmered in singing waves, and the little gem burned. He turned his hand, making the red reflection dance like a fairy over the opposite wall. He looked up to find the brown girl staring at him with a look of utter horror on her beautiful soft features.

"Oh—I'm sorry," he apologized, he knew not what for. "You said to put it on. Here." He tugged at it, against his wrinkling knuckle.

"A muleteer?" she whispered, still with that aghast look. "My ring has brought me a stinking *muleteer*? A big stupid German lout—"

"Swiss," Thur corrected, still tugging. A big stupid Swiss lout, yah. She must have been watching him from the window when Pico's packtrain arrived. He grew scarlet, like the gem. His knuckle was red and white, and swelling. "Excuse me. It's stuck." He twisted the ring around in embarrassment, but it still jammed. "Maybe some soap. I have a bit of soap in my pack. You can come with me. I'm not trying to steal your ring, Madonna. I was going to Montefoglia. My brother has apprenticed me to a goldsmith there, or he was going to, but now I don't know what's happening. My brother Uri is a captain in the Duke's guard, you see, and I don't know . . . I'm afraid . . . I don't know if he's alive or dead right now." He twisted and pulled more frantically as her face, stunned, began to crumple with tears, but it was no good. The ring was stuck fast. "Sorry. Can . . . can I help? Can I help you, Madonna?" He opened his hands to her, offering—well, he didn't have much. Offering his hands, anyway.

To his alarm and distress, she sank to the floor, hands to her face, weeping. Awkwardly, he levered himself down beside her. "I'll get the ring off somehow, if I have to . . . to chop off my finger," he promised recklessly.

She shook her head helplessly, and gulped out, "It's not that. It's the whole thing."

Thur paused, and spoke more gently. "That really is your father in the smokehouse, isn't it? I'm sorry. That innkeeper is a bit of a monster, I'm afraid. I'll break his head for you, if you like."

"Oh . . ." She put her hands out flat on the floor, and leaned on them wearily for support. She stared down at them, then looked up at Thur, searching his face. "You don't look much like Uri. I didn't expect his younger brother to be so much bigger. And you're so blond and pale, compared to him."

"I worked in the mines most of this winter. I scarcely saw the sun." He must look as repulsive to her as a white worm winkled from under a rock . . . his thought stuttered, jerked about. "You know my brother Uri?" And, more urgently, "Do you have any idea of his fate?"

She sat up straighter, and held out a hand to him in

sad irony. "Hello, Thur Ochs. I'm Fiametta Beneforte. Prospero Beneforte is my father. You have arrived just in time to become apprenticed to a smoked corpse." Her lips compressed on an angry sob.

"Uri's letter didn't mention a daughter," Thur blurted in surprise. He grasped her hand quickly, lest she take it away again. "His letters are always too short, Mother says."

Her voice lowered. "I last saw Captain Ochs take a sword thrust through his chest, while trying to defend little Lord Ascanio from Ferrante's murdering men. I don't know if he's alive or dead, or if he got away with the other wounded to the healers at Saint Jerome. But it was no small wound." She released his grip and plucked jerkily at the wrinkled velvet of her skirts, bunched in her lap. "I'm sorry I have no better news, nor more recent. My father and I fled away for our lives. Or we tried to."

"What happened?" His belly was cold, cold. . . .

In short, blunt sentences she stammered out a nightmare account of her last four days. Thur remembered the grief and loss of his own father's death in the mines. He'd been at school with Brother Glarus that winter day; the news of the cave-in had come at breathless second-hand. After days of frantic, fruitless rescue efforts, the priest had consecrated the shaft and the lost men been left buried, and Thur had never looked on his father's face again. Fiametta had had to wrestle with her dead alone in the night. Thur felt both horror for her, and a strange envy. Dead her father was, as his, but at least not cut off from the last services survivors could bestow, though smoking and curing was not exactly on the usual list of comforting ritual pieties properly due a paterfamilias.

". . . and the second time he tried to twist it from my thumb, I kicked him in the knee and barricaded myself in here. That was . . . that was yesterday," she came to the end of her tale, and rested her head on her knees, face turned to his, rocking a little. "How did you come here?"

Briefly, he described his brother's letter, and how he had found a guide and company in exchange for his labor with Pico.

"But how *here*? To this inn, just in time to meet me?"

Thur blinked. He had an extraordinary knack for finding things, yes, but surely it would be some kind of arrogance, in front of a real mage's daughter, to claim supernatural meaning for a mere knot in his belly and catch in his breath. "Pico always stops here. It's the only place between Bergoa, on the border, and Cecchino."

"Have I wrought true after all?" she breathed in bewilderment. Her hand closed. "You put my ring right on. . . ."

Thur twisted it. "I'll get it off. I promise."

"No." She sat up, and spread her fingers, pink palms down. "Keep it. For now. Anyway, fat Catti won't try to wrest it from *your* hand."

"I can't take this, it's much too valuable!" Not that he seemed to have much choice, till his knuckle shrank again. "I tell you what, Madonna Beneforte. I have a few coins. I think I have enough to ransom your father's body from that greed-head innkeeper. Get him out of the smokehouse, at least, and help you get him properly buried."

She wrinkled her brow. "Yes, but where? The ignorant peasants here all fear to have him planted on their property, because he was a mage. And I won't have him buried in the middle of the road."

"I passed through the village of Bergoa yesterday. There's a little parish church there, and a priest. He'll have to take your father in. I'll help you take him there tomorrow."

She bowed her head, and whispered, "Thank you." Freed of the stiffening from her isolation and fear, Thur could see her weariness was near to overwhelming her.

"I . . . I'll have to go south, after that," Thur said. "I have to find out the fate of my brother."

Her head came up. "It will grow dangerous, the closer you try to go to Montefoglia. Lord Ferrante's mercenaries will be out marauding, pillaging for their needs, killing any who resist or . . . or compelling them to their service. Or do you think to volunteer your service to the Duke's guards, if they still hold Saint Jerome against Ferrante?"

Thur shook his head. "I have no calling to be a soldier. Unless I were defending Bruinwald, the way the men of Schwyz fought off the Armagnacs at the battle of St. Jakob an der Birs. But I can't go home to our mother without sure news of Uri. If he's hurt, I must try to bring him away."

"And if he's dead?"

"If he's dead . . . I must know," shrugged Thur. "But it's certainly too dangerous for you down that way, Madonna Beneforte. Maybe the priest at Bergoa will know of a safe place for you to stay till I—we—return."

"Return?"

He smiled in an attempt at reassurance. "Your ring will be your surety. If I can't get it off, I'll have to bring it back, won't I?"

Her generous mouth pursed in plaintive puzzlement. "Isn't that the wrong way around, for a surety?"

"A debt is a bond. It must be paid."

"You are an unusual man. Muleteer. Miner." Her brow lifted. "Mage?"

"Oh, I'm no mage. I meant to apprentice to your father, yes, but I figured to haul wood and lift ingots, mainly. Just a workman, really."

"I am my father's only heir." She bit her lower lip with strong white teeth. "Your apprentice's contract— had it been drawn up—would now be a part of my inheritance. I wonder how much of the rest has been looted by the Losimons, by now?"

"There you go, then," said Thur cheerfully. "Well met, Madonna, though the times are ill."

"Well met, Muleteer," she whispered. Her twisted smile was not unkind, her brows quizzical, as if she were growing used to him, or to the idea of him. "Though the times are very ill."

He lumbered to his feet, and gave her a hand up. "Come. Let's get something to eat. I don't think Catti will refuse my coins."

"No, but with his wife gone, the food could be chancy," Fiametta warned. "I gather she did all the cooking, and a great deal more besides."

"You can have my toasted sausage by Pico's fire, if you will. You can share our camp. Pico won't mind."

She grimaced. "I'd rather sleep under a tree than spend another night under Catti's roof, that's certain."

They started for the stairs, that gave onto the front taproom. Men's talk echoed up. At the head of the stairs, Fiametta suddenly froze, and held up her hand to stop Thur. "Shh," she whispered, and listened intently, head cocked to one side. "Oh, God, I know that voice. That spitty sound it has. . . ."

"A friend?" said Thur hopefully.

"No. It sounds like the man who led Ferrante's bravos, the night they killed my father."

"Would you recognize him, if you peeked through the staircase?" The wood below the rail had decorative trefoil holes cut in it.

She shook her head. "I never saw his face."

"They don't know me," murmured Thur after a moment. "Crouch here, and I'll go see what's happening."

"Turn the ring inward. They might recognize it,"

she whispered, and he nodded and turned the lion mask to his palm, letting his hand curl.

She sank to the floor, slipped a little way down the staircase, and put her eye to one trefoil cutout. She drew in her breath, and her hands clenched to fists; apparently she knew the man after all. Thur walked openly into the taproom.

Three or four local folk had drifted in, and sat on the benches nursing mugs. By their work-stained tunics and leggings, they were farmers or laborers. In addition, two strangers stood, quaffing pots of ale and talking to Catti. They were clearly horsemen, travelers, wearing mud-splattered boots, short cloaks, doublets, and heavy hose. In addition to the usual dagger that every man carried, each bore a steel sword. They wore no badge or colors identifying them as Lord Ferrante's men or any other lord's. When the senior, bearded one put down his mug after a last up-tipping draught, Thur could see he was missing several front teeth. Thur hung in the background, blending in with the local peasantry.

"Take us to him, then, Innkeeper, and we'll see if he's the thief we seek," said the bearded horseman, wiping his lips with his sleeve.

"For the price of his ransom, you can have him," grumbled Catti. "I knew something stank of old fish. This way."

Catti lit a lamp and led the two strangers through the inn to his back yard. Thur, and after a moment two other of the curious yokels, tagged along. The sky was still luminous with late twilight, though the evening star shone above the western hills.

Catti, with the lamp, and the bearded man ducked into the smokehouse. They emerged again very shortly. The bearded Losimon spoke to his stubble-shaved companion. "Found him. Get the horses."

The younger man glanced around uneasily at the

gathering dusk. "Sure you don't want to spend the night here, and go in the morning?"

The bearded man's voice fell to a growl. "If we're late, or botch this again, you'll *wish* for hobgoblins. *Without delay*, he said. Get the horses."

The younger man shrugged, and trudged off around the corner of the inn.

Catti rubbed his hands together happily. Thur drifted over to him. Catti looked up. "Did you get the she-cat out of my best room?" he asked.

"Yes."

"And where is she?"

"She ran off up the road."

"In the dark? Damn! I wanted that ring. Well, I have the horse. Good riddance. It looks like I'll be quit of both my problems in a moment."

The younger stranger returned, leading three horses. Two were caparisoned with light cavalry saddles. The third bore an empty pack saddle. The younger man laid out a large piece of old canvas on the ground, and tossed some rope down beside it.

"Who are those men?" Thur whispered to Catti.

"Guardsmen from Montefoglia. That dead graybeard in my smokehouse turns out to be a thief. Stole a valuable gold saltcellar from the castle, they say. They're taking him off my hands."

"I'd think they'd want the saltcellar, not the body. Isn't it a little late for a hanging?" said Thur. The two men entered the smokehouse. After some thumping sounds, they came out with the old man's body on its board. They pulled the board away and began rolling the corpse up in the canvas. "What do they want it for? And whose guardsmen are they, the Duke's or Lord Ferrante's?"

"Who cares, if their coins are good?" Catti murmured impatiently.

The two men bound the canvas round with rope,

and lifted the long package. They grunted, forcing it to bend over the pack saddle. While the bearded man tied the canvas-covered shape firmly to its carrier, the younger man ducked back inside the smokehouse and came out with two hams, which he slung over his saddle bow.

"This is wrong, Master Catti," Thur whispered urgently. "You mustn't let them take him. Here—I have some coins in my pack. I'll get them right now. I'll ransom him from you, instead."

"I'll take their coins in my hand, thank you," snapped Catti. "They offer a better bargain."

"Whatever they offered, I'll give you more."

"Not likely, muleteer." Catti waved him away, and approached the strangers, smiling. "I see you fancy my hams. You won't regret them, I guarantee. Now, let's see. The ransom, plus two pots of ale, plus two hams, comes to . . ." He counted on his fingers.

Thur saw it coming. He dropped back by the smokehouse and snatched up a long billet of wood from the stack alongside.

The younger man swung aboard his horse as the older man grasped the counting Catti by the shoulder and pulled him toward himself. "Here's your payment, Innkeeper." The steel of his dagger flashed in the folds of his cloak, as he stabbed Catti in the stomach.

Catti cried out in pain and astonishment, and stumbled backwards, hands clutching his belly, as the bravo flung him away. The two watching locals started toward him, their reactions slow. The bearded man grinned, dark-mouthed with his missing teeth, and vaulted aboard his horse. His subordinate was already spurring toward the road, yanking the packhorse along. Futilely, Thur flung his billet at the younger Losimon's back with all his strength. It rotated through the air and bounced off the cloak- and doublet-padded man with little effect. Clods of dirt spun up from the horses' hooves as the bravos fled into the gathering shadows.

Thur pelted around the building in their wake, but by the time he reached the front gate, the hoofbeats were only a fading echo in the twilight. Fiametta was standing in the middle of the road amidst the dust hanging in the air, peering south after the vanished horsemen. Her face was drawn, eyes big and dark.

"They stole your father's body," Thur panted. "I couldn't stop them."

"I know. I saw."

"*Why?* It's madness! They took two hams as well. Surely they don't plan to eat him!"

"Oh . . . ," she breathed. Intensity of thought struggled with dismay in her face. "I have a guess. A monstrous guess. He cannot—I have to stop—" She stepped down the road a few paces, fists clenched, as if in a trance.

Thur caught her by the sleeve. "You can't go running down the road by yourself in the middle of the night."

She rotated in his grip, looking across to the pasture and the dim glimmer of her white horse among Pico's mules. "Then I'll ride."

"No!"

She stared at him, brows lowering. Her eyes flamed. "What?"

"I'll go. Tomorrow." And, as her breath drew in angrily, he added hastily, "We'll both go."

She hesitated. Her hands uncurled. She stared around into the vast uncertain darkness. Her shoulders slumped. "I don't know what to . . . how to . . . yes. You're right. Very well." Looking stunned, she turned to follow him back into the inn.

Chapter Six

The uproar in the inn was augmented by two families of refugees from Montefoglia who arrived just as the wounded Catti was carried indoors by the big blond Swiss and the locals. The chaos did not die down till Catti's wife returned, fetched by a breathless neighbor. Fiametta hung back uncertainly, as the woman who had been kind to her bustled within. But Madonna Catti, though she frowned deeply, spoke no blame. Instead she drafted Fiametta's aid, carrying and arranging bedding, water, and washbasins for the mob of new guests while she tended to her husband. She emerged from her bedroom several times, to keep her stableboys hustling, and to direct the Montefoglians' servants to put together a meal of bread, cheese, smoked sausage, wine, and ale, served all round. Fiametta did not partake of the smoked meats.

At Madonna Catti's request Packmaster Pico brought his mules, his cargo, and his sons within the walls of the compound, and the gates were firmly locked for the night. The Montefoglians were distressed to learn that the marauding soldiers from whom they'd fled were ranging this far north, and made plans to move on in the morning. In the meantime, counting up the fathers, brothers, servants, Catti's stablehands, the Picos and the Swiss, there were fourteen armed men within the walls tonight. Nothing less than a large mounted patrol would offer threat. *But Lord Ferrante already has what he wanted,* Fiametta thought with numb certainty. *They won't be back tonight.* Not till Ferrante marched up the road a conqueror, at the head of a troop no country inn was likely to resist.

Fiametta kept moving like a clockwork doll. Work was better than thinking, or feeling. But inevitably, she came to the end of her chores. The babble and excitement faded, and people blew out their candles and went to their beds. Catti's wife emerged from their bedroom with bloodstained bandages and Catti's shirt to put to soak in cold water, which Fiametta drew for her from the well in the yard. They set the bucket down outside the back door in the lantern light.

"How is Master Catti doing?" Fiametta asked guiltily.

"If the wound doesn't go bad," Madonna Catti sighed, "he'll probably live. His fat belly saved him from the dagger going too deep. If he asks for food, don't give him any." She pushed the bundled cloths down into the bucket, straightened wearily, and wiped her hands on her apron.

"I'm sorry to have brought these troubles upon you."

"If the greedy old ass had set you on the road to the priest at Bergoa that second morning, as I begged him to do for charity's sake, these troubles would have gone elsewhere," Madonna Catti said tartly. She glanced up at her inn, bulking in the dark; her mouth flattened. "If he truly feared a dead sorcerer's ghost, he should have buried him decently, not put him up in my good smokehouse. My smokehouse will be accurst, now. I shouldn't wonder if all my meat goes rotten and maggoty."

"My father was never a man to overlook an insult," Fiametta admitted reluctantly. "But I think—I fear—his spirit has greater troubles just now." Her hand kneaded the folds of her skirt.

"Oh?" Madonna Catti studied her sharply. "Well . . . go to bed, girl. But go from here tomorrow."

"May I have my horse?" Fiametta asked humbly.

"Horse and all. In fact, I don't want you to leave anything here that you came with." She shook her head. Fiametta followed her back indoors.

A second-floor porch or loggia overlooking the back yard of the inn, usually used for drying laundry, had been converted into a dormitory for the female servants of the two Montefoglian families. Fiametta had laid a bedroll for herself closest to the railing. She now picked her way over the snoring forms of the exhausted women. She slipped off her overdress and laid it atop her blanket, and pulled down her linen underdress, bunched a bit above the snakebelt she'd worn concealed from Catti's greed. Despite the night chill, she leaned on the railing and looked out over the inn yard.

The moon, waning and dull, rode a quarter of the way up the sky. Along the far wall, Pico's mules stood strung along a horse line, fodder piled at their feet to keep them content. Smoke still seeped from the smokehouse, a layer of haze in the dimming moonlight. Pico, his sons, and the Swiss were bedded down in a little bastion formed of the pack saddles, near the mules. She could see the blond man's bowl-cropped hair gleam as he shifted and turned over in his bedroll. She curled her fingers around her ringless left thumb, rubbing the empty place. *What have I done? Did my*

*ring draw him to me? Is he really supposed to be my
true love? Does he know this?*

Thur wasn't what she'd pictured, when she'd cast
the ring and its true-love spell together on the first
day of spring. She could scarcely say what she had
pictured, in her inarticulate longing to be loved. She
stared down at the blanketed lump in the yard and
tried to feel ardent, or swept by passion, or at least
impressed. Nothing. It wasn't that she disliked him.
He was just sort of there, alarmingly solid and real.
Friendly, certainly, after the manner of a big spoiled
mastiff pup who'd never been cuffed, snuffling up to
be petted.

It had never even crossed her mind that she would
not immediately love her true love back. But she'd
been expecting someone . . . shorter. Older. More
sophisticated. Better dressed, at least. And richer.

He really doesn't smell all that bad, for a muleteer.

She felt a frustrated urge to rip her ring from his
hand and tap it on the nearest tabletop, as if something
stuck inside her spell could so be loosened. But she
could still feel it, even now at this distance, the same
quiet, tiny hum of magic. The spell had emitted
scarcely a ripple when the Swiss had slipped the ring
on, curling around his finger and purring like a smug
and comfortable cat fed on fish and cream. A well-cast
spell was a barely discernible thing even to the inner
eye of a trained mage. Only when badly botched or
thwarted was magic obvious to ordinary senses, a jan-
gling discord that wasted power. Teseo's first efforts
had been almost painfully loud, emitting visible sparks.
But one scarcely knew Master Beneforte's spells were
there, flowing as much as possible with nature, not
wrestling against it.

*You see, if a corpse is preserved unshriven and
unburied, the new-riven spirit can be harnessed to the
will of a master. . . .*

Did Lord Ferrante seek a new spirit ring? A murdered master mage must be a fount of great power. The ironic symmetry must appeal to Lord Ferrante, to compel the man who'd destroyed his ring to become its replacement. And if Ferrante had ransacked their house, God knew what else he'd found to rivet his power-hungry attention.

She turned the days over in her mind. A night and a day for the Losimons to ride back with their injured to the castle, and return the magic saltcellar to their master. A day for the siege-preoccupied Lord Ferrante to awaken to the fact that they'd left a greater treasure of sorcery to rot in a field. A day for them to return and find their prize gone, a day to ask up and down the road after a conspicuous corpse. . . .

She rubbed her aching temples. Surely her fears for her father should have ended with his death. The dead were supposed to be beyond pain, healed and comforted in the bosom of Lord Jesus and the saints. That first night, mixed with her grief, she'd felt a curious lightness to her spirit, as if an unrealized weight had been removed from her shoulders. As if her world had suddenly enlarged, a vast vacated space above her freed to grow into. Her life become, unexpectedly, her own to choose and order. Her heart had pulsed with a subdued joy even while her throat choked on sobs. Surely that joy was a great sin. She should feel only grief, and fear of the world, with her protector removed. Only grief. Not resentment.

Now Master Beneforte's troubles flapped back in to settle on her life like a great flock of carrion crows, weighing her back down. *It's not fair. You're dead. I should be free of you.* Now not death but eternal damnation loomed, and the danger of a black magic far beyond her depth.

What can I do? I'm only half-trained. You yourself

neglected to train me. It's your fault I don't even know where to begin. I'm only a puny girl.

Tomorrow, she would attach herself to the servants of the Montefoglians, and run away to the north. Let the big stupid Swiss go in any direction he chose but the one she took. Let him lumber into the nearest ditch, for all she cared. She never wanted to see him again. Nor Montefoglia. Nor her house. Nor her own little bedroom, warm and cozy. . . .

Shivering, her nose clogged with unshed tears, she rolled up in the blanket and buried her face as best she could in the thin pillow. Her spinning thoughts bogged at last in sleep.

Fiametta woke out of a troubled dream of wandering in a strangely labyrinthine version of their house in Montefoglia. The place was deserted, in ruins, boards of the gallery rotting treacherously underfoot, shutters hanging half-off, walls crumbling. She'd been trying to light a fire, but couldn't, and armed creditors banged at the door calling for payments Master Beneforte had hidden and Fiametta could not find, though she searched frantically from room to room. . . .

Her pillow was damp and cold and her blanket wet with dew over the inner pocket warmed by her body. The waning moon was at zenith, casting its sickly insufficient light down into the inn yard. Still drenched with the unease of her dream, she rolled over and peered through the railing slats, glancing along the outer wall of the compound. No menacing men's shapes moved atop it; the wide night sky swallowed sound. Only her fears drained the scene of peace, though the line of hip-shot sleepy mules radiated a comforting animal warmth. Yet something was subtly wrong. She stared into the darkness for a full minute before she realized what.

The last trailing smoke from the smokehouse was

curling *down*, not up, collecting in a pool like a misted pond in the middle of the inn yard. Thickening. Contracting. The formless, seeking substance . . . Her heart lumped against her ribs. She caught her breath. She scrambled onto her knees, careless of the cold, and pressed her face to the slats.

The silver-gray smoke coalesced to man-form, legs in hose, a pleated tunic, a big cloth hat wound round like a turban with a jaunty fall of smoke-fabric to the side. The hat tilted upward, toward Fiametta on the loggia. A faint smoke beard curled beneath the brim. Moonlight picked out a gleam, like the edging of silver on a high cloud, from smoky eyes.

"Papa?" Fiametta whispered. The word stuck in her throat. She swallowed.

The figure beckoned to her, with palpable effort, smoke wisping off its arm as it moved. The knot in her belly dissolved in a strange cockeyed pleasure. *I'm glad to see you.* . . . Weren't ghosts supposed to be fearful manifestations, instilling terror? But Master Beneforte looked so . . . himself. Impatient and annoyed, as ever. She could almost hear his voice, ordering her about, threatening to beat her for clumsiness or delay, a threat he almost never carried out except when he was seriously short of money, and on those days she'd learned to be careful. The translucent figure beckoned again.

Fiametta swarmed over the railing, hung from the porch's edge by her hands, and dropped into the inn yard. She ran to the apparition, then stopped, longing yet afraid to touch it; clearly, he was holding the smoke together with great difficulty. She could see it in his expression, that familiar tense absorption that transformed his face when he worked his subtler spells. His gray hands opened to her, and he mouthed words.

"Papa, I can't hear you!"

He shook his head, mouthed more. Nothing. He pointed south.

"What are you trying to tell me?" She danced from foot to foot, mirroring his frustration.

Idiot child, he mouthed; that one she could make out, through long familiarity. But what followed was too rapid and complex. Her hands clenched, like his.

Pico's younger son, wakened by her voice, sat up, rubbed his eyes, and peered at the smoke-man over a packsaddle. He yelled in fright, dove for his father's bedroll, and burrowed under, waking Packmaster Pico with a floundering snort. Open-mouthed, Pico drew his blanket up over his boy all the way to his own chin. Thur, dressed still in his same tunic and leggings, sat up, then stood, staring. Pico's older boy Tich snored on, oblivious.

Thur took a deep breath and trod warily toward her. He came up beside her, rather paler even than his usual whiteness, and looked back and forth between her face and the moon-gray one. "Is it your father, Madonna Beneforte? What's he saying?"

The hazy figure, agonized, was beginning to shred away in the night wind. His dissolving arms reached for her, and she for him. Then the smoke abruptly contracted to a white sphere the size of a French tennis ball. It exploded outward again with a single word.

"Monreale!"

The word and the smoke both passed away down a puff of breeze, and the inn yard was empty once more.

"Monreale?" said Thur blankly. "What does he mean?"

"Monreale!" Fiercely, Fiametta stamped her foot. "Of course, Monreale! *He'll* know what to do. He'll know how to rescue Papa if anyone does. Except . . . ," she faltered, "if those gossipy maids speak truth, he's on the wrong side of a besieged wall."

The Swiss nodded solemnly, as if he failed to grasp this was not just an interesting fact, but a fatal flaw.

"A wall surrounded by Ferrante's soldiers," Fiametta amplified.

"I'm starting to dislike Ferrante's soldiers," he remarked mildly.

"I'm sure they'll be quite alarmed by that news," Fiametta snapped. "No doubt they'll run away and let us right through."

He smiled in embarrassment, palms out. "We'll figure out something. First we have to get there. Or I have to get there, anyway. Don't you think you'd be better off, and safer, going north with those other Montefoglians tomorrow?"

"You aren't going to dump *me* in a ditch!" she cried, outraged. He took a step backward, making little negative flaps with his big hands. "This is my business. I just might . . . might *let* you come with me, is all."

"Thank you, Madonna," he said earnestly.

Fiametta's lip curled in suspicion. "Don't you dare mock me!"

He opened his mouth, closed it, then settled on that same safely stupid friendly smile he'd favored her with when she'd threatened him with the chamber pot. She realized she was shivering violently, her thin linen rippling in the night breeze.

The maids in the loggia were awake, crying and praying. An uproar almost equal to the one following Catti's stabbing spread from them through the inn, till three-fourths of its occupants were roused. By the time the story of the ghostly apparition had been told and retold by those who'd seen to those who hadn't, gaining drama, Madonna Catti was in despair.

"This will ruin my business!"

"I doubt he'll be back," said Fiametta through her teeth.

"I'll call for the priest, and get my smokehouse exorcised!"

"What, that same priest you couldn't afford to have bury him?"

The two women exchanged tight-lipped frowns. The maids babbled hysterical nonsense. Tich was loudly irate that no one had wakened him to see the show. Fiametta went back to her cold bedroll and pulled the pillow over her head. No one dared approach her.

The interminable night gave way at last to a foggy pinkish-orange dawn. Fiametta's head throbbed vilely, her mouth felt full of fustian, and her eyelids scratched like sand. She dragged on her ruined velvet overdress. She wanted nothing more than to be gone from this place, the sooner the better.

At least Thur made no demur or delay. Dressed already, he had his bedding rolled and packed within a minute of his rising out of it. They sat on the benches in the tap room and washed down a breakfast of dry bread with ale. Catching the white horse from the pasture proved to be the greatest obstacle to their quick start. The innkeeper's wife, after watching them lunge through the dew-wet grass after it for several minutes, shook her head and came out with a basin of oats to entice it, and bridled it herself. She handed the reins to Thur, who handed them to Fiametta.

"Can't you ride a horse?" Fiametta demanded of her would-be cavalier.

He shook his head. "My mother only kept a few goats. We couldn't afford a cow, still less a horse." He added after an uneasy moment, "I could lead you on it, though. Like the mules."

"Well . . . all right," Fiametta said doubtfully. She stood beside the animal, her nose level with its withers. "Lead it to the fence, and I'll climb on."

"Oh, that's easy," said Thur. He picked her up around the waist and popped her aboard as if she'd been a three-year-old. At her outraged look, he added apologetically, "You're much lighter than an ox hide full of rocks, Madonna Beneforte."

She wrestled her skirts around her legs, wedged Thur's pack in front of her, took up a handful of long greasy mane, swallowed, and nodded. "Lead on, then."

The white horse was loathe to leave the green pasture, but once out on the road seemed to become reconciled to its fate, and plodded on beside the Swiss. Madonna Catti watched them out of sight, as if to make certain they and their bad luck were really departing. The early morning light was level and golden, setting the lingering wisps of mist ablaze in the meadows, casting knife-dark shadows across their feet from the poplar and cypress trees along the road. The damp warming air was redolent with spring flowers, and with the green scent of the little rocky streams that crossed the road as it dipped into shaded dells, then climbed again. The sun and the horse's warm back began to drive the night's chill from Fiametta's bones. If she weren't so tired and aching, the ride would have been pleasant.

Thur strode along easily beside the horse, petting it encouragingly on the neck now and then. He at least seemed no worse worn for the night's disruptions. He glanced over his shoulder at Fiametta, as they crested a little hill.

"Your father said *Monreale*. You called him the Abbot—is he the same as the Bishop Monreale my brother mentioned sometimes in his letters?"

"Yes, there's only one of him. Except unlike the Roman bishops, he actually serves both of the benefices he holds, Papa says. Said. Abbot Monreale's father was a Savoyard nobleman who married a Lombard lady. Monreale was a younger son, so he went off to seek his fortune as a captain in the armies of France, back when they drove the English from Bordeaux.

Your brother Uri used to like to get him to talk about
it, and it was never too hard to persuade him to remi-
nisce, though he pretends to be ashamed of it now.
Monreale kept trying to persuade Uri that he'd be
better off turning monk himself, and serving God
instead of Duke Sandrino. It got to be a kind of running joke between them, except that it wasn't quite a
joke." Fiametta bit her lip. It was no joke now, that
was certain.

"Papa and the Abbot were gossips, somewhat. At
first because of their being the two best magicians in
Montefoglia, I suppose, and Papa of course had to
stay on Monreale's good side to get his ecclesiastical
license from Monreale as Bishop. But I think they
really liked each other. When Monreale came to town
to the cathedral to tend to the affairs of the Diocese,
they would sometimes sit in our courtyard and drink
wine and talk. And sometimes they would go fishing
together on the lake. Papa was more practical, wanting
to master material magic. Monreale was more interested in the theory of sorcery, with an eye to his spiritual duties about it, I suppose. Sometimes Papa would
go to him for ideas, when he was stuck working out a
new spell. Monreale must know about spirit-magic,
he'd have to study it to fight it, at least."

"Spirit-magic?"

"Black necromancy." She described the silver putti
ring Lord Ferrante had worn, the casket with the salt-
shrivelled baby, and the connection Master Beneforte
had feared, found, and severed between the two.

"That's a level of sorcery over my head, I'm afraid,"
said Thur humbly.

"Yes, I can see that," Fiametta sighed. But to be
fair was compelled to add, "Over my head too." But
not over Monreale's. Nor Master Beneforte's—there
could be no concealments now, though Fiametta was
near-certain her father had never confessed his experi-

ment in Florence to the Abbot-and-Bishop. If Fiametta's vague understanding was correct, her father's spirit dangled now over damnation on Lord Ferrante's string. His soul risked being cut off from God even at this late hour. "I hope Abbot Monreale is not too busy with the siege to attend to one poor lost spirit."

Thur frowned thoughtfully down the winding road. "If Lord Ferrante succeeds in compelling your father's ghost to serve his will, and if this spirit-magic is as strong as you think, it would put all those people Monreale is trying to protect into greater danger. Your father's fate is near the center of his troubles. He'll attend." Determination stiffened his face. "All I have to do is get you there. Right."

Fiametta hung on tightly as Thur and the horse picked their way across a rocky brook at the bottom of the hill. The hazard cleared, she asked, "What is your magic, Thur? Your brother must suspect you of some talent, or he wouldn't have sought to apprentice you to a mage."

Thur's mouth screwed up in uncertainty. "I'm not sure. I've never been tested by a real master. I can find water with the dowsing-stick. And I have a knack for finding things, Mother says. I once found a little girl, the mill-wright's daughter Helga, who was lost in a snowstorm. But we were all out searching, so maybe I was just lucky. And I've long thought . . . ," he cleared his throat, as if embarrassed, "thought I could sense the metal ore, in the rocks. But I was always afraid to speak, for if I was wrong, the men would have been very angry with me. A false stringer is the devil to work." He hesitated, then added shyly, "I saw a kobold once, not long ago." He seemed about to add more, twisting the lion ring around his finger, but then shook his head. "And you, Madonna Beneforte? You must be skilled."

Her brow puckered. She *should* be skilled, yes. But.

"I'm very good with fires," she offered at last. "Even Papa has me light his. And my Latin pronunciation is good, Papa says—said." She brightened in memory. "The best thing I got to work on so far was, Papa let me help cast a spell for fertility for Madonna Tura, the silk-merchant's wife. She'd had no children, though she'd been married for four years. The spell required a balance of male and female elements, you see. We made it in the form of a belt of little silver rabbits. He let me design and shape the rabbits, all different. I got to keep two real rabbits for models. White French. Lorenzo and Cecelia. They had baby bunnies, which I adored—they were so soft!—it was part of the spell. But then they had more baby bunnies, and they kept digging out of the run in the back garden, and they ate all of Ruberta's herbs, and left rabbit droppings all over the house, which Papa made *me* clean up. So when the spell was finished, Papa said we had to eat all the rabbits. I suppose thirty-six of them really were too many, but I didn't forgive Ruberta, our cook, for weeks. Rabbit stew, rabbit ravioli, rabbit sausage . . . I went hungry," she said virtuously, but then rather spoiled the impassioned account of her pets' martyrdom by adding, "Except I helped eat Lorenzo, because he always bit me."

She frowned at Thur's grin, which immediately muffled itself. "I sneaked Cecelia out and let her go at the edge of town."

"And did it work?" Thur inquired, as she fell silent.

"What? Oh, the spell. Yes. Madonna Tura was delivered of a boy just last month. I hope they're all right." A silk-merchant's shop would be a likely target for looters. But perhaps Madonna Tura had escaped to other relatives.

He held up the lion ring to the sunlight, and wriggled his fingers to make it sparkle. "And is this a magic ring, Madonna?"

His words gave her a chill, nearly identical as they were to those of his—dead?—brother. "It . . . was supposed to be. But it didn't work, so I just wore it as jewelry."

She glanced down at him warily, but he merely remarked, "It's very beautiful."

She had been surviving hour to hour, not looking ahead. As a result here she was, alone in the wilderness, or at least passing through somebody's woodlot, with almost-a-strange man. A week ago, she would have thought it terribly compromising. Those careful social safeguards seemed flimsy and false as a stage-setting, now. Yet what fate was she riding toward?

Her marriage portion was supposed to have come from the great bronze Perseus, which Master Beneforte had not lived to cast, nor Duke Sandrino to reward him for. She would inherit the house, presumably, though it was surely stripped by now. Unless Papa's creditors sued for it, and wrested it from her and divided the money among themselves, leaving her destitute. . . . Worse had happened to unprotected widows and orphans in the courts of law. That free future she faced was a frightening thing, without money. A rich young woman had a control over her life equal only to control over her funds. A poor young woman . . . the same. Only different.

But if Lord Ferrante's conquest of Montefoglia succeeded, all hope was futile. Only if Ferrante fell did she have a chance of regaining any of her inheritance.

She watched Thur, marching along. His hair gleamed brighter than the lion ring as they emerged from the insect-humming woods into the sun again. She felt a flash of guilt, for worrying about money when his brother Uri's fate was still uncertain. Was it really so uncertain as she had made out, in her anxiety to soften the news? The thrust had looked mortal enough. At least the uncertainty had them both heading in the same direction. If he'd known his brother was dead, what reason would he have had to accompany her? She scarcely believed her ring's testimony. *How can you be my true love? You don't even know me. You must be dazzled by some magic illusion of me, and when you find out what I'm really like, you'll hate me.* Her eyes blurred with tears. *Idiot child. Stop your blubbering,* she thought sternly to herself.

Late in the morning they came to the meadow and coppice where Master Beneforte had been murdered, or died. The horse ate grass while Thur rested his legs and Fiametta walked about. But she gained no sense of Papa's presence here now. The meadow seemed only innocent and beautiful in the daylight. They went on.

Thur told her a little about his own life, as he walked through the warming noon. There didn't seem to be that much to tell, though clearly Thur was not naturally voluble. He'd had some schooling with the village priest—Fiametta was relieved to learn he could at least read and write. A younger sister had died of plague, possibly, judging from the dates, in the same bad year's outbreak that had carried off Fiametta's mother. His father's death in the mines had cut short his schooling and sent Thur to hard work in the valley, and his brother Uri off to the more glamorous life of a mercenary. The mines sounded tremendously tedious. She'd never guessed so many men's hands, so many steps, so many trees burnt, were required to bring the little shining bars of metal to their final destiny in her father's workshop. Thur had never seen a city—never been out of the valley of Bruinwald before. He seemed astonished and awed to learn that she'd lived in both Rome and Venice. He stared around at the rolling hills and ordinary little farms as if they were wonders. For practical purposes, the man was a babe, Fiametta realized with dismay.

Uri had made an excellent Perseus. She studied Thur, wondering what statue he'd make a model for. She couldn't think of a matching Greek hero. Ajax was too warlike, Ulysses too crafty, Hercules maybe *too* dim. Hector had been a solid family fellow, unlucky in his brother . . . that would be a bad omen, considering Hector's unfortunate end. Some northern hero, then, Roland or a knight of Arthur's? A Biblical figure, a saint? No, that would be even more bizarre. Somehow, Thur resisted the heroic mold. Fiametta sighed.

In the early afternoon the valley broadened, and they neared the northern end of the lake and the village of Cecchino. Thur declared himself willing and able to push on. Fiametto was reluctant to stop at the village, lest she be recognized, though at this point she had little left to steal and no reason to think any ranging bravo or anybody else would have an interest in her beyond the usual idle malice. Fiametta held the horse's reins and let it graze out of sight from the road while Thur went into the village to buy food. He came back with cheese, bread, new radishes, boiled eggs, and wine. It was almost like a picnic, in better times; he encouraged her to eat up, and in truth, she did feel better afterwards. But sleepiness lost to anxiety, and they took to the road again soon after their meal.

As evening came on, they were still six or seven miles short of Saint Jerome. They stopped to nibble the remains of their food, and shared the last of the watered wine.

"It must grow more dangerous, from here on," Fiametta said doubtfully as the shadows deepened. "Lord Ferrante's sure to have a guard posted on the road somewhere between here and the monastery."

"Yet his men were spread thin, you thought?"

"He only had fifty to start with. He may have called more horsemen from Losimo, but his main body of foot soldiers can't possibly have arrived yet. And he'll have to keep some in the town."

"It sounds like tonight is the best time for us to try to get to the monastery, then. If we can't see them, they can't see us."

"I don't know. . . . There's a little postern door in Saint Jerome's east wall, near to the woods. I think it's our best chance. The main gate will be better watched. We can circle around through the sheep pasture and the vineyards."

"Lead on, then."

"Yes, but I don't know how soon to get off the road. The later, the better, but . . ."

Thur sniffed the air. "Not yet, I think. I smell no campfires."

"Oh."

They trudged wearily onward. The lake was a darkening gulf beyond the trees on their right. The little farmsteads to their left were shut up dark and eerily silent. Frogs croaked in the reedy margins of the lake. The cooling air grew clammy with the moisture from the water. The old horse was getting balky and stiff, and Thur had to practically tow it. Fiametta dismounted and walked, her own legs aching. This trip had certainly been easier by boat. She sniffed, experimentally, from time to time. She and Thur stopped short at the same moment.

"Roast mutton," Thur whispered. "South, upwind."

"Yes, I smell it too." She hesitated. "That fieldstone wall up ahead is the monastery's outlying sheep pasture. We're almost there. But how are we going to sneak this stupid great horse through the woods?"

"Leave it in the pasture," Thur suggested. "It'll be happier there. I don't think anyone in their right mind would steal it to ride. And the soldiers aren't likely to eat it till they run out of sheep."

Thur was perhaps as tired of dragging the beast as

it was of being dragged. But the idea seemed practical as any. Senses straining, Fiametta led them off the road to a low place shaded by oaks. Thur made the waist-high wall lower by quietly removing the top couple of courses of stone. At last they were able to coax the reluctant horse to step over. Fiametta removed its bridle and stuffed it into Thur's pack, which he shrugged onto his shoulders. The horse wandered off, sniffing suspiciously at the sheep-cropped grass. Fiametta felt much less conspicuous.

Keeping low beyond the wall, she led Thur up the hill and around the vast pasture. Peering over the stones, Thur pointed silently to a dell on the far side. The orange glow of a fire reflected up from it, men's shadows moved, and voices drifted downwind with the smoke. Some of Ferrante's men were at a late supper of stolen holy mutton.

With only a few clinks, Fiametta and Thur climbed over the next wall and took to the concealing rows of the vineyard beyond. The long vineyard carried them in turn to the woods, which Fiametta skirted to the east, above the slope. Their cautious footsteps pushing through the weeds sounded like scythes, to her ears. At last, she calculated, it was time to drop down through the trees, hopefully to emerge by Saint Jerome's back door. She peered into the dark leafy shadows with deep unease. There must be more guards concentrated nearer the monastery's wall. Thur, after several tries on deadfall branches, picked up a stout stick with enough sap left in it to lend toughness. *Oh, Mary. Why didn't I run away north while I still could?* Holding Thur's other hand, Fiametta slipped with him into the woods.

Chapter Seven

They were doing well, till they fell over the sleeping guard.

The man was lying on the ground with a gray blanket wrapped around him, and in the dim moonlight and shadows looked much like a fallen tree trunk. He was positioned in just the lookout spot for which Fiametta naturally headed, a hollow at the edge of the woods with a clear view of the cut field behind the postern gate. Two lanterns burned brightly on the stone wall above the little door, casting a pool of illumination on the green grass. Clearly, the entry was guarded by men wary of night attack. Fiametta was so fixed on her goal, which was so near, so hopeful, so thank-God easily found, she was already in her mind running across the greensward. She didn't even look down till the log she stepped up on for a better view sank squishily, convulsed, and lumbered up cursing. She fell back with a squeak of fear. The ominous scrape of sword steel drawn from a scabbard skirled painfully in her ears. Images of the banquet massacre flooded her mind, shining metal piercing flesh.

Thur dropped his pack and stepped between Fiametta and the swordsman, his grip tightening on the log in his right hand. The swordsman yelled "Losimo! Losimo!" at the top of his lungs, and swung a powerful blow at Thur's neck. Thur caught the blade in the log; it stuck, and he wrenched the sword almost from the man's hand. Then the half-cloven wood broke. Thur leapt within the sword's arc to grapple with the man, his hands clamping around the sword wrist.

The guard kept yelling; he must have comrades nearby. Thur, fighting silently, tried to butt the Losimon's mouth with his forehead. As the two men wrestled, grunting, for advantage, another guard came running from a concealed position at the woods' edge several hundred yards to the south. He carried a crossbow, cranking it as he ran. The rachet clattered like bones. He stopped at near-point-blank range, and loaded it with a heavy short bolt that glittered in the moonlight. Raising the crossbow to aim at Thur, he hesitated for a line of flight that would not risk his comrade. Thur, at Fiametta's scream of warning, saw the crossbow and wrenched the swordsman around between them.

The crossbowman was a hairy fellow, with a bushy scalp and a thick curling black beard. His teeth gleamed in the midst of the thatch as he grimaced for his aim. The only thing Fiametta could think to do was set his beard afire. As he circled the wrestlers to regain his shot, Fiametta began to muster the oft-practiced domestic spell, her eyes squeezed to slits and her hands clenching in concentration against her terror.

Her father's voice whispered in her ear. "No, Fiametta! 'Tis sin!"

Her mouth fell open, and she whirled, but saw nothing, no smoke-form—

Out of the ground in front of the crossbowman, dirt and dust and leaf litter and little sticks arose and became the figure of a man. A whirl of detritus and decayed beech mast formed legs, pleated tunic, a big cloth hat—*Papa!* With an astonished yelp the crossbowman fell back a pace, his trigger released, and his deadly bolt flew wide into the woods.

With a crackling pop of wrist bones, Thur's grip shook the sword from the swordsman's grasp. The swordsman screamed in pain. The crossbowman howled as the leaf-figure dissolved into a cyclone that whirled around his head, casting dirt into his eyes and sticks into his beard. Thur stooped to grab up the dropped sword and sprang back, shoving his man away. The Swiss whipped the sword around in a wild figure eight, inexpert but menacing in its momentum. The crossbowman clutched at his eyes.

"Run!" Master Beneforte's voice came out of nowhere.

Fiametta darted forward, grabbed Thur's free hand, and yanked. "Run for the gate!"

Gasping for breath, he nodded. They bounded out of the hollow. His long legs soon had the advantage of her, and she leapt into the air at each stride and let him pull her along. Her shoulder blades cringed with the expectation of the *thunk* of a crossbow bolt, heavy steel shattering ribs, biting deep into her lungs—

It seemed to take forever to reach the postern door, floating in its pool of light like a receding mirage. Fiametta fell on it, pounding, and wheezing "Help!" but her words seemed a whisper and her blows weak as a babe's. Thur's pounding made the oak shake on its hidden iron hinges. "HELP!" he did not disdain to bellow.

"Who goes there?" came a man's growl from overhead.

Fiametta fell back, and craned her neck upwards, but could only make out blurred dark heads, one tonsured, one helmeted, against the bright lantern light. "Help! Sanctuary, for the love of God! We must see Abbot Monreale!"

The helmeted head craned outward in turn. "Why, I know the girl. It's the Duke's goldsmith's daughter. I don't know the man, though."

"His name is Thur Ochs, brother of your Swiss captain," Fiametta called back urgently. "He's come to seek his wounded brother. Oh, let us in, hurry! They'll be after us!"

"We are forbidden by the abbot to open the door," said the tonsured head.

"Then let down a rope," said Thur, in what started out as a reasonable tone, but rose to a yelp on the word *rope* as a crossbow bolt whanged off the stone a yard from him and ricocheted into the dark. They made beautifully illuminated targets. Thur stepped between Fiametta and the night.

"We could at least let the girl in," said the helmeted head.

"Sinful, to have her in here. Better the man."

"Bah! Your hospice is full of crying women right now, Brother. Don't quibble."

"Don't *delay*," shrieked Fiametta as another metal bolt whacked into the oaken door and stuck there, vibrating with a deep bass hum.

A knotted rope came curling down at last. Thur boosted her halfway up it; indeed, her puny girl arms could scarcely lift her own weight. But she must climb quickly, so he could climb in turn. Skin scraped from her palms, but she flung herself over the top of the wall on her stomach and rolled across in an awkward bundle of skirts. "Hurry, Thur!"

The soldier and the monk were standing on a mere wooden platform, none too solid, hastily raised to overlook the postern door. The helmeted soldier peered into the night, raised his own crossbow, and with a curse fired a quarrel in return for one that hummed close over his head. "Maybe *that* will keep the bastards' heads down," he growled, ducking below the stone.

Thur rolled in turn over the top of the wall and fell to the platform, making it shake. The monk yanked the rope up hand-over-hand. The soldier peeked back over the wall, just the top of his helmet and his eyes exposed. Fiametta searched Thur in panicky haste for blood, but none gouted from his back or anywhere else. The crossbowman's eyes must still be half-blinded with dirt; judging from the force of his quarrels' flight, he'd followed them close to the wall.

"I must . . . see the abbot," Fiametta panted to the crouched monk. "It's an emergency."

The soldier snorted. "God's bones, that's the truth."

The monk frowned. "Just because we're granted dispensation from our rules of silence doesn't mean we're free to use displeasing language in the cloisters."

"I never took a vow of silence."

The monk grimaced; it was evidently an ongoing argument. He turned to Thur. "What does she want to see the abbot for?"

"It's my father," Fiametta answered him. "I'm afraid he's in terrible danger. Spiritual danger. We witnessed Lord Ferrante using black magic."

The soldier crossed himself; the monk looked disturbed. "Well . . . tell her to follow me," he said to Thur. He climbed down the platform's triangular braces into the yard below, which proved to be the monastery's cemetery.

"Why don't *you* tell her? Should I come, too?" asked Thur, sounding confused.

"Yes, yes," said the monk impatiently.

"He's trying not to speak to a woman," Fiametta whispered in explanation.

"Oh." Thur blinked. "Doesn't he trust his abbot's dispensation?"

Fiametta smiled sourly down on the shaved scalp. "Perhaps he's a disobedient monk, in his heart."

The monk looked up and shot her an outright glare, but then looked doubly unsettled. They both followed him, Thur first, helping her jump down safely the last few feet. The monk, silent again, beckoned them through another gate to a corridor, through an even darker room, and out into a cloister-courtyard. He led them up steps to a gallery and knocked on a door. After a moment another monk opened it and stuck his head out. Orange candlelight flowed from the gap. Fiametta was relieved to recognize Abbot Monreale's secretary, Brother Ambrose, a big man with a kindness for cats, rabbits, and other small animals, whom she had met several times in the Abbot-and-Bishop's company.

Old habits dying hard, their guide monk pointed silently to Thur and Fiametta.

"Fiametta Beneforte!" the secretary said in surprise. "Where did you come from?"

"Oh, Brother Ambrose, help me!" Fiametta said. "I must see Abbot Monreale!"

"Come in, come in—thank you, Brother," he dismissed their reticent guide. "You may return to your post."

He ushered them into a small chamber, the abbot's study or office. It was furnished with a scriptorium-style desk with a brace of beeswax candles casting light across a paper and quill the secretary had apparently just put down. Another candelabrum burned brightly on a tiny altar below a small carved wooden crucifix hanging on the opposite wall. Abbot Monreale got up from his knees in front of it as they entered.

He was dressed now in the gray habit of his brothers, the cowl pushed back, only his belt with its keys marking his rank. His craggy face looked weary and worried. Tonsured hair made a gray fringe around his scalp that almost exactly matched his garment. The robes made him look bulkier than he was; his body was burned lean with years of ascetic moderation.

As he turned to them his gray brows shot up in surprise. "Fiametta! You escaped! I'm glad you are unharmed." He came toward her with a warm smile and took her hands; she curtsied and kissed his bishop's ring. "Is your father with you? I could use him now."

"Oh, Father," she began, then her face crumpled with exhausted tears. It was the sudden sense of safety, in Monreale's presence, that unstrung her; she'd done all right in the woods. "He's dead," she gulped.

Monreale, looking shocked, led her over to sit on a bench against the wall. He glanced curiously at Thur, and gestured him to sit also. "What happened, child?"

Fiametta sniffled, and regained control of her voice. "We got out of the castle, before you, I think."

"Yes."

"We fled in a boat. Papa became very ill, suddenly. I think it was a sickness of his heart, brought on by the banquet and the running and the terror."

Monreale nodded understanding. Though not a healer himself, as the regulating supervisor of Montefoglia's healers he was well experienced in both the physical and the spiritual infirmities of men.

"Papa bought a horse in Cecchino, and we rode on it into the night. But some soldiers Lord Ferrante dispatched overtook us on the road. Papa fought them while I hid. I found him in the field, dead—unwounded—I think his heart burst. They'd stripped him. I took his body to an inn, where Thur found me—oh! Ask after your brother, Thur. This is the younger brother of Captain Ochs," Fiametta explained hastily. "He was on his way to Montefoglia, and—ask, Thur!" Hers was not the only mortal anxiety here, though the Swiss had been more patient.

"Have you seen my brother, holy Father?" Thur asked. His voice was steady, though his hands fiddled with the lion ring. "Is he here?"

Monreale turned his whole attention on Thur. "I'm sorry, son. I saw your brother fall, but he was not among those we carried away. I ... thought it was a fatal blow he took, but I was hurried off just then, and can't swear to his last breath. I'm afraid I can't counsel you much hope for his life, though you must hope for his soul—he was a very honorable man—if that's a help to you. But ... it's barely possible he may still lie with other wounded in the castle. His body was not returned with the others during yesterday's parley. I— in truth, I have not heard. There's been much to occupy me."

"That's all right," said Thur. He looked a little numb. He'd expected to be freed of his fears one way or another; now, it seemed, he would be forced to bear them further. His shoulders bent, and his right thumb absently stroked the ring. Monreale studied him thoughtfully.

"Parley?" said Fiametta. "What's going on?"

"Ah. Well, Duke Sandrino's remaining guards surrounded us, myself and Lord Ascanio. We fled through the gate, though in hindsight I think we should have stood and fought them there ... speaking militarily. We fought rearguard through the town, and retreated to Saint Jerome. A multitude of refugees have sought sanctuary here since. We're very crowded." He shook his head. "So much bloodshed, so sudden. Like a judgment. I must stop it, before it spreads like a plague from man to man all over Montefoglia."

"What are you doing now?"

"Lord Ferrante also seeks to stop this unlooked-for war. He sent to treat with me, as *de facto* chancellor to poor little Ascanio. The lad's asleep in my room right now."

"A truce with Lord Ferrante?" Fiametta repeated, appalled.

"I must consider it. We're not in a good position, here. The Duke's guards were a match for Losimo when Sandrino led them, but now they're scattered, demoralized, separated from their commanders."

"Can't you send for help—somewhere?"

Monreale's lips thinned bleakly. "That is precisely the problem. For years, Duke Sandrino walked a very careful line between Milan and Venice. Call either of them in now, to an unmanned dukedom, and gobble! snap! Montefoglia would be eaten in a trice. Call in the other to eject the first, and Montefoglia becomes a battlefield."

"Would Lord Ferrante really attack the monastery?" said Thur, sounding shocked. "How could he get away with such a deed?"

Abbot Monreale shrugged. "Easily. Monasteries have been razed before, by violent men. And if he succeeded—who's to punish him? If he establishes his rule in Montefoglia and Losimo, he'll be too strong to readily dislodge. Except by either Venice or Milan, who would then keep Montefoglia for themselves— what gain to Lord Ascanio in that?"

"What about Papal troops?" said Fiametta, seizing on a hope.

"Too far away. Even if the Gonfalonier would dispatch them, involved as he is now with the troubles in the Romagna."

"But the Duchess Letitia is the granddaughter of a pope!"

"Wrong pope," sighed Monreale. "Perhaps, at the next election, her family's star will rise again, but not under His present Holiness's rule. The Curia will be swayed by arguments of order over right. Why should they spend troops to restore a weak woman and child to the Duchy when, if they do nothing, a strong, experienced man who's a known Guelf will assume the government?"

"Is that your decision too?" Fiametta demanded hotly. "Order over right?"

"It's practical politics, child. I don't know if I can save Ascanio's dukedom, but I think I can save his life. Ferrante treats to send Ascanio, his mother, and sister to exile in Savoy, with a stipend, in exchange for peace. It's more than a minimal offer. In the circumstances, almost generous." Monreale looked like a man biting a lemon compelled by courtesy to pretend it sweet.

"No! That gives Ferrante everything!" Fiametta cried, outraged.

Abbot Monreale frowned at this outburst. "Shall I fight to the last—monk? I'm sorry, Fiametta, but most of my brothers are not ready for such a contest. I would not hesitate to urge the least of them to martyrdom for the sake of the faith, but to sacrifice them to wrath serves no holy purpose. I cede Ferrante nothing he could not—all too readily—take for himself."

"But Lord Ferrante murdered the Duke!"

"You can't expect an ordinary man to not defend himself. When Duke Sandrino attacked him, Ferrante could not help but draw in return."

"Father, I *witnessed* it. Duke Sandrino flung only words, if bitter ones. Lord Ferrante drew first, and stabbed him outright."

Abbot Monreale's attention was arrested. "That was not the story I was told."

"By Ferrante's emissary? Lady Pia was with me. We both saw. Ask her, if you don't believe me!"

"She's not here. As far as I know, both she and the castellan were taken prisoners along with the Duchess and Lady Julia." Monreale rubbed his neck, as if it ached, walked to the casement window, and stared into the dark. "I don't disbelieve you, child. But it makes little practical difference. The troops from Losimo are on the march, and once they arrive our defying Ferrante will only make the final outcome worse. I've seen sieges, and what they do to men."

"But Lord Ferrante used black magic! Didn't you see the dead baby at the banquet?"

"Didn't I see *what*?" Monreale, pacing, jerked around as if wasp-stung.

"The baby in the box. Ferrante's footstool, that broke open when Uri kicked it off the dais just before he was stabbed." She tried to cudgel up a precise memory of that chaotic moment. Monreale had been beyond the upturned table, managing Ascanio, his crozier, and a flurry of assailants and helpers, seeking an exit, while retreating over the far side of the platform.

"I saw the footstool. I didn't see it break open."

"*I* saw. It spilled right across my feet. My skirt was caught under the table's edge. The footstool was full of rock salt, and this horrible dried-up shrivelled infant. Papa said its spirit was enslaved to that ugly silver putti ring Ferrante wore on his right hand. Didn't you sense anything? Ferrante used the ring to blind a man, and he tried to use it on Papa, but Papa did—something—and the ring burned Ferrante instead. Papa said he released the baby's spirit, but I don't know how."

Abbot Monreale turned, agitated, to his secretary. "Brother Ambrose, did you see?"

"I was on the other side of you, Holy Father. A Losimon was trying to hack off your head with his sword, and I was fending him off with a chair. Sorry."

"Don't apologize." Monreale paced. "The ring. The ring! Of course! Damn!—I mean, God bless me. *That's* what it was."

"Then you *did* sense something." Fiametta was relieved.

"Yes, but I should have sensed much more! What can Ferrante have done to conceal . . ." He headed for his massive bookcase as if drawn by a string, then turned back, shaking his head. "Later. I wish your Papa were here now, Fiametta."

"What did you see in that ring, Father?"

"It appeared to embody a simple spell to ward off lice and fleas, of the sort anyone might carry in an amulet bag in his pocket. I thought it an odd vanity to cast such a humble thing in silver. It felt wrong, though—I thought it poorly cast. But if the vermin-warding spell was masking another, a spell to ward off *attention* . . . then beneath *that*. . . ." He hissed through his teeth, looking sick. "What did you sense in it, child?"

"Ugliness."

"From the mouths of babes. You humble me." He smiled sadly. "But then, you are your father's daughter."

"That's what I was starting to tell you. Lord Ferrante's men came back, to the inn where I'd sought help with Papa's body—" Quickly, Fiametta described her unpleasant adventures with Innkeeper Catti, his greed, and his smokehouse, the bravos' bizarre theft, and the manifestations of Master Beneforte in smoke and dried leaves. Thur confirmed the details of their journey. Much more hesitantly, Fiametta repeated what Master Beneforte had confided to her of his previous experience with spirit rings, though she concealed the names of Lord Lorenzo and Florence. The Medici must be responsible for his own confession. She explained her sharp fear that Lord Ferrante meant Master Beneforte's ghost for his new and more powerful slave. Abbot Monreale's shoulders sagged as her story piled up.

"Papa called for you," Fiametta finished. "He cried

out for help from you. Holy Father, what do we do next?"

Monreale sighed deeply. "Just before you arrived, child, I was on my knees praying for guidance, some sign that my decision to make this truce was correct. That's the most frightening risk you take, with prayer. Sometimes, God answers." He nodded wearily to his secretary. "Tear up the treaty, Brother Ambrose."

Delicately, the big monk picked up the paper on which he'd been working when Fiametta and Thur had entered, and tore it slowly in half. He let the pieces drop to the floor. His eyes met Monreale's in an affirmation tinged with fear. "So much for surrender. Holy Father, what *do* we do next?"

Monreale squeezed his eyes shut, and rubbed his wrinkled brow. "Temporize, Brother. Return soft answers and temporize." He looked up at Thur and Fiametta. "Take these exhausted youngsters to the hospice, betimes. I'm going to the chapel to meditate, before Lauds. Assuming we've anyone to spare to sing the night psalms." He added under his breath, "At last I realize why the Rule of our Order puts so much emphasis on training monks to do without sleep."

His secretary murmured *Amen,* picked up a candle, and gestured Fiametta and Thur out of the room ahead of him.

On the way to the hospice, which was situated near the front gate, they passed through a courtyard with a covered well. Even at this late hour, past midnight, two monks, a soldier, and a woman stood waiting to draw up water. A monk had his hand on the crank, but was not turning it.

"How goes it, Brother?" asked Brother Ambrose in passing.

"Not good," the monk at the crank replied. "It's

coming up muddy. We're waiting for it to settle between buckets, but it's taking longer and longer."

He began cranking at last, and poured the well bucket out into vessels held by the soldier and the woman. He let the rope down and began waiting again. Brother Ambrose followed after the soldier.

"A water shortage?" asked Thur.

"Unless it rains and refills our cisterns," said Ambrose. "We normally house about seventy brothers. Now we've taken in some fifty or sixty of Duke Sandrino's guards, many of them wounded, their families, others who've fled from the violence in town—there are over two hundred people packed in here right now. The infirmary is overflowing. Abbot Monreale is considering giving the hospice entirely over to the women, and putting the wounded in the chapel, if we get any more."

The water-lugging soldier turned aside as they passed the infirmary. Fiametta peeked after him through the door into a long, stone-arched dormitory. Straw pallets were set between wooden-framed beds, most occupied by blanketed forms. In the dim light of a couple of oil lamps a man's open eyes, glassy and feverish, gleamed in his stubbled face. A hooded monk moved among the beds; toward the end of the row a man in pain moaned continuously, like a cow lowing.

Brother Ambrose guided them through another door and into the area of the hospice proper, ordinarily the only area of the monastery open to visitors. He handed Fiametta off to a tired-looking older woman, dressed in night robes with her gray hair in a braid down her back. Fiametta recognized her as a lay sister from the Cathedral chapter in town. Ambrose took Thur off with him through the visitors' refectory toward the men's sleeping area. Thur glanced back uncertainly over his shoulder at her, as he passed around the corner, and waved a left-handed good-bye.

The women's dormitory was another stone-arched chamber similar to the infirmary, but smaller and more crowded. Again, its original beds were supplemented with woven straw pallets and even hastier piles of loose straw with blankets atop. Some twenty-five or thirty women and perhaps twice that number of children and young girls were bedded down every which way. The older boys were presumably housed with the men.

Fiametta picked her way past the strewn bodies, through a door at the far end of the room to an over-worked and odoriferous latrine. She began to realize why the abbot considered holding out through a long siege, even without having to repel attack by Ferrante's infantry reinforcements, a dubious proposition at best. This time last night, she'd imagined that if only she could win through to Monreale, he would somehow fix everything. And it seemed she wasn't the only Monte-foglian with that idea. But now . . .

When she emerged from the latrine the lay sister guided her to a pile of loose straw, already occupied by two sleeping girls. Fiametta peeled off her ruined shoes and flopped down between them. It was bed enough for now.

Chapter Eight

Uri. Thur blinked open bleary eyes to see the dim vault of the men's dormitory ceiling, and stretched himself on the thin bedding, loose straw with a blanket thrown atop. The evil dream from which he'd wakened vanished away like mist even as he tried to remember it. By the aching spots all over his body, the straw had done little to protect him from the stone floor, though to be fair most of the bruises had been administered by that terrifying Losimon swordsman he'd fought last night. How much pain did Uri, far worse than bruised, lie in right now in the prison of his enemies? How much terror? Thur had straw and a blanket and freedom. Perhaps Uri had only bare stone.

Some men were up and moving, some still slept. Beside Thur, a stubble-faced Montefoglian guard smelling of several days dried sweat squeezed his eyes shut, rolled over taking the blanket with him, farted, and started snoring again. Creakily, Thur rose and went to join the line for the latrine. At least Uri's prison could scarcely be more crowded than this.

He had no problem getting dressed; he'd slept in his clothes. His only clothes, since he'd lost all his possessions in the fight last night. Well, he fit right in here among the possessionless monks, even though his poverty was accidental rather than vowed. He would dedicate his poverty to God like the brothers, along with a prayer to please make it as brief as possible.

A monk in the refectory was portioning out brown bread, ale, and watered wine when Thur entered. The servings were not large. It was good bread, but under the circumstances Thur hesitated to ask for more. The ale was a blessing, washing out his gummy night-dry mouth.

As soon as his voice was his own again, Thur began questioning men who looked like they might have known Uri. They welcomed him with interest for Uri's sake, and told Thur their own gruesome stories of fight and escape, but none of them had any later sight or better guess of their Swiss captain's fate than had Abbot Monreale or Fiametta. The morbid uncertainty made Thur's neck ache.

There were women in the refectory, but Fiametta was not among them. Their voices were subdued, but for one sharp female whose complaints sounded with nasal clarity, till she sat abruptly on the floor and started crying. Another woman led her away to their dormitory. Thur rubbed the lion ring, and wondered if he might approach a woman to ask after Fiametta. But as he was working up his nerve, Brother Ambrose appeared and touched him on the shoulder.

"Thur Ochs? Abbot Monreale would like to see you."

Thur licked the last stray crumbs from his fingers, drained his mug, and returned it to the hosteller. He followed Brother Ambrose.

The secretary-monk led him through a courtyard and corridors, across the cloister, and up first stone and then wooden stairs. They came out on a flat roof above the office where Thur had met the abbot last night. The buttresses of the chapel arched just to the north. A wooden dovecote occupied one end of the roof. Monreale, his hood pushed back, stood next to it. Brother Ambrose paused, signalling Thur to wait.

A speckled gray dove fluttered uneasily on the abbot's hand. Monreale seemed to be speaking to it; he touched his lips to the bird's head, then held his hand aloft. With a burbling coo and a thrumming of wings like a drumroll, the dove climbed into the sky, circled the chapel twice, then flew away to the south.

Thur and Brother Ambrose crunched across a light peppering of sun-dried guano toward the abbot, who turned at the sound of their footsteps, smiled briefly at them both, and scanned the sky.

"Have any returned yet, Father?" Brother Ambrose asked deferentially.

Monreale sighed, and shook his head. "Not one. Not one! I fear for my flock."

Ambrose nodded appreciation of the double meaning, and they both gazed southward into the pale morning blue, their hands shading their eyes. With a downward fist-closing gesture Monreale at last indicated an end to it, and led them back down the stairs to his office and through another door into an adjoining chamber.

Thur stared around in fascination. The chamber was well lit from the north through large high windows, and lined with chests and boxes for books. Shelves held a riot of brass, ceramic, and earthenware jars, colored glass bottles, and mysterious little boxes with labels in Latin. Two big worktables stood, one in the center of the room and one against a wall, strewn with clutter and stacked with papers and well-used cloth-bound notebooks. In one corner a narrow barrel held staves of various woods, and, snout up, the long stiff form of a dried and mummified crocodile, its leathery lips wrinkled back on a jaw half-emptied of teeth. Bags hung from the beams, including one of red silk netting holding a delicate tangle of papery dried shed snake-skins. A corner featured a plastered fireplace. The bee-hive form of a small furnace, just the size to fit in the fireplace, sat cleaned and ready for use on the slate hearth.

Brother Ambrose took a round mirror the size of a platter, framed in wood, from a cupboard and set it on the center table. Beside it he placed a small round tambourine of stretched pale parchment. Monreale cleared away clutter and placed bunches of dried herbs at the cardinal points around the two objects, murmur-ing under his breath in Latin. Brother Ambrose closed the window shutters, making the plaster-walled room cool and dim. Ambrose gestured Thur, hanging back in a mixture of politeness and caution, to step up to the table and watch, but put a finger to his lips to enjoin silence.

From a little blue glass flask, Monreale let one drop of a clear fluid fall to the middle of the mirror; it expanded in a bright blink to the edges. Monreale blew on the surface, and the mirror began to glow with a light that was no reflection of anything in the room. Thur craned his neck to see, barely breathing.

A dizzy, jerky whirl of colors danced in the glass. Thur squinted, trying to make sense of what appeared at first to be yellow and orange confetti. Then he real-ized he was looking at tile roofs—looking *down* from above upon a town. The town turned in the mirror with the inhuman speed of a bird's flight. Yellow stone and brick castle walls arced into view. With a dipping swoop the view sped to the top of a castle tower then, blessedly, stopped for a moment. Thur, engrossed, swallowed a slight nausea. He caught a jerky look down into a courtyard with an elaborate marble staircase, then the tower's twin was framed in the glass.

Atop it two crossbowmen were cranking their winches, and a thin, dark, clean-shaved man in a red robe leaned on the crenellated yellow brick and pointed. Thur had to quell a startled fear that they were looking straight at him. The slight man shouted, and the crossbowmen took aim and fired. The view jerked, turning again. Another crossbowman, behind the bird on the first tower, was much closer. Thur saw and heard his strings twang with the force of his quarrel's release, then the view in the mirror flared and went dark. Thur realized suddenly that the sound had actually come from the tambourine, but somehow his mind had attached it to the images in the mirror. Monreale grunted, like a man struck in the stomach.

"No, not another one," groaned Brother Ambrose.

Monreale's fists clenched, leaning on the tabletop. His lips pinched on words that did not sound quite like prayers. "They were waiting. They were set up and waiting," he said angrily. "Somehow, they must be able to tell my birds from the others." He turned and paced the room with an impatient stride. "Tonight I shall try bats after all. Not even Ferrante has a bowman so quick he can take a bat out of the air in the dark."

"We'll see little ourselves, in the dark," said Brother Ambrose dubiously.

"But hear better."

"Snores, mostly."

"Mostly. But if Lord Ferrante is indeed as far up to his neck in black magic as he is accused, night in the castle may be a busier time than we think."

Brother Ambrose made a wry face, crossed himself, and nodded. He went to open the shutters again.

Abbot Monreale straightened his sagging shoulders

and turned to Thur with a forced smile. Monreale's face was pale and lined, the skin beneath his eyes puffy with fatigue. Thur had slept on straw and stone, and found it a penance. He began to suspect Monreale had not slept at all, and decided not to complain about his bedding.

"You've plunged me into a real dilemma, boy. You and Fiametta," Monreale observed. "Neither prayer nor reason have yet shown me the way out of it. So I pray more, and seek to give my poor weary reason some new premise to work upon. But as you see, my birds do not come back to me."

"They are magic spies?" Thur asked. The mirror reflected only the beamed ceiling now.

"They are supposed to be. They seem to be meeting the fate of spies discovered, certainly." He rubbed the deep crease between his eyes. "Ambrose, did you recognize that man in the red robe on the tower?"

"No, Father. Did you?"

"No . . . that is, I feel I do. But I can't put a name to him. Perhaps I met him in a crowd, or long ago. Ah, well, it will come to me. My poor doves." Monreale turned to Thur. "I need a subtler spy. A human one. I need a volunteer. Someone whose face is not known in Montefoglia."

Thur glanced around the room. No one here but himself and Ambrose, and somehow he didn't think the abbot was addressing Ambrose.

"You should know, it's dangerous. My birds were not my only trial. I'm missing a brother."

Thur swallowed, and spoke up with an effort that sounded unnaturally loud in the quiet chamber. "Father, so am I. What do you want me to do?"

Monreale smiled, and clapped Thur on the shoulder. "Well spoken. Bless you, boy." He cleared his throat. "It's reported that Lord Ferrante's troops are combing Montefoglia for metalworkers, and Ferrante has posted a reward for any foundry master who will come to him at once. Your brother talked of the mines and smelteries of Bruinwald. Do you think you could pass yourself off as a foundryman?"

"A worker, yes. I don't think I could pass for long as a master."

"A worker would do. I want this to be as simple as possible. All you need to do is gain entry to the castle. As you move about whatever work you are assigned, look for inconspicuous places to put some small objects I will give to you. Places where men stand to talk—guardposts, the dining hall. If . . . if you can get to the Duke's study, or whatever rooms Lord Ferrante now frequents, that would be ideal. If you can somehow smuggle one in to Duchess Letitia . . . well, it's not likely that a foundry worker would be permitted in the prisoners' tower. But if you can, do so."

"What will these objects be, Father?"

"I must think on that, and prepare them. We'll let you down over the wall tonight, under the cover of darkness and a spell I will devise. Once you are away from the monastery, enemy troops should be few. You can try to get into Montefoglia when the city gates open at dawn."

"Why does Lord Ferrante want metalworkers?"

"I wish I knew. Maybe you can find out, eh? My best guess is that it's to repair some of Duke Sandrino's cannon. There was a cracked bombast that would make short work of poor Saint Jerome, if it could be made sound again. The lighter cannon are all with Sandrino's bastard's mercenary company in Naples, or they would be pounding us now. Who could have forseen what a bad time this would be to hire out the army? They're farther away than Papal troops right now. Yet Milan was at peace, and Venice too busy with the Turks in the Adriatic to threaten Montefoglia this year, and Losimo was about to be united with ties of blood. I should have . . ." Monreale trailed off, staring blindly into the infinite regret of the might-have-been. "Ah, well." He shook off the blackness. "What have you to wear, son?"

Thur turned his palms out. "Just this. I lost my pack last night outside the walls."

"Hm. Perhaps Brother Ambrose can help you find something less . . . rural, among the men here. Some clothes to help you look your part. By the way." Monreale paused. "How did you come by that ring?"

Thur touched the little lion mask. "It's not really mine, Father. It belongs to Madonna Beneforte."

"Ah! That explains a great deal." Monreale brightened. "Prospero Beneforte's work, is it? I should have realized. I urge you to leave it with Fiametta. It's not the sort of thing a foundryman normally wears. You should do nothing to bring extra attention to yourself, you see."

"I can't get it off, Father." Thur tugged at it, by way of demonstration.

"Hm?" Monreale took Thur's left hand, and bent over it, peering. The shaved part of his scalp around the edge of his tonsure was bristly with new growth, but the center was naturally hairless, smooth and shiny. "Ah, ha! The true love spell of the Master of Cluny, I wager." He straightened, smiling. "And it's working."

"Oh," said Thur. "You must tell Fiametta. She'll be so pleased. She thought her magic was a failure." He paused. True love spell? *What* true love spell? "Working how?" Vague fear washed through him. Had his new longings been manipulated by magic? That was an unsettling thought, but no. Real panic came with the notion that Fiametta might somehow be taken from him. But she didn't belong to him. His left hand clenched possessively.

"Fiametta cast this? Not Master Beneforte? Excuse me, I must have a closer look." He took Thur's hand again, but instead of peering, shut his eyes tightly.

Thur's brows wrinkled. Abbot Monreale was silent for a long minute. When he straightened again, opening his eyes, his expression was grave. "Brother Ambrose. Please fetch Fiametta Beneforte."

Alone with Thur, Monreale crossed his arms and leaned against his worktable. He sucked thoughtfully on his lower lip, gazed at his sandals, then glanced keenly at the young man. "So how do you like the girl, son?"

"I . . . like her very well, Father." Thur replied sturdily. "At least . . . I think I do. I know I do. But what's the ring doing to me?"

"To you? The ring isn't doing anything to you. You, however, are doing something to it. Completing it, I suppose would be one way of putting it. Cluny's spell is reputed to reveal true love, but that is not perfectly accurate. More precise to say it reveals a true heart." He gave Thur an odd smile, above intent eyes.

Thur breathed relief. He was not enspelled. Well, he hadn't really thought he was.

"But are your intentions honorable?" asked Monreale. "Cluny is not always clear on that point."

"My intentions?" Thur repeated, confused. "What intentions?"

"Do you think of marriage, or are you in danger of drifting into the sin of lust?" Monreale clarified.

Marriage? The word had the weight of a rock hammer, swung from behind, meeting his head. Thur blinked. Himself, a husband? Like . . . like a grown man? A dizzying gulf of maturity yawned before him, quite unexpectedly. "But . . . I don't . . . Father, if all had been as it was, as I'd been expecting when my brother's letter fetched me to Montefoglia . . . Uri had arranged for me to be apprenticed to Master Beneforte, you see. As a poor apprentice, I could not have hoped—not for years, and by then she would have been married off to some rich fellow. Aren't we too far apart? Dare I think I could . . . have her? It's true, Madonna Beneforte needs someone. . . ." Thur trailed off, his head whirling. Lust? In marriage he could have all the lust he wanted, presumably, and be blessed for it.

"Given the death of her father, Fiametta needs someone very much," said Monreale. "She has no relatives here. No woman should live alone, with no master to her household. Particularly not a young woman. And Fiametta Beneforte still less. A situation fraught with danger. There is a gap of rank between you, true, but the testimony of this ring is . . . unusual. What you are, though, is very young and poor to be thinking of setting up a household."

He hadn't *been* thinking of it, till Monreale brought it up.

"Yet not too young for me to send into a danger I fear could be . . ." Monreale trailed off. "God help me." That was intoned as a prayer. His voice firmed. "It's a rare and happy man, son, who ever finds his true vocation, his true love, or his true faith." He nodded to the ring. "There is no evil in this for you."

Footsteps sounded in the outer room, and Brother Ambrose ducked into the inner chamber, followed by Fiametta. Her wildly curling hair was subdued this morning in a thick braid down her back. It made her look serene, older, an effect slightly spoiled by a few stray wisps of straw sticking here and there to her filthy red velvet dress. Thur wanted her to look less tired and worried. She had laughed once, on the road yesterday, at something Thur had said. He wanted her to laugh again. Her laughter had been like water on the hot day. His distress for her weariness and worry became all mixed up in his head with a sudden picture of her, laughing, in a marriage bed, her smooth brown limbs flashing in some froth of nightgown. . . .

Monreale composed his face into stern lines. He pointed at the lion ring. "Did you make this, Fiametta?"

She glanced from Monreale's face to Thur's and back again, and said faintly, "Yes, Father."

"Under your Papa's supervision?"

She swallowed. "No, Father. Well, yes and no."

Monreale's gray brows rose. "Which? Yes, or no?"

"No." Her sculptured chin lifted. "But he knew of it."

"It seems to be a Beneforte trait, to dabble in questionable rings," said Monreale in a dry tone. "You know Master Beneforte had not licensed you as his apprentice."

"I've been learning the jeweler's craft for years. You know that, Father Monreale."

"The metalwork is not my concern."

"You knew I assisted him in his spells."

"Such assistance as was proper, under a licensed mage. This, however, is not a work of assistance. Neither is it the work of a clumsy amateur. How came you to know so much?"

"I *often* assisted him, Father." After a long, expectant silence, she added reluctantly, "I found the spell written out in one of Papa's books. Investing it in the ring was no problem, I already knew the gold-casting part. I just followed the directions very carefully. There didn't seem to be much to it. No flash. I was disappointed, at first, because I didn't think it had worked, because . . . because Uri didn't put it on. I tried to give it to him."

"Ah!" said Monreale in a professionally interested tone, that he converted to a more neutral throat-clearing noise.

"But then I gradually realized that no one could put it on. That soldier, and the thieving innkeeper both tried hard to steal it for its gold, but they couldn't."

She glanced covertly at Thur. "Um . . . *is* it working, Father?"

"We will discuss that later. So, you read your Papa's books. With his permission?"

"Uh . . . no."

"Fiametta, that is the sin of disobedience."

"No, it wasn't! He didn't forbid me. That is . . . I didn't ask. But I found out later he was watching me all the time, and he didn't stop me. So that's almost like permission, isn't it?"

Thur could have sworn that Abbot Monreale suppressed a smile at this sophistry, but the flicker of expression in the stern visage was gone again almost at once. "Master Beneforte never applied to me for your license."

"He was *going* to. He was just so busy, lately, with the saltcellar and the Perseus and all his other commissions. I'm sure he was going to."

Monreale raised his brows again.

"All right," Fiametta sighed, "I'm not sure. But we did talk about it. I begged him to, countless times. Father Monreale, I want to be a mage! I can do good work, I know I can! Better than Teseo. It's not fair!"

"What it is not, is properly approved," said Monreale. "Not properly supervised. I've seen souls lost to such hubris, Fiametta."

"So approve me! Papa's not here to ask for me, I suppose I can ask for myself now. Who else? I want to be good, let me be!"

Monreale said mildly, "You ran ahead of me. First comes contrition, confession, and penance. Then absolution. I haven't even finished my sermon on contrition yet."

Fiametta's brown eyes heated with a sudden glimmer of anticipation, at the leakage of humor and hope from behind Monreale's firm facade. She straightened alertly, almost bouncing. "Oh, get to my penance, Father, quickly!"

"Your penance will be to go to the altar of Our Lady in the chapel and pray, on your knees, for patience and obedience. When you feel your prayer has been answered, go eat your noon meal, then come back to me here. I urgently need a talented assistant in addition to Brother Ambrose, who is as exhausted as myself. I have a project to complete this afternoon, before Compline."

"In magic? You're going to let *me* help *you*?" Her voice thrilled.

"Yes, child."

She danced around him, and hugged him hard, habit and all. He fended her off, smiling despite himself. "You must truly compose your mind in prayer first, remember. Demanding, 'Mother Mary, grant me patience and grant it right now!' won't do."

"How do you know?" Fiametta's eyes sparkled.

"Hm. Well. You can try it, I suppose. Who am I to say what the Mother of God can't do, in her infinite mercy? The faster she speeds you to patience the sooner I can put you to work. Ah. One other thing, first. I'm sending your friend Thur here on an errand, and I fear that big gold ring would be too conspicuous on his hand. I can draw it off with a little spell, but you can just draw it off."

"But . . . it's stuck. I saw it. How can I draw it off if he can't?"

"Put simply, he doesn't want to."

"But I really tried, Father!" Thur said.

"I know you did. I will discuss the inner structure of the Master of Cluny's spell with you in some less hurried time."

Frowning in puzzlement, Fiametta turned to Thur. Obediently, he held out his hand. Her tapering brown fingers closed over the lion ring; it returned to her palm as smoothly as if greased. "Oh," she said, startled.

Monreale handed her a long thong. "I suggest you keep it around your neck, out of sight, Fiametta. Till you come to give it back." He gave her an indecipherable look.

Thur's finger felt empty, light and cold without his—no, *her*—ring. He rubbed at the lonely spot, already missing the reassurance that touching the lion had given him.

The shuffle of sandaled feet came from the outer room; a monk knocked politely on the doorframe, then stuck his head through. "Father? Lord Ferrante's herald is at the outer gate."

"I come, I come." Monreale waved him out. "Thur, I want you to rest in the afternoon. I'll send a brother to rouse you when it's time. Fiametta, I'll see you here after the noon meal. Go along now." He herded them ahead of him, out through his office, pausing to attend to something at the desk with Brother Ambrose. Thur followed Fiametta down the stairs into the shade of the cloister walk around the courtyard. A few doves paced solemnly about on the lawn in the sunlight, pecking vainly for food bits in the grass.

Stone benches lined the walkway between the arched stone pillars. Enticed, Thur sat down on one. Fiametta alighted on the other end. Her fingers touched the stiff new leather thong around her neck, faltered to her lips, then settled to the cool stone.

The sighing of wind in the nearby woods, the low twitter and occasional liquid warble of birdsong, and the muted voices from the monastery gave a temporary illusion of peace. Thur wished it were real. The beauty of the day seemed a cruel hoax. Sweating, grunting, stupid menace of the sort he'd wrestled last night patrolled right outside the stone walls. He wanted to keep that menace far from Fiametta.

Fiametta was still bright-eyed and bouncing, reminding Thur of the lid on his mother's kettle. "Abbot Monreale takes me *seriously*," she chortled. "Wants me to help—I wonder what with?"

"Perhaps those scrying things," said Thur.

"Scrying things?"

"He wants me to disguise myself as a workman and take some scrying things into the castle at Montefoglia, and drop them here and there. His spy-birds aren't getting through, you see."

"He wants you to go outside? Through the siege?"

"We got in through the siege all right." *Just barely.* "He's going to send me out after dark."

Fiametta went very still. Thur imagined her about to say *Be careful,* in the tone of voice his mother used every day when he went off to the mine. But instead she said slowly, "My father's house is on the other end of town from the castle. It's not likely you'd have a chance to get over there and see what's happened to it, but if you can . . . it's the last house on Via Novara. The big square one." She paused again, her voice at last growing worried. "Abbot Monreale doesn't want you to do anything very *complicated,* does he?"

"No." He looked away from her, into the brightness. Out on the lawn, a very young kitchen cat was stalking the doves. It had big ears, gray and black striped fur, and somewhat outsized white paws. Its whiskers cocked forward and its eyes almost crossed with the intensity of its gaze. It crouched, hindquarters wriggling in earnest preparation.

Marriage. The heated softness of this girl, all his to possess? But what if . . . surely Abbot Monreale would have said something if . . . He blurted, "Madonna Beneforte, you're not betrothed already, are you?"

She drew back, and gave him an unsettled look. "No. Why do you ask?"

"No reason," he gabbled.

"Good," she said in a rather faint tone. She rustled to her feet and retreated around the bench. "I must go to the chapel now. Good-bye." She skittered away, out the end of the cloister.

In the grass, the cat pounced and missed. The dove burst away in a flurry of wings. The cat stared upward, tail lashing and teeth chattering, till all hope vanished over the rooftops. The cat padded off stiffly, embarrassed, and came and plunked down by Thur's feet. It looked up at him and emitted a loud and piteous meow, as if Thur could produce flightless pigeons from his pockets on demand, like a magician at a fair. Thur felt very far from being any kind of a magician at all, right now.

He picked up the cat and scratched its ears. "What would you do if you caught it, anyway, catkin, hm? The bird is bigger than you are." The cat purred ecstatically, and butted its head against Thur's hand. "There are birds in my mountains that would make a meal of *you*. You must grow up some more." Thur sighed.

Thur spent the rest of the morning offering minor assistances to the harried monks. He cranked the well windless, carried water to the guards on the walls, and helped set up the trestle tables for the noon meal and take them down again afterwards.

He thought he would be too tense to sleep, but in deference to the abbot lay down on his straw bed anyway. The dormitory was cool and quiet in the warm afternoon. The next thing he knew, a monk was shaking him awake from another sweaty dream he was just as thankful not to remember. The last red rays of the sun touching the western hills fingered straightly through the window slits, orange dust motes dancing in their beams.

After an evening meal consisting mainly of fried

bread with a thin sprinkling of cheese and garlic, Brother Ambrose led Thur off to the laundry to try on some clothes. They found a short padded tan jacket and real knitted hose dyed red that were large enough to fit. The clothes were not new, but had been washed fairly recently. Thur had never owned a pair of hose before, only the bias-cut leggings his mother made "loose for room to grow." He stared down at his red thighs in unease, feeling gaudy and exposed. A round red cap topped it all.

They left the laundry and passed through the maze of the monastery. Brother Ambrose paused when they came out in luminous twilight into a small courtyard at the foot of the chapel's belltower. A monk, his robe tucked up into his belt and his white legs scrambling, was clambering awkwardly down the thick ivy growing up the tower's side. He clutched a large linen bag in his teeth. Ambrose caught his breath as one sandaled foot slipped, but the climbing monk caught himself and completed his descent safely.

Gasping from his exertion, the monk straightened his robe and thrust the lumpy bag at Ambrose. The lumps were moving. "Here's your bag of bats. *Now* may I go eat?"

"Thank you, brother. That wasn't so hard, was it?"

The monk shot him a look of unbrotherly unlove. "Next time," he wheezed, "*you* try it. I was almost killed grabbing for them, and two bit me." He displayed minute wounds upon his fingers, squeezing them for blood to prove his assertion. " 'Sing the song,' you said, 'and they'll fly right into the bag.' Ha! They did not!"

"You have to sing the spell with true loving kindness," Brother Ambrose reproved.

"For *bats*?" The monk's lips screwed up in outrage.

"For any of God's creatures."

"Right." The monk sketched him a mocking salute.

"I'm going to get my supper—if there's any left—before the abbot decides he wants a bucket of centipedes." He marched away.

Brother Ambrose held the wriggling bag carefully, and led on.

Abbot Monreale's workroom was candle-lit. Fiametta sat on an upturned barrel by the center table, resting on her elbows. Thur regarded her anxiously. She looked tired, but not unhappy. The abbot paced.

"Ah. Good," he said as Ambrose and Thur entered. "Thur. I want you to look around the room and see if you notice anything new."

Baffled but willing, Thur walked around the table. The dried crocodile still grinned from its corner; if Monreale had moved his clutter about, Thur couldn't tell. "No, Father."

Monreale smiled rather triumphantly at Ambrose. "What was sitting on the table in front of Fiametta? Don't look!"

"Uh . . . a tray."

"And what was on the tray?"

"I . . . I can't say."

"Good." Monreale passed his hand over Thur's eyes. Thur immediately looked again.

Arranged on the tray were a dozen tiny white parchment tambourines, small enough to fit in a palm. Thur could have sworn they hadn't been there a moment ago. "Did you make them invisible, Father?" Thur picked one up and turned it over.

"No. I wish I could have. Or made them smaller, or disguised them as some other common thing. Prospero Beneforte would have thought of something cleverer, I'm sure." Monreale sighed regret. "We ran out of time for experiment. But at least they are very hard to notice. Nevertheless, when you place them, try to place them out of sight. With nothing touching or damping the membrane. They must be free to vibrate."

"What do they do?"

"They are little ears. Ears and mouths, in sympathetic pairs. What each ear hears in Montefoglia castle, its mouth will speak to a listening monk here at Saint Jerome. Since each mouth takes a monk to maintain, please try to put them where something important is likely to be said, eh?"

"I'll try, Father. How long do they last?"

"Only a day or so. I must seek some way to make this spell less volatile. So don't activate them until you actually place them. This is a variation of the scrying spell I use with my birds, but I've never heard of anyone attempting it without a live creature at the other end. I considered cockroaches, but they tend to scuttle away, unless they are crippled, and then they tend to die."

And Thur had thought that remark about the centipedes was a joke.

"I wonder if anyone has tried this before, and failed, or part-succeeded and kept it secret. . . . There is too much secrecy in this work. If all sorcerers pooled their knowledge for the common good, instead of each hugging his secrets to himself, what practical advances might be made! Even in the Church, pride and fear divide us. I've been mulling this notion for a time, but until it was suggested today to exfoliate the parchment and divide the twinned halves between ear and mouth, to harness their natural congruency, I had not solved the problem of how to get an ear to hear with life on only one side. But now the two are one, or the one is two."

"Shouldn't I carry a mouth for you to speak to me?"

"Alas, I wish you could. But you are no trained mage, to continually enspell it to speak loud enough to hear." He frowned in worry. "I hope they will span the distance. We could only try it across the cloister. I pray it will be strong enough to carry from Montefoglia Castle to Saint Jerome."

Monreale began placing half the tambourines in an old canvas carry-bag, nestled in a pile of clothes and other oddments that a foundryman looking for work might own. Gently, Ambrose hung his linen bag from a ceiling beam. Thur spoke to Fiametta.

"Did things go well for you today?"

"Yes," she said cheerily. "Though it was much the same sort of work I used to do for Papa. It seems he'd been using me as an apprentice without paying the licensing fee for quite some time." Thur wasn't certain if she was pleased or annoyed, but a subdued self-confidence glowed in her eyes. He found himself smiling back at her. She whispered behind her hand, "Peeling the parchments apart was my idea. I got it from something Papa used to do with leather, to make a secret pocket in his purse."

Monreale held up the last parchment circle, and gazed absently upon it. "What a boon it would be . . . Suppose, every year, the Church were to publish a book of the best new spells men had devised, and send copies to every Diocese. Men might be willing to give up their secrecy, to compete for the honor of such fame. . . . Ah, well. So," Monreale closed Thur's new pack, "do you have any other questions?"

No questions, really. It was all plain enough. There wasn't anything Monreale could do for the sick knot of worry in his belly. But the kobold had promised, if he went to the fire, he'd live. What was a kobold's word worth? "Father Monreale, should I trust the word of a demon?"

"*What?*" Monreale spun around, astonished. "What demon?"

"A kobold. We call them mountain-demons. I spoke with one, in the mine."

"Oh." Monreale huffed relief. "Don't frighten me like that, boy. A kobold is not a demon."

"It's not?"

"Not at all. Kobolds—and sprites and dryads and all their ilk—are, er, natural supernatural races. So to speak. They have a command of material magic, each according to its nature, but it is inherent, not learned. None can transcend their nature, as a human mage who combines spirit and material magic can learn to do. The Church Fathers have determined them to be a separate creation of God, but neither of the body of Christ as men are, nor under the dominion of men as, say, horses are. They're just . . . other. They are long-lived, compared to men, some of them, but they are mortal. Of the nature of their souls, there are several theories and heresies, but no certainty. God made them, they must have a purpose, but then, God made lions, wolves, and head lice, too. We need not allow them to be a nuisance. Fortunately, the Church's spirit magic can banish their material magic at need." Monreale was animated; clearly, Thur had tapped an enthusiasm.

"But then what is a demon?"

Monreale faltered, turning grave. "Ah. I'm afraid demons are to us more as Turks are. Brothers. Demons have a human origin, and so their evil is immeasurably more dangerous to us than the little malicious tricks of the shy folk."

Fiametta glanced up sharply. Fear narrowed her eyes, a fear of something Thur barely dared to guess at. "What *exactly* are demons, Father?"

Monreale frowned, looking troubled. "Fiametta, understand. You are not to discuss this subject without proper spiritual supervision, lest you fall into heresy or error. You must be very clear in your thinking. If you go on in the practice of magic, as you hope to do, you will be exposed to certain . . . temptations that do not trouble the ignorant."

"Does this have something to do with Papa?" she demanded.

"Alas, yes." Monreale paused. "Demons are ghosts."

"Papa's not a demon!"

"Not yet, no. But he may be in danger of becoming one. You see, shriven spirits go to God. Some fair souls go on even without any such ministrations. But in a few cases—almost always a sudden untimely death, accident or murder—the spirit lingers."

"So Papa said."

"Yes. Of these, most fade in time, like smoke on the wind, lost to man and God. Or at least, to man's sight. Such can be enslaved to a spirit ring or other material matrix for a time, fed and maintained."

"Maintained how?"

"Oh, there are a plethora of rites. What's really effective gets mixed in with a lot of damned nonsense, harmless or horrible—a good bit of the sin of maintaining a spirit ring, besides impeding a soul's ascent to God, is in these rites. When the would-be mage imagines that great crimes will give great powers. He is often addled or mistaken, which must surely make Lucifer laugh. Vast vile nonsense. I hate the rubbish. When the maintenance stops, the ring-bound spirit will begin to fade."

"Doesn't it go to hell?"

"Hell, as the great Saint Augustine revealed, is not a place. It is an eternity. Which is not the same thing as the end of time. Hell is right here, now. As is heaven. In a sense." He took in Thur's and Fiametta's utterly baffled stares, and waved a hand. "Never mind that now. There is one other category of ghost. Somehow, sometimes, a spirit becomes self-maintaining, without a body or a ring or any other material anchor. Some become sin-eaters, feeding on fear, anger, despair—and seek to increase such sins in order to sustain themselves. Some seek out witches and magicians and attempt to seduce them to their aid. That is the origin of the true demon. They are, thank God, extremely rare. Much rarer than the reports of overexcited common folk would have you believe."

Monreale rubbed his face, pressing out the deep apprehensive grooves. "Yet as you describe the apparition, Prospero Beneforte's ghostly strength is already nearly that great. To create a temporary body even from something so insubstantial as smoke was a feat. In Ferrante's hands, enslaved to a ring, fed ... the things he would be fed, he could become terrible."

"Papa won't do evil!"

"Prospero Beneforte was a man. A fairly good man, as men go. Little troubled by sloth or gluttony ... perhaps a trifle too subject to pride and wrath. And avarice. We are all, even the best of us, still sinners. He may resist Ferrante for a time. But sooner or later the allure of life, or at least, continued existence in the world of will, must prove overpowering. I could not resist such a reward, out of my own strength. I could only throw myself upon the mercy of God and pray for rescue."

Fiametta sat chill and stiff. Thur could see her wrestling with this new and subtle dread. "He called for you," she repeated.

"Yes," Monreale conceded. "I hope he has not mistaken me for God. I shall set you some special prayers, Fiametta. And in the meantime we'll see what we can do to stop Ferrante by all the other means God gives us."

Abbot Monreale took Thur to a spot on the south wall away from both the postern door and the main gate. They had to clamber over the laundry roof to reach it. There was no moon, and Brother Ambrose had darkened his lantern. Thur peered, willing his eyes to see into the nearby woods. If he couldn't see any soldiers, maybe they couldn't see him.

Monreale and Ambrose could have been shadow-monks. Only Fiametta's white linen sleeves made a pale blur. Thur had been hoping Monreale would produce a cloak of invisibility, but Monreale merely intoned a spell over him. Perhaps he was becoming more sensitive, with all this magic about, for this time he felt something, if only a vagueness, settle over him with Monreale's words.

"Can they see me at all?" Thur whispered.

"Not readily," Monreale murmured back. "This is akin to the spell I laid on my little ears. It will pass off in a few hours. If Ferrante's men see a shape or hear a sound, they will attribute it to animals, or nerves. But if you blunder right into one as you did last night, the spell can't help you. So watch yourself."

Had it only been last night they had arrived at Saint Jerome? "Yes, Father." Thur took the rope, tested it, swung his legs up, and sat athwart the stone. He jammed his cap on more firmly. Fiametta stood on the roof, her arms wrapping her torso against the chill, skirt a dark billow. Thur could not see her face.

"Thur . . ." she said. "Be careful. Uh . . . your new clothes look nice."

Thur nodded, cheered. He let the rope ease through his hands, and began his descent.

Chapter Nine

Thur dozed away the last hours of darkness behind a tree near the road, a quarter-mile from Montefoglia's northeast gate. Golden dawn glowed up at last from the eastern hills. He rolled over and watched the dusty road. He did not want to be first through the gate, nor second. Too conspicuous. Third, maybe. The road stayed abnormally quiet for this hour of the day, so near such a large town. Everyone who could was staying as far from the soldiers as possible, Thur guessed. But eventually a horseman passed—likely a Losimon— and then an old man trundling a wheelbarrow full of vegetables. Thur slipped down onto the road in his wake, well back.

Thur swallowed, as the town wall bulked up. Squared-off stone and brick of various ages ran down to the lakeshore and up and around, cradling Montefoglia from harm. A mile of wall at least. Was Rome like this? In the clear morning light the city looked magical, exciting—*men built this? Then what other wonders might men do?* True, the wall was in need of repairs in a few spots, stones starting to tumble down. His heart lifted still. Why had he stayed so long in Bruinwald when this had been waiting on the other end of the road? Uri had tried to tell him. . . .

The thought of Uri, perhaps lying wounded for days among brutal enemies, ill-tended, made Thur lengthen his stride till he overtook the man with the vegetable barrow. The gate was an arched doorway in a tall square tower topped with red tile. The barrow-man was stopped there by three guards, an unarmed man wearing the livery of the city, and two sword-girded Losimons. Both still wore the fancy livery issued for the betrothal procession, festive green and gold striped tunics and green tabards embroidered with Ferrante's arms, now dingy and worse for the unexpected wear of a fight and a week of siege and occupation duties.

"Radishes?" said the city guard in a worried tone, poking through the contents of the barrow. "All you bring us is radishes?" In fact, the barrow contained lettuce and spring onions tied in bunches as well.

"Our men will bring in something, one way or another, if the countryside doesn't." The taller Losimon glowered at the old man. "Tell your neighbors that."

The old man shrugged, not daring any more open defiance, and trundled on through. The city guard turned his attention to Thur. "What's your business, stranger?"

Thur turned his red cap humbly in his hands. "I seek work, sir. I was told some men in the castle wanted to hire foundrymen."

The city guard grunted, and wrote Thur's name, which Thur gave as Thur Wyl, and business down in his record book. "And where are you from?"

"Meissen. Altenburg," Thur threw out at random. He'd once met a crippled miner from the Altenburg, hands eaten away and half-blinded from the corrosive cadmia. It seemed a good place to be from, far from.

"German metalworker, eh?" said the shorter Losimon. "They'll be glad to have you."

Thur turned eagerly to him. "Do you know where I should go and who I should see, sir?"

"Go to the castle—right and straight up the main street—and ask for Lord Ferrante's secretary, Messer Niccolo Vitelli. He's doing the hiring."

"Thank you, sir." Thur ducked away.

The streets were narrow, like ravines between the tall stone houses and shops all crammed together. The sky was squeezed overhead into a blue ribbon. Thur recognized nothing of the town at this new angle but the colors. There were not many people in the streets this morning. On a sudden, urgent impulse, it occurred to Thur that it might be easier to check on Fiametta's house first, before he became caught up in God-knew-what labors in the castle. He stopped a man bent under a load of firewood, and asked directions to Via Novara.

Thur turned the opposite direction from the castle. A dry gutter ran down the center of the cobbled main street. Near the eastern city wall he found Via Novara, and turned upslope to its end.

That big square house? It seemed almost a *palazzo* to Thur's eyes, all of cut stone. Fancy cast-iron bars decorated with leaves and vines guarded the downstairs windows; larger windows protected by wooden shutters ran in a course high above. How right a setting it seemed for Fiametta. This house would protect her like a human jewel at its heart, like a little Lombardy princess. No wonder she was worried about it.

A thick oak door was set in an archway framed in white marble blocks, contrasting brightly with the yellowish native stone of the walls. The door stood open, guarded by a green-tabarded Losimon, armed. A fresh-faced young Losimon groom stood in the street nearby, holding the reins of two horses. One animal wore a plain leather headstall. The other, a big glossy chestnut with a snowy, showy blaze and white legs, had a long-shanked, gilded bit and gold-studded, green leather reins, with a silk-tassled breastband and crupper to match. Thur paused uncertainly.

"What do you want?" the guard, seeing him loiter, asked suspiciously.

"I was told Lord Ferrante's secretary, Messer Vitelli, wished to hire foundrymen," Thur began, letting his northern accent thicken. He was about to add, *But I got turned around and lost in the city,* when the guard relaxed and waved an understanding hand.

"Go right in."

Startled, Thur sidled past him. He paused in the stone-flagged hallway to let his eyes adjust to the dimness. To his right a door led into a deserted workroom, with workbenches and a clutter of tools strewn about—thrown about, Thur realized from the empty brackets on the walls. The benches were shoved out of place, one upturned. Looters had evidently given the room a once-over, but not yet stripped it of all tools and function. Thur walked forward into the brightness of a large inner courtyard.

The courtyard had its own well. A little pool was now dry. The court might have been originally designed as a garden room, but was very far from gardenlike now. It more resembled an infernal workshop, housing some satanic project interrupted and abandoned. Thur's eye picked out meaning from the apparent chaos of cranes, brickwork, digging, and scaffolding.

Master Beneforte had built a raised smelting furnace, right in his courtyard. Below it, in a deep dug-out depression, stood a huge clay lump, stuck about with thin tubes and fenced with iron bands and gird-ers. The lump was vaguely manlike, an elemental

swamp-monster struggling toward form. It could only
be the great Perseus Fiametta had spoken of. Char
in the pit revealed where the wax had been melted
out of the mold, drying and readying it for its molten bronze. Around the figure was built up a bank
of earth, pierced here and there with clay pipes. The
whole was tented over with canvas, to keep the
nonexistent rain off the baked clay.

From the wooden gallery circling the courtyard
above came a man's deep voice calling, "No luck
here." Footsteps echoed, and Thur turned to see the
man lean on the rail and stare down at him in turn.

He was a powerful-looking fellow in his thirties,
wearing military garb, chain mail over a padded coat,
tough leather leggings below for riding. An officer, by
his sword and confident bearing. Dark hair was cut
plain to fit in a smooth cap under a helmet. He was
clean-shaved, though a natural heaviness of beard
darkened his jaw. His face was redeemed from heaviness overall by alert dark eyes that studied Thur without
fear, measuringly. His right hand, resting on the railing, was wrapped about with a white gauze bandage.

More footsteps, and another man appeared on the
gallery opposite. Thur schooled his face to reveal no
twitch of recognition. It was the red-robed little man
he had seen atop the tower in Monreale's mirror,
directing the crossbowmen's fire. "Nothing here,
either," he said, then looked down and noticed Thur.
He frowned. "What's this?"

Thur doffed his cap again. "Excuse me, sir. I'm a
metal-worker. The guard at the town gate told me
to see Messer Vitelli."

"Oh." The little man grew less stiff. "They sent you
on, eh? Well, you've found me."

It seemed to Thur that his damnable talent for finding things lacked discrimination. He was not at all sure
he was ready to deal with Messer Vitelli. Yet the fellow

was slight, clerkish, not too well endowed with chin, bright-eyed and jerky as a blackbird. Why should he make Thur uneasy?

"Are you a foundry master, by chance?" asked Vitelli.

"No, Messer."

"Pity. Well, you look strong enough. You're hired. How are you at solving puzzles?"

"Eh?"

"Strong, but not too bright. Come up here."

Obediently, Thur mounted the stairs to the gallery and presented himself to the man in red. The soldierly fellow strolled around to join them.

"We're looking for something," Vitelli told Thur. "A book, or possibly a bundle of papers. It will be well hidden."

A pile of books and papers overflowed from a chest that sat waiting on the gallery. Thur pointed to it. "Not one of those, Messer?"

"No. But similar. Those are valuable, but they're not what we seek."

The soldierly man rumbled, "How can you be so sure it even exists, Niccolo? I think you have us on a wild goose chase. Or Beneforte may have burned it, years ago."

"It must exist, my lord. If he'd had it, he wouldn't have destroyed it. No mage could. Not if he'd already gone so far."

My lord? So this was Lord Ferrante himself? Thur wondered if he should pull out his little dagger and attempt to assassinate the man on the spot. His dagger was more used to cutting bread at dinner. The soldierly man scarcely looked the devil incarnate that Thur had been expecting. An ordinary man, even attractive. And Ferrante's mail protected him, nor did he turn his back. That seemed a quite casual habit, as he slid past them toward the next room. But he didn't let anyone, not even Vitelli, get behind him. Then another green-clad guard came out of the room, and the moment of opportunity was gone.

"Help him." Vitelli directed Thur to the guard. "Tap every brick, try every board. Don't skip a one."

"Yes, Messer." The bored-looking guard motioned Thur to follow him.

And so Thur found himself ticking on stone and knocking on plaster, and crouching on the floor sliding his dagger between the boards, inch by inch. They did one room, then another.

Vitelli stuck his head through the door. "Finish this floor. We're going to try the cellars."

I'd go up, not down, thought Thur automatically, and choked the words on his lips. Now was not the time to let his talent, or luck or whatever it was, shine forth. Of that, he was certain. He bent his head to the floorboards and ignored the ceiling.

The next room, he realized with a little shock as they entered it, was Fiametta's own. The wooden bed had been broken apart, the mattress knifed open in the first excited search for the goldsmith's treasures. A couple of chests had been upended and emptied out, but nothing remained of their contents now except a few old linens strewn on the floor. Surely Fiametta had owned more clothes than that. The good cloth must have been taken. Disturbed by an obscure sense of violation, Thur righted the chests, gathered the undergarments back up, and clumsily folded them away. Had the soldiers laughed, clowned around with her women's clothes? Thur didn't want anyone to laugh at Fiametta, with her sturdy dignity so hard-held. He frowned deeply.

"Come on, here," the impatient guard, sensing shirking, demanded help. Thur dutifully started tapping the walls. There was nothing behind the walls, of that he was sure. One wall, two, three . . .

"Ah, ha!" cried the guard, from the floor in the corner. "Got it!" He jimmied a short floorboard out of its slot with the tip of his dagger. A bundle of paper tied about with silk ribbon rested within the space. He snatched it out and brandished it triumphantly, grinning, and hurried out to find his master. Thur followed.

They found Lord Ferrante and Messer Vitelli in the kitchen, just climbing out of the root cellar, looking dirty and disgusted.

"Here, my lord!" The excited guard thrust the bundle of papers forward.

"Ha!" Vitelli snatched it, ripped off the ribbon, and spread the papers across the kitchen table. The cracks of the wood were yellow with the flour of many batches of bread and noodles. Vitelli read eagerly, turning papers over, then his face fell. "Damn! Rubbish."

"That's not it?" The guard, who'd been fingering the flat purse at his belt, said in discouragement. "I found it hidden under a floorboard. . . ."

"It's not Beneforte's writing. It must be the girl's diary. Peh! Notes on magic, yes, but it's all apprentice's rubbish. Gossip and love spells and like muck." Contemptuously, Vitelli flicked the papers away.

As Ferrante and Vitelli turned away, Thur surreptitiously gathered the sheets back up, wound the ribbon around them, and tucked them back out of sight in a cupboard housing dinged and battered old pewter. Ferrante paused to let Thur and Vitelli and the bitterly disappointed guard exit the kitchen first.

"That's all the time I can waste this morning," said Lord Ferrante as they walked into the courtyard. "You can take some men and try again this afternoon, Niccolo, if you insist, but then we'll just have to go on without it."

"It must be here somewhere. It must," said the secretary doggedly.

"So you say. Maybe he kept all his notes in his head, eh?"

Vitelli groaned at the thought.

Ferrante stared absently around. "Perhaps when I'm Duke here I'll give you this house."

"That would content me, my lord," said Vitelli, growing a shade more serene.

"Good."

Vitelli wandered into the sunlight, and glanced under a pile of canvas. "Should I have these pigs of tin moved to the castle along with the books, my lord?"

The gleaming metal bars in the stack weighed about a hundred pounds each, Thur estimated, doubtless the only reason they hadn't been carried off in the first wave of looting, before some officer had arrived to assert Ferrante's rights.

"Leave them for now," Ferrante shrugged. "They're not going to march away. Until we can find a foundry master who can cast a cannon that will be more dangerous to our enemies than to ourselves, they might as well sit here as anywhere." Ferrante turned away. "Come along, German."

Thur picked up his pack. Ferrante paused at the oak door to speak to his guard posted there.

"I know you've been poking about in here, looking for jewels."

"No, lord," said the door guard in a shocked voice.

"Eh. Don't lie to me or I'll have you stretched. You and your friends pocket a garnet or a coin or two, I don't care. But if I find that anyone has carried out a single scrap of paper, even if it's an inventory of the chamber pots, I'll have his head on a stick before sundown. Understand?"

"Yes, my lord." The guard stood frozen to attention till Ferrante and Vitelli swung aboard their horses. Two breast-plated and helmeted soldiers who had been searching the garden and toolshed appeared when the groom ran to fetch them, and fell in behind the two horsemen. Thur's guard and the boy groom marched ahead.

At Ferrante's hand motion, Thur walked beside his stirrup through the town. The guards glowered suspiciously at any citizen who strayed too near the little procession. The Montefoglians in turn tended to fade away at Ferrante's approach, turning in to shops or side streets, or stepping back to flatten themselves against walls. No one hissed, no one cheered. It was as if a circle of silence surrounded Lord Ferrante, moving as he moved.

Only four guards? Was Lord Ferrante so brave? He rode straight-backed, not deigning to glance about like his escort. Thousands of Montefoglians lived in this city. If they all turned out into the streets at once, surely Ferrante and his men could not stand against them despite the disparity of weapons. Why didn't they? Thur wondered. Had Duke Sandrino been so unloved? Was one tyrant the same as another to the citizens, for all practical purposes? Maybe Ferrante's abrupt reversal of status, from son-in-law to usurper, friend to foe, was simply too sudden to assimilate. What hold had Ferrante on the Montefoglians? Fear, clearly, but . . . all very well to imagine a mob of irate citizens taking to the streets to avenge their duke, but who would volunteer to be the first to run up on the enemies' swords? Thur was an outlander; this wasn't really his fight. Was it? *Does Uri live?* A bend in the street brought the castle into view, on its steep-sided rocky hill, and Thur's belly shivered.

"So, German," Lord Ferrante spoke agreeably from his horse. "What do you know of cannon foundry?"

Thur shrugged, adjusting his pack more comfortably on his shoulders. He tried not to think about what was in the pack. "I've worked in smelteries, my lord, parting metals and ores. Cleaned the furnaces, and helped stack the fuels and metals. Run the bellows. I've helped with some casting in sand pits, but only little things, plaques and candlesticks ... except I once helped with a church bell."

"Hm. How would you repair a cracked bombast? If you had to."

"I ... it would depend on the crack, my lord. If it ran lengthwise, I've heard of heating iron tyres and binding the barrel around. If the crack ran crosswise, maybe use the old bombast as a pattern, and remelt and cast it. You would need some fresh metals to add, because of the waste in the furnace and channels."

"I see." Ferrante regarded him with mild approval. "I've seen military engineers do the trick with the tyres. You seem to know your work. Good. If I can find no other master, you may find yourself promoted."

"I ... would do my best, my lord," said Thur in an uncertain tone.

Ferrante chuckled. "I'd make sure of it."

He seemed in a fairly mellow mood, for a murderer. Thur ventured, "What were you looking for, in that house, my lord?"

Ferrante's smile thinned. "No concern of yours, German."

Thur took the hint, and stayed silent. They were nearing the hill where the road climbed to the castle. From the corner of his eye, Thur saw a man dart and crouch behind a water trough. One of a group of three young men waiting by a cross-corner was staring hard at Ferrante. The others seemed deliberately turned away. Ferrante became conscious of the starer, though he did not return the look; his chin rose and his jaw tightened. He switched his reins to his bandaged right hand. His left touched the hilt of his sword. Another group of half a dozen young men, seemingly drunk, were lurching down a side alley, singing. They bumped and jostled each other, but their voices were too subdued.

Ferrante's guards bristled like dogs, but did not draw, glancing to their master for orders.

Thur looked around for someplace, any place, a shop or alley, to duck away in. Nothing. The building on his right hand was solid, doors and shutters locked. Ahead, the three men joined the six, and they all lumbered into the street. All had swords out. None were smiling or joking or singing now. Determination, anger, fear, and second thoughts flickered in their faces. One boy, no older than Thur, looked so green-white Thur half-expected him to bend over and start vomiting.

A couple of the gang members made little rushes forward, then stepped back again when their company did not follow fast enough. A few began shouting insults at Ferrante and his guards, more to encourage themselves, Thur feared, than to annoy their enemies. Ferrante's face was set like iron. He nodded; his guards drew their swords. Vitelli, who bore only a dagger, reined in his horse.

Ferrante's veterans kept a silence more ominous than the attackers' shouted threats. The guards were tense—they might be illiterate, but at least they had enough arithmetic to know the difference between six and ten. Yet they seemed more intent than fearful, as if they faced an unpleasant but familiar and well-practiced task. Ferrante's boy-groom drew his dagger, and glanced back over his shoulder at his master for reassurance; Ferrante gave him a nod. Thur gibbered in his throat. Should he draw his knife or not? He was on the wrong *side*. . . .

The street gang surged toward Ferrante at last, prodded by a screaming leader who switched his colorful insults from the Losimons to his unforward comrades. The three guards rushed ahead and engaged them with a clang and scrape of steel.

A well-dressed young man in blue doublet and

bright yellow hose slipped between the embattled guards, his eyes on Ferrante. The little groom ran forward to meet him, brandishing his dagger. The contest was unequal, the dagger parry futile. The Montefoglian's sword buried itself in the boy's chest. The little groom screamed. Yellow-hose paused, as if shocked and astonished by his own effect.

Ferrante turned scarlet. "Coward!" he bellowed, snatched out his sword left-handed, and spurred his flashy chestnut horse on. His hot dark eyes focused on Yellow-hose with terrifying concentration. Yellow-hose took a look at his face, yanked his sword from the little groom with a spatter of blood, turned, and ran.

He almost succeeded in drawing Ferrante out from his screen of guards. Hands reached up to grab for the horse's gilded bridle, and the street men roared. Ferrante swung at them, and spurred again. His horse reared and kicked, squealing, connecting at least once with a solid, juicy *thunk*. The guards ran forward to catch up.

A Montefoglian swordsman popped up in front of Thur. Thur whipped out his dagger and knocked the blow away barely in time, and then, not knowing what else to do, lunged forward and wrapped his assailant in a bear hug, trapping the sword arm. His prisoner heaved and struggled, and they gasped garlic and onion, exertion and terror, onto each other. "Not me, you idiot!" Thur groaned into the Montefoglian's nearby ear. "I'm on your side!" The Montefoglian tried to butt him with his head.

A flash of color and movement to the side—Thur wrenched his prisoner around just as another Montefoglian thrust at him. The man's sword ran clean through his comrade's back and pierced Thur's belly. Thur sprang back with a cry of pain and surprise, and the man he'd bear-hugged slumped to the cobbles. The second swordsman wailed, and drew his sword out hurriedly, as if he might so take back his misaimed, disastrous blow.

Thur touched his belly. His shaking hand came away red as the stain spread on his new tan tunic. But it was only a surface cut; he could feel it, no organs touched. He could straighten and move, and did, shuffling backwards. The Montefoglian didn't follow up but, crying, tried to drag his injured comrade away.

Thur whirled around as a scraping clatter grew deafening. It was the scrabble of hooves on the cobblestones. Half a dozen green-clad Losimon cavalrymen were riding down from the castle to succor their lord. They slammed into the street men from behind, scattering them and totally disrupting their attack. Each man turned from the assault on Ferrante and began to try to save himself. Losimons chased them severally up the alleyway. Thur felt around himself; he had not, thank God, dropped his pack nor spilled its incriminating contents across the cobbles.

Ferrante, breathing heavily, soothed his pawing horse. The animal's eyes rolled white, nostrils flaring with the scent of blood. The boy-groom, whey-faced, eyes fixed and staring, lay now across Ferrante's lap. Ferrante sheathed his sword and, murmuring, turned the boy's head around to his. He stared for a stunned moment into the dead face, then growled like a wolf.

Two of the guards were injured. Three dead Montefoglians lay on the stones, including the one Thur had wrestled. Two dismounted cavalrymen held the struggling Yellow-hose a prisoner.

Ferrante's face went from red to livid gray. He pointed to the prisoner, and spoke to his cavalry captain. "Squeeze that one. Find out the names of his accomplices. Then hunt them down and kill them." The chestnut horse danced uneasily beneath its rigid rider.

"My lord." Messer Vitelli resheathed his dagger,

which he had not used, and pressed his horse up beside Ferrante's. "A word." His voice fell. "Hold this one, yes. Learn what he knows. But don't spend men pursuing them now. It would just plunge their families into vendetta against you."

Thur breathed covert relief. A voice of reason and mercy, to stop this monstrous cascade of violence . . . his respect for Vitelli rose a notch.

"When your troops arrive, *then* take the assassins and all their relatives at once," Vitelli went on. "Leave none alive to seek revenge. It will make a good strong first impression, after which your rule will be less troubled."

Ferrante's brows went up; he studied his secretary as if slightly bemused. At last he grunted assent. "See to it, Niccolo."

Vitelli on his restive horse bowed his head briefly in acknowledgement. "That reminds me. We should let the late Duke's enemies out of the dungeon. We're going to need the space."

"Take care of it," sighed Ferrante. The excitement and energy of the fight were visibly draining from him, leaving a kind of lassitude. He glanced down at Thur. "You're hurt, German." He sounded, if not exactly concerned, at least mildly interested.

"It's just a scratch, my lord," Thur managed to choke out.

Ferrante's war-experienced eye summed Thur and concurred. He gave Thur a brief nod. "Good. I like a man who doesn't whine."

Despite himself, Thur felt inanely warmed by the man's approval. *Remember who he is. Remember Uri.* He gave Ferrante a stiff nod in return, which for some reason caused Ferrante to smile dryly to himself.

With a last thin-lipped look of grief, Ferrante smoothed back the boy-groom's hair from his white forehead and gave his body over to one of the cavalrymen. He frowned at Thur's palm, pressed to his red belly, and extended his left hand. "Climb up. I'll give you a ride to my surgeon."

So Thur found himself not an inch away from Ferrante himself, athwart the chestnut horse's muscular haunches as the beast climbed to the castle. His fingers clung to the saddle's carved cantle, not daring or wishing to grip the Lord of Losimo. Ferrante rode through the tower-flanked gate and let Thur down in the castle courtyard, and detailed a guard to guide him. "When you've got a patch on that belly, find my secretary. He'll show you the work."

Chapter Ten

Thur followed the guard across the courtyard. A servant led Lord Ferrante's horse in the opposite direction. On his left Thur recognized the elaborate marble staircase that he'd glimpsed in Monreale's mirror. Ferrante mounted the steps two at a time and disappeared into the castle. In his guide's wake Thur entered a much humbler portal on the north side of the court into what was apparently the servants' wing. They passed through a stone-paved, whitewashed kitchen where half a dozen sweating and cursing men wrestled with firewood and the carcass of an ox. A couple of frightened-looking old women kneaded a small mountain of bread dough. Beyond the kitchen a butler's pantry was taken over by a camp apothecary, and a few steps up and a turn through another corridor brought them to the late Duke Sandrino's state dining room.

It had been converted to a temporary hospital. A

dozen sick or wounded men lay on woven straw pallets. Upon the frescoed walls ruddy half-naked gods and pale greenish nymphs smiled and sported among the acanthus leaves, indifferent to the fleshly pain under their painted eyes.

While his guide-guard spoke with Ferrante's surgeon, Thur anxiously scanned the pallets. All strangers. Uri did not lie among these men. So. And how many men had Thur seen? Counting the troops besieging the monastery, more than Ferrante's original honor guard of fifty, surely. Some of the swifter cavalry must have already arrived from Losimo. How many days behind them did Ferrante's infantry march? He should try to find out these things, Thur guessed.

Ferrante's military surgeon was a squat swarthy Sicilian who moved with bustle. He seemed more a barber than a healer or mage, not at all like the learned and robed Paduan doctors who took pulses, sniffed urine, and pronounced gravely. This man looked like he'd be more at home digging graves. He wrinkled his full lips and shrugged when Thur removed his jacket to display his cut. The first profuse bleeding had stopped, and the elasticity of the skin pulled the edges of the wound apart. Thur stared with morbid fascination at the glimpse of his red-brown muscle sliding beneath the gaping gash.

The surgeon laid Thur down on a trestle table, muttered a perfunctory-sounding spell against suppuration, and sewed the edges of the cut together with a curved needle while Thur, eyes crossed and teary, bit on a rag, his breath whistling through his teeth. The surgeon had Thur sitting up again within moments, and tied a linen bandage around his waist.

"Cut the stitches and pull them out in about ten days, if the wound doesn't go bad," the surgeon advised Thur. "If it goes bad come see me again. All right, run along."

The pain dulling with use, Thur managed a "Thank you, sir." He folded up his bloodstained tan jacket and rummaged carefully in his pack for his spare, a shabby gray linen tunic. Should he attempt to plant a little ear in this chamber? Would it hear anything of value? But for its frescoes this seemed much like the infirmary in the monastery. The men all looked the same, stubbled and shocked or flushed and fevered; the smell was the same, sweat, drying blood, the tang of urine and feces, a burnt whiff suggesting some recent cautery.

The surgeon's back was turned. Thur palmed a little parchment disk and looked around for a place to hide it. A mess of equipment was piled in a corner behind the trestle table: a dented cuirass, somebody's empty pack, a pike, and a couple of stretcher poles. Thur started to stoop, but was stopped abruptly by the twinge of his belly. He caught his breath, murmured the activating words Abbot Monreale had given him, and dropped the little disk in behind the pile. He straightened up more carefully.

The surgeon finished putting his needle away in its little leather case, which contained even larger and more unnerving implements of the sort, and stuffed the bloody rags into a laundry bag. Thur laced up his jacket and asked casually, "How many of these men are Lord Ferrante's, and how many are your prisoners?"

"Prisoners? Up here?" The surgeon raised bemused black brows. "Not likely."

Dare he ask after Uri by name? "Did you take many wounded prisoners?"

"Not too many. Most ran off after that militant abbot, and we traded back all the ones that were so bad off as to be no further threat to us. Let them consume the enemy's resources. Just as well. I'd rather serve my own."

"Uh . . . where are they now? The few you did take."

"The dungeon, of course."

"Officers too? Even the Duke's captains and officials?"

"All the same enemy." The surgeon shrugged.

"Won't . . . Lord Ferrante risk criticism, for such harshness?"

The surgeon barked a short, humorless laugh. "Not from his soldiers. Look—you read, don't you?"

"Yes, sir. A little."

"Thought so. Or you wouldn't be repeating such priests' and women's twaddle. I got my start as a surgeon in the camp of a certain Venetian condottiere— I will not foul my lips by naming him. We were pursuing some Bolognese. Dogged 'em for days. Caught up with them by a marsh—and our dear commander stopped and let them *prepare* for our assault. He got a reputation for chivalry out of it, and retired rich. I got a tent full of dying men who should never have been wounded. A fiasco. Peh! Give me a captain who puts his own men first. The enemy can have the crumbs of any sentimentality left over."

"Then you admire Lord Ferrante?"

"He's a practical soldier. The older I get, the better I like that." The surgeon shook his head.

Thur puzzled this over. "But now Lord Ferrante has to be more than a soldier. Now he has to be a ruler."

"What's the difference?" The surgeon shrugged.

"I'm . . . not sure. It just seems there ought to be one."

"Power is power, my young philosopher, and men are men." The surgeon smiled, half-sour, half-amused.

"I'm a foundryman."

"You reason like one." The surgeon clapped him on the shoulder in a gesture copied, Thur could swear, from Lord Ferrante. "Just make us some cannon, Foundryman, and leave the aiming of them to your betters."

Thur smiled dimly in return and, clutching his pack, escaped the painted chamber.

*   *   *

He found himself wandering through a bewildering succession of rooms, some bright and panelled and frescoed, others plain and dim. In a tiny hall a couple of Losimon soldiers dozed atop their blankets in the heat of the afternoon, while a couple more pursued a desultory game of dice. They barely glanced at Thur. *Down. I must find a way down, somehow.*

Beyond the soldiers Thur found a larger-than-usual chamber with a marble-paved floor. Double doors stood open to the breathless air and a hazy brightness. Thur peeked through into a garden bounded on the other side by a high wall. Insects hummed sleepily in the white afternoon. A few wilted crossbowmen manned turrets atop the stonework. Thur oriented himself by the shadows; the garden wall must run along the cliff which fell sheer to the lake. There was little fear of assault from that quarter. There was very little fear of assault from any quarter, Thur admitted grimly to himself. But perhaps Lord Ferrante didn't know that.

Off the larger chamber stood a smaller one, wood-panelled. A desk with piles of papers, shelves of books, and a map-strewn table marked it as a study. Duke Sandrino's office? Jolted by his opportunity, Thur glanced around and nipped inside. He dug a little ear from his pack and stared about.

Peculiar brown stains were spattered over the wooden floor, caked in the grain of the oak. A set of shelves stood taller than Thur. He reached up and swiped a hand across its top, and found only dust. Footsteps sounded on the marble outside. Hastily Thur murmured the words and pushed the little round tambourine out of sight above. A man would have to be half a head taller than Thur to see it. He stepped away from the shelves.

Messer Vitelli entered the study, and frowned suspiciously at Thur. "What are you doing in here, German?"

"Lord Ferrante told me that you would show me the work, Messer," Thur replied, trying not to sound too breathy.

"Huh." The little man rummaged among the papers on the map table, found the one he was looking for, and motioned Thur out into the sun-heated garden. Thur bit his lip in frustration and followed. He glanced back at the bulking brick and stone of the castle. *So close. I must find a way down.*

Vitelli led Thur to the bottom of the garden, opposite to the stables through a locked gate. A couple of sun-reddened workmen, naked to the waist, torsos shiny with sweat, were slowly excavating a hole. Nearby piles of sand, woodstacks, brick, and broken brick indicated a foundry-in-the-making. A bronze bombast, weathered green, sat on a sledge, its wide black mouth gaping to heaven. "That's the piece." Vitelli pointed to it.

An ogre's stewpot. Thur knelt beside the cannon and let his hands trace over its scale-encrusted ornament, animal masks, knobs, vines cast in relief winding about the barrel. The crack was obvious, a jagged spiral that ran halfway around. The damage must have propagated while the ordnance was cooling after a bout of firing. A flaw that severe which occurred when the bombast was actually being fired would have torn the bronze apart and killed its artillery master. Another firing would do just that. But an iron ball belched forth from that pot could crack stone as thick as Saint Jerome's walls, no question.

"How often could it be fired?" Thur asked Vitelli.

"About once an hour, I'm told. Its previous owner tried to exceed that limit."

Such a battering, kept up night and day, could breach Saint Jerome in less than two days, Thur guessed. The spiral path of the crack made quick and easy reinforcement with iron tyres a doubtful proposition, or Duke

Sandrino's artillery master would have already had it done. The bombast had obviously been set aside to await recasting.

"What do you think, Foundryman?" Vitelli was watching him closely, Thur realized.

Might he tell Ferrante's secretary the bombast could be bound with iron, and so lure the enemy into blowing it up themselves? No, Thur decided regretfully. From the preparations it was clear the Losimons already knew what had to be done. But a complete recasting would take time, and much labor, and Ferrante was man-short and many things could go wrong. Of that, Thur realized, he could make sure. He was no foundry master, but for such sabotage he scarcely needed to be. The clumsier the better, in fact. He brightened. "It will have to be recast."

"Can you do it?"

"I've never done anything that large before, but— yes. Why not?"

"Very well. Take over. Make a list of what you need to finish the job, and bring it to me. And, Foundryman . . . ," Vitelli's secretive smile twitched a corner of his mouth, "our artillery master has an iron chain about six feet long. One end will be bolted to the caisson. The other ends in a manacle that will be locked around your ankle. It will be your honor to light the match, the first time your new piece is fired. Immediately afterwards you shall be given a purse of gold."

Thur grinned uncertainly. "That is a joke . . . Messer?"

"No. It is Lord Ferrante's order." Vitelli favored Thur with a small ironic bow, and turned back toward the castle. Thur's grin turned to grimace.

The two workmen, Thur discovered upon inquiry, were already digging the pit for the proposed sand casting. Thur fended off the pointed offer of a shovel by displaying his new bandages, and poked around the piles of supplies trying to look shrewd and unimpressed, like Master Kunz. Plenty of brick, though the firewood was scant. A couple of barrels of good clay, well-seasoned. The sand pile was clean and dry, but should be covered with canvas in case the rain the monks were praying for to fill Saint Jerome's cisterns ever came. Thur tilted his face up, blinking. The sky was cloudless, if hazy. All right, canvas to keep out foreign matter. Thur still remembered Master Kunz's plaque casting the time the village cats had gotten to his sand pile, and the workmen had failed to sift the sand before shovelling it into the pit. Molten bronze had met cat turd, instantly creating a steam explosion. The casting had been ruined, the workmen beaten, and Master Kunz had spent the next two weeks heaving cobbles at any stray cat unwise enough to show its whiskers near his shop.

Or perhaps Thur ought to salt Ferrante's sand pile with, say, old fish heads? *Here, kitty, kitty. . . .* Thur recalled Vitelli's six-foot chain, and set the idea aside. For now.

His preliminary inventory finished, Thur returned to the castle in search of Messer Vitelli, reminding himself to look for more good places to conceal the little ears. As soon as he had them all distributed, he could be gone, and the devil take Ferrante's cannon foundry. As soon as he found Uri.

Unfortunately, Thur found Vitelli in the first place he looked, the Duke's study. Ferrante's secretary was penning letters by the window in the last light. He turned his paper face down as Thur entered. "Yes, German?"

"You asked for a list of needs, Messer."

Vitelli took a fresh quill and a scrap of paper. "Say on."

"A crane, or the long timbers, fittings and chains

needed to build one. Iron pipes for the channels. Enough canvas to protect the work in progress. And scrap bronze, or new copper and tin to add to the melting, to make up the waste in the melting and the channels and vents. More firewood. What's there will only be enough to dry the mold. Charcoal, and fine lute clay to line the bricks of the furnace. A rammer. A couple of good big bellows made of oxhide, and enough strong workmen to take turnabout to keep them pumping during the tricky parts. Six men would do."

"I can lend you some soldiers for that. How much more bronze?"

"I'm not sure. A couple hundred pounds at least." At Vitelli's pained look Thur added, "What's over, too much, you can recover from the channels, but if you're under the casting will fail. And the mold will be destroyed, and since the old bombast would be melted down by then, you could not make another."

"More bronze, then." Resignedly, Vitelli bent his head over his scratching quill. Thur schooled himself not to glance at the top of the shelf across the study. Vitelli frowned up at him. "Carry on, German."

No escape from this pantomime yet. Thur retreated to the garden, where he marked out the dimensions of a furnace on the high side of the pit, and directed the workmen to begin building up its base with their dirt pile. By then it was nearly twilight, and the workmen led him off to the kitchen where a curt camp cook issued them fried bread, a few scraps of meat, and cheap wine. Thur, ravenous, ate his portion out of hand as they took him to the workmen's dormitory over the stables, shared with the grooms. Thur found an uninhabited straw pallet to claim for his bed. At least, he trusted it was uninhabited—he peered suspiciously into its weave for signs of life. In an unobserved moment he concealed another little ear under the foot of the tattered quilt he was issued by a senior groom, and tucked the remaining three into his gray tunic. Leaving his pack, he escaped his new acquaintances' offer of wine and a game of dice. "I have to go talk to Vitelli about cranes." He excused himself.

Actually, the unnerving little secretary was the last man Thur wished to see again right now. He descended the ladder from the dormitory and passed uncertainly through the stables, crowded with Losimon cavalry horses. A few overworked grooms carted fodder and water. These could only be a portion of Ferrante's horses, Thur realized, counting under his breath; the rest must be pastured outside of town somewhere, with yet another complement of guards.

The stables opened onto the entry court, with its two massive towers and its marble staircase. The red tile fringing the tower tops blazed like enamel in the last high light of the setting sun, then faded to a shadowed earthy tone against the cool sky. A couple of helmeted heads moved in the crossbowmen's platforms, crenellated brick boxes open to the air that stuck up out of the skirts of sloping tile.

A faint golden glow of candlelight reflected from two shadowed slots halfway up one tower. Did it mark the chamber where the Duchess and Lady Julia were kept prisoner? Nothing thicker than candlelight or a crossbow quarrel was likely to escape from those pinched stone mouths.

Soft and insistent as a heartbeat, Thur's sixth sense drove him onward, through the service entry on the other side of the courtyard. This time he turned away from the kitchen into a dim stonework corridor. At its end he found a thick wooden door. A tired-looking Losimon with a short sword sat on an upturned barrel, his pike leaning against the wall.

The pikeman gave Thur a hard stare, his hand going to his sword hilt. "What d'you want, boy?"

"I'm . . . Lord Ferrante's new foundryman. I'm . . . supposed to check the bars and metalwork down there, and submit a list of repairs to Messer Vitelli." There. That was the likeliest lie Thur could come up with. If that one didn't work . . . Thur eyed the pike. *Uri, I'm coming.*

"Oh. Yes. I know the cell they mean." The guard nodded knowledgeably. "I'll take you to it." He rose from his barrel and pushed the door open.

A shout echoed up the stone stairs beyond the door. Another Losimon guard was toiling upward, holding a lantern. He paused to catch his breath when his comrade appeared at the head of the stairs. "Carlo! The lunatic's out again. Keep a watch up there."

"He hasn't come this way."

"All right, then he must still be hiding down here. We'll keep looking."

"I'll lock this door till you find him." The first guard motioned Thur through. "Here's my lord's workman, come to check the cell."

"Good." The second guard beckoned, and turned back down the stairway. Thur descended, bewildered. But as his shoe leather scraped across the gritty stone, every step echoed his certainty. *Down. Yes. This way.* Behind him, the thick door swung shut in the gloom, and its iron bolt grated home into its slot.

The two men went down a second turning, and the corridor's walls changed from cut and fitted stonework to solid native sandstone. The corridor narrowed, then turned again and flared to accommodate a guardpost and a garderobe. A barred window overlooked the lake, admitting the dim blue light of early evening. The window had to be cut right into the cliff face, beneath the garden wall. The garderobe's stone chute for slops tunneled through nearby.

The corridor sank a little further, and passed a row of unusual doors. Each cell door was a rack of vertical iron bars, their iron hinges set deep into the sandstone. The cells, too, had tiny barred windows, making them not so airless, damp, or horrible as Thur had expected. In conjunction with the airy ironwork of the doors, the ventilation was excellent. But the cells were crowded, four or five men in each. Thur slowed, trying to make out faces, forms . . . Ferrante only held about twenty prisoners here. Uri was not among these. . . .

"Here, workman." The guard frowned back at his laggard steps, and Thur hurried to catch up. On his left, he passed another narrow corridor leading . . . up into the castle? Too dark to tell. The guard pointed into an empty cell at the end of the row. "This one."

"What's wrong with it?" Thur asked. It looked identical to the others, except for being empty.

"Nothing, I wager," said the guard darkly. "*I* think it's magic. Magic and madness." Glumly, he rattled the door on its hinges, took a key from his belt, and unlocked it. "See? It was locked, just like this. Yet the madman has—dare I say—flown."

Nervously, Thur entered the cell. A vision of the guard clanging the door shut behind him with a cry of *Ha! Caught you, spy!* flashed in his mind. But the guard merely rubbed his nose and stared, helpfully hoisting the lantern high. Thur stepped to the cubit-square window, and traced over and shook the iron bars set therein. Solid. There was a couple of feet thickness of solid stone between the cell and the cliff face. The window was like a little tunnel. A slice of lake glimmered in the gathering gloom; in a tiny patch of sky, one star shone. Thur jerked his hand back as a large centipede scuttled from a crack and flowed over the stone, to disappear over the outer edge of the window tunnel.

Thur gazed around the whitewashed walls of the cell. The chamber was small, but not inhumanly so; there was room for a taller man than Thur to lie down on the usual woven straw pallet, and, standing up, Thur's head didn't brush the ceiling. The walls seemed solid. Thur chafed under the gaze of the guard. *Go away, you.* He was close, close to Uri, he could feel it, if only he could win a few moments unobserved.

Rough voices echoed down the corridor, blended with a much stranger noise—laughter? A high shriek rang, "Eee, eee, eee!"

"Ah. They got him." The Losimon guard grimaced. "He doesn't get far. But how does he get *out*?" He shook his head and backed out of the cell. Thur followed, dogged by the darkness that seemed to seep from the corners as the lantern was withdrawn.

Two Losimons were manhandling a third fellow toward the cell. Their prisoner was a middle-aged man, tending toward stoutness. In another time, he might have been grave and stately. The torn and soiled velvet tunic, decent skirts to the knee, and silk hose he wore marked him as a man of rank, his graying hair as a man of dignity. But now his hair stuck out wildly, uncombed, and his beard-salted jowls were shrunken. Red-rimmed eyes stared out from bruised hollows. He shrieked again, twisted, and flapped his hands below the guards' solid grip on his arms.

"Where did you find him?" asked the guard with the lantern.

"Downstairs again," panted the younger guard. "Same corner. We missed him first pass, but he was crouching there the second time I looked—God! Maybe he does turn into a bat."

"Don't *say* the word, you'll just start him up again," began his partner, their sergeant, but it was too late. Excitement flushed their prisoner's face, and he began to jabber and mutter beneath his breath, his body jerking.

"A bat. A bat. A bat's the thing. The black Vitelli is a false bat, but I am a real one. I'll fly away. Fly away from you, and you'll be hanged. Fly to my wife, and you won't stop me—vermin! Murderers!" His conspiratorial grin gave way to incoherent rage, and he began to buck and fight in earnest. The two guards flung him into the cell and slammed the door shut. He banged into it with a velvet-covered shoulder, over and over, while the two junior guards leaned against the bars to hold it closed while their sergeant thrust the key into the lock—it took three tries—and turned it. The Losimons stood away from the door, relieved, as the bolt caught.

The madman continued to bang and shriek his wordless bat-cry, alternated with stamping in circles and shaking his whole body as if he were a bat flapping its wings. It was absurd, but somehow Thur didn't find it funny. Tears leaked down the man's ravaged face as he piped his strange cries, and his indrawn breath churned in a raw throat. "I will fly. I will fly. I will fly. . . ," he trailed off at last. He crouched to the floor, then sat heavily, weeping and exhausted.

"Who is the poor fellow?" Thur whispered, staring through the bars.

"He was the dead Duke's castellan, Lord Pia," shrugged the sergeant, catching his breath from the wrestling match. "I think the battle and the bloodshed turned his brain. He doesn't half care for being locked in his own prison, I can tell you."

"But he doesn't *stay* locked in, is the trouble," muttered his younger comrade. "How does he do it? Vitelli swears there's no trace of magic on the lock."

The prisoner's eyes flashed up at the secretary's name, a scarlet, lucid, malevolent glare that crossed Thur's startled eyes, then buried itself in downward-looking muttering again. *Is he really mad? Or only pretending?* Or perhaps the castellan was both . . . strange thought. It was no wonder he was kept alone, though, even as crowded as the prison was now.

Thur examined the iron door. The bars were oiled, free of rust and corrosion. The hinges were deep-set in solid rock, and sound. He tapped down the long vertical rods. All rang true, no hidden hollows for a secret slide. He was no locksmith, but there was nothing wrong with the lock that he could see.

"We've done all that," said the guard with the lantern impatiently, watching Thur.

"Have you searched him for a key? Searched the cell?"

"To the skin. Twice."

"To the skin. Um . . . I don't suppose he could have . . . that is, uh, did you——"

"No, he didn't stick a key up his ass," said the guard sergeant, dryly amused. "He didn't swallow and gag it up again, either." Thur decided not to ask how he knew. "Somebody's just going to have to watch him, day and night," the sergeant went on.

"I've got to go fetch dinner," said the younger guard nervously.

The sergeant eyed him in an ominous sergeantly manner, but then shrugged. "We're short-handed all around. I'll ask the captain to assign us a convalescent. It would be easy duty. Just sit on a bench opposite the door and watch. And stay awake."

"I wouldn't sleep down here," said the younger guard fervently.

"Afraid of the spiders?" his comrade with the lantern mocked. "Or the rats? We ate the rats roasted, in the prison in Genoa."

"And fried the spiders in garlic and axle grease, no doubt," his comrade returned testily, nettled by what was apparently an oft-told tale of manly endurance. "It's not the spiders that bother me. But there's things in the walls. Uncanny things."

It disturbed Thur a little that no one denied this, nor accused the guard of drinking.

"Leave me the lantern," Thur suggested, "and I'll watch him for a while. Maybe I'll get some clue as to how he does it." The castellan was seated cross-legged on the floor now, rocking from side to side, gaze fixed on nothing, face like stone.

The guard sergeant nodded, and his subordinate yielded the lantern to Thur.

"Don't get too close. He can grab you through the bars."

"I'll yell."

"Only if he doesn't grab you by the throat."

The guards returned to their immediate duties. Under the close eye of the sergeant who held a cocked crossbow, they traded dinner pails into the crowded cells in return for full slops buckets, which they carried off to empty in the garderobe. None of the prisoners seemed inclined to try a violent escape attempt this evening, though.

Thur watched the rocking castellan a while, then leaned against the wall opposite and closed his eyes. He hardly required the lantern now. He could find his destination with his eyes shut, he was certain. It thumped in his head, so close. *Down. Down.*

At a moment when the guards were thoroughly busy at the far end of the corridor, out of sight in the garderobe or their guard post, Thur picked up the lantern and trod silently into the dark cross-corridor. The walls brushed his shoulders, and the cut rock seemed to slant up toward the castle. For a moment he doubted his underground intuition, as the lantern cast a pool of orange light on the rising floor in front of him, but then he found the stairs, one set going up, one down. He went down.

A narrow hall at the bottom had four doors leading off it, all solid wood this time. Two were not locked. Neither unlocked door was the one he wanted, Thur was heart-certain, but he peeked within anyway.

Storage chambers. Barrels of flour, dusty wine casks ... provisions for the castle against a siege of man or weather. Green sparks flung back his lantern light from a corner, the jewel eyes of a scuttling rat. Spider webs festooned the corners. The spiders were smaller than the rats, but not as much smaller as Thur would have preferred.

He returned to the hallway. *This* door. He tried it again, rattled it futilely, then attempted to force it with his shoulder. The iron lock groaned, but held. He should have borrowed some tools from the other workmen and tucked them into his tunic before he'd started out. If he went back and got some, could he bluff his way back in here a second time? How long before the guards above noticed his absence? *Now. Now or never. Uri, I'm here.*

He squatted, trying not to pull his aching cut, and called softly under the crack of blackness at the bottom of the door. "Uri? Uri. . . ?" *Why do I fear an answer?* The twisting sensation in his gut had nothing to do with his gash.

The dust on the floor beneath his nose moved, swirling. There was no draft. Thur lurched hastily to his feet, sending a hot flash of pain ripping along his stitches. He stepped back till he was stopped by the stone wall, icy against his shoulders. He swallowed a cry and stood silent, heart pounding. *Wait and see.*

The dust swirled upward, each tiny mote spinning in the lantern light, into a familiar, tenuous figure ... big cloth hat, curling beard. . . . *Don't think of him as a ghost. Think of him as ... as your future father-in-law,* Thur told himself wildly.

"Hello, sir," Thur whispered. Panic and politeness squeezed his throat. "M . . . Master Beneforte. I came . . ."

The faint suggestion of a hat seemed to dip in acknowledgement.

Thur pointed to the lock. "Can you help. . . ?" How powerful a poltergeist was the dead mage? Could this be the secret of the mad castellan's escape? It was only slightly better than imagining Lord Pia turning himself into a bat and slipping between the bars.

The ghost of a figure seemed to shrug, like a man girding himself for a difficult task. The dust-features anticipated pain. A moment of preparation, and the dust contracted and fell from the air. Inside the lock, metal scraped, stopped, scraped again. A clank, and the door fell open a finger's breadth. Then silence, utter as the stone.

Thur took a deep breath, reached, and pulled the door open. Holding tightly to the lantern, he stepped over the threshold, and softly drew the door almost shut again behind him.

The room was larger than the other storage chambers, and had a barred window tunnel to the cliff face like the cells above, allowing good air. A trestle table was shoved against one wall, cluttered with boxes, jars, books, papers, a brazier . . . it all reminded Thur uncomfortably and exactly of Abbot Monreale's magic workroom. A leather-topped footstool in the shape of a small carved chest sat among the papers. Two iron candle racks held a dozen thick, fine beeswax candles, half-consumed. Good work lights, for things done in the night. Thur eased his tallow candle from the lantern and lit a few. Only then did he force himself to cross the room and examine what lay along the opposite wall.

Two oblong crates lay side by side, each upon a pair of trestles. The crates were about six feet long, cobbled together from coarse pine planks. The pine lids were held on only by a single rope circling the middle of each crate.

Cautiously, Thur touched one rope. It did not rise to wind about his neck or any other trick of ensorcellment. He yanked the slip knot and the rope fell to the floor. Thur had no cloth tucked in his tunic to press to his face, so he merely held his breath, and slid the lid aside.

Well. Not altogether unexpected, this. The body of Master Beneforte, still wrapped in the gauze from its smoking, lay in a bed of glittering rock salt. Thur wondered vaguely why the apparition always appeared in the clothes he'd died in, and not this thin shroud, which seemed more ghostly. Maybe the velvet court dress was a favorite. The smell was not nearly so bad as Thur had feared, mostly the clinging, not-unpleasant scent of applewood. Still—Thur counted over the summer-heated days—Ferrante or Vitelli must have added some powerful spell of preservation. The tanned and bearded face was chill. No ghost could animate this thick and heavy clay the way it animated weightless dust and smoke. Thur searched his heart for superstitious dread, but the object before him seemed more sad than fearsome. A battered old naked man, who'd lost everything, even his vanity. Thur covered him back over with the pinewood lid.

Reluctantly, he turned and tugged the slip knot of the second crate, then stood a moment, screwing up his ... not courage, exactly. Hope. *Maybe it isn't Uri. Many men have died this week in Montefoglia.* For one moment longer, he could hope. Then he would know.

You know already. You've known from the beginning. And *No! It won't be him!* Thur shoved the lid back on a huff of decision.

His brother's face jutted from its matrix of salt, both familiar and alien. The once-handsome features were all there, undisfigured. But the animating humor, the sparkle and shout, hungers and ambitions, quick wit ... how empty this strange, drawn, pale visage was without them. *He died in pain.* That quality alone lingered in the stiff face.

Thur looked down the nude body. A single wound gaped darkly in its chest, of which Thur's hot belly cut seemed a thin parody. *He died swiftly. Days ago.* At least that half of the nightmare, of Uri suffering as a prisoner, could be laid to rest. *If only you could have waited, brother. Hung on. I was coming. I was. . . .*

There was no shortage of new nightmares to take the emptied place. What did Ferrante intend this chamber and its strange equipment for? His own face feeling nearly as numb as his elder brother's, Thur walked around once more. A cleared area in the center of the stone floor bore traces of chalk, and less-identifiable substances. Black necromancy indeed. Grimly, Thur took a little tambourine from his tunic, whispered its activation, and, on tiptoe, found a place for it on a high shelf behind a jar. There. That one ought to give Monreale's listening monks an earful.

He returned to his brother and, for the first time, touched the cold face. Only a husk. Uri was gone, or at least, gone from this clay. But how far? Thur stared blindly around the chamber, realizing abruptly that both his nightmares were literally true. Uri was dead. *And* Uri was a prisoner in this terrible place. *How do I release you, brother?*

The muffled reverberation of a bass voice, and the stony echo of a brief laugh, sounded from beyond the chamber door. Appalled, Thur hastily pulled the plank cover back over Uri's crate, banging his thumb painfully between box and lid to quiet the clatter. Too late to escape? He turned around, eyes raking the chamber for cover.

The candles blew themselves out all at once, without a puff of breeze, plunging the room into darkness scarcely relieved by the night glimmer of starlight reflected up from the lake through the deep barred window embrasure. A hand that Thur did not think he could have seen even in daylight grasped his shoulder. "Down, boy!" a whisper that moved on no breath tingled in his ear.

Too frightened to argue, he crouched and shuffled under the table. The door clicked closed and the lock snicked shut. Thur shrank back against the wall, and a piece of cloth poked into his hand with the insistence of a dog snuffling up to be petted. It was light and soft, like linen, and he pulled it up over himself.

A real and solid iron key scraped in the lock, and the bolt clacked back again. Thur peeked over his cloth cover at the wavering yellow glow reflecting from a hand-held lantern. The guards, come looking for him?

Two men's footsteps crossed the floor, one's booted, one's slipper-soled. *I wish it were the guards*, he thought in sudden sick perception.

Messer Vitelli's voice rang hollow in the stone-walled chamber. "Do you smell hot wax, my lord?"

Chapter Eleven

Fiametta rubbed her drooping eyelids and stretched her arms high in an effort to fight off drowsiness. The watered wine and bread she'd had for supper was not so grand a feast as to induce torpor, but she'd slept poorly last night, turning over and over on the crackling straw, worrying about Thur, constantly disturbed by the rustling and coughing and movements of the other women in the overcrowded dormitory. Not to mention the fleas. She scratched a red welt on her elbow.

Abbot Monreale's workroom was warm, the plastered walls of the second-floor chamber still retaining the heat of the day, and the light from the single candle beside her was golden and cozy. She wriggled her hips on the hard perch of her barrel-seat, planted her elbows on the table, and let her chin sink back into her hands. On the tray before her the three remaining tambourines, the mouth-twins to the little ears Thur carried, remained stubbornly mute. Were they still working. . . ? Yes, her day's practice at keeping them enspelled had made it an almost automatic process, like absentminded humming. They conveyed nothing because they had nothing to convey.

In the next room she could hear Abbot Monreale pause to cough, pace, and continue his dictation to Brother Ambrose. A letter to the Bishop of Savoy, describing their desperate situation, calling for help, magical if not military. A futile letter. How did Monreale propose to dispatch it? The day had passed in an ominous, overheated quiet, without even the usual desultory exchanges of curses and crossbow bolts between the besiegers and the defenders on the monastery walls. No new herald or emissary had come to the gates today, no new refugees. No one at all. It was as if Lord Ferrante's grip tightened chokingly around them.

She stared at the little circles, willing them to speech. Three had come to life today, two in the afternoon and one at dusk, when she'd been gone to supper. Initiate brothers had taken each one off to their cells, where they sat with quills and paper ready to take note of important secrets. She trusted the brothers were all staying awake, too. But anyway, Thur had still been alive and free at dusk.

She stifled a yawn; if Monreale glanced in and saw her fading, he would send her to bed, and she might miss the next word from Thur. Why didn't the big fool think to speak into the ear-tambourines when he activated them and report on himself? She gritted her teeth on her next yawn. The white parchment circles swam before her eyes.

Then, without other warning, one—*flared*, Fiametta supposed she must describe it, though it was not an effect she saw with her eyes. She took a deep breath of anticipation and sat up straight. Thur's voice, whispering his badly accented Latin, drifted up from the tambourine to her straining ear. *Talk to me, Thur!* But there followed only a scraping sound, as of a jar shoved across a shelf. Footsteps crossed a stone floor, then a sad, meditative silence fell. Desperately, Fiametta tried to generate a picture in her mind from the mere sound. Stone floor, harsh echoes: a stone chamber? Rock walls—the Duke's dungeon? True intuition, or self-delusion? Her hand pulled at the thong around her neck, drew the lion ring from its warm hiding place between her breasts, and closed over it. What was Thur seeing? *Talk, you Swiss lout!*

But the deep buzz of a voice that came suddenly from the tambourine was not Thur's. She could not make out words. A tenor laugh followed, then a muffled clatter, hasty steps, a clunk and a clack. Words rang in her mind that did not come through her ear— *Down, boy!* She stiffened in panic. *Papa?* The sound of a door opening, then, and a stranger's light voice: "Do you smell hot wax, my lord?"

My lord? Where was Thur? Had he fled? Her heart hammered.

"From your lantern, Niccolo." The bored bass voice was Lord Ferrante's; his Romagnan accent was distinctive.

She heard an odd muffled thunk, as of something heavy being placed on a wooden table. "I think not," returned—Niccolo's?—voice. "These candles are warm." Then, "Ow!" A scuffle of slippers, as of a sudden recoil.

"Did you do that, Niccolo?" asked Ferrante in an interested tone.

"No!"

Ferrante laughed unkindly. "Beneforte is playing his little tricks again." His voice went mocking; Fiametta's imagination supplied a sweeping, ironic bow. "Thank you, my servant, for lighting my way."

A sucking sound—burned fingers being licked? "He's not our servant yet," growled Niccolo.

"Abbot Monreale," Fiametta whispered frantically, then reminded herself that sound only flowed one way through the little ear-and-mouth sets—could that be altered?—"Father Monreale!" she shouted. "Come quick! It's Lord Ferrante himself!"

Monreale hurried through the door from his adjoining office, followed, after a scrape and crash of a chair falling and being righted again, by Brother Ambrose, still clutching his inky quill. They bent over the tray of tambourines.

"Are you sure?" asked Monreale.

"I remember his voice from the banquet. I don't know the other man's voice, though. Ferrante calls him Niccolo. I think they are in a chamber beneath the castle."

"Ambrose, take over." Monreale nodded toward the mouth-tambourine.

I can enspell it as well as he can, Father! Fiametta, wrenched, held her tongue, and passed the spell-keeping to Ambrose. His lips moved silently a moment, then he settled in.

Ferrante's voice asked, "How much more dare we strengthen him, then, before I do control him?"

Niccolo replied grumpily, "He must be fed. And the very feeding brings him nearer to us. It's under control. I admit, I wish we could find his own damned notes on spirit rings. We could catch him by his own magic most finely. But he can't know that much more than I do. We'll have him under our thumb soon enough."

"None too soon for me. I've had about enough of this midnight skulking." Ferrante spat, eloquently.

"Great works require some sacrifices, my lord. Hang the three bags on those hooks. Take care with the leather one."

"To be sure."

Rustling noises followed, as the two men arranged whatever mysterious burdens they had been carrying. Abbot Monreale's eyes narrowed, and his lips parted in concentration, like Fiametta trying to guess at actions from their sounds. "Talk some more, blast you," he muttered under his breath.

"Oh, for a dove now," mourned Ambrose.

"They would not fly in the dark. And there's no time to launch a bat, nor could it see or hear much more than this. Sh!" Monreale waved him to silence as the tambourine spoke again.

"Well," said Ferrante's voice. "Shall we conjure Beneforte now, and compel him to tell us the secret of this saltcellar of his?"

"I'm certain I understand the secret of the salt, my lord. Our trials with the animals and the prisoner were most convincing. Alone, its ability to detect poison would make it a treasure for your table, but its ability to purify as well—pure genius!"

"Fine and good. But I do not understand the secret of the pepper. And I am not inclined to trust my life to something that holds secrets from me. Salt is white and pepper is black. What more logical than that the salt embodies a white magic and the pepper a black?"

"Slander!" Fiametta hissed. "Fool! Does he think Papa would—" Monreale's hand on her shoulder tightened, and she swallowed her outrage.

"Possibly," allowed Niccolo. "Beneforte would have had to smuggle it past inspection by that prig Monreale, though."

"Monreale should have been an Inquisitor. He has the long nose for it."

"He lacks the stomach for it."

"So he would have men believe," said Ferrante sourly.

"I *know* that voice," muttered Monreale by Fiametta's ear. "Niccolo. Niccolo what?"

Ambrose offered, "Lord Ferrante has a secretary named Niccolo Vitelli, Father. He's said to be Ferrante's shadow. I was told he's been in Ferrante's employ for about four years. Ferrante's men are wary of him—I thought it was for his slyness, but now it seems there's more to it."

Monreale shook his head. "That's not what I . . . But I suppose this Vitelli could be the reason that Ferrante, who was never rumored to have any use for magic in his condottiere days, seems to be up to his ears in it now."

"The pepper did no harm to the animals." Lord Ferrante's voice came persuasively from the parchment.

"Of course not," Fiametta muttered. "They have no power of speech."

"—and the spell engraved on the bottom of the saltcellar worked fine for the salt," Ferrante continued. "The second one *must* work for the pepper. I think we should try it again, upon a subject more capable of reporting subtle effects than Lady Julia's lap dog."

"We?" said Vitelli in a suspicious tone.

"I will speak the spell," said Lord Ferrante, "and you shall place the pepper on your tongue. But don't swallow it."

"I see." An unenthusiastic silence was followed by a "very well. Let's get it over with. There are more urgent tasks waiting tonight."

Now Fiametta could picture the chinks and thunks as Ferrante squinting at the bottom of her father's saltcellar by candlelight, returning it to its ebony base, and installing a bit of pepper in the little Greek temple under the golden goddess's hand. In a rapid whisper, she interpreted the sounds for Monreale and Ambrose. Sure enough, Ferrante's voice soon intoned the Latin prayer of the pepper-spell.

"Try it now," ordered Lord Ferrante.

After a moment, Vitelli's voice reported, in the odd muffled intonation of a man trying not to dislodge a pinch of pepper from his tongue, "I feel nothi'g, my lor'."

"It *can't* be doing nothing. Pepper. Tongues. Do you feel inspired to eloquence, perhaps?"

"No."

"Hm. Do you feel you could sway men's minds? Tell me a lie, and convince me of its truth. What color is my hair?"

"Black, m'lor."

"Say, 'red.'"

"Rrr . . . black." This last was sputtered out so as to almost lose the pepper.

"But say red."

"I *can't*. Black!"

A brief silence. "My God," whispered Ferrante. "Can the pepper compel truth?"

"Took you long enough," muttered Fiametta.

"Truth is not something that much springs to his mind, it seems," observed Ambrose.

"No, don't spit it out yet," Ferrante's voice ordered firmly. "I must be sure. What . . . what is your age?"

"Thirty-two, m'lor."

"Your birthplace?"

"Milan."

"Your—oh, your name."

"Jacopo Sprenger."

"What?" Ferrante's voice from the tambourine blended in astonishment with Monreale's, as the abbot slammed his fists to the table and cried, "*What?* It can't be!"

Fierce sputtering sounds emanated from the parchment circle, and muffled noises as of a man frantically wiping his mouth out with a cloth.

"*Does* the spell compel truth?" Ferrante's voice demanded of his secretary.

"It seems so, my lord," said Vitelli/Sprenger in a distinctly surly tone. After a short pause filled by who-knew-what boiling glance from the Lord of Losimo, the secretary went on reluctantly, "I took the name Vitelli . . . in my youth. After a . . . little difficulty with the law in Bologna."

"Well . . . so it is with half the scoundrels in my army. But I didn't think you had any secrets from me, my pet." Ferrante's tone was judiciously forgiving, but with a dangerous hint of steel underneath.

"All men conceal something." Vitelli shrugged uneasily. His voice went bland. "Would you care to try the pepper for yourself, my lord?"

"No," said Ferrante. The irony in his voice matched his secretary's. "I do think I believe you. Or believe Beneforte, anyway. But God! What a treasure! Can you imagine how valuable this could be when questioning prisoners? Or people who are attempting to hide their gold or goods?" The excitement of this vision sharpened his voice.

"God," Abbot Monreale moaned, in quite a different tone. "Is any magic, any intention of men, ever so white that it can't be perverted? If even truth itself isn't godly . . ." His lips drew back on a grimace of pain.

"Who is Jacopo Sprenger?" Brother Ambrose whispered, apparently, like Fiametta, unable to quell the secret conviction that if they could hear Ferrante, Ferrante could hear them.

"Is it possible. . . ? The fellow on the tower—but he's grown so thin! I'll tell you—later. Sh." Monreale bent his ear to the tambourine again, trying like Fiametta to guess what the rustling noises of Ferrante and Vitelli's next preparations meant. This time the occasional muttered word or order, or scraping sound, seemed to convey more to Abbot Monreale than to Fiametta, for he began to murmur interpretive guesses for Ambrose and Fiametta's benefit.

"I believe they are drawing a sacred diagram upon the floor. Lines to contain the mystic forces of the planets, or of their metals . . . sacred names, to compel or contain the forces of their spirits. A peculiar combination of higher and lower magics, I must say."

"Are they going to try and enslave Papa's spirit to that awful putti ring now?" asked Fiametta unhappily.

"No . . . not tonight, I think. I don't hear anything that sounds like them setting up a furnace, do you? The ring must be new-cast from molten metal at the time of the investment, you see. The metal must be fluid to take up the internal form of the spirit."

Fiametta, remembering the making of her lion ring, nodded.

"They could not recast that putti ring for your father anyway," Monreale went on. "Silver is for a female spirit. They should use gold for Prospero Beneforte, ideally. If they have any idea of what they are doing. Which, unfortunately, they seem to. If Vitelli is Sprenger, that's no surprise. . . . He was a brilliant student of—" Monreale broke off as voices began again.

"The black cat for the sorcerer, the black cock for the soldier," said Vitelli. "Hand me the bag with the cat, my lord, across the lines, after I enter the square and close it." His voice went off into another string of Latin, far more purely intoned than Thur's or even Ferrante's.

"He enspells his blade," Monreale muttered.

"What is he going to do with it?" asked Fiametta tensely.

"Sacrifice a cat. Its life—I hesitate to call it its soul, but anyway, its spirit—will be given to your father's ghost, to . . . strengthen it. Like a meal."

"Is it still alive?" demanded Vitelli's voice uncertainly.

A weak and piteous meow, full of suffering and pain, was made to answer him. "Just barely," said Ferrante.

Fiametta and Ambrose exchanged a look of horror. "Unlucky cat," said Ambrose. His thick hands wrung.

"Just what are they doing to it?" asked Fiametta.

"Enough for two men to burn for. Sh," said Monreale impatiently.

The cat's voice rose to a terrified squall, cutting across Vitelli's Latin drone, then went abruptly silent.

"Surely Papa would refuse such an unclean offering," said Fiametta. "He wouldn't . . . eat? The poor kitty!"

Monreale shook his head, face grim as granite. But his brows wrinkled in puzzlement as Vitelli's chant started up again. "What are they . . . can there be *two*?"

The mysterious scene was reenacted, but this time it was the squawking and flutter of a cock that fell to silence at the bite of Vitelli's darkly blessed blade. A familiar name flashed past, embedded in Vitelli's pure Latin.

"Uri Ochs?" Fiametta repeated in horror. "Oh, no! Is he—is Captain Ochs dead, then?"

"He must be," said Monreale blackly, "to be a recipient of that spell. That would explain why he was neither among the wounded prisoners or the dead who were returned. . . . Ferrante fancies a spare ring, it seems."

"Poor Thur. . .," breathed Fiametta. Where *was* Thur? He'd had scarcely time to escape, between the time his breath had activated the little ear and the time Ferrante and Vitelli had entered the chamber of dread. Yet he must have escaped, or he'd have been discovered by now.

"No. . .," Monreale corrected himself judiciously, "Captain Ochs must have been selected first, by Ferrante, on the very day he fell. He had no known relatives in town, to demand his body for burial. It was your father, Fiametta, who was added as an after-thought."

"There." Vitelli's voice sounded satisfied; slapping sounds followed, as if he were rising and dusting chalk, and worse, from the knees of his robe.

"How much longer must we spend on this ped-antry?" Ferrante asked querulously. "I want my rings. Events of State will not wait on your thaumaturgic fiddling."

"Beneforte's is a very dangerous ghost to attempt to invest, my lord. He is hostile, and he knows far too much. One little mistake . . ." Vitelli paused reluc-tantly, then added, "I think we can invest the soldier as early as tomorrow night. That is the sensible order of things, for then we can use him to help control the mage. You bring the new bronze for the ring. I'll see to the fuel. Then you will have at least one ring, ah, to hand."

"I'd rather have the Swiss anyway," Ferrante remarked in a brighter tone. "He's not such a tricksy weasel as the Florentine. As a soldier, he will doubtless under-stand obedience better."

"Perhaps I should keep the mage's ring, then," sug-gested Vitelli, in a casual tone that did not quite hide an eager quaver. "There are two rings, two of us—it would be difficult for you to manage both."

Said Lord Ferrante distantly, "No, I don't think so."

The silence after that was distinctly sticky, till Vitelli broke it with a curt, "Let us be done. If you will take down the leather bag with the adder, my lord."

The next noises were very hard to interpret, until Vitelli said, "Are you quite certain you have the *head* end pinned through the leather this time, my lord?"

"Yes," snapped Ferrante impatiently. "Open the bag and reach in. Or would you rather I did?"

"I—well, if you wish, my lord. I'll get the knot."

"Ah . . . ha! Got him. Right behind the head. See him grin for you, Niccolo? Heh-heh."

"Ah—not so close, if you don't mind, my lord. His venom would be wasted on me. Come along. We're almost done for tonight, and I am weary to the bone."

Ferrante grunted reluctant agreement. A clattering sound, like pine boards being wrestled about, was followed by actions Fiametta couldn't even guess at, plus more of Vitelli's Latin, sprinkled with some Hebrew, or perhaps it was outright gibberish. Fiametta could scarcely tell.

"What are they doing now?" she asked Monreale.

"I believe it is a spell based upon the principle of contrarity." Monreale listened intently. "It seems to be quite original. . . . I believe they are forcing the puff adder to, er . . . I'm sorry, Fiametta—bite the corpse, or the corpses. It seems to be part of the preservation spell."

More rattling about, and then, suddenly, a shout: "Watch out! It lashes—" "Don't drop—" The rapid scuttling of feet, "*Catch* it!" "*You* catch it!" "It's going under the table!"

A brief silence.

"You have boots on, my lord," said Vitelli suggestively.

"They will not protect my arms, reaching under there in the dark, if that is what you are implying," said Ferrante coldly. "You reach under there for it. Or enspell it out. My little mage."

"I am exhausted with spells." Vitelli's voice sounded like it, low and slow.

Ferrante spat again, but did not deny this. After a pause he said, "Come back and clean this place up in the morning. When you can see better. Catch it then. Or perhaps by then it will have escaped, slithered under the door. Come down from there, now."

"Yes . . . my lord," said Vitelli wearily.

A careful thump—Vitelli letting himself down from

a tabletop?—was followed at length by a bit more rustling and rattling, footsteps, a door closing, and the grating of a key in an iron lock. Then unbroken quiet. When a nightingale warbled from outside Monreale's own workroom windows, Fiametta jumped. The candle guttered low.

Ambrose shook himself from his concentration, and went to light new candles from the old before it went out. The added illumination seemed to bring everyone back to the present. Monreale rubbed his face, grooved deep. Fiametta stretched muscles gone rigid with tension. The tambourine spoke no more; surely Thur must have somehow escaped the chamber before Ferrante and his pet sorcerer had entered. Fiametta could only be glad he could not have witnessed the dreadful abuse of his brother's corpse and spirit.

"Papa resisted that horrible offering Ferrante made . . . didn't he, Father Monreale?"

Monreale made no immediate answer, though he gave her a small strained smile. "The two necromancers thought their effort a success," he said at last. "But they could be mistaken. Self-delusion is a common fault of those who dabble in the black arts."

Fiametta judged this weak reassurance to be the desire to comfort her, warring with honesty; Monreale being Monreale, honesty had the edge. In a way, she was glad.

Ambrose drew up a wooden chair for the abbot, and a stool for himself, and sat heavily, his brow channeled with dismay. "Who is Jacopo Sprenger, Father? Besides, apparently, Niccolo Vitelli the clerk."

Monreale settled back wearily, looking deeply disturbed. "For a moment, I thought he must be a demon himself. Till more natural explanations occurred to me.

"About ten years ago, the Order sent me to study advanced spiritual thaumaturgy at the University of Bologna, under Cardinal Cardini, that the Church might qualify me to issue licenses to such master mages as your father, Fiametta. In my college at that time was a brilliant young student from Milan named Jacopo Sprenger. He was of humble origins, but had completed his bachelor's work in the seven liberal arts, and was close to being qualified as one of the youngest doctors of theology and thaumaturgy ever. Too young, in my opinion. Brilliant, but not . . . wise. That happens, sometimes." Monreale sighed.

"He was training to be an Inquisitor. Again, too heavy a burden for his age, though I fear his intellectual pride was such that he would have been the last to recognize it. He was drawn into a deep study of black witchcraft, ostensibly to aid the Inquisition as a specialist witch-smeller, to stamp out the evil of witches perverted by the service of demons. He was working on a treatise, which he meant to dedicate to the Pope, that he'd titled "The Hammer of Witches." The subject excited him greatly. Too greatly, we finally recognized—too late. He fell into the temptations of the object of his study, as wizards sometimes do; he began to actually experiment with demonology, and it soon got out of hand. Who shall guard the guardians?" Monreale stared into the candle flames, and rubbed his exhaustion-numbed face with both hands.

"I fear I had not a little to do with the discovery of his, er, after-dark career. He was expelled, and brought to trial very quietly, so as not to damage the reputation of the school. I testified against him. But before the verdict was issued, he suicided in his cell. Swallowed a poisonous sublimate smuggled in to him—or so I was told. Now I think his body must have been carried out still alive, counterfeiting death through some combination of medical and magical means.

"A committee consisting of Cardinal Cardini, myself, and a doctor from the college of law took up the problem of his papers. Cardinal Cardini thought at first merely to put his book on the Index, until we examined it more closely. Sprenger had a hungry mind and a phenomenal memory—his accumulation of spells, anecdotes, folklore and hearsay could have filled ten volumes. But he had no *sense*. His style was facile, even compelling, but his scholarship was weak, his credulity unlimited, his practical understanding of real courts—the doctor of law threw up his hands. Sprenger seriously recommended that accused black witches be compelled under torture to name accomplices! I know the tortures the Holy Inquisition uses, and the sort of men that apply them—can you imagine the spate of wild accusations that would result, each triggering more arrests, more accusations—why, in a little time an entire district would be in an absolute uproar! It was all incendiary to the point of hysteria. I think it represented Sprenger—the daytime Sprenger—struggling desperately against his night-self. I recommended the book and all his notes be burned."

Ambrose, himself a scholar in a minor way, winced. Monreale spread his hands. "What would you have? Better to burn the book than the poor old hedge-witches, who in my experience—yours too, you've worked in the country districts—are nine times out of ten either mumbling old women with foggy minds, or the malice of a neighbor trying to fix blame for the death of her maltreated cow or for some perfectly natural event like a hailstorm. And the book was bad theology, to boot, ignoring the power of the name of Christ . . . tremendously dangerous. We burned it all. Cardinal Cardini was not so sure, but I felt like a surgeon who had successfully stopped a gangrene through a timely amputation.

"Be that as it may, Sprenger himself was by the time of his—we thought—death, utterly corrupt, his will given over entirely to the pursuit of demonic power. Yet I felt I'd personally lost a soul for God, the night

I heard he'd suicided, and the Devil laughed at me."
Monreale shook his head in memory.

"What are we going to do now, Father?" Fiametta
asked, as the silence lengthened.

An ironic smile, full of pain, twisted Monreale's lips.
"God knows. I can only pray He will confide it to me."

"But you have to do something to stop them!" quavered Fiametta. "It's black magic, it's in your holy vows
to fight black magic! Tomorrow they mean to enslave
poor Captain Ochs. Then Papa. And then Ferrante's
troops will arrive, and then there will be no chance!"

"If we are to try . . . anything, it must be before the
Losimon infantry arrives," Ambrose agreed diffidently.

"I don't need you to tell me that," snapped Monreale. He controlled his nervous irritation with a visible
effort, squaring his slumped shoulders. "It's not a simple problem. It's hard to conceive of a force sufficient
to stop Ferrante that does not itself partake of black
magic. Some evil intent, seeping through to imperil
the soul."

"But . . . everyone's depending on you. Like a soldier.
Soldiers do awful things, but we need them, to protect
us from . . . from other soldiers," said Fiametta.

"You need not tell me what soldiers do," said Monreale dryly; Fiametta flushed. "I'm well acquainted
with the whole vile argument. I've seen it used to
justify crimes you can scarcely imagine. And yet . . ."

Fiametta's eyes narrowed. "There *is* something. You
have it in mind, something you can do, don't you.
Something magical."

"I must pray on it."

"You pray a lot. Will you still be praying when Ferrante's army marches to the gate of Saint Jerome and
batters it down? When Ferrante commands spirits with
the wave of his hand?" Fiametta demanded hotly. "If
all you're going to do is pray, why not hand over Lord
Ascanio and everything now? Why not yesterday?"

"We might," said Brother Ambrose slowly, "live to fight another day. Lay charges of black magic later upon Lord Ferrante."

"And what Herculean sergeant-at-arms shall we send to arrest the miscreants, after they have made themselves undisputed lords and masters of two states?" said Monreale softly, staring again into the flames. "Sprenger must remember me, as surely as I do him. I know he must, he's been so very careful to keep from my sight. I wonder if I would live to lay charges anywhere."

"Well, then!" said Fiametta.

His fingers told over the beads in his lap. He glanced up at her from under tufted gray brows. "I am not . . . a powerful mage, Fiametta. Not as powerful as your Papa, or even some of the lesser mages here in Montefoglia . . . God knows, I tried to be, once. It has been my burden to have an understanding greater than my talent. Those who can, do. Those who can't . . ."

Ambrose interjected a little negative huff, spreading his hands in denial. "Not so, Father!"

One corner of Monreale's lips twisted up. "My good Brother. By what standards do you imagine you judge? Did you think it was only a monastic calling that holds me here in Montefoglia? First-rate talents go to Rome, go to the Sacred College. Lesser men find themselves buried in rural provinces. In my youth, I dreamed of being a Marshall by the time I was twenty-five. I put away those military follies only to replace them with dreams of becoming a Cardinal Thaumaturge before I was thirty-five. . . . God gave me humility at last, for God knew I needed it.

"Sprenger—if Vitelli is indeed he—had a talent stronger than his understanding. Now, after it has had ten years to grow cunning in dark and secret, he's found a powerful patron, who protects him, funds him, lends him his animal vitality—for Ferrante has great strength of will, make no mistake. Add to that a spirit-slave of the order of Master Beneforte, and their potency will be . . ." He broke off.

Ambrose cleared his throat. "I confess, Father, your words unsettle my stomach."

"My calling is to save souls, not lives." Monreale's fingers worked.

"Souls can be saved later," Fiametta pointed out urgently. "When you lose lives, you lose lives and souls both."

Monreale shot her a peculiar grin. "Have you ever considered taking up Scholastic studies, Fiametta? But no, your sex forbids."

An insight shook her. "You're not afraid of losing your soul. You're just afraid of *losing*." Afraid of having his self-accusation of second-ratedness finally confirmed.

Ambrose drew in his breath at this blunt insult, but Monreale's grin merely stretched. His eyes were lidded, unreadable.

"Go to bed, Fiametta," he said at last. "Ambrose, I will send Brother Perotto to watch and maintain this ear through the night. Though I suspect the show is over for the moment." He stood up, shook out his robes, and rubbed his face. "I'll be in the chapel."

Chapter Twelve

Thur sat very, very still. The puff adder's earlier agitation had passed off, but now instead of burrowing under Thur's crossed legs as if beneath a little cave ledge, it had looped itself entirely around his calf and thigh. For warmth, presumably. Thur could feel the cool waxy scales through his fine hose as the snake hitched itself up another couple of inches. As long as Thur remained the best source of heat in the room, the viper seemed disinclined to move away.

Thur dared not even move the dark linen cloth still draped stuffily over his head and body. He needed to piss, and his nose itched abominably. He dreaded a sneeze. He tried to wriggle his nose, twitching and stretching his lip, but it didn't help greatly. How much time had passed, since the two necromancers had left this rock-cut chamber? An eternity? Still the pitchy darkness was unrelieved by the slightest gray hint of dawn. If he could just see the cursed reptile, he would match his hand against the speed of its strike and try to grab it behind the head. But to grope for it in the dark. . . . Yet he could not sit like this much longer. The cold stone floor stole the heat from his numbing buttocks, and his leg muscles, unrelieved for too long by any change of position, threatened to spasm.

Movement, when it came, was not the prayed-for departure of the adder, but the scrape of a key in the lock again. The snake's coil tightened around Thur's leg. Light booted footsteps crossed the floor, and stopped at one side of the room. A faint crockery clatter was followed by a tiny gurgle, as of someone pouring liquid from a jug. Then—Thur froze, if possible, more still, though his heart beat faster—Vitelli's voice, in a brief Latin chant. The snake twitched. A pause: in more impatient tones, Vitelli repeated his words. The snake unwound a little more, but made no move to leave Thur's lap. Well, it was probably just a country snake. Maybe it didn't understand Vitelli's fine school Latin. Thur suppressed an hysteric giggle.

Vitelli swore under his breath. "Damned stupid snake. Probably escaped by now. Have to send a pig-soldier to Venice tomorrow to buy another." The footsteps departed in an irate shuffle; the door was locked once more. The snake vented a surly hiss. Thur blinked tears of frustration and fear, which trickled maddeningly down the inside of his nose. He must try a grab. . . .

A tiny scuttling noise crossed the chamber. Only in this stone-silence and night-stillness could Thur have heard it, exacerbated though his senses now were. The snake seemed to hear it too. Its head rose, and wove from side to side; then, coil by coil, it slid from Thur's leg and out from under the linen cloth. It seemed to take an age for it to remove its entire length. Thur held his breath for several more seconds, then let it go with an explosive huff. In a frantic, fluid motion, he rolled out from under his cramped table-prison, and vaulted atop it instead. He grabbed for a dislodged iron candelabrum, felt but scarcely seen, before it could fall with a clang. His eyes, straining in the utter darkness beneath the cloth for so long, could actually make out dim shapes in the faint starlight reflecting from the lake through the deep window: his table, the crates on their trestles. The light was not good enough for him to see the adder, though.

"Master Beneforte," he quavered, "will you light me one candle?" No response. More hesitantly, "Uri? Please?"

His hands shaking, Thur felt along the tabletop. Papers, knives, cool metal tools. A little box. A tinder box? Thur opened it, but found it contained only a soft powder. He almost licked his fingers to try to identify it, but on second thought wiped them on his tunic instead. Odd scrabbling noises came from the floor, clicking, and a weird, tiny animal shriek, which Thur tried to ignore. Could snakes climb table legs? He'd heard of snakes in trees. . . .

Another, heavier box proved more lucky. Flint and steel made familiar weights in his hands. He struck sparks, found the tinder in their light, and managed after several tries to ignite a splinter. It almost went out before he could raise it to a candle wick, but after dying to a tiny blue globe, the yellow flame flared up from the wax. Thur, kneeling on the tabletop, decided it was the most beautiful flame he'd ever seen. He reignited the splinter and lit the entire candelabrum, six short slagged and nearly spent beeswax lumps. Then he looked around for the adder.

No wonder the snake had seemed to go on forever. The creature was four feet long. It was coiled to one side of the floor near a saucer of milk. Its jaws were stretched wide, its throat distended; the back half of a very large rat stuck out of its mouth. The rat's rear legs spasmed, and its tail twitched.

In a wild leap, Thur sprang upon the snake, grabbed it tightly with both hands around its stuffed throat to keep it full of rat and unable to twist and bite, ran to the window, and crammed it out through the bars. After a moment, a faint splash echoed back from the lake below. Thur sank to the floor, gasping for breath. Several minutes passed before his other troubles began to crowd back into his mind again.

Looking around, Thur decided Vitelli must have brought the saucer of milk for the snake. It certainly couldn't have been meant for the cat. Thur grimaced at the gruesome pile of animal parts left to coagulate in the center of a complicated diagram drawn on the floor in red and white chalk. Stepping carefully around the marks, he tried the door. The lock did not open from this side without the key, either. How much time had really passed? The guards upstairs must have missed him by now, searched—though not in here. Thur was fairly sure no one came in here voluntarily except Ferrante and Vitelli.

"Master Beneforte?" Thur whispered. "Uri? Master Beneforte? Can you open this lock again?"

No response from the spirits this time either. Yet Thur had *seen* Beneforte, earlier. His intense sense of Uri's presence had driven him down here. Thur eyed the papers scattered over the table. A conjuring compelled a spirit to appear whether it wanted to or not. Thur didn't suppose he'd be so fortunate as to find such a recipe jotted down. He turned the papers over. More Latin, mostly; he knew words here and there. "Master Beneforte, *please.*"

"*What?*" The irritated tone was sick, shaken, but somehow stronger. Not so effortful as Beneforte's earlier, desperate attempts to communicate. Thur turned, staring into every corner of the chamber, but no dust-ghost wavered in the draft that fluttered the candles. Only the voice.

"Where . . . where is my brother? Can you see him, from where you are? Why doesn't he speak?" Thur asked the emptiness.

A long silence; Thur began to fear that Beneforte's ghost had fled the chamber and left him, when the reluctant reply whispered, "He is a weaker shade. He has not had the lifetime of the spiritual manipulation of the world of matter that my profession, my art, gave to me. Now my clay has dropped away, my blind eyes are opened to such visions . . . but oh, I did not think I would miss the sensations of my gross flesh so much. . . ." The slow voice died away in longing. It seemed to be centered in a position over the chalk diagram.

"How can I rescue you? What should I do? Vitelli says he means to enslave my brother tomorrow night!"

"Ferrante might not be so bad a lord to serve," Beneforte's voice murmured judiciously. "Ferrante, Sandrino, Lorenzo . . . a prince is a prince. Service is service. . . . Ferrante talks of having my Perseus cast."

"I'd think he'd be more likely to melt it down for cannon!" said Thur.

"True, he's been more a patron of the art of war than the art of sculpture. But he is not immune to the attraction of glory in that form. Glorifying himself with my Perseus, he would immortalize me. . . ."

"But you're dead," Thur pointed out inanely. "Three nights ago you cried for help as if to save your soul!" *Literally.*

"Well, souls, now . . ." The ghostly voice trailed off. "Why hurry to that world, after all?"

"Can you . . . see another world?" Thur asked, awed. Frightened.

"I glimpsed a light . . . it almost hurt. *Did* hurt."

But you're supposed to go there. Not stay here. This

was not the urgent apparition of three nights ago speaking now, Thur realized with a chill. How much had the necromancers' black rites already sapped Beneforte's will?

"Vitelli is no prince. Do you itch to serve *him*?"

"That Milanese dabbler! Second-rate scum—I could have him under my . . . ." A glow like a dazzled afterimage in the eye zigzagged through the chamber. A flash of . . . anger? Pure will? *Your Papa could be in danger of becoming a demon. . . .*

Thur felt a cold knot twist in his gut. If Beneforte's spirit was already becoming corrupted, for how much longer could Thur trust him? He scarcely seemed to be struggling against Ferrante any more. *Not too late, no!*

But what could Thur do? The bodies—Vitelli and Ferrante seemed to need the bodies, to complete their vile rites. Could Thur steal them away somehow? He could not lift even one of those salt crates by himself, let alone two. And there were the stairs to climb and the guards to get past. A wild vision of setting the chamber afire and reducing the corpses to ash foundered on an obvious lack of sufficient fuel. If the bodies were only partly destroyed, could Vitelli still use them?

Thur was crouched before the lock, smiling in his desperation, when an oddly familiar flicker tickled the corner of his eye. He tilted his head, staring into the wavering candle-cast shadows across the room. Could Beneforte—or Uri—be struggling to take up material form? That liquid, moving shadow by the wall was no rat, nor (unsettling thought) another snake. The shadow stepped from the wall, taking on dimension as it did so, and skittered to hide coyly behind a trestle leg. A little mannikin, not two feet tall. . . .

"Good God," said Thur in startlement. "I didn't know you had kobolds here!"

"There's quite a little colony of them in the hills west of town," Beneforte's ghostly voice remarked, eerily conversational.

"I thought they only lived in mountain wastes. Didn't go near men's towns."

"That's generally true. But they are attracted to magic. I had rather an outbreak of them for a while. They came up under my house to spy on my doings, in my shop. Pesky, and they move things about, but not malicious if you don't attack them."

"Yes, that's the way ours are in Bruinwald," agreed Thur. The shadowy little figure flickered to shelter behind a nearer trestle leg. Beady eyes flashed at him.

"I trapped one once," Beneforte reminisced. "I made it bring me some raw silver, and beryls. It claimed there is no gold to be had in the ground in these parts. I finally let it go, and after that its kin grew wary and stayed away from my shop, and I was not troubled further."

"I thought they were mainly attracted to milk, which they cannot get underground. Or so it is in the mountains. They sometimes steal from unguarded pails, after the cows or goats are milked. And there was a wet nurse in the village who got in a lot of trouble when she was found to have silver nuggets in her possession—she was accused of stealing them, or of lying with the miners who had stolen them from work. But she claimed she was trading her milk to the kobolds."

"Milk, yes," came a thin hopeful voice from behind the trestle. "We *like* milk."

"I used milk to bait my kobold trap," Beneforte confirmed. "At home they mainly eat a bread made from fungus, which they grow underground in their colonies. Milk is better than wine to them. I never heard of them stealing wine."

"My mother leaves milk out for them in secret on All Hallow's Eve," Thur confessed. "With a prayer for safety in the mines. Brother Glarus would not approve. It's always gone the next day."

"They swim through the rock as a man might swim through water. Strange . . ." Beneforte's voice hesitated. "I can see them now. Though my eyes are . . . See all around, see through the rock. There have been half a dozen of the rock-folk hanging around under the castle since Vitelli arrived, and began his . . . activities. I think Vitelli worries them, a little."

Vitelli worries all of us.

A twiggy finger pointed from behind the trestle toward the saucer of milk. "Not a trap, my lords?" it inquired. "You don't want it, yes?"

"It's not my milk," said Thur. "You can have it, for all of me. Vitelli put it there for his snake. But I can't guarantee it's not poisoned or something."

"You need my saltcellar," Beneforte said smugly.

Thur glanced at the table. "They took it with them." Solid gold, Ferrante would hardly have left it lying about even without its magic properties.

"Do I even need the salt now, to focus . . . ?" Beneforte's voice went meditative. "My eyes are wide, if I dare see. . . ."

Thur saw nothing, but a felt *presence* near the saucer of milk made the hairs stir on his arms. The opaque white surface of the liquid shivered.

"Vitelli has laced it with an opiate, to stun the snake," Beneforte's voice reported. "Can I . . . *dare* I . . ."

A blue flame rose from the surface of the milk, and burned off in a long streamer.

"It's purified now," said Beneforte. His voice was elated. "I couldn't have done that, when I was clouded by my flesh."

Thur glanced uneasily at the diagram and its spent, unclean offering on the floor nearby. *You could not have done that yesterday, I'll wager.*

The kobold crept warily out to the saucer. "Thank you, my lord," it addressed Beneforte. Wherever he was.

A second kobold, and a third, oozed up out of the stone beside the first. They all knelt down on their gnarled little hands and lapped at the milk, for all the world like three scrawny barn cats around a bowl. These hill-kobolds were lighter in color than the granite-gray little men of Bruinwald, with a yellowish cast to their skins like the Montefoglian sandstone. The two new ones were naked, though their leader wore an apron much like its mountain cousins. The milk level dropped rapidly; the leader picked up the saucer, as large as its head, and licked it clean. It gave Thur a black-eyed stare over the rim of the crockery, then, abruptly, all three melted down into the stone and were gone without even a thank-you.

Thur blinked, and tried the door lock again. It still held fast. "Master Beneforte? How should I save you? And my brother?" *And myself?*

"I grow weary . . ." the ghostly voice breathed. "I cannot speak any more."

Evasive, is what Master Beneforte's shade grew, Thur decided unhappily. Not good. He tried to think through the haze of exhaustion that numbed his face and filled his head with fog. He was swaying on his feet. He felt in his tunic. He still had two little ears left. Three, should he chance upon some better place to hide the one he'd left in the grooms' loft. Abbot Monreale had explicitly urged him to try to smuggle an ear to the imprisoned Duchess, if he could, up in her tower. Well, he'd made his way down to the dungeon, right enough. It was Monreale's job to fight black magic. It was Thur's job to follow Monreale's orders. If he could. His jaw tightened.

He could not get past the guards till he solved the problem of getting out of this room. Enough odd tools

were scattered on the table and shelves; if nothing
else he could simply take the blasted lock apart. But
when Thur approached it with a hastily grabbed awl
in his hand, he found he could not make the metal
penetrate the keyhole nor dig beneath the nails. The
lock was ensorcelled, protected as if by some invisible, unbreakable glass. Beneforte's ghost, of course,
had not had a problem with it. Beneforte's ghost
walked through walls, if it chose. Thur ground his
teeth.

"Mater Beneforte." Thur made his voice placative,
plaintive. "Please let me out."

No response.

"For Fiametta's sake?"

All he couldhear was the blood beating in his own
ears.

"Uri, if you love me!" He swallowed the harsh edge
of panic. In the unanswering silence the horror of
being trapped in this cell with the dead and the subtle
aftershock of black sorcery bore in upon him. "Help
me!"

This time, the felt presence was not Beneforte's
cool, coherent power, but something raw and wild.
A strange blue glow like miniature lightning writhed
over the iron lock. When the bolt clacked back the
presence fell away like something wounded. *Pain*. The
action had cost pain, and will. Uri was truly here.
Mute, but by no means impotent. And *not* Vitelli's
creature, not yet.

Thur bowed his head. "Thank you, brother," he
whispered. Staggering a little, Thur relit the guard's
tallow-candle lantern. It had sat on the floor by the
table the whole time, unnoticed. Why should Ferrante's eye be caught by something so humble and familiar as his own army-issue equipment? Thur blew out
the remains of the beeswax lights and slipped from
the chamber as silently as he could. He pulled the

door shut behind himself. *I'll be back somehow, Uri. With a plan. With the abbot. With an army.*

It took Thur a moment to reorient himself in the hallway. He trod cautiously up the narrow stairs, his ears straining for the slightest breath or creak of a guard waiting in ambush. None waited in the corridor to the prisoners' cells. The stairway twisted around itself like Vitelli's snake, rising into the castle. In the pitchy darkness at the top Thur found a solid oaken door. Locked, of course. He retreated to the corridor on the prison level.

It was his aching bladder that finally decided his course of action. From the pungent aroma, the dark space at the end of this corridor had been used as a makeshift garderobe by men before Thur. He relieved himself in the same spot, trying to splash quietly. He then blew out the lantern, tiptoed down the corridor, set the lantern down, lay on the stone floor, pillowed his head on his arm, closed his eyes, and pretended to be asleep. Weirdly distorted images of the night's events flickered through his imagination as he waited for a guard to discover him. He told over his tale to himself for practice, but his thoughts tailed off in darkness. . . .

An explosive curse brought Thur blinkingly awake. His body ached with the cold and pressure of the stone; his first attempt to lumber up was sabotaged by twinges of pain. A booted foot kicked him, though not very hard.

"What? What?" Thur choked blearily, his disorientation only half-feigned. He had slept in truth. The guard sergeant was looming over him with a lantern and a hard frown; his shout brought a second guard running with a drawn dagger. Thur sneezed.

"Where did you come from?" demanded the guard sergeant harshly. "Where have you been?"

A volley of sneezes delayed Thur's answer long

enough for him to get his thoughts in order. "Mother of God," he wheezed, with feeling. "I have just had the *strangest* dream!" He sat up, rubbing his eyes and nose. "Did I ... fall asleep? I'm sorry, I promised to watch—the madman's not *out*, is he?" Thur clutched the guard sergeant's boot.

"No."

"Oh. Good. Thank God. For a minute there I ..."

"For a minute you what?"

"For a minute I thought it was real. My dream. What time is it?"

"Almost dawn."

"It *can't* be. I just went down the corridor to piss a couple of minutes ago."

"You disappeared. You've been gone all night."

"No! You were just serving the prisoners dinner. I went down the corridor, and I was coming back. I heard the pails clanking. And then ... and then ..."

"Then what?"

"I felt so tired all of a sudden. It was as if something came over me—I just lay down here on the floor for a moment. And I had this wonderous dream, and then you found me and woke me."

The two guards eyed one another uneasily. "What was your dream, Foundryman?" asked the junior man.

"The mad castellan changed into a bat, before my eyes. And then he changed me into a bat, too. We flew south, to Rome. Absurd. I've never been to Rome." Thur ran his hands through his hair in a dazed way. "We could see it all at a glance from the air. Watchlights gleaming on the Tiber ... the Pope, all in glowing white robes, was standing on the balcony of a great palace. The castellan—still in the form of a bat, with bat-ears, but he had the face of a man—landed on His Holiness's shoulder and whispered in his ear. And the Pope whispered back, and touched him with his ring. And then we flew home," Thur ended simply. He stopped his tripping tongue just short of adding, *Oh, my arms are tired!* Ferrante's guards had good reason to be credulous of the uncanny, but not infinitely credulous.

"But we've been over this corridor ten times!" said the younger guard. "You weren't—"

"Quiet, Giovanni!" the sergeant cut across him. He hauled Thur roughly to his feet. The sergeant was shorter than Thur, but strong. He stared at Thur with angry, worried eyes. "Do you think you might have been ensorcelled, Foundryman?"

"I . . . I . . . don't know. I've never been ensorcelled before. I thought it was a dream."

"I must have you checked. By an expert."

That was not in Thur's plan. "Almost dawn? My God. I've got to get to work. Lord Ferrante demands his cannon without delay."

"Where will you be working?" inquired the sergeant, narrow-eyed.

"In the garden, or back courtyard, or whatever you call it. I must build the furnace tomorrow—today, that is."

"Very well. So long as I know where to find you. Giovanni, escort my lord's foundryman to his work, eh? Speak of this to no one. I'll do the reporting."

Thur had a strong sense that he had not much time left. He found his work mates from yesterday just rising to go to a kitchen-breakfast of hot mutton wrapped in bread. Whatever Ferrante's other sins, he made sure that his men were well-fed. Thur took care not to bring up the topic of where he'd spent the night.

Thur and the laborers went out in the cold dawn fog to the foundry site at the end of the walled castle garden. The trampled grass was slippery underfoot. But the moisture was a tease; when Thur looked directly overhead he could see through the mist to the high blue vault of a cloudless heaven, already illuminated by a sun that had yet to clear the eastern hills. Glad as Thur was to see light after the night's dark doings, he wished time would slow down. Pink rays touched the castle towers, Thur's new goal, all too soon.

Thur directed the workmen automatically, all the while trying to figure how to get away from them and into that tower. He stacked bricks around the proper curve of the oven-to-be's walls, and tried to think through a throbbing head. He must deliver an ear to the Duchess—hang the extra two—and be gone from this accurst castle by noon at the latest. Then make it, somehow, back to the monastery and demand magical help for Uri. Could they sneak a boat with muffled oars to the base of the cliff wall, after dark? Climb, or levitate, to the tomb-chamber's window? And then what?

Or should Thur try to assassinate Vitelli, this afternoon, before he could perform the next set of vile rites? Ferrante, though he was involved to the eyebrows, did not seem to be the driving will behind this wholesale foray into the black arts. Thur shivered at the thought of a blade in his hand, driving into the thick resistance of a man's flesh. Was it even possible to murder a mage? Foolish question—think of Master Beneforte. Death came to mages as to other men. Or . . . perhaps not quite as to other men. Would another murder create another malevolent ghost, or worse? Maybe Monreale could shrive it, and send it on its way. Shrive them all.

Thur fitted the bricks for the furnace floor and plotted his escape, as soon as he reached the end of this row, by excusing himself to go to the garderobe. A pounding noise came from the heavy timber gate to the stables at the end of the garden. Someone was unblocking it with a mallet. Thur looked up. A couple of big, loud Losimon soldiers in steel and leather backed through pulling on a rope. Their whoops seemed too good-natured to go with some combat, and Thur's work mates, after first freezing at their shovels, relaxed and leaned on them to watch.

Following the Losimon soldiers came a train of mules, roped together pack-saddle-to-halter. The first mule was a distinctive gray, the second honey-brown with a cream-colored nose—the gaily-striped saddle blankets were all too familiar. Oh, Jesus, it was Pico's mule train. Would the packmaster blurt out recognition of Thur? Would Thur be dangling by his neck from the castle wall, hanged as a discovered spy, within the half-hour? Thur crouched down in his half-built furnace and stared wildly. Damn it, Pico had said he was going to cut over the hills to Milan. What bad angel had inspired him to bring his load of copper to sell in Montefoglia, instead? Now, of all times?

But the eighth mule walked stiffly through the gate with no sign of Pico, or of his two boys. Only a quartet of dismounted Losimon cavalrymen tugged the animals along. Thur stood up from his crouch, wary and confused.

"Hey, Foundryman!" shouted the lead soldier. "Where do you want us to put this?"

Thur almost answered, *Stack the pigs in pairs over there*, but gulped down his mistake and said instead, "Put what?" He walked toward the mule train.

The mules were sweaty and dirty under their harness. Iridescent green flies were already plaguing new pink raw spots showing under the edges of the leather straps. One mule had been limping, and now stood with a hind hoof held gingerly tiptoe. All dove their heads to the grass and weeds at their feet, smacking dry and thirsty lips.

"My lord's new copper." The soldier flicked up the

canvas of a pack-saddle and pointed proudly to a thick metal bar.

Thur stared at the lathered and exhausted animals. Pico would never have permitted—"Where is Pi—is the packmaster?" Thur demanded. Dread lent his voice an unaccustomed harshness.

"Gone to God," grinned the soldier. "He left us these in his will, eh?"

Thur swallowed. "Where did you find them?"

"We were on patrol, foraging up north of the lake yesterday. Too damn far from home, we were just about to quit and go back, when we came upon this fellow's camp in the hills. Our lieutenant fancied this'd be a gift to my lord's taste, so we took 'em. We ran them all night to get here. Stubborn beasts, we had to beat 'em with the flats of our swords to keep 'em moving, toward the end."

Yes, several of the animals' haunches showed long bloody welts. Thur had to allow, Ferrante's cavalrymen were just as cruel to their own beasts, and to each other. The sweat-stained, filthy soldier's features were lined with a fatigue scarcely less than that of the drooping mules. But the mules lacked his greedy elation.

"Pi ... didn't the packmaster ... I take it the packmaster objected?" Thur struggled to keep his voice cool, disinterested.

"A length of my officer's Spanish steel settled the argument soon enough." The soldier paused thoughtfully. "Didn't much care for what he did to the boy. The lad wouldn't stop trying to fight us, after it was over. Half-mad, I think, though his elder brother had a better head, and tried to hold him. Well, t'was no worse than some of the things that happened after the last siege of Pisa."

"Did he ... what did he do to the boy?"

"Half chopped off his head. It stopped the scream-ing, right enough, which was a relief."

"Killed him?" Thur choked.

"Outright." The soldier spat reflectively. "Could've been worse."

Thur gripped his hands behind his back, to hide their trembling. "Did he . . . kill both boys?"

"Naw. The smarter one ran off." The soldier glanced up. "Ah. Here we go."

Thur followed his gaze to the doors to the castle. Just descending into the garden was Lord Ferrante, dressed in the same fine mail tunic and leather leg-gings as yesterday morning. A clean white linen undercollar shone at his neck, and a gold badge in his green hat winked diamonds in the sun. Flanking him stamped another dirty and fatigued cavalryman. A dusty black beard framed a dark smile missing several front teeth. Thur stiffened—but there was no reason to suppose the man would recognize him from Catti's inn. It had been dusk in the innyard, and Thur had hung in the background till things went so terribly wrong. *I should have recognized the man from his methods, though,* Thur thought wearily.

"So," said Ferrante bluffly, coming up to Thur. "What value have we here, German?"

Thur walked to a saddlebag, and pretended to exam-ine its contents. "Finest Swiss copper, my lord."

"Is it fit for our needs? Is it sufficient?"

"More than sufficient." Thur fingered Master Kunz's mark, stamped on the soft red bar. "I've . . . heard of this forge. Very pure."

"Very good." Lord Ferrante turned to his men, and took a purse from his waist. He poured gold coins into his hand, held them up for all to see, poured them back, and handed the purse to his gap-toothed minion for distribution. The men cheered.

"Unload these beasts, then send your men to eat,"

Ferrante directed his lieutenant. "Deliver the mules to my quartermaster's constable, outside the walls." Ferrante frowned, walking down the line of mules. "See that they get water and hay, and their harness off, before you eat. Tell my head groom to check that dun's off-hind hoof. *My* mules must be made to last."

Ferrante wheeled away, and strode back into the castle. Under Thur's wooden direction, the hungry men made short work of unloading and stacking the copper pigs on the ground beside the furnace. Laughing and joking about their new-won gold, the soldiers led the mules back into the castle stable.

A bird trilled from the white blossoms of a plum tree espaliered to the garden wall. The workmen returned to their digging, shovels scraping through the hard-packed earth. The line of light creeping across the ground as the sun rose higher reached the stack of copper, edging it with blinding red fire. Thur swallowed nausea.

"I'm . . . going to the garderobe," he said, turned, and stumbled from the garden.

Chapter Thirteen

Thur really did go to the garderobe, a slit cut into the castle wall at the back of the stables and used by the grooms and the workmen. But he exited again without, as he had at first feared, being violently ill. He leaned shakily against a stall partition and listened to the steady munching of a horse eating its hay. The presence of the big animals soothed him, a little. The dumb beasts were innocent. Though God had made Balaam's ass speak out against injustice, or so Brother Glarus had told the story. Why not Pico's mules?

An unfamiliar trembling shortened Thur's breath. Hatred. *Wrath*, as the list of the seven deadly sins had it. The murder of Pico's boy Zilio, so bluntly described, burned in his imagination, angered him almost more than the death of Uri. Uri had been a man, taking a man's risks. The Losimons hadn't any call to kill a child. They could have knocked him aside, or tied him up, or something. . . . His righteousness died as an image of the whey-faced boy groom across Ferrante's saddlebow troubled his mind. He shook his aching head in bewilderment.

He made his way to the stable door into the main court. A couple of grooms had taken Pico's mules outside, and tied them to ringbolts in the wall in the narrowing shade. They had watered them and stripped them of their harness, and now were rubbing them down and daubing goose grease on their sores. The mules snatched at little piles of hay, and grumpily laid their long ears back and nipped at each other. Thur squinted into the heat of the courtyard, and the light reflecting blindingly off the bulbous marble staircase. The sun was higher. Did it always climb this fast, of a morning? Across the pavement at the base of the northern gate-tower, two guards stood flanking a small entry arch.

Thur felt in his tunic for the two remaining ears, and studied the men. They looked harder-faced, more alert than the fellow who'd been sitting tiredly by the dungeon door last night. Dare Thur try his thin story about checking the bolts and bars a second time?

While Thur stood trying to muster up his courage, the little door swung inward and the guards came to attention. A Losimon officer exited, followed by three women who stood blinking in the light. Two women and a girl, Thur corrected himself. The first was a dark-haired, prettily plump matron of perhaps twenty-five, wearing a crocus-yellow linen gown. The second, older woman wore black and white silk. She was a little, faded blonde; sandy-haired, sandy-complexioned, her face drawn and stiff in the shade of a brimmed hat. The girl, almost as tall, wore pale green linen and a close cap, a braided rope of gold hair falling from her nape. She clung tightly to the faded woman's arm.

The officer gestured them onwards, palms open like a man herding sheep. Frowning at him, they scuffled across the courtyard and up the marble stairs, disappearing into the castle. Thur bit his lip, then walked quickly back through the stable and climbed over the rear gate into the castle garden. His work mates made a few sharp comments about shirkers as he hurried past the brick pile. But he had not strode half the length of the garden when the women reappeared at its main entry and then descended into the open, still dogged by the officer. Thur hesitated, and bent to pretend to knock a bit of gravel from his shoe. The silk-gowned woman went to sit on a marble bench under a grape arbor, the tender green leaves making a woven shade. The girl and the dark woman in crocus-yellow linked arms protectively, and strolled upon a gravel walk. The noble prisoners were being aired, it seemed.

For how long? Dare he just walk up to them? The officer lingered close by, within hearing. Confused by this ambiguous near-opportunity, Thur retreated to his brick pile and made to lay on another course, all the time watching down the garden. The Duchess's hat turned toward him once, then away; the strollers paused by her bench. Then they strolled toward him. Thur held his breath. The officer made a step to follow, but then changed his mind and waited near the Duchess, leaning on an arbor post with his arms crossed.

The two young women drew nearer. The girl must be Lady Julia, the matron some sort of lady-in-waiting. One of the workmen made a coarse comment under his breath.

"Lamb or mutton, it's all for my lord's table," his companion murmured back with a sour grin. "Not even a scrap for us, I'll wager."

"Shut up," Thur growled. The laborer frowned back but, perhaps daunted by Thur's size, swallowed whatever insubordinate jape was on his tongue and bent again to his shovel. Thur walked around his furnace-base with a judiciously measuring glance, trying to look like the man in charge. He evidently succeeded, for upon coming up the dark-haired woman inquired of him, "What are you doing here, workman, tearing up our poor garden?"

Thur ducked his head in a clumsy half-bow, and immediately trod nearer to her. "We're building a furnace, Madonna. To repair that bombast yonder." Thur pointed to the green pot.

"By whose order?" she asked, stepping back.

"Lord Ferrante's, of course." Thur gestured expansively, and stepped close enough at last to lower his voice. He blurted out quickly, "My name is Thur Ochs. Brother to your guard captain Uri Ochs. Abbot Monreale sent me. I'm only passing myself off as a foundryman."

The dark woman's hand tightened on the girl's arm. "Go fetch your mother at once, Julia."

"No," Thur began to protest, but the girl was already scampering away. "We mustn't be seen to be conversing in secret, it will give all away." He turned, and began pointing at various parts of the foundry operation as if still explaining its function. The workmen, just beyond earshot, turned their curious eyes away to follow the gestures, and Thur slipped a little ear from his tunic and whispered its activation spell into his palm. He let his concealing hand drop casually to his side, flashing it briefly toward the woman. "This is a magic ear. When you talk into it, Abbot Monreale and his monks at Saint Jerome will be able to hear you. Hide it, quickly!"

Staring at the bombast, she pulled a handkerchief from her sleeve, and touched it to her face as if she were feeling the heat. It fell from her hand. Thur bent to retrieve it. Ear and handkerchief disappeared into her sleeve again. She gave him a polite nod of thanks, but stepped back as if repelled by his peasant stench.

Or perhaps she really was repelled by his peasant stench. His gray tunic was stained with the sweat of the hot morning's labor.

Duchess Letitia arrived in tow of Lady Julia. The older woman at least had the wit to gaze out over the work site first, instead of directly at Thur.

"This foundryman claims to be an agent of Bishop Monreale's," the dark-haired woman murmured. Thur swallowed, and made an unfeignedly awkward bow, Work-lout Introduced To Duchess; the play might well pass, at a distance.

Letitia's red-rimmed, faded blue eyes grew hard as steel. She stepped to Thur and gazed up into his face. Her hand clutched convulsively at his sleeve. "Monreale?" she breathed. *"Does he have Ascanio?"*

"Yes, Lady. Safe at the monastery."

Her puffy eyelids closed. "Thank God. Thank the Mother of God."

"But . . . the monastery is besieged by Losimons. I have to get back there, to get help. My brother is killed, and Ferrante and Vitelli are trying to enslave his ghost to a spirit ring. I have to stop them, but I don't know how."

The Duchess's eyes opened again. "Killing them would do it," she observed dispassionately.

"I . . . haven't had a good chance," Thur stammered, only half-truthfully. He'd had chances, they just hadn't been good enough. *I bet they would have been good enough for Uri.*

"If I could but lay hands on my ebony rosary, I swear I would make my own chance," Letitia stated. Her eyes turned away, once again concealing the intimacy of this conversation. The woman in yellow folded her arms.

"Beg pardon?" said Thur.

"See you, man—do you think you could make your way in secret to my chambers? There is an ebony rosary in my escritoire. Or there was, if it hasn't been looted by now. It's very distinctive, with gold wire flanges. On its end hangs a little ivory ball, cunningly carved. If you could find it and bring it to me—"

"The cracked bombast itself will be melted down to make up part of the metal," Thur interrupted her loudly. He widened his eyes at her, desperately signalling. Lord Ferrante had just exited the castle. He looked around and spied the women, waved away his officer's salute, and started down the garden; the guard followed, to take station discreetly beyond hearing, leaning up against the outer curtain wall. Ferrante held a small, rather scruffy dog with protuberant brown eyes under his arm. Thur continued, "The rest we shall melt new. Lord Ferrante deals us no shortages in our work."

Julia at first shrank nearer to her mother, but then saw the little dog. "Pippin!" she cried.

The dog wriggled frantically; Ferrante scratched its ears to calm it, then bent and released it. It ran to its mistress and jumped up on her skirts, yipping, then tore around the garden in circles. It returned to Julia's calling at last, and she picked it up and cradled it in her arms, dropping kisses on its head.

The dark-haired woman made a scandalized face. "Don't kiss the *dog*, Julia!"

"I thought he'd killed poor Pippin!" A fierce glower toward Ferrante identified the accused. Tears sparkled in her eyes.

"I only said I wished to borrow him," said Ferrante in a reasonable, indeed, kindly tone. "See, here he is back safe and sound. You must learn to trust my word, if we are to get on, Lady Julia."

All three women gave him identical repelled glares, as if forced to look upon a centipede or a scorpion. Ferrante shifted, and grimaced.

"Are we to get on?" inquired the Duchess coldly.

"Consider the advantages," Ferrante shrugged. And added with a matching glint of ice, "Consider the disadvantages, if you don't choose to."

"Strike some devil's bargain with my lord and husband's murderer? Never!"

"Never is a long time. Life goes on. You have children to provide for. It's very true, we have all suffered an unfortunate accident. It's not one I looked for, and I'm sorry I lost my temper, but I was goaded. What would you? Wrath is a man's sin!"

"Yet you dare still suggest I bind Julia to a life under that threat?" snapped Letitia. "To become the next victim from my family to your wrath? And how *did* your first wife die, my lord? Truly, you are mad!"

Ferrante's jaw clamped. He produced a strained smile, and drew a leather ball from the figured purse hung from his belt. "Here, Julia." He turned to the girl, his voice deliberately gentled. "I brought you a ball for, er, Pippin. Why don't you take him down to the other end of the garden, and see if he will fetch it for you? I wager he will."

Julia glanced uncertainly at her mother, who had locked eyes with Ferrante. "Yes, love," Letitia agreed thinly. "Do that."

Reluctantly, the girl put down her dog and obeyed, with a backward glance or two. Pippin danced around her, following.

"My lady?" The woman in yellow raised her brows, with a nod after Julia.

"Stay by me, Lady Pia," said the Duchess. "I would have a witness to this man's next crime, whatever it turns out to be."

Ferrante rolled his eyes in exasperation. "Think, Letitia! What's done is done, and no one can call it back. You must look to the future, and let the past go!" His hand tightened, then stretched out carefully flat on the leather legging of his thigh, next to his sword. His eye fell on Thur, standing there trying to look invisible. "Go back to work, German." Ferrante waved him curtly away. Thur bowed and retreated to the nearest spot, his broken brick pile, crouched, and pretended to be sorting them by size. Ferrante glowered over the work site a moment, then followed, lowering his voice. "So, Foundryman. When will my cannon be cast?"

Never, you bastard. "If I work steadily through the day, my lord, I might have the furnace built by sundown. Then it must be lined with clay, and the clay dried and fired."

"Could you do that tonight?"

"I could, but to fire it while still damp risks cracking."

"Mm. Risk it," Ferrante ordered, with a quick glance at the sun. Time bit at his heels too, it seemed.

"There's still the bombast mold to make, my lord. The furnace may as well dry slowly while that's being done."

"Ah. Yes." Ferrante frowned at the brickwork, his face abstracted. Was he seeing, in his mind's eye, his bombast battering down the walls of Saint Jerome? And then what? The breach in the wall fought for, taken; monks and Sandrino's soldiers slain. Women— Fiametta, God!—tormented, refugees chased from corners, put to the sword while crying futilely for sanctuary in the chapel? Would Fiametta be among them? Surely she would fight like a cat, and be killed for it, not prettily. Thur did not think Fiametta had the knack of surrendering. A frightened Ascanio dragged out from under the prior's bed to have his throat slit . . . *like Pico's boy.* Though neither guards nor stone walls had defended Zilio. Not that it seemed to alter the end result.

Killing them would do it.

Thur was alone beside Ferrante. His knife in its sheath on his belt pressed against the small of his back like a compelling hand. *What more chance do you want than this?* Ferrante wore mail, true, but his neck was bare as ... as a boy's. But could Thur escape, afterwards? Over the stable gate, say, out through the entry court, before the alarm went up? An image of the black-mouthed cavalryman's lance driving between his shoulder blades as he fled down the road made Thur's muscles stiffen. He did not want to die, on this bright morning. Maybe Ferrante did not want to die either. *This isn't my calling. I came to Montefoglia to make beautiful things out of metal, not corpses out of living men. Oh, God.* Thur stood up.

But Ferrante had already turned away, and was striding back to the Duchess. Another chance lost. Right or wrong? Did angels weep, or devils gnash their teeth? Thur bent and worked around his brick pile to keep Ferrante in sight, straining his ears to catch the next words.

"We can yet arrange things, my lady, in good public form," Ferrante continued to the Duchess, his voice and temper controlled again. "Sandrino's death was an accident. He fell on the knife in a scuffling fall. We had both drunk too much unwatered wine at the banquet. My lieutenant misunderstood the situation."

"We all know those are lies," said Letitia flatly.

"But we are the only ones who know," Ferrante argued smoothly, after a glance at Lady Pia's stone face apparently convinced him denial would be fruitless. "If we all say otherwise, why then, so it will be, as far as any outsiders know. You can save your family's honor and position, in this awkward event. If I wed Julia, and become Ascanio's guardian, why, it will be clear to all that Sandrino's unfortunate death was an accident. You lose nothing, not even your home, and gain a protector in me."

"So you can go on to cheat my son out of his patrimony? So you can murder him at your leisure?"

"I could murder him at my pleasure right now!" Ferrante snapped. "Give me credit! I am trying to save you all!"

"You are merely trying to save yourself. From the just retribution that must fall on your head, if God has not abandoned the world altogether!"

Ferrante's nostrils flared, but he reaffixed the smile that had slid from his face. "I'm not inhuman. I desire your goodwill. See, I have even brought you your rosary that you asked for. My men and I are not the thieves you accuse us of being." He pulled a string of polished black beads from his purse, and held them out just beyond her reach.

Letitia turned pale, controlled her hand in mid-snatch, and accepted the gift with a small curtsey. "Thank you, my lord," she stammered. "You can't know what these mean to me."

"I think I do," smiled Ferrante. She drew the beads through her soft white hands, came to the end—a black bead stopped with a gold flange—hastily reversed the string, and came to the other end, also a plain black bead. Her face came up, wide-eyed with anger, as Ferrante held up a small carved ivory ball between his thumb and finger. "Do you seek this?" he inquired sweetly.

"Give me—" Letitia surged forward in a hiss of silk, then stood still, hands clenched to her sides.

"A very interesting object, this. I've had Vitelli examine it thoroughly."

Lady Pia crossed her crocus-sleeved arms tightly under her breasts, but remained standing sturdily behind the Duchess.

"A fascinating spell," Ferrante went on, hugely ironic. "A way for a woman to kill a man many times stronger than herself. A poison that is neither food nor drink, against which my saltcellar would be quite useless. The woman holds the poison locked in this little ivory ball, under her tongue. Then she induces the man who is her enemy to kiss her. Was that task to be yours, or Julia's? Or Lady Pia's, here? A pretty scene, to be seducing me while her husband lies imprisoned below her very feet. She whispers the word which unlocks the ball, and breathes into her unsuspecting lover's mouth. The poison flows into him in the form of a snake made of smoke. He dies strangled, unable to breathe. I suppose she must take care not to inhale while this operation is in progress, eh?" His fist closed around the ivory sphere.

"If ever a man deserved such a death, it is you," hissed Lady Pia.

"Oh, were you to have been my executioner?" purred Ferrante. "I'll remember that. But no. When you add this to the evidence of a very curious painted cabinet, kept locked in your boudoir, my lady Letitia, it seems to me a very convincing charge of black witchcraft and poisoning might be got up against you. Think on that."

"By you? You hypocrite! God cleave your lying tongue!"

"One would think God is your personal bravo, the way you call on him," snarled Ferrante sarcastically. "You keep your secrets well. I had no hint before this that you had a talent for the black arts. But this," he rolled the little ball between his fingers, "is quite a pretty piece of work."

"I didn't make it," denied Letitia.

"Then however did you come by it?"

"I had it from a girl who burned for it. She had it from a Moorish magician in Venice. She had used it to kill her unfaithful lover. I visited her in her cell, the night before her execution, for mercy and our Lord Jesus's sake. The Inquisitor himself, for all his hot irons, never found out how she did it, but she confessed it to me. She gave it to me. I kept it for . . . a curiosity. To make such a thing is quite beyond my power." Letitia pressed her lips tightly together.

"You must of course say so. But look at it from my point of view. A man who has his mother-in-law privately strangled must expect harsh social disapproval from her numerous cousins, however much envious men may secretly applaud the deed. But a pious fellow who has her publicly burned for black witchcraft against his life can only gain solemn sympathy."

"Judicial murder," said Letitia frozenly, "is murder still." Lady Pia was pale, breathless.

"But my hands will not be stained with it, eh? And hasn't there been enough murder in Montefoglia? Come, my lady. Let us cry peace. Today, I ask humbly, and grant you the dignity of free compliance." Ferrante's effort at goodwill was brightly strained.

Letitia turned her face away. "I have the headache. You have kept me too long in the sun."

Ferrante's voice hardened. "Tomorrow I shall have the means to compel cooperation. And you'll wish you'd struck your best bargain while you could."

"I wish to go in." Letitia's face had less animation than one of the marble statues tucked among the garden walks.

"So that you can continue to poison your daughter's mind against me!" Ferrante tucked the ivory ball away in his pouch, and gave her a courtier's bow. Letitia and Lady Pia glanced down the garden to where Julia now sat on the bench, fearfully clutching her lap dog. Ferrante followed their gaze, his eyes lidding. "I think the time has come to separate her from you and your so-loyal handmaid. Before you force me into the same rough courting our noble Roman ancestors used to gain their Sabine wives."

It took a moment for the import of this threat to sink in. Letitia's eyes went luminous with anger. "You dare—!"

"And would you then dare deny me permission to wed her, afterwards?" Ferrante's brows drew down, considering this inspiration. "Perhaps not. Is this the solution to your stubborness, Letitia? Drastic, but if you force me to be cruel to be kind—"

"Monster!" cried Lady Pia, and swung a clawed hand at his face. He caught her arm easily, and wrenched it downward, his lips compressed with annoyance. A white circle fell from her crocus sleeve, and bounced on the dry ground. She gasped, and stamped her foot upon it, too late; a liquid orange light flared around her slipper, and was gone.

"What's this?" Ferrante asked, holding Lady Pia one-handed at arm's length despite her struggles. He stooped to retrieve the crushed tambourine, shoving her away.

His part as spy must be revealed in moments. Thur stood up, and felt for his knife hilt. He'd last used it to cut roast mutton at breakfast. It needed sharpening. Why hadn't he thought to sharpen it? He could not breathe.

He drew and lunged, just as Ferrante straightened up. Too far a strike; the guard by the wall, starting forward, cried a warning. Ferrante half-turned and flung up a mail-clad arm, deflecting Thur's thrust. The blade skittered across the links and grazed the side of Ferrante's throat. In a desperate bid to recover the chance Thur turned the blade and recoiled. It bit the back of Ferrante's neck. But Ferrante's grip, astonishingly strong for the awkward angle, was already wrapped around Thur's wrist, and the knife did not bite deep. They wrestled for the hilt. Then Thur's groin exploded with blinding pain, like lightning chewing up his nerves, as Ferrante's combat-experienced knee hit its target with force and precision. A boot met Thur's chin as he sank, snapping his head back. It was worse than meeting a rockfall. A second kick found his belly; his stitches burst, and the hot cut bled anew.

The tip of a long, shining sword pressed into the hollow of Thur's throat as he lay blinking up at the bright blue sky and Ferrante's dark face swimming overhead. Ferrante pressed a hand to the side of his neck, glanced at the sticky blood staining his palm, and cursed. He swung his sword up and stepped back a pace as a couple more guards came running up and, redundantly, began kicking Thur.

The noblewomen were screaming and clutching one another. Fiametta at least would have picked up a brick and tried to help bash Ferrante's head in. Thur deeply regretted his shyness. If only he had been more forward, he might have won a kiss from her, or more, before this death. . . .

Ferrante leaned on his sword, breathing heavily, the whites of his eyes showing. After a minute, when it was quite plain Thur would not rise to try again, he waved the guards back. "Take them to the tower." He dispatched two men to remove the crying women. Gathering up the terrified Julia and her dog, the officer-guard hustled them from the bright garden.

Thur blinked madly watering eyes, and tried to memorize the sky. He wanted to fall up into it, go to God. He'd rather his last sight be the face of Fiametta, but he certainly did not wish her here, so blue sky must do. The faces of enemies wavered over him. There was Ferrante's, blurred and doubled, brick red with rage and fear.

"Why, German?" Ferrante grated. The bright sword pressed Thur's throat again. It looked like the chute to heaven, foreshortened in the sun. You could slide up it into the blue sky. . . .

"Swiss," Thur corrected thickly. His mouth was numb and gritty with dirt.

"Why did you just try to kill me?"

Why. Why. Well, it had seemed like the proper thing to do. Everyone had wanted him to. He hadn't really wanted to. He wanted Uri back far more than he wanted Ferrante dead. "You killed my brother," Thur spat out in a gobbet of blood.

"Ah? Not Sandrino's Swiss guard captain!" Ferrante's teeth gleamed in a weird satisfied grimace. Apparently vengeance for dead brothers was reason enough to make more dead brothers, in his world. Did Ferrante have a brother? Would this chain go on forever?

Vitelli the secretary, his red robe flapping, came running up. "My lord!" he cried, in a voice edged with panic.

"It's not as bad as it looks, Niccolo." Ferrante's voice was controlled again, a bored drawl.

"You're bleeding—"

"It's not deep. You there. Go fetch my surgeon."

"Let me staunch it. . . ." Vitelli passed a hand across Ferrante's neck, and the bleeding slowed to a dark ooze.

Ferrante scratched carefully around the cut with gory fingernails, his face screwed up in irritation. "That was too damned close. Search him for hidden weapons." He nodded to a soldier, who knelt cautiously by Thur and began prodding around his bruises. He discovered Thur's thin purse tucked in his tunic, which he handed up to the secretary. He laid a white parchment circle absently on the ground. Thur moaned.

Vitelli himself had to look three times. "What . . . ?" He bent to pick it up. After a moment, he swore. His hand closed on the parchment tambourine, crushing it; the orange light leaked briefly between his fingers. "Where did you get this?" he demanded of Thur.

Thur smiled dreamily, afloat in a sea of pain.

"Answer!" a guard yelled, kicking him again. Thur

grunted, and paddled after a receding darkness that would take him away from all this.

"Never mind." Vitelli put out a hand to stop the guard's helpful efforts. "If there are more, I can use this to find them."

"What are they?" asked Ferrante, taking and comparing the crumpled circle with the other.

"I believe it is some kind of device for eavesdropping, my lord. It's . . . rather fine work. I feel there are more about."

Ferrante glanced from the tambourines to Thur, pursing his lips. "He is a spy?"

"Without doubt," said Vitelli.

"He said he was Sandrino's guard captain's brother. Of course, he could be both." Ferrante beckoned to his soldiers. "Hang him from the south tower. On the side where he can be seen from the north tower."

Guards reached for Thur's arms, to drag him upright. Thur dimly recalled praying to God to save him for hanging. *I take it back.* Surely he'd been promised death pressed in earth and water, not death dangling in the air.

"Wait, my lord. . . ." Vitelli advanced to peer down into Thur's swollen and bloody face. "Brother to Captain Ochs? Really? They don't look much alike. Well, perhaps the chin."

"Does it matter?"

"There is an opportunity . . ."

"What?" said Ferrante in exasperation. "I get no pleasure in dragging this out. He is a spy and an assassin; fine, let him be executed at once, as a warning to others."

"Execute, yes, but . . . I believe we can make better use of his death. Below-stairs. Eh? Cats and cocks are but trifles, compared to a man. And if the man be truly a brother to . . . another, why then . . . I will have to recalculate all my diagrams. Oh, it's excellent, my lord!"

"Oh." Ferrante rubbed his chin thoughtfully. "I see." He stood a moment in uncharacteristic indecision. "I wonder if he has another brother, who will come popping out of the dark at me? Well . . . he is a condemned criminal, after all. Too bad. I rather liked him."

"All the better, my lord." Vitelli's eyes glittered.

Ferrante's lips thinned, but he turned to his soldiers. "Take him to the dungeon. We'll question him later, and execute him privately."

Two Losimons forced Thur to his feet. The garden spun around him in slow jerks, and his stomach heaved. His new gray tunic was all spoiled with bloodstains too, now, he saw with tearful regret. Mother would be unhappy. . . . They frog-marched him up the garden. The dimness of the castle swallowed the day. The hollow echo of plastered corridors floated past him. He stumbled down stairs into a perpetual stone night. Around a corner, past familiar barred cells. An argument hurt his ears, irritated voices: ". . . too crowded." "Not in there!" "Why not, we have to watch him all the time, anyway. Maybe this will stir something up." "Don't want him stirred up!"

The world, in the form of cold stone, came to rest at last, pressing against Thur's face. His hands felt across the gritty chill, and he turned his aching head carefully to the side. A little dim blue daylight reflected through a tunnel in the wall above him. Somewhere, a metal lock clanked shut, and footsteps receded.

A thick warm hand gripped his hair, and turned his face around. Thur looked blearily into red eyes in an unshaven face, a beard like salt and pepper scattered across sagging jowls. Tufted brows rose.

"A bat's the thing," the mad castellan advised him kindly, opened his hand, and let Thur's cheek slap back to the stone.

Chapter Fourteen

"There goes the last of them," said Brother Perotto grimly. A haze of orange light evaporated from the surface of the parchment tambourine on the table before him. The haze flickered uncertainly in the cool northern daylight of Abbot Monreale's work chamber, and was gone.

"All that work," moaned Brother Ambrose. The other monks ringing the table, each clutching a now-silenced mouth, grimaced in agreement. Fiametta fingered the last tambourine, before her place. Dead. It had never even started to speak, but now its magic aura was not merely inactive, it was gone without trace. *Where are you, Thur?*

Fiametta had just turned over to Monreale the mouth speaking, alternately clear and strangely muffled, from Lady Pia's sleeve, when it had emitted a cry and cut off abruptly. Monreale had hastily gathered his other listeners together to follow Vitelli's destructive progress through the castle; Sandrino's office, the infirmary, the groom's dormitory. The words the little mouths emitted before going dead had been few and businesslike: "Here's another, my lord." "Under the blanket. Ha!" Till the last, damning one, found on its shelf in the chamber of necromancy. Fiametta understood that mouth had kept Brother Perotto tinglingly awake last night even after she had gone to bed by Monreale's orders, but Perotto had been maddenly vague about the events it had reported, at least to her.

Vitelli's last whispered message had been brief and horrible. "It is you, Monreale, isn't it? I recognize your style. It's done you no good. Your fate is sealed, and your stupid spy shall die directly." A crackling, cut off, and the mouth in front of Brother Perotto had given up its so-painstakingly-invested magic.

Monreale sat bent over, pale, as if pieces were being torn bit by bit from his belly. Brother Perotto sat back, and turned his palms out in helpless frustration. "What happened, Father? It seemed to be going so well, and then . . ."

"I greatly fear for poor Thur," said Monreale lowly into his lap.

Fiametta wrapped her arms around her torso, pressing the lion ring secretly between her breasts. She could still sense its warm, musical hum, its tiny heartbeat. If Thur's real heart stopped, would she know? She stared around the table at the array of gray-cowled men, solemn, authoritative, and helpless. "What's the use of you?" she demanded in sudden anguish.

"What?" said Brother Ambrose sharply, though Abbot Monreale merely looked up.

"What's the *use* of you? The Church is supposed to be our defense against evil. Oh, you ride about the countryside, terrorizing old hedge-witches about a plague of lice in their neighbor's hair or some stupid love potion which half the time doesn't work anyway, and threatening their souls with hellfire if they don't cease and desist, you're fine at pestering men at work in their shops, but when real evil comes, what good are you? You're too afraid to fight it! You persecute the little crimes of little people, that's safe enough, but when great crimes march in with an army at their backs, where is all your preaching then? Strangely silent! Great stupid louts of—of *boys*—are hanged while you sit and *pray*. . . ." Tears were running down the inside of her nose, and she sniffed mightily, wiped her sleeve across her face, and bit her lip. "Oh, what's the *use*. . . ."

Brother Perotto began an angry lecture on the proper humility due from ignorant girls, but Abbot Monreale waved him to silence.

"Fiametta is partly right," he said in a distant tone, then looked around the table and smiled bleakly. "All virtues come down to courage, at the sharp end of the sword. But courage must be tempered by prudence. Courage wasted by misdirection is the most heart-breaking of all tragedies. If there is an eighth deadly sin, it ought to be stupidity, by which all virtues are run out into dry sands. Yet . . . where does prudence end and cowardice begin?"

"You sent Thur in there alone," said Fiametta breathlessly, "to confirm my charges of black magic and murder. Since my ignorant girl's word was not good enough against so great and *virtuous* a lord as Uberto Ferrante. Now my charges and much more are confirmed, through their own mouths. What do you wait for now? There is no reason to wait, and every reason to hurry!"

Monreale laid his hands out flat, palms down, upon his worktable, and regarded them gravely. "Quite." He sucked a little air through his teeth, then said, "Brother Ambrose, fetch the prior and the lieutenant of Sandrino's guards. Brother Perotto, Fiametta, you shall assist me. Begin by clearing all the rubbish from my table."

For all her passionate plea for action, Fiametta was taken aback by this sudden response. Her belly fluttered with fear as she busied herself scurrying around the chamber putting away, ordering, and fetching the objects of his art at Monreale's over-the-shoulder directions. Monreale was prepared, mentally at least; apparently all that time in meditation had been spent on more than prayer. When the lieutenant of the refugee Montefoglian guards arrived, Monreale sat him down with a map of the town and exact instructions for coordinating their magical and military efforts.

The ring of Losimon besiegers encircling Saint Jerome was known to be thin. Monreale urged the Montefoglian guards to leave just enough crossbowmen to keep the enemy away from the walls, and, breaking through the ring, make a sally toward town. With Ferrante and Vitelli incapacitated by the spell he planned to cast, and in the face of this sudden attack, Monreale hoped the Losimon troops would be thrown into confusion. Sandrino's—now Ascanio's—men could then rouse the townsfolk to their support.

"The Losimons have made themselves odious enough," Monreale judged. "All our people need is some real hope of success, to quell their fears of reprisal, and they will pour into the streets for you. Drive all the way through to the castle and the Duchess on the first rush, if you can. Though with their leaders gone, the Losimons might be willing to surrender on terms even from behind sealed gates."

Fiametta grew chill, listening to this. Well, Ferrante's Losimon bravos were ruthless, but perhaps their loyalty did not run to self-sacrifice. They wouldn't hesitate to sacrifice others, though. The complexity of the military situation daunted her heart. There was more to fighting their way out of this monstrous coil than merely waving a magic wand. Yet if anyone could pull all the disparate threads together, it was surely Abbot Monreale. Even Papa had called on him.

Monreale blessed his empty worktable while Brother Ambrose, chanting, circled the chamber with a thurible dribbling incense smoke. "To clear away the lingering echoes of previous spells," Ambrose explained. Fiametta nodded; her father had practiced a similar sort of housecleaning now and then, before casting particularly important, delicate, or complex commissions. Or ones of which he was not too sure of the outcome. The ritual seemed to order the mind more than it did the room, Fiametta reflected, coughing in the smoke.

Monreale himself laid out the props of his intended spell. "It is to be a spell of spirit over spirit as much as spirit over matter. The symbols must be chosen correctly to concentrate the mind. Still, I could wish for some material connector. A lock of hair, an article of clothing actually worn. . . . I might as well wish for the Papal army to appear over the hill while I'm at it." He sighed, then brightened. "Still, I have Vitelli's true name. This would have miscarried for certain without it, and I would not have known why." He took a new stick of white chalk, and began to laboriously trace a diagram upon the tabletop.

When he'd finished the chalk pattern, Monreale laid a knife with green and gold thread tied around it parallel to a wand of dry willow circled with threads of red and black. Ferrante and Vitelli, the soldier and the spiritually sapless mage. Monreale stood back and studied them. "Is it enough . . . ? Such a distance we must carry, over a mile."

They should be crossed, upside down, to represent their entanglement and their evil, thought Fiametta, but did not speak. Her father had severely chastised her for daring to offer suggestions in public. Surely Monreale knew even more about what he was doing.

Monreale folded a gauze cloth beside the knife and wand. It was actually a piece of cheesecloth fetched from the monastery kitchen. "Silk would be better," Monreale muttered. "But at least it is new."

Spider-silk would be even better, Fiametta thought, but she quailed at the thought of volunteering to go collect some, though there were plenty of odd corners in the monastery where spiders might be obtained. Very odd corners.

"It will be a spell of deep sleep," Monreale explained, "the same basic spell as that used by our healers, when a patient fears some little surgery. Powerful enough, but we must strive to make it more powerful, to overcome two men at once, neither anxious to cooperate and one fully capable of the most strenuous resistance. And he may have set wards . . ."

Why not enspell them one at a time? Vitelli first, of course.

"My greatest worry," Monreale muttered, "is to this spell's quality of whiteness, or spiritual benignity. It's very doubtful."

"What," said Fiametta, "why? It won't kill them— unless one is leaning over a balcony as it strikes, which seems unlikely—it won't even hurt them. They just go to sleep. A healer's spell, what could be whiter?"

Monreale's lip twisted. "And in the end—if we win—both men must eventually burn at the stake. Hardly harmless in intent, even if legal in means."

"If *they* win, are they even likely to bother with legality?"

"To hold what they have taken, they must wrap their crimes in some cloak of public pretense. Eyewitnesses to the contrary will be . . . in very grave straits."

"That includes me," Fiametta realized with a shiver.

"It includes enough by now to guarantee a very

massacre." Monreale sighed. "Well, I am ready. Until the lieutenant reports his men assembled, let us compose ourselves in prayer."

I might have predicted that. But Fiametta settled herself upon her knees before the crucifix on Monreale's office wall without demur. She did not lack things to pray about. She thought sadly of all the prayers she'd wasted in the past on her small desires . . . a lace cap, a silver bracelet like Maddelena's, a pony . . . a husband. Yet, in a backhanded way, all had been forthcoming; the cap and the bracelet from Papa, the white horse . . . Thur? What was this strange girl-power, to make the intractable world spit forth her wishes? *Oh, I wish it were over.*

At length, Sandrino's surviving senior officer returned, to confer briefly with Monreale. The soldier's eyes glinted grimly in the shadow of his steel helmet. His dented breastplate was dull and leaden. More determination than enthusiasm tightened his jaw, but perhaps that was the more durable emotion, under fire. The ten-year-old Duke's offer to lead his troops himself had been tactfully turned down, the lieutenant reported; but the man's spine seemed to stiffen in memory of it. Monreale blessed him and sent him on his way with a slap to his cuirass that echoed hollowly in the plastered office.

Monreale then led Perotto, Ambrose, and Fiametta into his workroom. The prior followed as a witness. The prior was more an administrator than magician or healer or even, Fiametta suspected, monk, but he had been Monreale's practical right hand throughout the crisis, managing men and space and the daily bread.

Monreale arranged his brothers standing around the table laden with the simple set for the spell. He bent his head in one more blessedly brief prayer, and extended his right hand to Ambrose and his left to Perotto. "Brothers, lend me your strength."

Fiametta stepped to the table's fourth side. "Father, I will gladly lend mine."

Monreale frowned, his brow furrowing. "No . . . no," he said slowly. "I don't want you exposed to the danger of the backlash, if this effort fails."

"My little mite could be the difference between failure and success. And not such a little mite as all that, either!"

Monreale smiled sadly, though Brother Perotto frowned repellingly. "You are a good girl, Fiametta," said Monreale. "But no. Please do not distract me further."

His raised palm blocked her protest, which she swallowed back into her tight throat. She stepped away from the table to the prior's side, and locked her hands behind her back.

"Ambrose, Perotto, join hands," Monreale instructed, and they reached across to each other to complete the ring. Monreale's grip tightened. "The first strike requires all our hearts, to overwhelm Sprenger." He bent his gaze to the symbols on the table, knife and wand, and began to chant in a healer's low drone.

Fiametta could feel the power build, as if an invisible sphere were forming above the table. Monreale's control seemed very precise, meticulous, almost finicky, compared to her Papa's flowing, sweeping gestures. *Monreale wastes nothing.* And yet . . . his economy wasted time, and attention, it seemed to Fiametta. *Abundance can afford to be daring.*

The sphere began to glow with a visible, corruscating white fire, shimmering in waves both upon its surface and within its heart, as its power built up and up. Now, *that* was wasteful. Papa had always insisted that a properly cast spell should be heatless and invisible. Perhaps it was some inevitable friction from trying to combine strengths from Ambrose and Perotto. Fiametta held her breath. *Oh, strike now, or Vitelli will feel it and be warned!*

Still Monreale held his hand, building up his power. The lacy sphere cast the monks' shadows on the walls. Then the light began to pour down like water into the vessels of knife and wand. They filled; the knife blade gleamed like moonlight. Soundlessly, the gauze lifted and drifted across the two glowing objects, and settled gently over them.

Monreale's eyes opened; he breathed the last syllable of his chant. Ambrose grinned in triumph, and even surly Perotto's eyes lighted. Monreale inhaled, smiling, to speak.

The dry willow wand exploded into flame, which flashed across the gauze, consuming it to crumbling blackness. White fire tainted with red flared up into Monreale's face like a powder flash from a misfired hand cannon. His features, lit from below, contorted. Red and green afterimages swirled in Fiametta's eyes, and she squinted futilely against them, her hands pressed to her mouth to stifle her scream.

Monreale's eyes rolled back, and he fell, unaided, since Ambrose's hands were clapped to his eyes and Perotto, too, was toppling. Monreale's forehead cracked the table as he collapsed. All three men's faces were reddening from the burn.

Fiametta and the prior jostled each other in their rush around the table. The prior knelt beside Monreale's bleeding head, but hesitated to touch him, still fearful perhaps of being guilty of interrupting some magic in progress. But there was nothing left to interrupt. Fiametta could feel it. The circle and the spell were broken.

"Father Monreale? Father Monreale!" cried the prior in anxiety. Monreale's face was dead white, mottled with red patches. His singed eyebrows gave off an acrid whiff of burned hair. Overcoming his hesitation, the prior pressed his ear to Monreale's robed chest. "I hear nothing. . . ."

Fiametta ran to the cupboard and snatched up a fragment of broken mirror stored there, and thrust it under Monreale's nose. "It clouds. He breathes. . . ."

Perotto moaned; Ambrose lay as oddly as his abbot.

"What happened?" asked the prior. "Did Vitelli counterattack them somehow?"

"Yes, but . . . Vitelli's counter-surge might have been contained. Should have been contained. It was the excess heat, and the tinder-dryness of the willow. Abbot Monreale let too much heat build up."

The prior frowned at this critique, and wiped the blood away from the rising lump on Monreale's forehead. He palpated the skull. "Not broken, I think. He should come around soon."

I don't think so. It wasn't just the crack on his head that was incapacitating Monreale. It was the spell, turned back on its source; she wasn't sure how Vitelli was doing it, but it was almost as if she could see a dark hand pressed to Monreale's face, as a man might hold his enemy under water. Strange. She shook her head to clear it of the ghostly impressions. She'd been steeped in too much magic of late, it was as if her senses for it had been sanded to an almost painful new receptivity. Maybe Ambrose could lift the spell hand, when he recovered. If he recovered.

Brother Perotto sat up on his own. Brother Ambrose's eyes opened at last, but he was dazed and incoherent. After another moment of uncertain observation, the prior ran to fetch the senior healer, Brother Mario. The healer directed several more monks to gather up the stricken men and take them to their beds. Fiametta waited for Mario to ask her what had happened, but he didn't, so she tried to tell him.

"You!" Perotto, supported between two brothers,

turned on her. "You ruined the spell. You don't belong in here!"

"Me! Abbot Monreale ordered me to be here!" said Fiametta.

"Impure . . . ," moaned Perotto.

Fiametta drew up indignation. "How dare you! I am a virgin!" *More's the pity.* And doomed to remain so, for all the rescue Thur seemed likely to receive now. At least until the Losimon soldiers took the monastery by storm. Ought she to suicide, before Saint Jerome was overrun? But that way lay damnation, too. Her heart burned in rage, and outrage. Why should *she* have to die and be damned for the crimes of men? She would rather fight, claw, and run away from the dismal fate of women and orphans.

The prior took her by the arm and steered her out onto the gallery overlooking the cloister. "Yes, yes, he meant no insult. But truly, it is improper for you to be in this part of the building. Go back to the women's quarters, Fiametta, and stay there."

"Till when? Till the Losimons come over the walls?"

"If the Abbot does not regain his senses from that knock soon . . ." The prior licked dry lips.

"He is *enspelled.* He won't come round until the spell is lifted. It must be possible to determine how to lift it. Vitelli labors under the same disadvantages of distance as we do."

"I will have the healers do what they can."

"It will take more than a healer!"

"Be that as it may, healers are what we have left, unless Ambrose recovers first."

"What will you do if neither man recovers soon? Or at all?"

The prior's shoulders bent, as the full weight of Monreale's burdens seemed to fall on them. "I will . . . I will wait the night. Perhaps the morning will bring better counsel. But if Ferrante's emissary returns to plague us again . . . perhaps it would be better to surrender on terms. Before it is too late."

"To Ferrante? You think he would honor his terms for five breaths?" cried Fiametta.

The prior's hands made impotent fists, by his sides. "Go back to the women's quarters, Fiametta! You understand not the first principle of the affairs of men!"

"What first principle? Save your own head, and let the devil take the hindmost? I understand that very well, thank you!"

"Go to—!" the prior began to roar, then dropped his voice to hiss between clenched teeth, "Go to your quarters! And hold your tongue!"

"Will you at least let me try to lift the spell of sleep, if the healers fail?" Fiametta begged desperately.

"Perotto is right. You do not belong in here. Go to!"

In a moment, he would beat her in his frustration, and call it a just chastisement; Fiametta could see it coming. She bared her teeth at him and ducked away, and stalked stiff-backed out of the cloister. She should have kept silence. She should have spoken up. She should have . . . she should have . . .

In the women's quarters, two children were puking, three were crying, and a sharp argument between two mothers over the last of the clean swaddling cloths had degenerated into hair-pulling and shrieking. Fiametta fled again. Her attempt to see Abbot Monreale in the infirmary was turned back sternly by Brother Mario. A Montefoglian guard in the refectory tried to squeeze her breast, in passing, and whispered a lewd jest into her ear as she twisted away from him. The old lay sister in charge, capped and kirtled, gave him a box on the ear and a sharp rebuke, invoking his mother by name. He fell back, grinning and holding his nose, as Fiametta dove into the chaotic, infant-squalling, vomitous sanctuary of the women's dormitory.

She flung herself down upon her pile of straw, and

burrowed her face into it, her teeth gritted against tears. A stick poked into her neck, and a flea jumped upon her sleeve and then into her hair before she could crush it. Turning over, she was elbowed by the girl next to her.

"Keep to your own side, blackamoor!" The girl's snarl was angry, but her pale face was furrowed with suppressed grief and fear. Strained with the waiting, along with the rest, to be murdered.

Fiametta almost set her hair afire with a word. She clamped her lips on the heat boiling off her tongue, and curled in a tight ball, trembling. *In the practice of magic,* Monreale had said, *you will be exposed to temptations that do not trouble the ignorant.* Indeed. Yet what of the spell embodied in her silver snake belt, still concealed under her velvet bodice? Its effect had been far from benign, though it fell short of lethal. Had her Papa allowed himself to be just a little bit damned after all, as the price of his magic? If he could do it, why couldn't she?

Mother Mary, keep me from harm. At Monreale's order Fiametta had prayed to the Virgin for patience, settling to the pavement in the chapel and arranging her skirts and gazing up earnestly at the serene white marble face of the statue holding the Child. Patience was apparently another one of those women's virtues, for she could not recall it as ever being one of Papa's. Fiametta's eyes fell now on that same velvet skirt, bunched in her fist, stained and tattered. *Mother Mary . . . Mama, who were you?*

This red dress was less faded than the fragmented images in Fiametta's mind of the woman who had first worn it. Her mother had died when Fiametta was eight, in Rome, of the fever that had carried off so many. A bad year, and August had been its worst month, with hard times upon them, Papa imprisoned in the Castel Sain' Angelo upon those deadly dangerous charges. . . .

Fiametta could not remember anything about her mother's death. Someone else must have been taking care of her for the sick woman. She held only a scrap-vision of following the cheap and simple bier through hot, stifling, smelly streets, dressed in stiff and uncomfortable clothes and holding some big woman's hand.

It bothered Fiametta that she could recall so little of Rome. Venice, now, she could picture clearly, even how Papa had taken her there perched upon the pack-horse. The excitement of the journey, the wonder and glitter and arrogance of the city . . . but there had been nothing of Mama in Venice. Fiametta had watched from her upstairs window as gaudily turbaned Moorish merchants were poled down the canal in their gondolas, or the occasional blackamoor slave of some great lord or lady, city-smooth and almost as proud as their masters, and once, the floating entourage of an Ethiopian ambassador. But none of these seemed to have any connection to Mama, the slim dark witch from Brindisi. . . . Fiametta was accustomed to thinking of her Papa as the powerful one, but Mama had been a sorceress too. Fiametta touched the lump of the snake belt. The silver work was Papa's, yes, but the original spell . . . ? *Was it Mama's? Yes. . . . Indeed?* The dark woman smiled at Fiametta over the shoulder of the beneficent white statue.

Mama, why did you give up your power to marry Papa?

I traded it for you, love, and never regretted the bargain. Magic is power, but children are life itself, without which there is neither magic nor any good thing. . . .

Papa regretted I was not a boy. Did you?

No, never. Fear not, Fiametta. The fullness of her power comes late to a woman. You must live your way to it, grow, and get more life . . . then all that was mine shall be yours, at the still center.

No. Not all the power had been Papa's, for he had circled that center as if swung on the end of an unbreakable silver cord. Till death had broken it. Fiametta's drifting calm was swallowed by panic. *But I need power now. Power, not patience. Mama. Mother Mary . . .*

The two faces, cool white marble, soft brown smiling flesh, fused together in a kind of maternal sisterhood. *You are my golden child. . . .*

Fiametta snapped awake at the wail of an infant, shocked at her fleeting dream, soggy with weariness, appalled anew at the noise. The edgy din in this crowded chamber would surely drive her mad. The light of the setting sun was knifing through the window slits on the western wall. Fiametta rolled back off the pallet and visited the latrine, which stank. Even there she was not alone. She eyed the dark squares of windows cut high in the wall for ventilation, just under the eaves, and wished they were larger. The other two women left. Another screaming argument started in the adjacent dormitory. Dizzy with tension, Fiametta reached high over her head and curled her hands around a dirty ledge, and heaved herself up and half through. She hung on her belly over the stone, and stared around.

The eaves of the leaded roof overhung these tiny windows like a tent, concealing them from outside view. Beams from the ceiling thrust out to meet the roof, making triangular braces. Far below Fiametta's nose, the monastery's outer wall met the ground, weedy, rocky, deserted. With difficulty, Fiametta wriggled her hips through the little window, and laid her body across the bridging beams. Narrow, precarious, but might it make a hiding place if the monastery were overrun by Losimons? Maybe, till the beams burnt and the roof collapsed.

But at least she was alone, the mind-numbing

uproar of the women's dormitory muffled to a blur of sound. She allowed herself to weep at last, though silently, lest some guard stationed on the roof above or the ground below overhear and investigate. Her tears dropped away and fell in the sunset light like molten gold in her Papa's shop falling into the basin of cold water to make the tiny round beads. The droplets puffed into the dust far below. The tears became pearls, then disappeared in the shadows as the light went. Her head and chest and belly ached with pent sobs.

Every dependency had betrayed her. Her trust had been mocked by one failure after another: Papa, Monreale, Thur . . . poor Thur. Drawn all unprepared into this. It was hardly his fault. . . . A large spider, making its web in a triangle to the west of Fiametta's head, dropped upon a strand of silk and bobbled a moment before reclimbing the thread, reminding Fiametta horribly of a man hanged. A blond young man, all blue-eyed and feckless and unlucky in love.

I could have fetched such a spider for Abbot Monreale, Fiametta decided. *So what if I'd had to touch it.* If only she had spoken up. Maybe it would have made the difference in the abbot's spell.

The spider sat upon its web, which was moving gently in some faint draft. The creature was fading to a black blot as the shadows deepened.

I'm only a puny girl. Somebody is supposed to save me. I'm not supposed to have to save myself.

Or them.

She could do nothing, clapped up in this stone pile of a monastery. Master mage or puny girl, demonstrably one had to get closer to the target. Risking the journey. Risking . . . what? Death? She risked that staying right here. Torment? Likewise.

Damnation?

Not a worry that stopped Ferrante, obviously, or even slowed Vitelli down. Nor their murdering bravos. *I'd fight those bastards with steel, if I were a man.* If she were a man, a priest would sprinkle holy water on her bloody sword and pronounce her forgiven before the bodies had cooled. But she wasn't a man, and she doubted she'd get ten paces with a sword in her hand. *Not man, but true mage.* And if God wanted to damn her for using the only strength He'd given her, that was God's choice.

Her belly filled with fires of resolution, in the gathering dark. She reached out and closed her hand over the faint suggestion of a spider hanging before her nose. It wriggled and tickled the flesh of her palm. There was more to a spell than pure will. There was focus, and the accumulation of power within symbolic structure.

"*Bene*," she whispered to the spider, "*forte.*" Barely able to see it, she squeezed its abdomen. Fine silver thread spun out from her hand, looping around a beam. She kicked her skirts free, and dropped upon the spider's thread toward the iron-hard ground. Her arm yanked up as the thread stretched, and held. She rotated, once, twice; her feet struck the ground with a thump, and she staggered for her lost balance.

The drop should have broken both her legs. Her impromptu spell had *worked.* She opened her right hand upon a gooey, crunchy, smeared blob.

Oh. I'm sorry, spider. A wave of nausea nearly overwhelmed her, and she rubbed her palm hastily upon the warm rough stone of the monastery wall to scrape off the remains.

Dizzied with the drop and the afterburn of magic along her nerves, it took her a moment to realize she was standing openly in the dusk against the wall, a clear target for any Losimon crossbowman sharp enough to have noticed the movement of her controlled fall. The spider thread, its enchantment consumed, had blown to dust upon the wind; she could not climb up it again. Nor make that poor squashed spider spin another. She dropped flat to the ground, panting. *Oh, God. Are You revenged for my pride already? Mother Mary!* But no quarrel hummed viciously above her head; no shouts rained down. Only the first croakings of frogs and the last twitterings of birds floated upon the cooling darkness. She waited several minutes, rigid with fear. The darkness deepened.

Now you've done it. You can't get back in. You have to go on. She wriggled around until she freed the silver snake belt concealed under her bodice, and wound it back openly around her waist. She took a breath, swung to a crouch, bundled up her skirts, and scurried toward the woods.

The shade was blacker, under the trees, but her footsteps crackled among the leaf litter, weeds, and sticks. She stepped as carefully as she could. If she could slip through the Losimon lines and reach the road to town—

She did not scream, when the dark man in soldier's leathers leapt upon her. It wasn't as if she weren't expecting something of the sort. Still her breath caught in her throat, and her heart pounded as he spun her around. "Ha!" he cried. "Got you!"

"No. I have you," she stated, then stopped, taken aback. Even in the dimness it was clear that the man was bald as a plate, and clean-shaved. But he wore a woolen shirt under his leather vest; she could smell the dried sweat in it. "*Piro,*" she said clearly.

His sleeves burst into flames, twining around his arms like orange flowers in the dark. Fey, she walked off into the wildly wavering torch shadows while he was still screaming and rolling on the ground. She didn't even run. His cries would bring his comrades to his aid; even now she could hear them crashing through the brush behind her. But not, she thought, after her. Few among the Losimon rank and file would be fool enough to chase an unknown sorceress through the dark fast enough to risk actually catching her. She strolled on awash in a kind of disconnected lassitude, very much like the times she'd drunk too much unwatered wine. She was without fear, and wanted to sleep. Her fingers felt thick as sausages; her legs felt like wood.

This woodlot to the south of the monastery featured a ravine which ran down to the lake, where the ground flattened out and the road crossed. She slipped and scrambled down the slope, scraping her hands on the rough tree bark to slow herself. She could feel stickiness from the blood, but her hands seemed numb to pain. At the bottom a nearly dry stream oozed slimy black around pale blotches of rocks. She picked her way among them.

She froze, crouching among some fallen logs, her white sleeves crossed under her breasts, when a couple of Losimon soldiers clanked past, swords drawn. Intent on the shouts echoing faintly from the vicinity of the monastery uphill, they ran by without seeing her. They must have been guarding the road, for when she reached the dusty track, a vague ribbon in the moonless dark, it was deserted. The lake lay like black silk.

She turned south and started walking home.

Chapter Fifteen

After an age, the reverberations of pain through Thur's body died away enough for him to uncurl from around his throbbing crotch and try to sit up. The north-facing window of the cell admitted no creeping patch of sunlight to mark the time, but the deep blue color of the bit of sky he could see suggested that the afternoon was waning. Gingerly, he put his hand to his swollen lips, touched loose-moving teeth, and winced. Sheer chance he had not bitten his tongue in half. His sides and back and kidneys ached from booted kicks, almost eclipsing the clamor of yesterday's sword cut broken open again. His red cap was gone, likewise his shoes. His knitted hose were torn, and unraveling badly. By pushing himself up sideways he got his back to the wall and his legs out in front of him. He looked around at last.

Lord Pia sat cross-legged upon a straw pallet, which had its own scrap of blanket. The castellan rocked gently back and forward, and nibbled at the blanket's corner in much the same absent way as a man might bite his fingernails. His red-rimmed eyes were fixed unblinkingly on Thur. His fine silk hose were all riddled and ruined too, Thur noticed with a sense of dreary fellowship.

"Who are you?" Lord Pia husked, not dropping his unnerving stare, nor ceasing his rocking.

"My name is Thur Ochs," Thur mumbled, muffled by his puffy mouth. "Brother to Captain Uri Ochs. I came seeking my brother, but Lord Ferrante has killed him." His tale sounded almost mechanical in his own ears, leaden, so often had he repeated it.

"Uri's brother? Truly?" Lord Pia's stare sharpened. "He spoke of a brother . . . I saw him die."

"He mentioned your name, from time to time, in his letters, Lord Pia," Thur ducked his head respectfully. Both men had been Sandrino's officers; they must have worked together daily.

"Uri was a good fellow," Lord Pia remarked, staring now into the middle distance. "Sometimes he helped me to catch bats, in the caves west of the lake. He was not afraid of the caves, after the mines, he said." He fingered the silver embroidery on his tunic, the glitter, Thur realized upon a closer look, of tiny bats ranked wingtip to wingtip edging collar and cuffs. Had Lady Pia stitched them?

"Oh?" said Thur neutrally, remembering how mention of the little flying animals had set Lord Pia off last night.

"A bat's the thing, you know. Clever creatures. I think a man might fly as a bat flies, without feathers, if he could but devise wings light enough, yet strong. . . . The leather was too heavy, even for Uri's sword and shield arms, next time I shall try parchment. . . . Do you know, bats eat the marsh mosquitoes that plague us? Their fur is very soft, like a mole's. And they can be trained not to bite the hand that feeds them. Unlike men." The castellan brooded. "To think that men dare to call them evil, only because they fly in the night, when men do murder in the broad day—the hypocrites!"

"They are God's creatures too, I am sure," Thur said warily.

"Ah! So good to find a man who is not prejudiced by idle superstitions."

"I often saw bats in the old mineshafts. They do no more harm than the kobolds."

"You are a miner, eh? So Uri said. Not afraid of the dark, either? Good fellow." The castellan brightened. Lord Pia's fellow-feeling for the bats seemed more enthusiastic than irrational, but for a certain skewed intensity of gaze when he spoke of them.

"I . . . saw Lady Pia earlier today," Thur offered, even more hesitantly. "She seemed unharmed. She stays bravely by the Duchess and Lady Julia. Ferrante is keeping them all together in the north gate-tower."

"My apartments," said Pia. "Ah." He tensed, blinking tears, and bit on his fingers, red gaze becoming withdrawn.

Thur's hands flexed together. Mad or not, the castellan had demonstrably escaped this cell twice before. "My brother," Thur began, and stopped at a creak of leather and a smothered belch. A Losimon guard sat just outside the cell on a bench against the far wall, watching them and listening. His left arm was bandaged, and his face bore week-old bruises, but a short sword hung at his belt. Thur's lips tightened. What the devil, let him get an earful. "My brother's body lies in a chamber just below this one," he continued more loudly. "Ferrante and Vitelli practice some terrible necromancy upon him. Magic black enough to burn for." Even louder, "Aye, and burn those who aid them, too!" He wasn't certain, in the dim light, but he thought the bandaged guard flinched. "They have also stolen the corpse of Prospero Beneforte, the master mage. They mean to enslave his spirit to a ring for Lord Ferrante."

"Ah," said Lord Pia distantly. "I have seen that chamber. So that's what they are about."

"You'll all burn!" Thur yelled out to the guard, then huddled back, coughing from the effort. He doubtless looked and sounded as mad as the castellan. He lowered his voice to a whisper. "Lord Pia, help me! They hold poor Uri's spirit through his body, and mean to drag him to some damnation. He is a prisoner, imperiled even in death. I have to . . . free him, somehow. And Master Beneforte, too."

"Ah," said the castellan, arching his brows. "Free. That's the trick of it, isn't it?"

Thur paused, confused. The castellan hunched a shoulder, turning away on his pallet, and resumed nibbling on his blanket and staring into space. *He is mad. This is useless.* Thur sighed. He added tentatively, "Abbot Monreale holds Lord Ascanio—Duke Ascanio—safe at Saint Jerome, for now, but they are besieged by Losimons." But to this Lord Pia made no response. ". . . Abbot Monreale enspelled some bats to be his spies, but I don't know if they have come this way."

"Ah!" said the castellan. "They are good and gentle creatures, don't you see, to so serve the holy abbot. Monreale knows." Lord Pia nodded sagely, and gnawed wool. Thur lay back down on the stone and throbbed awhile, despairing.

He was roused by steps and voices from the corridor. A couple of big Losimons loomed beyond the door, followed by Messer Vitelli in his red robe. Vitelli held a small green glass flask padded with woven straw. The little man stared through the bars at Thur, yawned, and sucked on his lower lip. "Go ahead," he directed, and stepped aside to let the prison sergeant unlock the door. The sergeant, one eye on the castellan, waited warily for the big bravos to enter the cell. But Lord Pia never even looked up at this invasion.

One of the bravos got behind Thur, and yanked him to a sitting position, his arms locked behind his back. Vitelli leaned against the wall, yawning as if his face would crack, then touched something under his robe. He shook his head like a dog shedding water. "Damn the man," he muttered, and straightened up, inhaling deeply.

The hairs stirred on the back of Thur's neck, as Vitelli's dark aura disturbed something subtler than his senses. There was neither heat nor flash, sound nor scent, yet it was as if an aroma of magic rippled Thur's belly, without first passing his nostrils. Vitelli was maintaining a spell, not invested and constrained and supported in some symbolic object, but held in his own liquid thoughts, a spell powerful and oppressive. And yet he was still able to walk and talk, smooth and ordinary. The impression faded even as Thur grasped at it, giving him hallucinatory vertigo. Maybe it was just another aftereffect from his beating. He squeezed his eyes shut, and blinked rapidly, and the dark aura receded to linger on only in Vitelli's dark eyes.

The man behind Thur grasped his lank blond hair and pulled his head back, and the second stepped forward to force a stick between his teeth and pinch his nostrils shut. Vitelli unstoppered his flask, and sloshed its contents into Thur's aching mouth. It was a sweet dark wine with a bitter undertaste. Thur choked and sputtered and bucked and gagged. And swallowed.

"Good." Vitelli stepped back, and turned his emptied bottle upside down. A last drop shivered on its lip, and fell like a starburst of blood upon the cell floor. "That should do it, even for so large a lout. Return in half an hour and cart him downstairs." He exited the cell, leaving his men to lock it; the dark distracted look spread out from his eyes across his face again as he turned away. Their scuffling footsteps faded again down the corridor, leaving only the sitting guard. Thur's head, sinking inexorably, met the cool stone.

The castellan's face came up, and he giggled, quite distinctly. His giggles became hoots, then high screams. He jumped to his feet. "A bat's the thing!" he cried, snatched up the slops bucket from the corner of the cell, and skipped around the little chamber. With a cunning grin, he stopped by the door, yanked off the bucket's lid, and flung the reeking urine upon the startled guard.

The guard came up off his bench with an outraged yell, unfortunately meeting rather than dodging the vile wash. The castellan leaned through the bars, his hands opening and closing, then danced backward as the soldier drew his blade and lunged at him. Lord Pia pounced upon the sword arm and wrested the blade away, and waved it in the air, striking sparks from the ceiling. Swearing and screaming for the prison sergeant to bring him the key, he was going to kill this madman despite all, the guard retreated up the corridor, brushing at his tunic in disgust and almost crying.

"Quickly." Lord Pia dropped the sword and turned to the swooning Thur, who had watched the whole performance from a numbing huddle on the floor. Strange patterns, like watered silk, swirled and wavered across his vision. Lord Pia slapped the slops bucket upright under Thur's nose, yanked his head back by the hair rather less gently than had the Losimon bravo, and thrust his thick and filthy fingers deep into Thur's throat. He kneed Thur's belly for good measure.

"That's it, boy, bring it all up," he crooned encouragingly, as Thur retched into the smelly bucket.

Thur didn't even need a second stimulus to empty his stomach altogether. The sickly sweet wine, bile, and poisonous acridity of the drug filled his mouth, and he spat wildly, eyes watering, nose running. Lord Pia turned his head, listening, then grabbed the bucket away to toss its revolting new load quite accurately and neatly through the bars of the outside window.

"Before they get back. Listen to me!" Lord Pia pulled Thur up by the hair again, hissing. Thur's eyes still swam with tears. "Lie still! Pretend it is yet working upon you. Go limp as a slug, don't cry out even if they stick an iron needle into your flesh, and they will carry you out of here themselves. Then *keep* pretending, till I call you to rise and strike! Do you hear? Do you understand?" His red eyes were fierce. Thur nodded dizzily. It took no effort at all to pretend to swoon; a dark haze fogged his brain. At least the numbness muffled the pain of his bruises and knocks. He wiped his lips on his sleeve, eliciting another. "Lie still!"

Lord Pia snatched up the sword and bounced from wall to wall, waving it and ululating, as the guard and the sergeant returned. The sergeant peered through the bars, looking very annoyed. "Stupid fool, to let him disarm you! Now how d'you think I'm supposed to get it back for you from a howling lunatic? Ha? Wait for him to cut his own throat? I ought to—" Both men jumped back as the castellan on his breathless circuit clattered the sword across the bars. The iron continued to ring faintly as he stopped, tilted his head cunningly, and blatted his lips in the direction of the Losimons. The guard, wild, grabbed for the sergeant's key ring, but the sergeant slapped him down. "Witless nit, I'll have you flogged if you don't obey orders. Here, you!" This last was directed at Lord Pia who, with a weird snicker, danced to the window and stuck the sword out through the bars, and let it go.

The guard yelled in incoherent rage, shaking the door bars, and the sergeant cuffed him. "Ninny! Go and get it. You can wash in the lake while you're down there. In fact, you'll have to, that steel will be sunk ten feet down at least. And don't take all day!"

"I'll get *him*," snarled the unhappy guard, but was driven off with a stream of vicious invective and personal abuse from the sergeant, who then stared at the castellan, shook his head, and plunked down on the bench in weary obedience to his orders to keep the elusive madman under continuous observation. Lord Pia, wheezing and sweating, gray hair disordered, flung himself back down upon his straw pallet and stared at the ceiling with empty eyes.

Vitelli's two big bravos came back before the disarmed guard returned. The castellan ignored them completely as they stopped by Thur. One kicked Thur in the belly, not viciously, just testing; Thur could not help flinching, but he let his eyes roll back, and he stayed limp. It wasn't that hard. Trying to stand up, *that* would have been hard.

Night was falling. The light from the window was a strange salmon-pink afterglow. The sergeant held up a lantern like a smoky gold animal eye in the growing shadows. One Losimon took Thur's shoulders, the other his feet. It was good to be carried. He felt waterlogged, every breath an effort. As he was hoisted up Thur let his glazed eyes pass across Lord Pia's, who lay on his side and stared back expressionlessly, his fingers tracing and trapping out an odd little rhythm on the stone floor, as formlessly compulsive as his blanket chewing.

Why am I going along with this madman's plan? If he even has one. But here he was, just as Lord Pia had forecast, being carried out of the cell. His porters bumped him down the narrow stone stairs in the black dark to the familiar under-level with its four doors.

Too much to hope they would just lock him in with the wine casks ... no. They lugged him through the door into the magic workroom.

"Leave him there," Vitelli waved in the general direction of the room's center. They dumped Thur down ungently.

"Is there anything else, Messer?" one of the soldiers asked, cautiously deferential.

"No. Go."

They did not linger to be told twice. Their bootsteps scuffed up the stairs in double time.

Thur lay sprawled, his face mashed to the floor, and let one eye slit open. Vitelli was turned away, lighting a few more bright beeswax candles to add to an already brilliant array. The little man had exchanged his red robe for a gown of sable velvet. Gold embroidery glittered here and there in its folds. Symbols? Magical, or merely decorative?

Lord Ferrante entered, swinging a small leather bag in a way that suggested it did not contain wildlife this time. The cut on his neck had been cleaned and stitched closed with silk threads of extraordinary fineness. He wore a clean shirt, unstained with blood, but had donned his chain tunic and sword belt again, and leggings of black leather. "Do you have everything?" he asked Vitelli.

"Did you bring the new bronze?"

"Yes." Ferrante let the bag twirl on its strings.

"Then we have everything."

Ferrante nodded, and bent to lock the door. He placed the big, iron key back in the pouch hung on his sword belt. Thur almost moaned aloud. How the hell was he supposed to get out of here this time? *Pretend, till I call on you to rise and strike.* How the hell did Lord Pia think he was going to get *in*?

"Stay," said Vitelli, as Ferrante started toward the

salt crates. "I must divest this damned awkward sleep spell into something that will hold it for a little."

"Can't you just let it go? Even bound, it must distract you."

"Not nearly as much as Monreale would distract me, should he recover quickly enough to interfere at some critical moment. And it is easier to maintain than it would ever be to recast. Prudence. And patience, my lord."

Ferrante grimaced, hitched a hip on the tabletop, and let one black-booted foot swing. He frowned down bleakly at the little footstool-chest, beside him, and shoved it away. After a moment he drew a slagged silver ring from his belt pouch, and turned it broodingly in his hand. His right hand was no longer bandaged, Thur realized, though it still looked red and barely half-healed.

"For all your troubles, Niccolo, Beneforte set the spirit of this ring free most readily. A wave of his hand. And none of your antics with the corpse or ring since have sufficed to call the power back."

"Yes, I've told you we must find Beneforte's hidden notes on spirit-magic. I have said it repeatedly."

"I think it was no bargain," said Ferrante quietly, "to trade my damnation for so brief and volatile a power." He closed his hand over his palm.

Vitelli, facing away from Ferrante, rolled his eyes up in exasperation, then carefully composed his features to proper deference, and turned. "We've been over this, my lord. The infant was sickly. Its mother lay dying. It would not have lived the night. Would you rather have let that death go to waste? What merit in that? And it was only a girl-child anyway."

Ferrante said dryly, "I would hardly have let you persuade me to do that to my son and heir, Niccolo, sickly or no." He blew out his breath. "I want no more such sickly girls. You're a magician, how do I assure a strong son next time?"

Vitelli shrugged. " 'Tis said a woman's part is to supply the matter, and the man's to supply the form with his seed. All things struggle toward the perfect form, the male, even as metals in the ground strive to grow to be gold; but many fail, and females thus result."

"Are you saying I should have added more form?" Ferrante's brows rose. "She was too sick. Vomiting all the time. Revolting. I had no heart to plague her. Besides, there were plenty of women in town."

"It's not your fault, I'm sure, my lord," said Vitelli placatingly.

Ferrante frowned. "Well, I want no child-bride next time. The pale and whimpering Julia is unfit to bear."

Vitelli said sharply, "With Julia comes a dukedom. Give her a little time."

"I hold the dukedom now by force of arms, or will, shortly," Ferrante shrugged. "What other right do I require? What other right would even avail, if I had no army?"

"True, lord, but the Sforza did both, in Milan."

"And left too many Visconti alive, who now skulk about half the courts of Italy, trying to brew trouble." Ferrante turned the ring in his hand, without looking at it, as if wondering if it sought some such subtle revenge.

Vitelli paused, and said slyly, "Give me the silver ring, my lord, and I will try to see if anything may yet be salvaged."

Ferrante smiled, not pleasantly. "No," he said softly, but very firmly. "It was fair and just that my dead daughter's spirit serve me. No other. I would not bind one of mine to serve a base-born Milanese . . . damned dabbler."

Vitelli bowed his head, his jaw tight. "As you will, my lord. There will be other opportunities. Better ones." He turned to clear a place on the boards to his other side, dusted it with a gray powder, and then wiped it clean. He then arrayed a simple spell-set; a tiny gold cross, facedown, and a gauzy silk cloth. His features sharpened in concentration; he began murmuring. After a few moments, the silk gauze rose in the air like the head of a questing snake, and settled gently over the cross. Vitelli's muttering died away. He took a deep decisive breath and turned to Ferrante. "Done. It will hold Monreale for—long enough."

"Shall I light the furnace, then?" asked Ferrante.

"No, I'll do that. Strip the Swiss spy of his clothes. I'll help you hoist his brother momentarily."

Ferrante tossed him his purse, which he caught one-handed. A little jeweler's furnace sat upon stone blocks near the window. Vitelli had already laid in the fuel. Now he bent to the lower hearth opening and whispered, *"Piro!"* Blue flames licked the pine and charcoal, which caught and burned steadily. Vitelli emptied the chinking contents of Ferrante's leather purse into a new clay firing pot no bigger than his fist, and popped it into the oven.

Thur bore being stripped, willing his limbs to flaccidity, his breathing to a deep slowness. Ferrante was quick and businesslike—had he practiced on corpses in the field of battle?—though truly there was little left to take, just the ruined red hose and the gray tunic. The floor was chill on Thur's bare skin. Did drugged men shiver? This play could not go on much longer. He must throw off his seeming sleep and strike soon, or die. Or strike and die. One last chance. He was being given one last chance to be a hero like Uri. . . .

Vitelli pumped the furnace bellows a few times, then turned to help Ferrante lift Uri's stiff gray corpse from its bed of salt and lay it out, faceup, on the floor near Thur. A few dislodged salt crystals fell and bounced, scattering across the stone with a muted glitter. Ferrante returned to arrange Thur facedown. And where the hell was the ghost of Master Beneforte while all this was going on? Indeed, if only Beneforte *were* lodged in hell, none of this would be happening. For a mad moment Thur wished him there with all his heart. No helpful dust-man rose from the floor now.

"Take over the bellows," said Vitelli to Ferrante. A tense edge to his voice warned Thur that the enspelling was about to start in earnest. Vitelli arranged three sticks of new chalk, green, black, and red, in a fan in his left hand, and stepped forward to crouch beside Uri. His Latin chant sounded almost like a prayer. Thur didn't think it was a prayer, at least no prayer to God. Vitelli took a clay ring mold from his robe, and set it on the floor midway between the quick and the dead. He placed a long-bladed and very shiny knife with a bone handle near Thur's head. What kind of bone? It was getting very, very hard to keep his eyes from focusing and tracking, and Vitelli kept glancing at him. . . .

Murmuring again, Vitelli began to trace his chalk diagrams upon the floor around the two brothers. Thur thought of the cat, and the cock. This floor had been well scrubbed since last night, and not, he suspected, by any servant, unless Vitelli employed a man with his tongue cut out. The bellows wheezed steadily; the fire's husky sound deepened.

"The devil—!" Ferrante ducked. A bat had flitted in through the window, and was circling the room in rapid, silent swoops, as a child might whirl a toy on a string. Vitelli, engaged in his chant and unable to stop, gave Ferrante and the bat both a glare. Ferrante drew his sword, and swung at the flying target, missing three times. He swore, and lunged after it.

Vitelli came to the end of a stanza, and drew breath

long enough to snarl, "It's only a bat. Leave it, damn it!" over his shoulder, then resumed chanting.

Ferrante grimaced, pausing, but on the bat's next circuit his sword licked up again. Only half-aimed, in a lucky blow it whacked the shadowy animal out of the air. A wing broken, the bat chittered across the stones and one of Vitelli's chalk-lines, smearing it.

Vitelli's teeth clenched. He broke off his chant. His words felt to Thur like a line of marching soldiers stumbling into each other as their leader stopped without warning. Vitelli opened his hands, and let the terrible tension leak away, before moving.

"Clumsy—!" he cried to Ferrante in real agony. "We'll have to start over. You get the sponge and mop these lines." Face working, he strode over and stamped on the injured bat, killing it. He picked the little corpse up by one wing, holding it delicately away from his robe, and flung it out the barred window.

Ferrante was clearly not pleased by this abrupt order to a menial task from his subordinate, but, stiff-faced, he obeyed. Out of his depth in this complex magicking, perhaps. He did a neat job, though, and within minutes the floor was dry and ready again. Vitelli picked up the ring mold and the knife and started anew.

This time he had Ferrante stand within the lines, by Thur, as he drew them. Thur kept one slitted, white eye on that bone-handled knife. He must reach for it before Ferrante did, come what may. He wished desperately he were in better shape. Could he even stand up, let alone fight? The miasma of magic in the room was so thick he could scarcely breathe, as if Vitelli's dark aura had expanded to the walls. Vitelli appeared in the corner of Thur's vision with a pair of tongs clasping the cherry-red clay cup holding the molten bronze. Sweat trickled in shiny tracks down his face. When he poured, the ring would freeze almost at once—trapping Uri's spirit? The chanting rose to a crescendo. Ferrante's leather leggings creaked, as he knelt behind Thur, awaiting his signal to take up the knife. Thur must strike *now*—a scrambling noise, and puffing, came from the window that faced the lake. Much too loud for a bat—

"Rise and kill the bastards!" Lord Pia roared.

Ferrante wheeled, and drew his sword. *Rise* was not quite the word for it, but Thur lurched forward in a sort of frog-flop, fell upon the knife, and rolled. The bone hilt, in his hand, sent a paralyzing jolt up Thur's right arm, not-quite-pain, shuddering along his nerves. His hand spasmed open, and the knife clattered across the floor out of sight under the trestles. The chalk lines burned his skin like whips as he pressed across them. Ferrante's sword struck sparks and a white scar on the stone where Thur had just lain.

Vitelli bent and choked convulsively. The tongs fell from his grasp. The clay cup cracked on impact, and its molten bronze spattered across the cold stone floor.

The castellan squeezed from the window and stood, hair waving, eyes alight. The guard's short sword was in his right hand, and an iron bar from the window was in his left. His legs were bare and hairy. His lips were drawn back in a feral snarl.

Reaching a trestle that held a salt crate, Thur at last pulled himself to his feet. His legs shook, but held him. Ferrante started to lunge at Lord Pia, stumbled across the chalk lines, and recovered just in time to parry Lord Pia's sword with his own blade, then catch the murderously swinging iron bar with an upflung arm. Ferrante stepped back, absorbing the shock of Pia's onslaught in a hastily ordered defense. Pia was a soldier, yes, and a match for Ferrante with the sword. But older, and fatter. Already his breath pumped like the bellows.

Vitelli was half-sprawled, half-kneeling by Uri, doing something to Uri's mouth. Thur staggered over to him, grasped him by the padded shoulders of his velvet gown, and heaved him into the wall. "Win or lose, you will not have my brother!" Thur meant it to be a defiant shout; it came out a croak. He grabbed Uri's rigid ankles, and dragged him toward the window.

He glanced out, surprising a kobold shadow-man who was drawing the last iron bar down into the solid stone, like sinking a spoon into porridge. The kobold grinned at him, and melted away after its prize. Thur heaved Uri up and stood, his joints cracking and popping like the mine timbers. He aimed his brother at the little square window and charged forward as if he were carrying a battering ram. His aim was good. The corpse shot through the narrow opening without catching or dragging, and arced into the night air. After a moment a great splash sounded below. Thur pushed himself back upright from the window ledge, and turned to seek his enemies.

Lord Pia was still engaged with Ferrante, their swords clanging like a couple of demented blacksmiths. Thur, mother-naked, bore nothing to attack a swordsman with. What about a black magician?

Vitelli had regained his feet, and started toward Lord Pia, muttering, his hands gesturing. With one hand Thur grabbed an iron candlestick, and with the other he swept the spell-set of gold cross and silk gauze from the tabletop. Vitelli yelped, stumbled, and turned toward Thur.

Thur swung, doing his very best to take Vitelli's head off with the first almighty blow; he did not think he'd get a second chance. Vitelli ducked, and Thur was twisted off-balance by his own momentum. He came around just in time to see Ferrante stab Lord Pia through his sword arm, nailing him to the oak door. Pia did not cry out. Ferrante left his own sword quivering in flesh and wood, and caught Lord Pia's short sword as it fell. Without a pause, he whirled and lunged at Thur.

Thur knocked the sword aside with the candlestick, once, twice; Ferrante pressed him swiftly across the chamber. Backing him into the furnace. Thur could feel the heat on his bare haunches. He sidestepped to put the window behind him instead. Ferrante had regained his balance, moving smoothly and confidently; he almost seemed to study Thur at his leisure. Vitelli, moving up behind Ferrante, pointed a finger at Thur and began to scream in Latin. His dark aura spun around his head like a cyclone.

Thur did not think he had better be standing there when this spell, whatever it was, arrived. At Ferrante's next thrust he swung his candlestick with all his remaining strength, and knocked the sword wide. Ferrante still covered himself with a knife, not the bone-handled one, that had somehow appeared in his left hand. Thur spun on his heel and dove through the window after Uri. His aim was not so clean this time. The rough sandstone shredded the skin of his shoulders and knees in passing. Then he found himself flailing in the dark air. *A man might fly as a bat flies, without feathers*—had the castellan flown down? Where the hell was the *water*—

He smashed into it belly-flat. After the suffocating heat of the magic chamber, the cold was confounding. It closed over his head, and stopped his breath. He fought his way through a wash of tickling bubbles to the surface, and gasped for air. Cold but clean. It seemed to flush the dizzying sickly drug-torpor from his limbs at last. Thur kicked and turned about, trying to reorient himself.

The night was moonless, the stars muffled by haze. Fog tendrils steamed from the lake's surface, obscuring what vision was left. Against a looming black bulk, Thur made out a few dim gold blobs of candlelight, the cliff face with its windows and the castle wall, above. He had to get away from that. He paddled as silently as he could in the opposite direction, just his eyes and nose breaking the surface of the dark and quiet water. He bumped into a floating log.

No. Not a log. It was Uri's body. Somehow, in the frantic fight, Thur had imagined it sinking beyond Vitelli's reach, but it was quite buoyant. He tried to push it under, but it popped back up. Any Losimon with a rowboat could pick it off the surface of the lake tomorrow morning, and return it to Vitelli, and all this would be for nothing.

No, not nothing. Not nothing. But not enough. He had regained Uri only to lose Lord Pia. Mad, perhaps, but clever and bold ... as Abbot Monreale was holy, Duchess Letitia defiant, Ascanio innocent, and Fiametta ... Fiametta ... and all, all, sacrifices to Ferrante's towering self-conceit, his *fame*. What gave Ferrante the right to ride over all those lives?

Right has nothing to do with it. He fights to survive. And the more he drifts into wrong, the harder he will fight. Must fight. So spoke reason. Reason was no practical help.

Thur was drifting, too. He began to shiver as the chill lake water drew the heat from his body. At least it wasn't as killing-cold as the water in the mine. Would Uri become waterlogged, and start to sink or rot? Uncertainly, Thur began to kick, propelling himself and his brother log gently along. He was no longer sure where the shore was. No lights or lanterns shone bright enough to pierce the mist. But he achieved, after a little experiment, a sort of equilibrium, kicking just fast enough to keep warm, just slowly enough not to outpace his breath. He felt he might keep it up for hours. But then what?

By the time he bumped into the quay, he knew neither how far he had come nor how long he had been about it. He felt like he had paddled halfway to Cecchino. A town loomed beyond the steps and docks and pebbled beach. The stones bit his naked feet as he rose dripping and the water no longer supported his weight. He dragged Uri along horizontally as far as possible, then pulled him ashore like a fish. He was almost as slippery as one. Thur stood, his legs trembling, and stared into the dark tinged here and there with some faint illumination escaping through a closed shutter. Big buildings, too big for any village. A dog barked twice, and stopped. What town . . . ?

Damn. It was only Montefoglia. *Still* Montefoglia. Had he been swimming in circles? Quite possibly. He stared up and down the shoreline, mentally placing landmarks he could not now see with his eyes. To his right, the castle hill, to his left, the big docks, the lower walls, and the high outer town wall at the very end that ran right down into the harbor. Ahead lay narrow, winding streets, dark and strange. Well, they couldn't be any stranger than what he'd just escaped.

He stood a moment in indecision, water lapping his ankles. Where should he be trying to go, anyway? He had to hide Uri. He wanted . . . he wanted to talk to Fiametta. He wanted to find Fiametta, yes. Reason therefore said he ought to paddle back out into the lake and swim to Saint Jerome. He emptied his mind of reason, knelt, got Uri up on his shoulder, grunted to his feet, and started walking.

Up stone steps from the quay. His feet banged down hard with their doubled weight. Guards? There ought to be a guard—*there*. Thur ducked into the nearest alley as a man with a lantern appeared near the quay. An old man, a town watchman, not a Losimon. Thur walked on without looking back, placing his bare feet carefully in the dark. But suppose he did meet some urban danger in these passageways? He had a sudden picture of himself, a naked Swiss madman carrying a corpse. . . . Well, he had nothing to attract a robber, certainly.

Turn here. Turn there. Where the devil was he going? He would *not* go back to the castle, no matter how his sixth sense clamored. He stumbled over a blanketed lump in the alley, which gave a muffled cry; Thur, burdened, barely saved himself from landing hard enough to shatter his kneecaps on the cobbles.

"Damn it! No, be quiet. I won't hurt you. Forget you saw me! Go back to sleep," said Thur, panicked at the thought of an outcry.

"Thur?" said a familiar youthful voice. "Is that you?"

"*Tich?*" Thur stopped, stunned. "What are you doing here?"

"Why, you're all naked!" Pico's elder boy scrambled to his feet, his face a white smudge in the dimness. "What are you carrying?"

"Uri. My brother. You've met Uri, haven't you?" said Thur dizzily.

"It's a corpse," said Tich in horror, after a verifying touch.

"Yes. I stole him back from Ferrante's black magician. Why are you here?"

"Thur, those thieving Losimons—they killed my father and Zilio! They cut his throat like a dog—" His voice grew louder in his excitement—it had been a couple of days since he'd met any man he dared called friend, Thur guessed.

"Sh! Sh. I know. I saw your father's mules yesterday, when they brought them to the castle."

"Yes, I followed them. And they're *my* mules now. I want them back. I want to kill the bastards! I've been trying to figure out how to get into the castle."

"Sh, no. That accursed castle is no place to try to get into. I barely got out with my life tonight."

"Where are you going?" asked Tich, sounding quite as bewildered as Thur felt.

"I'm . . . not sure. But I cannot stand naked in the street till the dawn finds me!"

"You can have my blanket," Tich offered immediately, though in a rather dubious tone.

"Thanks." Thur wrapped it about himself, and suddenly felt much better, and not just for the warmth. "I . . . Look, I hate to take your only blanket. Why don't you come along with me?"

"But where are you going?" Tich repeated.

"To . . . a house in town that I know." The vision of Fiametta's home came clearly as he spoke the words aloud, finally unconfused by the overlapping call of . . . Tich? Yes. It was no accident, that he'd stumbled over Tich in the dark, any more than when he'd stumbled over little lost Helga in the snow. But he knew where he was going now. "There's no one home. Except maybe a Losimon guard," Thur added in sudden doubt. Maybe reason ought to prevail, just this once. . . .

"I have a dagger," said Tich. "If he's a Losimon, I'll kill him for you!"

"I . . . We'll see. It may not be necessary. Let's just get there first, eh? Um . . ."

"I'll . . . take his feet," said Tich reluctantly.

"Thanks."

Thur realized he was going to have to give up the blanket again. Awkwardly, they slung Uri between them, and walked on, not talking except for a few whispered directions from Thur. "Turn here. Down this street . . . right. Up this slope. We're almost there. . . ."

"Quiet neighborhood," Tich commented. "The houses are like forts."

The familiar walls of Master Beneforte's—Fiametta's—house rose up at last. There was the marble-arched oak door, glimmering even in the dark. No lights shone. It was surely both locked and guarded.

They set their burden down, and Thur borrowed the blanket back.

"How do we get in?" whispered Tich.

Thur was not sure he could even climb into bed at this point, let alone climb a wall. He stepped forward, and knocked on the door.

"Are you mad? You said it would be guarded!" hissed Tich.

Yes, he might be a little mad by now. But it wouldn't do to tell Tich so. Thur only knew he was very, very tired. "So, if there is a guard, this will bring him to us. Then you can kill him," Thur promised. He knocked again, and propped Uri's body up beside him, supporting him with a brotherly arm over his cold and waxy shoulder. He waited for the guard to greet them. And vice versa. He knocked again, harder.

At length came the sound of the bar being drawn back, and the snick of a bolt. Tich tensed, his hand clenching and unclenching on his drawn dagger. The door swung open.

Fiametta stood holding a lantern in one hand and a long kitchen knife in the other. She was still wearing her red velvet dress, missing its outer sleeves. She stepped back a half-pace, and her eyes widened as she played the lantern light over her visitors. Thur felt doubly grateful for Tich's dirty blanket, now wrapped like a skirt about his waist.

Fiametta looked back and forth between the two brothers. "Dear God, Thur. How do you tell which of you is the corpse?"

"Uri is better looking," Thur decided, after a moment's serious thought.

"I fear you're right. Come in. Come in. Get out of the street." Fiametta waved them urgently inside.

Chapter Sixteen

"What did you do to the guards?" Thur asked, staring blearily around the darkened entry-hall. He and Tich laid Uri down upon the flagstones as Fiametta locked and barred the door again behind them.

"Guard," Fiametta corrected, turning. "There was only one. He's locked in the root cellar under the kitchen, right now. I hope he's drinking himself senseless. I wasn't able to get his sword away from him." She glanced curiously at Tich.

"Did you magic him down there?" asked Thur, impressed. Tich's brows rose. "Oh," said Thur. "I'm sorry. This is Tich Pico. Don't you remember him from Catti's inn? The muleteer's son. A gang of Ferrante's bravos killed his father and brother, and stole his mules. Tich, this is Fiametta Beneforte. Her father was the master mage Catti smoked. This is his house. Was his house."

"Yes, I do remember seeing you," said Fiametta.

"We have a thing in common against Ferrante, then. All of us."

"Yes, Madonna Beneforte," Tich nodded. "Do you want me to kill that Losimon in the cellar for you?"

"I don't know. But he has to be better secured; I'm afraid he'll get out. Oh, Thur, I'm so *glad* you're here!" She flung her arms around him and hugged him.

Thur blushed with pleasure and grunted with pain. "Are you really?" he said, feeling suddenly shy.

"Did I hurt—oh, what a horrible gash! It should be closed and bandaged at once! You look terrible." She jumped back, but he managed to retain a clasp on her warm hands. He was still chilled from the lake and the night air. But he had to let go as his blanket slipped down further, to catch and clutch it to himself for decency. Fiametta paused in sudden puzzlement. "But *why* are you here?"

"I wanted to find you."

"But how did you know to come here? I wasn't sure I could get here myself, till an hour ago. Do you think . . . Is it still my ring?" She touched her chest. Yes, the ring hung there, under her linen and velvet, Thur was sure of it. But he had not thought about the ring.

He shook his head. "I don't know. This house was the only place I knew of in Montefoglia to hide. I mean, I knew—I felt this was how to find you. But I don't know how I knew. I'm good at finding things. Always have been. Lately, I've been getting better at it. I found Uri. . . ."

"It *is* a talent. It must be. Uri did right to apprentice you to my father. Oh, if only he had lived!" She rubbed her eyes, smeared wet with anger, weariness, and grief.

Hurriedly, Thur launched into a brief tangled account of his sojourn in Montefoglia's castle, culminating in his escape with Uri's body. Tich listened openmouthed; Fiametta's teeth clenched.

"We knew you were taken, this afternoon. Before he destroyed the last ear Vitelli used it to tell Monreale he was going to put you to death," she said. "I thought he meant to hang you. I didn't imagine anything so evil."

"But—how did you come to leave Saint Jerome?" asked Thur.

Her brows rose quizzically. "I was looking for you. I was going to save you from being hanged. I hadn't figured out how, yet. I thought they would do it at dawn."

A slow grin pulled up the corners of his mouth.

"Well, nobody *else* was willing to try—oh, dear." Strange thumping noises echoing distantly through the house interrupted her. "I think that guard is trying to get out. Come on." She picked up the lantern and led the way through the courtyard into the kitchen. Thur limped after, Tich bringing up the rear.

The wide polished boards flooring half the kitchen jumped as something hard struck them from below. The guard's head, Thur thought dizzily. Obscene curses drifted up, not quite muffled enough, as the Losimon heard their footsteps. After a moment, a sword blade thrust up through a thin gap between two boards, questing blindly for a target. Thur glanced down to make sure he was standing on the tiles.

"How did you get him down there?" Tich asked, also stepping cautiously around the wood.

"Not magic," said Fiametta. She lit a candle stub stuck in a bottle on the kitchen table from the lantern flame. "I was going to use magic. I was going to set him on fire. It's the only spell I know that I can work entirely in my head, without any material symbols to hold it. It's a talent. But when he came to answer the door, I thought I'd better get inside, first. So I told him I lived here, and I'd come back to see if any of my clothes were left. But then the talk went . . .

strange. He just let me in, and said he'd help me look for my dresses, if I'd let him . . . do things, to me."

Letting Tich kill the Losimon seemed suddenly a much better idea, to Thur. He set his teeth, then unset them again immediately as the loose ones twinged.

"I told him . . . well, I told him all right." Her hand touched the head of a striking silver snake belt looped around her waist. "But I told him there was a wine cask my father had hidden in the root cellar, behind the turnips, a special vintage. There really was one, you see. It might even still be there. When he went down to look, I clapped the trapdoor closed, and dragged the pewter cupboard across it." She nodded toward the large painted cupboard pulled out from the wall. "He almost pushed it up enough to get his fingers out, but then I jumped up and down on it. And then you came. I thought, if it didn't hold him, I must set his hair on fire—at least he *has* hair—and then try to stab him." She paused, as the sword thrust up again. "I could still set him afire. And *you* could stab him," she offered to Tich.

Thur, remembering his experiences with Ferrante, shuddered at the thought of little Fiametta attempting hand-to-hand combat with an infuriated Losimon veteran. "Just . . . wait a minute," he said. He borrowed the lantern and hobbled back to the courtyard. He recalled glimpsing . . . yes, there in a pile of tools beneath the gallery rested a good-sized sledgehammer. He carted it back to the kitchen. "At least let's get his sword away from him first."

For bait, he walked out on the floorboards, taking care not to step on a crack. Sure enough, the sword blade and curses came up through the slit again just in front of him. He raised the sledgehammer, familiar in his hands, to his side and swung it down hard. It clanged off the swordblade, and Thur almost toppled. He clutched again at his slipping blanket, and, light-headed from the effort, handed the hammer off to Tich, who caught on at once. Enthusiastically, he whacked at the bent blade as the Losimon tried futilely to withdraw it. On the third blow, the metal broke. A crash from below, and more curses, as the Losimon fell backwards.

"Why, Thur. That was *clever*," said Fiametta, sounding rather astonished. Thur's brow wrinkled. A little less astonishment would have been a little more complimentary.

"Now we're even," Tich grinned breathlessly, waving his dagger. "Let's get him."

"Wait," said Thur. "What do you have around here to bind him?"

Fiametta bit her lip in thought. "If they haven't taken it—it was only iron, not silver or gold, maybe they left—just a moment." She scurried out with the lantern. The Losimon stopped thumping. Fiametta returned in a few minutes, draped about with a long iron chain.

"It's a manacle my father was working on for the Duke. It doesn't have a key. It opens with a spell."

"Do you know the spell?" asked Thur.

"Well . . . no. I know where it is in Papa's notebooks, but Ferrante and Vitelli have taken all Papa's notebooks away."

"But do you need the spell to lock them?"

"No, they just lock. That's built-in."

Thur regarded the handcuffs, then stepped to the door to glance into the courtyard with its pillared stone arches supporting the wooden inner gallery. "All right." He returned to the kitchen to shout down through the floorboards, "Hey! You! Losimon!"

A surly silence resulted.

"There are two armed men—" his hand closed on the haft of the sledgehammer, "—and a very angry sorceress up here. She wants to set you on fire. If you come up and surrender without giving us any more trouble, I won't let them kill you."

A man's gruff voice responded, "How do I know you won't just tie me up and kill me?"

"My word," suggested Thur.

"What worth is that?"

"More than yours. *I* am not a Losimon," Thur snarled.

A long silence, as the Losimon crouching in the dark contemplated his options. "Lord Ferrante will have my head for failing him."

"Maybe you can desert, later."

The Losimon made an obscene suggestion, which Thur ignored.

Thur whispered to Fiametta, "Do you think you could, like, just warm him up a bit? Not really set him on fire. But demonstrate."

"I'll try." She closed her eyes; her soft lips moved.

A cry, and slapping noises, echoed from the cellar. "All right! All right! I surrender!"

Thur let Tich and Fiametta drag the pewter cupboard off the trapdoor, and stood with his sledgehammer raised. Slowly, the trapdoor creaked upward, and the Losimon cautiously poked his head out. He was a grizzled man, strong but no youth. Little red sparks still glinted in his curling hair, which gave off a singed stench. He did not bother to carry his broken sword hilt, but crawled out and stood empty-handed.

Thur had Tich clap one end of the manacle around the man's wrist and lead him to the courtyard, where he wrapped the chain around a stone pillar and attached the other cuff. Thur did not put down the sledgehammer until Tich yanked the chain to be sure the cuffs would hold, mashing the Losimon against the pillar. Tich put one foot to the pillar and held the man while Fiametta gagged him. He rolled his eyes at the sledgehammer, and did not attempt violence against the girl.

Fiametta led them back to the kitchen. "Here, sit on this chair," she said to Thur. "Ruberta had a healing salve for bruises. Oh, your sides look like a piebald horse. Are any ribs broken?"

"I don't think so, or I wouldn't have been able to get this far." Thur settled himself very cautiously.

Fiametta rummaged in the cupboards. Her voice wafted out, "That ugly gash won't heal unless the edges are held together. At least it looks clean. I'm no healer, but I know my needlework. If . . . if I can stand to sew it up, can you stand to let me?"

Thur choked down an anticipatory whimper. "Yes."

"Ah. Here's the ointment." She emerged from the recesses of a carved sideboard clutching a Venetian glass jar. A pale cream inside emitted a faint, pleasant scent, like wildflowers and fresh butter. Delicately, she daubed some upon Thur's ribs. A warm, relaxing numbness penetrated from the spots where she spread it. "I'll go get my sewing kit, if the Losimons haven't taken it." She set the jar down and hurried from the kitchen.

Surreptitiously, Thur scooped up a large glob of ointment and stuck his hand under his blanket to rub it on and around his aching, swollen crotch. It helped a lot, and Thur sighed relief.

"You should have gotten *her* to rub it on there," Tich snickered, settling cross-legged on the floor.

"That might have done . . . more harm than good," Thur grunted, charmed by the idea but offended by Tich having suggested it. Hell, he hadn't even kissed Fiametta yet, hadn't even tried to. He remembered his deep regrets about that, when he'd been facing death in the castle. "God, I hurt all over."

Fiametta returned in a few minutes carrying a small covered basket. "We're in luck. I found the curved needle Ruberta uses to sew up the stuffed goose when she roasts one."

"Sounds perfect," said Tich, his brows going up in black amusement.

Thur decided his lips hurt too much to smile.

"I think you'd better lie flat on the kitchen table," Fiametta directed.

"Just like the goose," Tich commented. Fiametta grimaced at him, half-amused, half-annoyed, and he subsided.

Thur climbed up and arranged himself while Fiametta threaded her needle. She studied the two stitches at one edge of the gash surviving from Ferrante's surgeon's work. "Yes. I can do that." Her lower lip stuck out in determination. She took a deep breath and made her first jab.

Thur sucked in his breath, gripped the table edges, and stared at the ceiling.

"Do you think anyone is going to come around and check on that guard?" Tich asked, standing up to watch. Fiametta shoved a candle into his hand to light her work.

"Not before morning," said Fiametta, tying a knot. She was neat, but much slower than Ferrante's surgeon.

"Maybe not at all," Thur managed in a strained voice. "They're undermanned, and this house has been stripped of valuables. Except Vitelli might come around to search it again. He's convinced—ah!—"

"Sorry."

"Keep going. He's convinced your father has hidden some secret notes or books on spirit-magic somewhere in the house. That's how I met them here day before yesterday."

"Secret books?" Fiametta frowned deeply. "Papa? Well . . . maybe."

"Do you know of any such?"

"No . . . if so, he's kept them secret from me."

Thur stared at the kitchen ceiling through eyes watering with pain. "I think they do exist. I think they're . . . *up*, somewhere. I felt it, when Vitelli had me trying to pry up boards. I didn't tell—ah!—Vitelli, of course."

Fiametta's eyebrows lowered in concentration. "Up. Huh." She tied off another stitch and glanced at the ceiling. Half done. Slow but sure. Slow, anyway.

"Vitelli wants them very badly. I'm certain he'll be back," gasped Thur. "But maybe not as early as tomorrow. He looked pretty sick, when I broke up his spell."

"That close to completion . . . so complex. . . ." Fiametta nodded thoughtfully. "I'll bet he's sick right now."

Silence fell as she worked her way meticulously across Thur's belly cut. The last one, at last. *Pale* was not in Fiametta's repertoire, but there was a distinctly greenish tinge beneath her toasted skin. She pursed her lips and rubbed a goodly handful of ointment across the cut, before sitting Thur up and tying a protective strip of cloth that looked suspiciously like a bit of former petticoat around his waist.

"That's . . . that's good," Thur wheezed gallantly. "Better than the surgeon."

A pleased smile curved her full lips. "Really?"

"Yes." He swung his legs off the table and stood up. Pink and black clouds boiled at the edges of his vision, and the room tilted. He found himself bent over, clutching the table.

"Tich, help!" Fiametta rushed to Thur's side; he waved her away, afraid he would crush her if he fell, but she ignored the wave and put her shoulder sturdily up under his arm. "You are going straight to bed," she decreed. "I'll put you in Ruberta's room; it's right off the kitchen here. It's the only bed the Losimons didn't break up looking for hidden treasure. Tich, the lantern."

By the time Thur's head had cleared they had maneuvered him into the housekeeper's bedchamber. "No!" he protested. "Your father's secret books, Fiametta. We've got to find them, to keep them from Vitelli. I'm sure it's important. I have to help you look."

"You have to lie down here." Fiametta pulled back blankets on the first real bed Thur had seen in weeks. It had linen sheets.

"Oh," murmured Thur, overcome. The bed seemed to suck him down. It was a little short, but wonderfully soft. Fiametta pulled the coverings over him and whisked Tich's blanket out from under them in one smooth movement. She gave the blanket back to its owner.

"But the notebooks," Thur said weakly.

"I'll look for them," Fiametta said.

"They were up. Above the second floor."

"This house only has two floors, doesn't it?" Tich craned his neck as though he might see through the ceiling.

"I have an idea or two," said Fiametta. "Go to sleep, Thur, or you'll be useless."

Persuaded, Thur sank back. Fiametta and Tich tiptoed out. Thur was weary beyond anything he'd ever known, but disorderly images from the past few days whirled in his thoughts. He'd rescued Uri, but Master Beneforte still lay in danger. The Duchess. Lady Pia. Lord Pia, with his strange passion for bats, stuck to the oak door with his blood running down. Vitelli's dark aura, growing in menace and power. . . .

But in a few minutes Fiametta returned, carrying a large clay mug. She set the lantern down as Thur, with difficulty, sat up.

"Have you eaten? I didn't think so. There's no food in the house right now but some flour and dried beans, and tired turnips, but I found that wine. Here." She sat on the edge of the bed and helped him get his hands around the mug.

She'd brought it unwatered. It was thick, red, dense, a little sweet. Thur gulped it down gratefully.

"That helps. Thank you. I was starving."

"You were shaking." She watched him with concern.

He watched her in return, over the rim of the mug. Their lives had been tangled together by this treachery in Montefoglia, and by the peculiar prophecy of her lion ring. Was the Master of Cluny's spell meant to be a prophecy of the self-fulfilling kind? Thur had been at first struck by Fiametta's prettiness, amiably inclined to love anybody who even suggested that she loved him. Yet now he was not so sure that she did love him, despite the ring. What *did* she think? He was uneasily aware that he had not more than half-won her mind. It was all so complicated. She was a complicated girl. Would life with Fiametta always be this confusing? He was beginning to suspect so.

He remembered staring up the length of Ferrante's shining sword, in the castle garden. Now, *that* had been simple.

Awkwardly, he slipped his free hand around Fiametta's waist, leaned forward, and kissed her. Their noses bumped, and he half-missed her mouth. Her big brown eyes widened, and he waited in resignation for her recoil.

Instead she kissed him back. Vigorously. And she managed to hit the target square. His arm tightened joyously around her shoulders. Her hand closed firmly over the silver head of her snake-belt. It felt strange, kissing through a bruised grin. When he broke off, her eyes were alight. *I did something right!* Thur thought in delight. *I wonder what it was?*

But before he could explore further, she jumped up. Considering his battered physical condition, this was perhaps just as well. She bent over and dropped a kiss on his forehead. "Go to *sleep*, Thur."

At least she left still smiling, a mysterious girl smile. Thur lay back. This time, sleep came almost simultaneously with the darkness.

He woke to an uncertain gray daylight seeping through the room's half-opened shutters. Creakily, he sat up. He hadn't been this sore since the day after the cave-in and flood at the mine. But he felt much better than last night. The sick dizziness was gone from his head. Still, he decided, another handful of that ointment would be welcome. He swung his bare legs out of the little bed.

At least he wasn't going to have to wear the quilt. Laid across the bed were clothes, of a sort, a threadbare man's gown of time-softened dark wool. Thur slipped it on over his head. It had clearly been made for a smaller fellow, probably Prospero Beneforte, for the hem, meant to brush the floor in a dignified scholarly sweep, rode at Thur's calves, and the sleeves wouldn't fit over his arms at all. He left the sleeves on the bed and tied a bit of cord around his waist to make a sort of tunic. He peeked out the window into the walled garden behind the house. Yes, there was the outhouse. The grayness of the sky was not dawn after all, but a steely midmorning haze. Had he slept too long? Worried, he walked into the kitchen, and stopped short.

A strange woman wearing a cap and apron and holding a wooden spoon turned from the blue-tiled stove to glance at him without surprise. "Ah. The young man." She gave him a cordial but measuring nod, as if he were a bolt of cloth she was considering purchasing, but was doubtful of the fastness of his dye. She was sturdy rather than stout, of middle years.

"Er," said Thur.

"The porridge will be a few moments yet." She pointed with her spoon to a black iron pot atop the stove. "There'll be a dried apple tart sweetened with honey, after. A lot of tart, not much apple, but one must make do. And I brew a posset of herbs that's better to drink in the morning than that strong red wine, which is all we have in the house. There is no ale." She nodded firmly, and bent to tease open the iron door to the stove's firebox with her spoon handle, and poke briefly at the coals.

Thur's mouth watered; the odors were delectable.

"You'll be wanting the outhouse first, I expect. Right out there." She waved the spoon vaguely toward an iron-bound door that led into the garden.

"Yes, I was heading there, uh, ma'am." Thur paused. "My name is Thur Ochs."

"Poor Captain Uri's brother from Bruinwald, yes, I know."

"Are you by chance Ruberta?"

"The Master's housekeeper, yes. Or so I was, before those thieving, murdering Losimons broke in upon us." She frowned tensely. "Crime upon crime . . . Prospero Beneforte was not an easy man to work for, but he was a great man, not another like him in Montefoglia. Run along now. When you get back wash your hands in that basin yonder and go fetch Fiametta to eat."

"Where is . . . Madonna Beneforte?"

"Somewhere about the house, trying to find what of her Papa's tools those cursed robbers somehow overlooked."

Thur did as he was told, returning through the kitchen to the courtyard. Their prisoner lay on a blanket, ungagged but asleep, a cheap wineskin clutched to his chest. Not the good red wine, Thur guessed. Someone had been out foraging since last night. Fiametta, probably. She must have fetched Ruberta. Thur hoped she'd had the sense to take Tich with her for protection. Not that a boy with a knife would be much help against swordsmen.

He stepped onto the flagstones in the entryway. Uri was not there. He glanced into the room on his right, which had its own fireplace in the corner, and rugs and chairs, clearly where important guests or clients were received. A sheeted shape lay upon a makeshift bier of boards laid across two trestles. Thur sighed, entered, and lifted the sheet to look upon his brother and, frankly, to check for rot. He was touched when he discovered that Uri had been decently dressed, in more of Prospero Beneforte's leftovers, knit hose, a shirt, a short tunic, not new or fine—or the soldiers would have taken them—but arrayed with care. The women's work, no doubt. Vitelli's preservation spell appeared to be holding. He covered his brother again, and crossed the hall to check the workroom opposite.

Fiametta sat perched on a high stool, her elbows planted on the worktable. She had not taken time to change her own clothes, but still wore her ruined velvet with the outer sleeves lost. Thur wondered if she'd taken time to sleep. Open upon the table in front of her was a large leather-bound book, and scattered in a circle about it was a litter of papers and parchments. She was frowning fiercely as she read.

She looked up at the sound of his footsteps. "Thur. You were right. I found them." Her face was haggard.

"Where?" He came to her side.

"Did you notice the little corner room with the two windows, off Papa's bedroom, that he had fixed for a study?"

"Yes. Vitelli did, too. He had it stripped out. I—the feeling was very strong in there, so I made sure not to look very hard."

"The ceiling is covered with squares of wood with rosettes carved in the centers."

"We tapped them all. They all sounded solid. We

even pried a couple down, then I persuaded the Losimon guard that they were all the same."

"If you'd pried them all down, you would have
found it. If you turn one of the rosettes, it releases a
latch, and a square comes down—it's the bottom of a
box. Not a very big box. It was crammed with all this.
No wonder it sounded solid." Her hand opened to
wave at the papers. "Papa would have been in serious
trouble if these had ever been found."

Thur cleared his throat. "A burning matter?"

"Not . . . quite, I think. Depending on the preju-
dices against Florentines of the Inquisitor. But enough
to endanger his license and his livelihood. There are
recipes for spells . . . records of experiments . . . jour-
nal entries about two night trips to graveyards, though
the results seem not to have been satisfactory. There
is a complete account of what I take to be the casting
of the great spirit ring for the lord of the Medici, with
a record of payments, though there are no names, just
initials. But the dates match the last time Papa lived
in Florence. Dangerous evidence against men who yet
live. Papa seems to have done some things with animals that were . . . most questionable. Not just rings.
Far beyond rings! My poor bunny—here," she opened
to a page in the book densely scrawled with Latin, "is
an account of how he invested the spirit of one of my
rabbits, to animate a brass hare he cast. Its nose
twitched, it moved—" Her finger stopped at a line,
and she translated, " 'It hopped upon my worktable
for a quarter of an hour before its spirit was consumed
and my spell failed. The stiffness of the cooling brass
seemed to tire it more quickly. Next time I shall
attempt to keep the casting hot to improve fluidity.'
Dear God, Thur, it's incredible! And he never so much
as let on—I mean, this very table! And we must have
eaten that same rabbit for stew, after! And I remember
the exquisite detail of that brass hare—it sat upon his

windowsill for a year and a half, until the Losimons looted it." Horror, pride, and exasperation mingled in her face. Her hand pressed possessively upon the notebook, whether to contain or retain it Thur was not entirely certain.

"What should we do with these notes, then? Turn them over to the Abbot? Your father is beyond earthly prosecution, I think."

"If we can. If we all live. I—there are things here— there is a lifetime's thought and work bound up in these pages. I could not bear to see them destroyed, but—Thur, the possibilities are horrid. Vitelli would not limit himself to rabbits! Suppose he decided to make an army of brass soldiers, spirit slaves? Papa speculates—an army of *golems*, he calls them; I do not know that word; I don't think it's even Latin. Papa danced so delicately, to try to use this magic power without damning himself, but others would see only the power, and reach for it regardless. . . ." She took a deep breath. "I'd give the book to Monreale before I'd see it destroyed. But I'd burn it myself before letting it fall into Ferrante's or Vitelli's black hands."

"All Montefoglia is falling into their hands," said Thur bitterly. "And nobody seems able—or willing— to stop them. I tried, God help me. And I failed. Even with a cowardly knife to the back. With a sledgehammer I might have done some good. You don't need me, Fiametta. You need a hero, like Uri, trained to the sword. The wrong brother lies dead in the next room."

"Thur, don't blame yourself! Lord Ferrante has been a soldier in the field for twenty years! How could you expect to best him in anything like single combat?"

"Lord Pia held his own, for a little. We almost had it, between us! Till I deserted him, left him nailed to the wall like a martyr surrounded by his enemies. But it was close, Fiametta. Lord Ferrante is not invincible.

Not till his army gets here, anyway. Tonight, tomorrow . . ." Thur grimaced.

"Not tonight," said Fiametta. "Ruberta says the rumors in the marketplace have it that the Losimons are held up getting their cannon across the ford at the border. But tomorrow—tomorrow they may be here." Wearily, Fiametta rubbed her face. "I found Ruberta this morning, at her sister's. I thought that's where she must have gone, if she'd lived. She told me what happened here. When the soldiers came that idiot Teseo panicked, and unbarred the door to them. Ruberta barely got over the back wall with her life. Well, it saved our poor door from being battered in, I suppose, and made no difference in the long run."

"Oh. Speaking of Ruberta. She says to come eat."

Fiametta sighed. "I suppose we must. To keep up our strength. Our strength to run away, if nothing else." Her face crumbled; she brought her clenched hand down on the tabletop with a bang, making the notebook jump. "*No*," she cried. "I don't *want* to run away! This house is the only dowry I have left, Ferrante's bravos have taken everything they could pry loose. I will *not* marry dowerless like a beggar's brat, like a slave . . ." Then she just cried.

"Fiametta . . . Fiametta . . ." Thur opened his hands, hardly daring to touch those shaking shoulders. "Your talents, your art and magic, are dowries in themselves. Any man must see, if he isn't a complete fool. And you're too good to wed a fool. Though I would wed you in a moment. But I haven't got a penny either. I haven't even got any clothes or shoes! If we could . . . live in Bruinwald, I could go back to the mines or the forge. I admit, there's not much call for goldsmiths in Bruinwald."

Fiametta raised a tear-stained face. "But . . . wouldn't you *like* to live here, Thur? I could take over Papa's shop, in a small way at first, but most of the tools are left—you could haul the wood, and move the furnaces, and carry out the big projects, and be my h-h-husband; the Guild Council would issue *you* the shop permits in a minute. As a minor orphan, the Guild would control my property, but if I were married, you would. And, and Ruberta could still come cook, and we could be happy here!"

Thur was taken aback by all the practical detail embedded in this picture of wedded bliss. She must have been thinking about it a lot. He'd scarcely dared let himself go beyond the vaguest physical longing— he had to admit, it was a wonderful house, as far above a miner's cottage as, as Montefoglia Castle was beyond a goldsmith's mansion. There were a lot of repairs to be done, after the looting, of course. He could do repairs, his hand and eye were clever enough for that. "I'd like it fine," he said. His mother would be astonished for him to marry so well, so soon. . . . "Could my mother come live here? Bruinwald winters are so cold and lonely." Yes, sooner or later, it must be his burden to tell her about Uri's fate. His stomach knotted at the thought.

Fiametta blinked. "Well, there's lots of room . . ." And more doubtfully, "Do you think she would like me?"

"Yes," said Thur firmly. He saw his mother dandling a grandchild on her knee, as Fiametta chinked away at some elegant goldwork, Ruberta cooked, and he ran a furnace, pouring pewter platters and candlesticks and other sturdy, practical things.

The colored vision faded at the thought of the advancing tramp of Losimon troops. Fiametta shared that dread; the light faded from her eyes. "All for nothing, if Ferrante wins," she sighed.

"Yes. Let's . . . go eat." Shyly, defying Ferrante and all the fates, he took her hand as they went out into the courtyard. She gripped his hand in return.

She paused to stare into the casting pit at the big clay lump, the fragile mold for the great Perseus. "So many works my father left unfinished. If I could do one thing to ease his poor shade, I would have this statue cast for him. Before the Losimons destroy the mold, or time and neglect crumble it away. We'll never get the metal for it, now."

Thur said glumly, "It's too bad we can't invest Uri into that old Greek hero, like the brass hare. *He'd* make Ferrante run."

Fiametta froze. "What?"

He stood very still. "Well, we can't . . . can we? I mean, that would be serious necromancy. Black sin."

"Any more sinful than assassination?"

Thur stared uneasily at her intent face.

"And suppose . . . suppose the spirit, Uri's spirit, was not bound against his will? Suppose he was invited— not a slave, but a free-will volunteer, like the spirit of Lord Lorenzo's great ring?" she said huskily. "Uri's spirit has already been strengthened for binding, if vilely, by Vitelli—we have the mold, the furnace, the wood, the spell is written out, oh, I *understood* it, Thur! It's not just words, it has an inner structure. . . ." Her shoulders slumped. "But we still don't have the metal. Not Vitelli himself could conjure a hero's weight of copper out of the air."

A vision danced and dazzled in Thur's mind like a lightning flash. A grinning kobold, drawing an iron bar down into solid stone as if it were porridge. . . .

"I can't conjure it out of the air." Thur's breathless voice seemed to his own ears to be coming from a great distance, as across a sea. "But I swear I can conjure it out of the ground."

Chapter Seventeen

"Now *this* is truly and straightly forbidden," said Fiametta, glancing around the front work chamber at her companions. Friends. Allies. Ruberta and Tich sat on opposite sides of a double diagram Fiametta had drawn on the floor in chalk. In the center of one axis lay Uri's body; on an absurd, indefensible impulse, she had placed a pillow beneath his head, as if he were sleeping. He didn't look asleep. That gray stiffness was unmistakably death. Thur sat cross-legged in the center of the other axis, looking scared but determined. The room's shutters were closed and locked; candles at the diagram's cardinal points gave practical as well as symbolic illumination. "If anyone wants to withdraw, you'd better do it now."

Tich and Ruberta shook their heads, identically tight-lipped. "I'm ready," said Thur sturdily.

We must all be mad, thought Fiametta. Well, if they were, Ferrante had driven them so. Thus evil bred evil. *Not all evil. I do not compel Uri's soul. I only beg of it.* She once more checked through the recipe for a séance in her father's notes. If he'd left nothing out, then neither had she.

"Are you sure I don't do anything?" asked Thur plaintively.

"You do nothing—in a, a *positive* sense. I think it must be harder than it sounds. You have to give up control." Fiametta reflected on this. "You have to really trust your . . . your guest."

Thur shook his head, smiling sadly. "Any other—guest, no. Uri, yes."

"Yes." She pursed her lips. "Abbot Monreale starts every spell with a prayer. It seems a little hypocritical here, but . . ." What to say? She could hardly ask for blessings upon this enterprise. She bent her head, and her companions followed suit. "In the names of Jesus and Mary we beg. God have mercy upon us, God have mercy upon us, God have mercy upon us all."

"Amen," murmured around the room. And an anxious, unvoiced *presence* assented, too.

She glanced for the last time at the notes, written in her father's flowing Latin hand. The spoken part of the spell was brief. She ran over the syllables in her mind, testing each one, and had a sudden insight. The substance of the spell was not in the Latin, but in a kind of under-structure of thought—was the insistence upon Latin merely a device to keep power from the ignorant? Uri did not speak Latin anyway, just German and Italian and a smattering of barracks-French. But now was surely not the time for experimentation.

Her lips formed the words anyway, a bridge of sound across a pattern held from second to second in her mind, of which the chalk lines were only a mnemonic reminder. "Uri, enter!" *These* were magic words, so blunt and plain? Her impulsiveness had spoiled the spell, they must start all over again—

Thur jerked, his eyes widened, his lips parting. His stoop-shouldered slump, partly weariness, partly a habit from ducking his height through unforgiving low mine tunnels, vanished. His spine straightened, like a soldier's on parade. An eager, hungry, almost frantic possession . . .

"Fiametta, I am here." It was Thur's voice, but with Uri's accent and intonation, polished smooth and mellowed by his time in the south. And his eyes—his eyes were intent, and bright, and very, very angry. "It's hard to stay. Hurry!"

"Oh, Uri, I'm so sorry you were killed!"

"Not half so sorry as I am." The flash of wry humor was all Uri, truly. His anger was not at her.

"It was my fault, I distracted you when I screamed."

"It wasn't you, it was what fell out of that accursed footstool. Horrible.'

A knot of guilty regret loosened in her heart. Uri/Thur's eyes closed. "Bless you, brother, for wresting me from the necromancers." The eyes pressed shut more tightly, as if in residue of some agony. "I *tried* to resist them. They did not . . . fight fair."

"I imagine not," said Fiametta faintly. "God grant you grace."

"It was hard to think of God in that dark place. Some men find grace in dungeons and mineshafts, as if the color and noise and distractions of life blind them, and only in the darkness do they see clear. But I came too late, and to the wrong dungeon. Vitelli's shadow is a darkness empty even of God." His face was set with the memory of that emptiness, of that dark.

"Shh . . . it's all right now." Well, hardly that, Fiametta thought, glancing at the gray corpse. "But could you—dare you—face him again?"

Uri/Thur flinched. "Vitelli?"

"Yes. But not so unevenly matched, this time. Uri—

we have discovered a spell of Papa's, a wonderful spell. Instead of casting your ghost into a ring, I think we can use this spell to open a way for you into the great Perseus. He *was* you, after all, but for the face and the pock marks. A body not of flesh, but of bronze, hurtless and immensely strong. It cannot be for long, though I plan to use my fire-spell to keep it hot and moving for as long as possible. But in that time you'd have a chance, one chance, to strike back at Ferrante and Vitelli. I cannot—I will not—compel or bind you in any way. But I will beg you. Uri, help us!"

"Make me a path to that end," breathed Uri/Thur, "and I will *fly* down it. Great Sorceress!" His eyes burned. "Sandrino trusted me with his life. And I stood *right there*, open-mouthed like a country buffoon, as Ferrante took it from him. I failed my oath, I was dishonored by surprise—I did not trust Ferrante, I should have been more forward, oh, Fiametta! To wash out my dishonor in Ferrante's blood, I'd give my soul for the chance!"

"Don't say that!" Fiametta cried, panicked. "I don't want that! But if the Crusaders can be soldiers for God, I don't see why you can't. Vitelli is worse than any Saracen. But we need even more help than that. Papa would have employed ten strong workmen on this casting. We have only four, three, because I will be attempting the spell. You were there, in the castle—can you tell us how Lord Pia compelled the kobolds in his aid?"

"Lord Pia has a long-standing friendship with the little rock people. That's why they are so thick about the castle. They had a mutual interest in caves, and in the creatures that live in them." Uri/Thur raised his hands, and made a little bat-wing-flapping gesture. "I once visited the kobolds' colony in Lord Pia's company. How *you* may compel them, I am not sure, especially to work, for they are lazy and flighty and would rather play tricks. They'll play nasty tricks on you, if you cause them pain. Trying to compel a kobold is a bad idea."

His brows-down expression became muddled, all of a sudden, and confused. Thur's voice pushed out of his own mouth with difficulty, slow and slurred. "Bribe 'em. Mother's milk. They'd do anything for it." His jaw opened, closed; then Uri was back, looking surprised.

"That would work better than stealing a nanny goat—it's not something they are often offered! They would flock to you!"

"But where would we get—oh, this is getting so complicated!"

"It is strange . . ." Uri/Thur's gaze grew distant, "what I can see now. More. Less. Other. Walls are like glass. Stone is like water. But I can see the kobolds in their shadow-form inside the rocks, and they seem oddly solid. People—you, in your flesh— are like shadows used to be, all garbled and distant and out of reach. Except right now, looking through these eyes. It's good to see you, once more." He smiled briefly, then grew grim. "All but Vitelli. His shadow is solid, inside his flesh. Solid and dark. Of him, I am afraid." Uri/Thur sighed, a long, controlled breath. "You must hurry. Even now Vitelli is moving toward binding your father in his ring. It's like a wrestling match. And Master Beneforte is losing! With your father's spirit bound to his will, Vitelli will own all his powers and knowledge. And who would doubt Master Beneforte's power to defeat his own spell, your spell, our spell?"

"When does Vitelli now plan to cast the ring?" Fiametta asked intently. "Do you know, can you tell?"

"Tonight."

"Tonight, oh, no! Can you see or speak to Papa at all? Tell him—"

But Uri/Thur's face writhed; a last, plaintive, "I cannot

hold! Good-bye—" broke from his lips, and he fell backward, gasping, all and only Thur once more.

"God. God." He almost wept.

"Did it hurt?" asked Fiametta anxiously.

"Hurt?" Thur shook his head from side to side in bewilderment, glazed eyes jerking. "I feel sick. Uri—Uri hurts. Vitelli has hurt him."

"Can we move now?" asked Tich breathlessly. "Is it safe?"

"Yes. It's over," nodded Fiametta. Tich stuck his legs out in front of him and bent and stretched, and Ruberta hitched around in her bundle of skirts and petticoats. "No. It's only beginning," Fiametta realized. "And we have so little time! It's grown so complicated. And Ferrante's soldiers might descend on us here at any moment, and oh—" She shuddered, nearly overwhelmed.

"We'll do it step by step, Fiametta," said Thur. "The last won't look so big, once the first is done. What's first? The copper. For which we must have the kobolds. For which we must have . . . hmm." He frowned at the ceiling.

"I don't think a wet nurse will drop down from the sky," said Fiametta tartly, following his gaze. "At least not one who would be willing to put a nasty little rock-demon to her breast. And we cannot involve an unwilling soul, which means we must reveal what we are doing. And if told, and if she does not agree, she could betray us—"

Ruberta snorted. "Oh, you children." Fiametta looked up, puzzled at her dry tone.

"Do you think you are the only ones hurting from this evil pass?" the housekeeper asked. "Ferrante's soldiers have been swaggering around town for days, making enemies for him. They don't act like the guard of a new lord, they've been acting like an occupying enemy. I could lay hands on a dozen unhappy women who would be willing to do far worse things to strike a blow in return. You leave this to me, girl." Ruberta grunted up and stood with her hands on her hips. "I'd do it myself in a trice, but that I gave up wet-nursing four years ago to become your Papa's housekeeper. I was getting old for it anyway. It's not a job for the squeamish. I don't know why they encourage maidens to be squeamish, there's no place in women's work for someone afraid to get her hands dirty." She nodded shortly, and marched out looking quite steely.

Tich raised his eyebrows, as if amused, or at least bemused, by her military stride.

"Don't you look like that at her," said Fiametta sharply. "Some of Ferrante's drunken men raped her niece two nights ago. Took her right off the street, when she ventured out to get food for her family. The girl was still in bed crying, all bruised and beaten, when I went there at dawn to look for Ruberta. The whole family's in an uproar."

Tich hunched contritely.

Thur took a deep breath, and heaved himself up. "Tich. We can start laying the wood in the furnace while we wait. And shift that stack of tin ingots."

"Right." Tich scrambled up, too.

Fiametta slumped, exhausted. "Oh, Thur. I feel like I've just kicked a pebble off the top of one of your mountains, and watched it start two other rocks, which struck five—a mountain is going to fall on someone tonight. Will it be us?"

"On Ferrante, if I can help it." He offered his hand to her; she took it and he pulled her to her feet as lightly as a straw doll.

She bent and gathered up the precious book. "I had better study the spell some more. And gather what I can of the necessary symbols. We'd best not go in and out of the house any more than we can help. The smoke from Ruberta's cooking fire will be put down to the guard, but what's going to happen when we light the smelting furnace? It's bound to attract attention."

"It will likely be dusk, by that time. It's past noon already," Thur pointed out. "You should also take a little time to rest, before."

"Yes." There was no more time for half-efforts or doubts. Fiametta squared her shoulders. She must dance atop this falling mountain, or they would all be buried in it. *May God have mercy upon us, amen.*

The knocking on the door from the street was unmistakably Ruberta, her habitual loud thump followed by three short taps, repeated impatiently. Fiametta hurried from the front workroom to let her in. The afternoon was waning. Truly, Ruberta had not been gone all that long, considering the complexity and delicacy of her errand, but the passage of time was making Fiametta frantic. Hardly the calm and ordered state of mind ideal for a master mage to cast a major enchantment, Fiametta thought drearily. But then, she was hardly a master mage. She hoped Ruberta had remembered the dried rue.

Tich, not knowing Ruberta's knock, had run to the entryway too, his knife clutched in his hand. Fiametta waved him back to work, and unbarred the oak door. She swung it open to reveal Ruberta, capped and shawled and burdened with a basket and a large jug. Behind her stood a tall silent woman in a long cape with a big hood pulled up over her head, shading her face. Ruberta gave Fiametta a reassuring short nod, as if to say, *This is it; I've done it.* Fiametta beckoned the women inside and locked and barred the door again.

"Hello," said Fiametta to the strange woman. Woman, not girl. There were gray streaks in her black hair, drawn back in a bun and braid. Lady, Fiametta refined her evaluation; her clothes were as finely made as Fiametta's had been, before the Losimons had stolen most of them. "Thank you for coming. Bless you for coming. Has Ruberta explained—oh, excuse me. My name is—"

Roberta held up an interrupting finger. "We have agreed to name no names."

That was understandable. Fiametta nodded. "I haven't a prayer of being anonymous, but you shall be as nameless as you wish. Call me Fiametta." The woman nodded back. "Has Ruberta explained what we ask of you?" Surely this lady was not a professional wet nurse.

"Yes. I handed off my babe to my mother-in-law, and ate well, before I came."

"I brought some good ale, to keep up her strength," Ruberta added, hefting the jug.

"Has Ruberta explained *what* it is we ask you to nurse?" Fiametta reiterated, making sure.

"Yes. Rock-demon, gnome, kobold, the Devil himself, I don't care what you call it, as long as it redounds to Uberto Ferrante's everlasting sorrow." She had that same burning-eyed look Fiametta had seen in all too many faces in Montefoglia of late. "The Losimons killed my husband on the first day. They murdered my first-born, my bonnie boy, my blooming young man, in a street fight these two days past. The plague took my middle two babes, years ago. Only the toddler is left, and now I shall get no other." Her hands clenched. Fiametta knelt, and kissed them each.

"Then you are as ready to start as I am." She rose again. "Come with me."

Fiametta led them through the courtyard toward the kitchen. She walked wide around the chained Losimon, who was awake and gagged again. He made a menacing lunge toward them, was brought up short by his chain, and sneered. The tall woman gathered her cloak away, not in fear, but as one might draw away from a leper, and gave him a direct and murderous stare. Despite his bindings he managed to return an obscene hand gesture, but then gave up and sat down sulkily as Thur appeared, hefting his sledgehammer. Thur and Tich accompanied the women into the kitchen, where Thur raised the trapdoor for them.

Fiametta lit the lantern, and led the woman down into the root cellar, a chamber half the size of the kitchen partly lined with shelves and stone jars. Thur also let himself down the narrow stair, almost a ladder. Ruberta and Tich watched anxiously from above. Fiametta upended a crate, and the woman seated herself on it as gracefully as on a velvet-covered chair.

The walls were surfaced with cobbles. The floor was beaten earth but for an outcrop of stone; Montefoglian soil was thin. Fiametta set the lantern down, and squatted next to Thur, who was staring at the rock as if he might see through it. However limpid it might look to Uri's ghost, the rock remained stubbornly opaque to her. Thur spread his hands out on the rough surface, and cocked his head as though listening.

"Smear some milk on the stone," Thur suggested after a moment. The nameless lady rose, undid her bodice, and leaned over to place a squirt of milk where he pointed. Fiametta rubbed it about and, rather desperately, called, "Here, kobold, kobold, kobold!"

"You're not calling a crowd of alley cats!" criticized Tich, looking down into the cellar. "Shouldn't you chant something?"

All the more stung because she was wondering the same thing, Fiametta snapped, "If you know so much about it, *you* chant something. Here, kobold, kobold, kobold!"

Dimness; the wavering glow of the lantern; silence. Not even the scuttle of a rat or the skitter of a roach. They waited. And waited.

"It's not working," said Tich, nervously biting his finger.

Fiametta glanced apprehensively at the tall woman. "Maybe just a little longer ..."

"I'm not in a hurry," the woman said. Patience for her vengeance dripped like vitriol from her voice; even Tich was quelled.

"*Here,* kobold, kobold, kobold," Fiametta tried again. Tich screwed up his face, apparently deeply offended by this dreadfully domestic, unsorcerous proceeding. But then his eyes widened.

Dark shapes twisted upon the wall, and upon the sloping outcrop, shapes not made by the lantern light. Two, three, four ... six ... twiggy little men rose up, as if instead of casting shadows they were cast *by* their shadows. Silently, they crept up around the tall woman, seated on her crate. The boldest reached out to touch her skirt, and tilted his head in a shy, sly smile. "Lady?" he piped. "Nice lady ..." She gazed back gravely, and did not flinch.

"You shall have milk," said Thur, "but not yet."

"Who are you to say, metal master?" asked the kobold leader. It frowned at him, thrusting out its bony chest.

"He speaks for me," said the tall woman quietly. The kobold hunched and shrugged, as if to say, *No offense meant.* Its bright black eyes were avid upon her.

Thur said, "In the garden court at Montefoglia Castle sits a stack of copper pigs. Each of you who helps to bring them through the earth to the courtyard of this house will be permitted to drink his, er, her ... its fill. When the copper is all transported. And not before."

"Too much work. Too heavy," whined the kobold.

"Not if you work together."

"We can't run in the sun."

"The day is cloudy, and almost done. The shadow of the wall is across that end of the garden by now."

"Just a little sip, on the lip, first, metal master?"

Thur wiped his fingers across the milk smear on the outcrop, and twiddled them under the kobold's nose. "You like this? Good? Then bring us the copper. First."

"You'll trick us, cheat us. Eh?"

The tall woman said, "If you do as he asks, you shall have your reward. You have *my* word on it." Her eyes held the kobold's. Its eyes darted away, as if scorched.

"Lady's word. You heard," it chanted to its comrades.

"Be careful, little ones," Thur warned. "Avoid the dark man called Vitelli. I think he could hurt you."

The kobold gave him a pained stare, its lips twisting. "This we know, metal master."

"Have you—" Thur's eyes went suddenly intent, "have you seen Lord Pia? Is he killed, or does he live?"

The kobold ducked away, crouching. "Friend Pia lives, but does not rise. Many tears are in his eyes."

"And Lady Pia? The Duchess and Julia, what of them?"

"They are kept too high in the air. Kobolds cannot venture there."

"Very well. Go. The sooner you return, the sooner you will have your reward." Thur sighed, and stood, mindful of his head on the beams above. They all climbed again to the kitchen, where Ruberta carefully wiped and poured ale into a Venetian glass, slapped Tich's hand away from it, and gave it to the tall woman, who sat and sipped obediently. Fiametta, Thur, and Tich went back out into the courtyard.

She and Papa used to take breakfast on a rustic wooden table in this courtyard, when they first moved to Montefoglia. The space had been almost a garden, cool and soothing, with potted flowers and a gurgling fountain. Now the Perseus project filled it from wall to wall. The old breakfast table was shoved away under the gallery, half-buried under a pile of tools and trash. The furnace, a beehive of bricks as tall as Thur, sat on a mound of rammed earth dug from the casting pit; the pretty paving stones had been torn up and incorporated into its base.

Fiametta peeked into the furnace. Thur had already laid in the first layer of seasoned pine. Tich had carefully swept and covered the channel, made of wood thickly lined with clay, sloping from the bottom of the furnace to the gates at the top of the mold. The big-beamed crane that had lowered the mold painstakingly into the casting pit, and was intended to raise the finished statue, was rotated out of the way for now. The huge clay lump was wound round with iron bands, just like a bell casting Papa had said, to prevent the mold from bursting when the great weight of molten metal poured into it.

Fiametta walked around the pit, planning her spell. She would lay Uri's body on the side opposite the furnace. No need to include the furnace itself in the diagram of forces. For one thing, Thur and Tich would have to cross and recross her lines, to add wood, stir the melt, and adjust the play of the bellows. There was no call for magic in the purely physical process of melting the bronze. The moment when Thur knocked out the iron plug at the base of the furnace and the metal flowed across her line, that would be the proper moment to start channeling Uri's urgent ghost into this creation. Fiametta realized she was really vague about cooling times. Those iron bands would have to be broken loose to release ... Uri, but if done too soon the mold might burst and the statue slump; if too late, it might grow too stiff. Scaling up was always a problem, Papa had said. And she was scaling up this spell with a vengeance. *I must be mad.*

An unexpected sharp noise came from the chained Losimon, that Fiametta finally realized was a shriek, pushed out around his gag. The startled guard had recoiled to the end of his chain. On the other side of his pillar two kobolds lugging a bar of copper recoiled from him with twittering cries. The Losimon tried to cross himself, and gargled through the cloth in his mouth, "Demons! Demons in broad day!"

"Ugly! Ugly Man!" squeaked the kobolds.

It was dusk, really, Fiametta decided, glancing at the sky. The courtyard was in shadow, and overhead thick clouds scudded across a purpling sky. It was growing chill. She could smell rain in the air.

"Over here." Thur motioned to the kobolds to bring their burden to the furnace. Tich ran to the kitchen with the news. By the time he returned with Ruberta and the nameless woman, a second pair of gnomes was emerging from the ground beside Thur's feet. There was something revoltingly organic about how the earth squeezed them forth, reminding Fiametta of the clown in the marketplace who extruded whole eggs from his bulging mouth for a trick. But they brought another copper bar. With a giggle, the first pair dove back headfirst into the soil. Then the third pair emerged, cheerful as cicadas.

Thur began stacking the copper carefully in the furnace, alternating with more wood. Master Beneforte had filled a downstairs storeroom with select pine, laid in to dry especially for this project. The Losimons had taken some—how closely had her father calculated his fuel? They would find out. More kobolds, or the same kobolds, popped up like weasels. Fiametta soon lost count, but Thur did not.

"That's the last," he said.

Fiametta came to his side as he backed out and closed the iron door to the furnace through which he'd been squeezing to load ingots and fuel. He rubbed his hair out of his eyes with the back of a dirty hand. He was big and warm, and his blue eyes were exhilarated. Even the absurd undersized robe he wore like a tunic, with his bare calves sticking out, could not quite make him look silly.

He could burn for this. For her There was a momentum in this moment that had nothing to do with Ferrante. She could feel it, the drive of art from the inside out, the determination to *complete*. She had hated her father, some days, for being as willing to consume others as himself to fuel that drive. And what she'd hated in her father she was not at all sure she liked finding in herself.

"Are you scared?" she asked Thur.

"No. Yes. I'm scared I might do something to spoil all this beautiful preparation. I mean, the furnace alone is a work of art. No wonder his ghost lingered, cut off so close to *this* being finished. It's a wonder he's not howling around it. If I can bring this off—it would be a bride-price for your Papa worthy of you. Poor miner's son be damned!"

Be not! "Thur, you realize—I have no idea what the effect on the statue will be when the spell wears off." *Nor on Uri.*

"The little brass hare was fine, you said. It's going to be magnificent. You'll see." He paused. "We can light the furnace now."

"That's a job for me." Fiametta brightened in a whiff of nostalgia. "I used to light all of Papa's fires for him."

They gripped hands, then Thur stepped back. Fiametta closed her eyes. *For you, Papa.* And for Abbot Monreale, and Ascanio and his Mama, and poor Lord and Lady Pia, and Tich and Ruberta and her niece and the lady with no name. For all of Montefoglia. *"Piro!"*

The furnace roared, then the sound dropped to a husky hiss. Thur started pumping one bellows, and on the opposite side of the beehive Tich began working the second pair. In a private spot beyond the furnace, sheltered by the gallery, the nameless lady sat, watching with interest. The first light from the furnace picked out an approving glitter in her dark eyes. She drew her cloak around a kobold, one of a cluster at her feet, who turned its wrinkled face up to her adoringly. In the twilight, one could almost imagine them as children. Almost.

A few sparks wavering in the heat rose from the furnace vents, but not much smoke. The wood burned hot and dry and clear, just as it should. Not . . . not *too* conspicuous, Fiametta hoped. *But we had better not be too long at this.*

She rounded up Ruberta, and together they carried Uri's bier into the darkening courtyard. Enough light leaked from the furnace to prevent stumbles, but Fiametta decided to have Ruberta hold a lantern for the next part.

"I can draw the diagram and lay out the symbols, and then rest while the bronze is melted. As long as we are all careful not to step on them. I'll draw them as close and tight to the bier and the pit as I can. You hold the light so I can be sure there is no break in the line."

"Where's your chalk, girl?" asked Ruberta.

"This spell doesn't use chalk." She knelt and took a small sharp knife from the basket of tools and objects she had made ready. She rolled up her right sleeve, and turned her palm out to expose her wrist. She studied her veins. "Um."

Ruberta held her hand to her lips in dismay, but suggested faintly, "Parallel to your tendons, dear, not across them. If you still mean to be able to write or do anything else, after."

"Uh . . . right. Good idea. Thank you." This was hard. *Think of it as practice for childbirth.* The lines

had to be drawn with the mage's own blood. No one
else's would do. She had to give Papa credit for that
one, anyway. No easy way; she dug the knife in point-
first and dragged it through her flesh. She had to do
it again before the blood was flowing freely enough
down her hand for her to write with her index finger.
She cleared her mind, stepped to Uri's head, and
began.

Her head was swimming by the time she'd murmured her way all around and closed her circle at
the starting point. Another problem of scaling up. She
stopped squeezing her arm and the blood oozed to a
halt. She sat a moment on the ground to recover.

"Is it melting yet?" wheezed Tich to Thur, sagging
on his bellows. "Is it time to add the tin?"

"Not nearly." Thur poked his head around the side
of the furnace and grinned at him. "If you add it too
soon, the tin exhales from the alloy and you lose your
trouble and expense. We've hours to go yet."

Tich moaned. But after a few moments of whispered
conversation, a couple of smirking kobolds crept out
of the corner by the lady and took over his bellows,
jumping and hanging off the handle like monkeys. Tich
sweated and rested by Fiametta. The rest of the
kobolds pitched in, alternated with diving in and out
of the furnace in their shadow-form, hooting and giggling. The orange glow from the flames lit the demonic
scene. The Losimon prisoner also saw it as a vision
out of hell, it seemed, for he had given up his surly
sneer and cowered, snivelling and weeping, on the far
end of his chain, the whites of his eyes wide in the
glare. Ruberta brought watered wine and bread and
hard garlic sausage all around. Fiametta ate gratefully,
but thought, *We have to speed this up*.

Papa. *It's a wonder he's not howling round this*,
Thur had said, in all innocence. A wonder, indeed.
Where was Master Beneforte? Why was his shade not

drawn to this, his obsession? She could scarcely imagine a more potent conjuring for him. It wasn't a problem of range. He had appeared as far away as Saint Jerome. She closed her eyes, and tried to empty her mind, to listen and feel. *Papa?* Nothing. If he did not come to this, it could only be because he could not. Bound, or partly bound—she pictured Vitelli winding him into smaller and smaller confines, a room, a diagram, finally to a finger's-breadth. How soon?

Very soon, she thought queasily. And what of Vitelli himself? There was enough to her quiet preparations to draw his supernatural attention, if he were actively looking. Vitelli and Papa must be fully occupied with each other, to be so conspicuously absent here. *It's like a wrestling match, and Master Beneforte is losing. . . .*

She opened her eyes, rose, and walked over to the furnace. Thur had folded down the top of his robe, and was now naked to the waist. His body glistened in the light and heat as he poked a long, iron stirring-rod through the access window.

"Is it melting yet?" Fiametta asked anxiously.

"Starting to."

She closed her eyes, concentrated deeply, and recited, *"Piro. Piro. Piro."* She stopped, dizzied; when she opened her mouth, her breath steamed. The furnace roared. Orange sparks spiraled up out of the vents into the night air, and were whipped away by the rising wind.

"Fiametta, save your strength." Thur's big hand closed in concern on her shoulder.

"We haven't much time left. I can feel it." *I am afraid.*

His grip tightened. "We can do this thing," he breathed in her ear. "It's going to be magnificent." In the bright blue light of his eyes, she could almost believe.

Tich staggered out under a huge double armload of

pine, which he dropped at his feet with a clatter. "This is the last of it," he gasped.

"What?" said Thur. "Surely not already." He peered through the furnace window again with troubled eyes.

"Sorry," said Tich. "Not another splinter."

"Well, let's load it in." Together, they heaved the wood into the furnace, while the kobolds manned the bellows. Thur stirred with the iron rod. "Maybe we'd better put in the rest of the tin now. It shouldn't be long, after that, Fiametta."

She nodded, and stood back. She watched the hot light play over his intent, absorbed face as he stirred the flux again. *He feels it too, the passion of making.* Her heart grew warmer, and her lips curved up in unexpected pleasure. *He is beautiful, right now. Like carved ivory. My muleteer. Who would have thought it?*

Suddenly, Thur's lips rippled back in a snarl. "*No,*" he groaned. He stirred harder, then stepped back, driven away by the heat. "It's *caking!*"

"What does that mean?" asked Tich, bewildered, but frightened by Thur's expression of despair.

"It means the casting is ruined! The metal is curdling. Ah!" He stamped his naked feet, threw the rod on the ground, and stood stiff and trembling. Tich slumped. Fiametta's breath stopped. Ruberta moaned. The kobolds chittered in confusion.

Thur threw his head back. "No!" he roared. "There must be something we can do to save it! More tin— more wood—"

"There is no more," said Tich timorously.

"The hell there's not. *I'll* give you more wood!" Fiercely, Thur rushed across the courtyard to the old rustic table and upended it, clearing it of its contents with a crash. Yelling like a madman, he took the sledgehammer to it. "Dry oak. Nothing burns hotter! More, Tich! Fiametta, Ruberta! Anything oak in the house! Benches, worktables, shelves, chairs, bring them! Hurry! Kobolds, to me! Pump those bellows, you little monsters! Shove these boards under the grating where the ashes fall, that the heat may rise up . . . !"

The next few minutes were like an orgy of destruction. Thur dragged a big shop workbench by himself with strength gone half-berserk, so that Fiametta feared he would burst her careful stitches again. Thur, Tich, even the kobolds helped whack the furniture apart. The kobolds seemed to enjoy it, squealing and shrieking. Ruberta even threw in her wooden spoons. The fire thundered, sparks and flames flying up out of the vents in a river coursing skyward. It must look like a signal fire, from outside.

Panting, Thur opened the furnace window and stirred again. His face fell, and his shoulders slumped; he crouched, his smudged, scorched face sagging almost to his knees. "It's not enough," he gasped. "It's over. . . ." He curled there, staring at nothing; Fiametta bent over a belly that ached in sympathetic synchrony. To come so close, and fail now . . . God did not wait for death to damn them to eternal torment, it was present in life. . . .

"Pewter," Thur whispered in the smoky silence.

"What?"

"*Pewter!*" screamed Thur. "Bring me every scrap of pewter you have in this house!" Not waiting, he galloped for the kitchen, to return juggling an enormous armload of old plates, platters, and porringers. He threw them through the furnace mouth as fast as he could, and ran back for more. Fiametta sprinted up the gallery stairs and through the upstairs rooms. She returned with a mug, a battered basin, and a pair of grubby old magic candlesticks that lit themselves with a word from anyone, that the Losimons had not recognized as valuable. Ruberta brought more spoons. In all, there must have been over a hundred pounds of metal. Thur stuffed it all into the furnace, crying, "Ha! Ha!" He stirred, jammed more oak into the grate, stirred again. The roar of the conflagration was omnivorous, ominous, drowning out the distant thunder that echoed across Lake Montefoglia.

"It's melting!" Thur howled joyously. His lips drew back in a demented grin. "It liquifies, oh, it's beautiful! Beautiful! Fiametta, get ready!"

She scurried to her chosen spot, the apex of a triangle halfway between Uri's head and the casting pit, and knelt on the churned earth. How she was supposed to think, evoke a master mage's serene control, in this screaming satanic chaos, she did not know. *That's why you memorized this spell. Don't think, just do.*

She touched the six herbs arranged in front of her, the knife, the cross. She touched the powders to forehead and lips. On impulse, she swiftly crossed herself, FatherSonandHolySpirit. God! *God be . . . God be praised for all wonders.* She closed her eyes, opened her heart and mind. Uri was a pressing force, a towering will hovering at her hand, three parts rage and one part terror, his dear humor almost gone. *I did love you, in some way.* She opened her eyes, looked at Thur, and nodded.

Tich swept the cloth cover from the channel. Thur grasped the crooked iron bar, and hooked the plug from the bottom of the furnace. White-hot fire streamed out, driving back the shadows. It ran down, biting through the line of Fiametta's drying blood, and poured into the gate of the great clay mold, a river of light as swift as hot oil.

Uri *flowed* through Fiametta. A thousand thousand images of memory, climaxing in the mortal wrenching dark of his death, all in the midst of motion— Her mouth opened and her back arched in agony. *It burns, oh it burns!* Mother Mary. *Mother . . .*

Above them, in the roaring rising heat, the wooden gallery caught fire. Yellow flames licked over the balustrade and railing. The door to the street began to shake with great blows, and the yells of men. Still the fire in Fiametta's veins coursed on and on. She dared not move, she dared not break, surely she was about to ignite like the gallery, explode like a human torch. . . . Tich ran to the stairs with a futile little bucket of water. Thur picked up his sledgehammer.

In the paved hallway, the door burst inward. Three Losimon soldiers holding a battering ram stumbled in on their own momentum. Behind them strode their shouting officer, his sword drawn. A bearded, savage, black-mouthed man, swearing furiously. In the channel, the last of the bright metal sucked away into the mold. Her spell released Fiametta as abruptly as an opening hand. She slumped to the ground, unable to move, barely able to breathe, and not even knowing if she had succeeded or failed.

The Losimons ran to the courtyard, and hesitated, doubtless stunned by the incomprehensible scene before their eyes: the burning gallery, the shrieking women, for Ruberta and the nameless lady were running after Tich with more water, kobolds flying every which way, the spasming chained guard howling through his gag and bucking wildly. Fiametta, her face sideways on the ground, giggled. Thur stood gently swinging his hammer. One man with a worker's tool against four swordsmen. Fiametta stopped giggling, and rolled over to gaze glassily into the casting pit. What had happened down there?

Let me out, something called. Fiametta didn't think she heard it with her ears. *Let me out!*

"Thur," she wheezed. "Jump down and knock off the hoops. The iron retaining hoops."

He glanced back and forth, at her, at the mold, at the advancing Losimons with their swords cautiously feeling in front of them as if for invisible enemies. He slid into the pit and began clanging at the clasps of the reinforcing iron bands. Fiametta's heart raced. Suppose it was too soon. Suppose the mold shattered, and white-hot molten bronze spewed out, drowning him. . . . One band sprang apart, then another, another. The point of a sword touched Fiametta's throat, pressing her to the ground. She looked up into a dark, bearded face devoid of humor, devoid of intellect, almost devoid of humanity.

"Put down that mallet and come out of there or I'll run her through," the Losimon lieutenant snarled. Thur, abandoning his hammer, lifted himself out and rolled away on the opposite side of the pit. He crouched froglike on his hands and knees, and grinned, eyes glaring, catching his breath.

In the pit, the clay began to crack apart with a sound like shattering crockery. It scaled away, fragmenting and powdering. Deep within the cracks, something glowed red as blood.

Something shrugged off its clay tunic like a dog shaking off snow. A severed head appeared first, at the top, clutched and brandished in a strong hand. Bronze snakes, cherry-red, writhed upon its mythic skull. Shoulders hunched, pulled back. A muscular arm holding a curved sword broke free. Then a winged helmet, and, with the jerk of his chin, a man's face. But not the serene face of the bland Greek, no.

It's Uri, thought Fiametta. *Complete with his pock marks.* She was insanely glad to see those pock marks.

The molten gaze rose, and found the gap-toothed lieutenant. *Remember me?* the burning eyes silently cried. *For I remember you.* The bronze lips smiled a terrible promise.

The Losimon broke at last, and ran screaming.

Chapter Eighteen

Fiametta pushed herself up to her hands and knees, then sat up on her heels. The gibbering gap-toothed Losimon was caught and held by two of his men, who had not seen what was happening in the casting pit. The third soldier finished breaking the prisoner's chain with blows from his sword against the stone pillar; the freed man repaid his comrade's pains by knocking him down in his rush for the exit. Thunder rolled close overhead in the midnight sky, shaking the house.

Uri's hands, burdened each with the curved sword and the fiery head of the Medusa, came up over the edge of the pit. Red bronze muscles rippled as he heaved himself out, a glorious nude hero. Even in the glare from the burning gallery he glowed with his own dark red light, except for his eyes which were yellow-white. It must be the magic, holding him together at that temperature, Fiametta thought woozily. His outlines were crisper, more perfect even than her Papa's fine wax copy of his body had been. Thur jumped lightly down into the vacated pit to retrieve his sledge-hammer, which evidently gave him quite as much comfort as it gave his enemy onlookers unease.

The hot bronze Uri gazed down upon the cold fleshly Uri, then raised his eyes to Thur. The two brothers exchanged a look, and even in the blank molten-yellow radiance of the metal Fiametta read regret, and sorrow, and something like love, mixed with the determination and rage.

Thur, his blue eyes flashing with the water standing in them, raised his sledgehammer in solemn salute. "Lead us, Captain Ochs. In the name of God, Bruinwald, and Duke Sandrino."

"Follow me, boy," Uri responded with a slow smile, "and I'll give you a show to tell my nieces and nephews. Mind you do." His bronze voice reverberated like a blast from an organ-pipe, deep, loud, with undertones to raise the dead, yet still somehow Uri. His yellow eyes found Fiametta, scrambling to her feet. "I haven't much time. Let us be about it."

"Lead. We follow," said Fiametta breathlessly. Her house was burning down. So what. She turned her back on it.

Uri bent his gaze upon the four Losimons who, supporting each other, had somewhat regained their nerve. They took a stand in a cluster, backs prudently to the exit hall. Uri's fingers flexed on his sword hilt, and he strode toward them. The churned earth blackened, steamed, and smoked in his deep footprints.

The black-mouthed lieutenant took his sword and his bravado and made a rush at the approaching apparition. His sword clanged off Uri's nude side, jolting his arm. Uri raised the head of the Medusa and brought it down upon his murderer's skull, smashing him to the ground. The Losimon convulsed once, his legs kicking, then lay without moving. The survivors retreated, crouching and covering each other in an almost orderly fashion, till they reached the shattered oak door to the street. The semblance of discipline burst as they sprinted away. Fiametta almost grabbed up the dead fellow's dropped sword, just in case. Uri's ruddy weapon was impressive, but she was uncertain how bronze, and heat-softened bronze at that, was going to stand up to weapons of tempered steel. Then she realized Uri could not exchange his sword. It was melded, one with his hand.

Thur hugged Fiametta around the shoulders as they followed Uri into the street. Fiametta stopped, taken aback by the sight of the crowd which was assembled there. A couple dozen people milled about, men, boys, even a few women, in every sort of dress and half-dress and nightshirts. Fiametta recognized the faces of several neighbors.

Lorenzetti, the notary who lived next door, rushed up to her. The Losimons had looted his house, too. His head was still bandaged from some ill-advised resistance. "Fiametta! What is happening? What have you done?"

"My house is on fire," she said numbly. With frightened cries, the crowd fell back from around Uri, though not very far back. They goggled, and shouted amazed queries. "We have made a bronze hero, a soldier to fight the Losimons for us and free Montefoglia. We're on our way to kill Ferrante now. Please stand back."

The three remaining Losimons had stopped and formed ranks again, in the dark street on the far side of the crowd. They hovered on the balls of their feet, watching and waiting. A man among Fiametta's neighbors, Bembo the wax chandler, held a torch aloft; more torches arrived, from where Fiametta did not know, and the fire was shared, doubled and doubled again.

Lorenzetti squinted, gaped, and stammered, "Isn't

that Uri Ochs, Sandrino's Swiss fellow? I played dice with him. He died owing me half a ducat. . . . Hey! Uri!"

Uri gave him a cheery salute with his sword hand in exchange for the recognition.

Lorenzetti backed a step, wild-eyed, and opened his hands in a bow. "Well, you have *my* blessing. Hey! Make way, there!" He gestured the crowd apart. The Losimons were suddenly framed by two ranks of their victims. An odd, abrupt silence occurred, half by chance. A cobblestone flew out, launched by an angry young man. It bounced off a Losimon's breastplate with a clank. The Losimon staggered. Uri began striding up the street between the people. Fiametta and Thur, holding hands like two children in the dark, followed close on his heels. A roar went up from the Montefoglians that reminded Fiametta of the furnace in full flux. The Losimons turned and ran this time in earnest, no stopping or looking back.

Shouts echoed through the streets. Above, shutters banged open and nightcapped heads crowded the windows. Cries of curiosity and fear rained down. Fiametta glanced over her shoulder. People were following them, first in ones and twos, then a stream, then a river. Doors flew wide, and more men issued. Knives and daggers appeared, and a few swords, and other weapons even more extemporaneous: axes and hammers, clubs, hoes, a mattock, a rusty sickle. One fat woman joined the throng armed with a large cast-iron frying pan. More torches sprang up, held high. Fiametta had no idea what the people at the back imagined they were following: half-parade, half-assault, exhilarated, ugly, determined, and confused.

And not at all the silent, secret midnight skulk through the streets of Montefoglia that Fiametta had pictured and planned. Uri could hardly march unseen anyway, fervid red in the dark like that. If the Inquisition ever brought her to trial for this night's work, there would be a thousand witnesses.

Lightning cracked the sky. The first few fat, cold drops of rain fell, slapping Fiametta's upturned face. They boiled off Uri instantly, and he trailed tendrils of gauzy steam. His feet hissed on the cobbles as they grew wet and shining. *Too cold,* Fiametta thought to the rain. *Stop, go back, not yet!* She stumbled, and Thur's grip tightened and held her on her feet.

They came to the base of the hill, and began climbing the road to the castle. No hope, no hope at all of sneaking in and taking Ferrante by surprise. Losimon soldiers were already running along the walls lighting torches. She could hear the rusty shriek of the portcullis being lowered. As she watched, the big heavy oak doors swung shut with a boom that matched the thunder echoing across the black lake.

"No," she cried, agonized. "Now what do we do? Ferrante can just wait in there until, until . . ."

Uri smiled over his shoulder. "Let us see." He paused a few yards from the castle gate. From above, a steel crossbow quarrel whacked into his shoulder, and stuck there. He shrugged, and brushed it away like a biting fly, and studied the gate. "Fiametta, warm me," he said.

"*Piro,*" said Fiametta, ordering the spell in her whirling mind with the greatest difficulty. But its familiarity steadied her. "*Piro. Piro.*"

Uri held up his sword-hand. " 'Tis enough, for now." He walked to the oak doors and leaned into them. The wood charred and burst into flame. He twisted his arms through the hole thus made and began elbowing and kicking the wood apart as if it were rotten punk. Burning chunks flew wide. Fiametta and Thur ducked and crouched in the ditch.

Uri stalked into the dark passageway between the two gate towers. A few paces further on the entrance to the courtyard was blocked by the grid of the portcullis. From the murder-hole above, a terrified Losimon soldier upended a pot of burning oil on Uri's head.

Uri threw back his face and laughed, a great bronze trumpeting. He turned under the stream of flame as under a refreshing shower, as a man might sport naked in a waterfall. In who-knew-what frenzy of mind the Losimons upended a second and third pot of oil after the first, before it dawned on some officer that it was doing them no good. Flames flared up, dancing and twisting, from Uri's glistening body as he swaggered, salamanderlike, to the portcullis.

He stuck his sword arm through one square of the cast-iron grid, wrapped it around a bar, and heaved backwards. The iron tore apart with a crack. Then another, another, another, till he could walk through upright, shoulders square. Fiametta picked up her skirts and dashed after him through the dying flames on the passageway floor, Thur on her heels. Thur paused to widen the gap in the portcullis with a few well-placed blows of the sledgehammer, for the convenience of those who came after. And there were men coming after, daring the few crossbow bolts from above that Ferrante's wit-scattered men managed to loose. They ran right and left, in groups of three and six, spreading into the castle to hunt down Montefoglia's tormentors. The mob behind them clogged the gate, then broke through.

Fiametta crouched on the cobbles, panting and watching. Uri strode into the courtyard, lighting it like a human torch. A gust of rain made him steam like a fumarole. "*UBERTO FERRANTE!*" he roared. The stones bounced back shuddering echoes. "Uberto Ferrante! Come out!"

Half a dozen Losimon swordsmen exited the castle door and spilled down the marble steps. Their offensive onslaught slowed and froze to defensive postures as they saw what called them. They glanced at each other in horror.

Lord Ferrante stepped outside, and swept his gaze over the court. He wore his gleaming chain mail, silver-gilt in the springing firelight, and his black leggings and boots. He wore neither hat nor helm, and a few raindrops glittered in his dark cap of hair like diamonds. He stood very still for a moment, then drew his sword with a slow, deliberate scrape that seemed to go on forever, and made Fiametta's teeth ache. He turned his head and shouted over his shoulder, "Niccolo!" He then raised his chin and stared briefly at the north gate tower, and lifted his blade in salute to someone Fiametta could not see, as if to say, *I dedicate this death to you.* Then, alert, sword ready, he stalked slowly down the stairs.

His guards, with backwards nervous glances, spread out in a screen before him. For a little time, till Uri raised his hands and started toward them. To a man, they broke and ran. Ferrante watched them go without surprise, a little ironic smile playing about his lips. But he did go so far as to open his mouth and bellow, "Niccolo!" again, louder. "Niccolo! To me, *now!*"

Did Ferrante sense himself to be outmatched? Fiametta thought so. And yet still he stood there on the last rain-silvered marble step, and did not retreat.

"He's evil," whispered Thur. "But . . ."

Fiametta felt it too. "Brave. Or fey." No wonder men followed this man. Fiametta had sometimes wondered why angels were reported to spend so many tears on sinners. *They do not weep for the evil. They weep for the good that is wasted in it.*

"So," said Ferrante, and moistened his lips. "Sandrino's incompetent guard captain rises from the waves like Venus. I thought we'd killed you."

"So," said Uri, with an attempt at matching irony.

"My incompetent murderer. Care to try again?" He lifted his red sword in invitation. Ferrante, Fiametta thought, did irony better. He had the style for it. But Uri's rage burned visibly, in rising waves of heat, and what his words lacked in bite they made up in power.

Ferrante cocked his head, half-smiling, and stepped off the stairway. "I think . . . you are in my secretary's department. But I shall do my best to entertain you till he arrives." And over his shoulder, his brows lowering and his lips rippling in irritation, "*Niccolo!*"

"What so occupies him, that he does not come running?" whispered Thur.

"I think I know," Fiametta whispered back, heartsick. But she could not yet race off through the castle searching for Papa; she had to stay with Uri, and keep him heated. Ferrante lunged.

The first flurry was brief. Ferrante's blade flicked past Uri's guard, but then clanged uselessly off the bronze skin. Ferrante skipped backwards, his stunned fingers flexing on his sword hilt, and the last irony left his face, to be replaced by an expressionless concentration. He closed again to try for a stab at Uri's yellow eyes, then recoiled, teeth clenched, hissing with pain, as Uri's attempt to brain him with the head of the Medusa brushed past his cheek and raised a swathe of instant white blisters.

"He cannot win, he's got to run. Why doesn't he run?" Fiametta whispered fiercely. She wanted Ferrante to run. Be a coward, yes, and utterly contemptible. But instead he closed on Uri again, clanging thrust and parry, parry—

"He's testing himself," Thur said suddenly. "He wants to be the best. He wants to *know* he's the best. And he wants everyone else to know it, too."

"He's mad."

"What is Uri about? Why doesn't he just pick up Ferrante and crush him?"

The method in Uri's attack came clear finally as he forced Ferrante to trip and fall backwards on the marble steps. Uri's sword lashed out and pinned him there, pressing into his chain mail in the identical spot to Uri's own mortal wound. Uri's face tightened in wrath, and he leaned on his sword with all the inhuman weight of his dense metal body.

"*Niccolo!*" screamed Ferrante. At last, a timbre of purely human terror.

He is brought down, thought Fiametta. *He is brought down.* But it gave her no joy.

The chain burst, and the sword drove through Ferrante's chest, searing flesh and quenching blade in one motion. Uri stood bent, holding Ferrante in place, for one long, long moment.

Vitelli flew out the castle door and cannonaded off the marble balustrade, his black, symbol-decked robe flaring. He brandished his right fist in triumph. Upon his index finger gleamed a gold band with a mask in the shape of the face of a bearded man. "My lord, I *have* it!"

Fiametta breathed a silent wail, her fists clenching hopelessly. *We were too slow. . . .*

Ferrante rolled his eyes up toward him and gasped out, "You're late . . . Niccolo. On purpose?"

"No, lord!" Vitelli screamed in horror, seeing him pinned there. A beat too late for conviction.

"Don't . . . lie to me, Niccolo. I hate a man who lies. I saw you, hovering in there. Waiting. Saw the whites of your eyes. Damn your eyes, Niccolo. . . ." His mouth opened and his face contorted in rictus agony as Uri put his foot to his chest and drew the sword back out.

For just a moment, Uri hesitated, staring warily up at the sorcerer with a face so strangely set as to almost make him appear inert metal in truth. Then, in two bounds, the marble cracking under him, Uri leapt up the stairs between Vitelli and the door. Vitelli launched himself one-handed over the balustrade, and jumped to the cobbled court. His knees bent, and he grunted with the force of his landing, but he straightened and danced back with room to move, his hands sweeping his velvet robe straight.

"I have you, simulacrum!" he screeched at Uri. "Cold will freeze you where you stand, and birds will nest in your ears!" He muttered, gestured; Uri, advancing determinedly upon him down the stairs, slowed. Uri's red glow faded, and his new bronze gleam shone instead, on his nose, ears, toes. With a tortured effort, he raised his sword arm.

"*Piro, piro, piropiropiro!*" Fiametta cried. Uri shook himself, red-hot all over, and began to move again, cat-footed across the stones, maneuvering for his cut. Fiametta fell to her hands and knees.

Vitelli shot Fiametta a look that said, *Later. And you'll wish that you'd never been born*, but then was forced to turn his entire attention upon Uri. He trod backwards, and rubbed his new ring. His low-voiced muttering became intent, then rose to a shout: "Thus I release you! Fly, unbonded, and be free!"

The bronze Uri stopped short. Vitelli, his eyes narrowing in triumph, straightened and strolled closer to inspect the frozen hero.

"*No,*" groaned Thur. "He has your Papa's spell, Fiametta! The one you said he used to release the baby spirit from Ferrante's first silver ring. We are undone! God help us, and Uri, too!" He hefted his sledgehammer, eyes rolling at Vitelli, and inhaled, ready to strike against the impossible odds. The smirking necromage circled around in front of the silent statue.

"No, wait," hissed Fiametta, scrambling up and clutching Thur's arm. "That's not right, it's not right, wait—!"

The bronze Uri grinned. His whisper reverberated off the castle walls.

"You cannot release me. *I am not bound.*"

In a vicious, whistling flat arc, he swung his sword full-force, and took Vitelli's head; but not before his words were heard and understood, so that the last expression on that black-browed face as it rotated through the air was of the most confounded dismay.

It landed, rolled, stopped.

Silence fell, and gusts of rain. Fiametta looked around. About a hundred people were watching, standing back all around the perimeter of the court. Three smudged white women's faces were pressed to the window slits in the north gate tower. Most of the witnesses were Montefoglian townsmen, with a few dazed Losimons being held at sword's point. Distant shouts, screams, and crashes wafted from odd corners of the castle as the last of Ferrante's men were winkled out by the mob. Vitelli's blood, pooling on the cobbles, steamed gently in the cold night air. Uri steamed, too, standing back in the rain; his red glow was darkening, and the gleam of metallic bronze beginning to frost his edges and surfaces. Cold, and a kind of lonely premonition, quenched the bright triumph of his eyes. He must go soon from his temporary metal body. *Go where?*

And where was Papa? She thought of the new gold ring on Vitelli's dead hand, and started toward it. She must retrieve it. Maybe Abbot Monreale would know what to do with it. It had to be possible to release Papa from the ring, and the ring from Vitelli's will, for how could one dead man be bound to another?

Ferrante too was crawling toward Vitelli's decapitated body, Fiametta saw with shock. The Lord of Losimo was not as dead as she'd thought. The hot blade must have cauterized as it cut, so that despite his crushed ribs Ferrante was not bleeding to death as fast as Uri had. His face was a clay-colored mask of determination and pain.

She raced him toward the ring. Thur followed with his hammer, though she did not think Ferrante was in any condition to offer further physical threats. Still there was a kind of weird glory in his unyielding will, that dragged his useless body across the rain-slicked stones.

But as she reached for Vitelli's right hand, a cold blast knocked her backwards with the force of a club. Ferrante, too, jerked back, one hand flung up to ward the invisible blow. The effort broke something loose inside, for he gasped once, then his dark eyes grew fixed, and closed no more. Fiametta crouched, open-mouthed, her eyes filling with the impossible.

A *form* was condensing over Vitelli's body, as if night were being made palpable. A dark man, a blackness much deeper than any shadow in this torch-lit court-yard. Inside the black man it seemed to Fiametta that she saw other little half-digested ghosts, dozens of them, deformed and agonized.

"Oh, no," choked Thur. "We've made another ghost! Will it never end?"

"No," breathed Fiametta, her chest tight with terror. "Worse. Much worse. We've made a *demon*." Where *was* Papa? Inside the dark man? One of those subghosts was very fresh, and in terrible pain.

The dark man's face awoke, sharpening into definite and familiar features. Vitelli's black eyes opened, and glittered with their own red glow. He looked almost as surprised as Fiametta. He turned his hands over, and stared at them in wonder. A shining light encircled one black finger. Vitelli threw back his head and laughed, as he realized his continued existence and power.

"It worked! I live! I am immortal now!" The dark man actually capered, and swept a wild ironic bow toward Uri, who stood freezing and stunned. "I thank you!"

She'd done it now, Fiametta thought miserably. Abbot Monreale, in one of his many sermons on the subject, had once described a sin as the making of a really irrevocable mistake, with permanent consequences. She stared out at her vast mistake, and thought: *The eighth deadly sin really is stupidity.* And ignorance. She had no idea how to fight a demon, none. But she was heart-certain that if Vitelli once escaped, the consequences would be dreadful.

"What have you done with my Papa?" she quavered to the Vitelli-demon.

She should not have attracted its attention, she realized as it bent those red eyes upon her. "His will is mine, now," Vitelli whispered in a voice like ice. "You are too late." It smiled a hellish smile. "*He* is too late, also." Its face rose toward the gate.

A horse's hooves clattered and scraped on the cobbles. Fiametta's heart leapt up, and she wanted to scream triumph and relief. It was Abbot Monreale, riding to their rescue on a white horse.

"Fiametta! Thur!" he shouted.

Her scream melted away in her throat as she took in the doubtful details. In the first place, there was the horse. She knew that horse. Even the cavalry saddle Monreale had borrowed from somewhere failed to conceal its swayed back. It stood wheezing and blowing, its nostrils red and round in its gray muzzle, its expression mournful and its legs trembling. Abbot Monreale must surely be a miracle worker beloved of God, for he had somehow forced the beast to trot uphill.

Monreale wore his gray monk's robe, rucked up with his bare legs sticking out and his sandals all awry from beating at the old horse's sides. His hands were a tangle, managing his crozier, the reins, and a couple of bottles. His hair stuck out as wildly as his bushy eye-brows, and he had a big lumpy purple bruise on his forehead. "Fiametta!" he cried again, and choked, as his eyes took in the tableau in the courtyard.

"I was going to say," he continued in a strange, mild, conversational tone, "Fiametta, whatever you do, don't kill Vitelli."

His gray eyes locked with the red ones of the dark man. Fiametta, gratefully, felt herself slide from Vitelli's dangerous attention. Everything about Monreale looked absurd, just now, except for his eyes.

Never breaking his gaze, Monreale swung his right leg over the white horse's sagging neck and jumped lightly down. He tucked the bottles into his robe, stood his crozier upright, and ran a hand thoughtfully down its length. He walked forward, then stopped with a jerk, as if feeling the same cold blow Fiametta had.

"Jacopo Sprenger. Though your spirit is parted from your body, you still partially exist in the world of will. While your will is free, you may yet effectively repent, confess your sins and profess your faith; I swear to you God is greater than any evil you can encompass. Stop. Stop now, and turn your face around!" Monreale's voice was anguished in its sincerity.

He had ridden through the night not to destroy Vitelli, but to save him, Fiametta realized. And she saw too a dreadful danger in it. Vitelli might try to trick Monreale, challenge him into dropping his guard. Despite all doubts, Monreale's own conscience would compel him to try Vitelli in all good faith. . . .

But Vitelli's pride in his power scorned to dissemble. The dark man crossed himself mockingly with an obscene gesture. The next gesture was something more effective, and when the swirling colors departed from Fiametta's eyes and the roaring from her ears, Abbot Monreale was on his knees, and *not* in prayer. He brandished his crozier, though, and counterattacked;

Vitelli seemed to shrink into himself, but only for a moment.

Uri could be no more help. He was freezing to cold bronze even as Fiametta watched, and there was not enough fire left in her spirit to make him hot again. She could not even stand up, but sank to her knees, then her hands and knees, and finally to the wet cobbles. Any passing Losimon could cut her throat this moment and she might do no more than look dully at him. Thur crouched worriedly beside her, and caught her shoulders.

The spirit ring. The gold gleamed on the corpse's hand, not two yards off. No wonder spirit-magic was so rare. So hard to acomplish, so fragile when invested! If only she knew her Papa's spell of unbinding—she pictured the moment, Ferrante's upraised hand, the crack and flash of the silver ring, the smell of burning flesh. . . .

But she *did* know rings. She had laid a little part of herself into the gold of her lion-ring. It was held there by . . . held there by . . . "Structure," she muttered muzzily. The spell had fallen into the molten metal like a seed crystal into the alum-water that the dyers used, and from it structure had feathered out like frost, intricate and beautiful. . . . The reverse must be . . . the reverse must be . . .

She rolled over on her face on the paving-stones a little way from that dead adorned hand. She had not enough power left to reanimate Uri, no. But she had some. Gold was a softer metal than bronze, and there was little more than a thimbleful in that ring. It was enough. It would do. . . .

"*Piro*," she whimpered. "*Piro*."

The gold mask sagged, slagged; the metal dripped as the flesh it encircled scorched, spattered, steamed and blackened. The acrid scent of burnt meat seared her nostrils.

The dark Vitelli screamed, as the band of light on his shadow-hand vanished. He whirled, his red eyes flaming rage, and focused on Fiametta. She smirked at him from the circle of Thur's arms, quite unable to move.

He seemed to inhale, towering up and up into a spindle of black smoke that slid sinuously into the open mouth of the bronze Medusa-head, held high in Uri's frozen left hand. The little snakes upon the skull turned cherry-red, and began to squirm. The head's eyelids slitted open in hot white lines. The face twisted slowly, and the ghastly eyes opened wide, and found Fiametta.

He will burn me to ashes where I lie. "Thur, get away! Get back!" She tried to twist from his protective arms, which tightened in distraught confusion.

And then, between her and that obscene head, the rain man appeared. He was made all of dense suspended diamond droplets, that glittered like tiny rainbows in the torchlight. He shone as bright and brilliant as the shadow-Vitelli was dark. He was amazingly beautiful. He wore a glittery pleated tunic, a big round hat like rain-brocade; his beard was fog, and his eyes were liquid and luminous.

"Papa," Fiametta breathed happily.

He blew her one kiss, or was it a raindrop landing chill on her skin? She rubbed her cheek in wonder, trembling.

A beam of incandescent fire lashed out in a double line from the Medusa's eyes. All the rain in its path turned to steam, boiling clouds of it, but the rain man reformed unharmed, only whiter for the added fog.

"Come *out* of there," demanded Master Beneforte querulously. "That's *mine*." He crouched, his hands cupped. With the slowness of tar, the black shape was drawn forth from the Medusa's mouth again. The rain man encompassed it. Fiametta could see it inside him, a spasming black mannikin, screaming in silence.

Master Beneforte turned to Abbot Monreale. "Quick, Monreale! Send us now, together, while I hold him! I cannot hold him long."

Monreale, his face stunned, levered himself up on his crozier. "Where . . . where does your body lie, Prospero?"

"The Swiss boy knows."

"Thur." Abbot Monreale turned to him. "Go at once—take these men"—for a couple of panting monks had arrived belatedly in Monreale's wake—"and fetch forth Master Beneforte's mortal remains. Hurry!"

Thur nodded, clutched his hammer, and ran across the courtyard, waving the monks to follow him. He disappeared into the castle by a side entry.

Gingerly, Monreale went to Vitelli's head, picked it up, and laid it beside the severed neck. He knelt, and made the rites, sprinkled water from one of his jars, and bent his head in prayer. The mannikin inside the rain-man convulsed, but then went quiescent.

When Monreale rose again, Master Beneforte remarked, "I liked your little sermon on will, just now. But then, I always liked your sermons, Monreale. They made me good for half a day after, at times."

"I would you could have heard them more often, then." A brief smile quirked Monreale's lips.

"You did warn us, how death comes suddenly to the unprepared. I was not prepared for it to come in this strange half-measure, though." He stepped closer to Monreale in a liquid shimmer, to be private, for the awed and astounded onlookers were venturing nearer. He lowered his voice to a whisper no louder than rain runneling on a shutter. "Bless me, Father, for I have sinned . . ."

Monreale nodded, and bent his head close. The voice rilled on until Thur appeared with a stiff, gauze-swathed shape, on a makeshift bier that looked like the lid of a pine crate. Monreale blessed the rain-shape, then turned to duplicate the rites upon the not-quite-abandoned body.

Fiametta crept to the rain man's side, and asked tremulously, "Did we cast it well, Papa? Your great Perseus?"

"An awful risk, for a couple of beginners—" he began, then stopped his critique in mid-word. He tilted his hat down at her, curiously, as if he were really seeing her for the first time, and half-smiled. "Well enough."

Only *well enough*? Well . . . that was Papa.

He added, "Marry the Swiss boy if you will, he's an honest young lout who will not betray you. You will not do better for any money. Speaking of money, Ruberta is to be given one hundred ducats, it is listed in my will, Lorenzetti the notary has it. Good-bye, be good—" His form wavered as the dark mannikin raged within. "And Fiametta, if you can't be good, at least be more careful!"

He turned to Monreale. "Father, your sermon is wearing off. Speed us. While I can still *will* to hold him."

"Go with God, my friend," whispered Monreale, and made the last sign of blessing.

The rain fell. And then there was nothing there at all.

Thur raised his hands in supplication to Monreale. "Father. Spare a blessing for Uri? My brother?"

Monreale blinked, and seemed to come back to himself. "Of course, boy." He turned awkwardly, almost stumbling; Thur caught his arm. Together, they inspected the statue. It was solidified in the pose in which it had first been cast, but the tiny glimmer of intelligence yet lingered, dimming, in its eyes. What sensations did that metal body bear him? The very heat that animated it made it impossible for Uri to embrace his brother, or kiss Fiametta good-bye.

Fiametta, on her knees, prayed for strength, and murmured "*Piro!*" one last time. Only the bronze lips flushed dark red.

"Father, bless me, for I have sinned," the hollow voice whispered like the faintest flute. "Though not nearly as much as I would have liked."

The corner of Monreale's mouth flicked up, but he murmured, "Don't joke. It wastes your little time."

"All my little time was wasted, Father," the fading voice sighed.

Monreale bent his head in acknowledgement. " 'Tis a fair complete confession. Do not despair, for it is a sin. Hope, boy."

"Shall I hope to rest? I am so tired. . . ."

"You shall rest most perfectly." By the time Monreale's hands had passed, nothing stood before them but a lifeless casting.

Not quite as it was first cast, Fiametta realized, looking up. The bland Greek face had not returned. Instead Uri's own distinct, alert, imperfect features were stamped permanently upon the bronze. There was even a touch of humor about the curve of the lips, most alien to the classic original.

And, she saw with a shiver, the Medusa's face too had changed. Black-browed Vitelli had the immortality he'd craved. Of a sort.

Chapter Nineteen

Thur held his palm near the statue's face. The bronze, though no longer glowing with its own light, was still too hot to touch. But Uri was no longer there to touch even if Thur could. The streaming rain would cool the metal soon enough. Thur raised his face to the sky, and let the cold drops mix with the hot ones from his eyes, disguising his grief before all these strangers. Their world would know Uri no more, would soon forget that he'd ever lived or laughed. *But I swear I will remember.*

When he'd blinked his vision clear, Thur saw that soldiers, Montefoglian soldiers, were arriving through the ruined gates. A couple of them pointed at the statue in startled recognition of their late captain's features, but then hurried about their work. Fiametta stood in the scintillating rain looking small, and exhausted, and very wet, her crinkly black curls escaping her braid only to be plastered flat to her skin. Thur wanted to offer her a cloak, but he himself possessed only the sodden old robe turned down around his loins. He rucked it back up over his shoulders and stood barefoot in the puddles and shivered, partly from cold, partly from reaction.

Fiametta turned her wan face to Monreale. "How did you come here, Father? When they carried you off to the infirmary at Saint Jerome under Vitelli's spell, you were lying almost as pale and still as a dead man yourself. Brother Mario wouldn't let me see you."

Monreale hung on his crozier, his sandaled feet apart. He tore his pensive gaze from the cooling bronze. "The spell was broken late yesterday evening. Was that your doing, Thur?"

"I . . . think it may have been, Father. I did not know for sure what spell was broken, but it distracted Vitelli when I swept a spell-set from the table. It was just before I escaped from the castle dungeon with my brother's body."

"Indeed," said Monreale. "I woke, but I was very sick. The healers kept me abed until morning, when I finally regained enough strength to ride over them. It was not until afternoon that I discovered you were gone from Saint Jerome, Fiametta, and no one seemed to know for how long. I sent out my birds, but could learn little except that Vitelli and Ferrante were not abroad, and Thur was not yet hanging by his neck from the castle tower.

"Sandrino's officers and I agreed we must attack, try as we'd planned yesterday. But I decided I must close the distance before attempting to grapple again with Vitelli. His powers had clearly grown to an extraordinary degree. We made ready, settling on a night assault to disguise our thin numbers." Wearily, he rubbed the back of his neck. His eyes narrowed and glinted with the press of these recent memories.

"We sallied out at dark, and had a sharp fight with

the besiegers that delayed us again. We finally broke through, and made for town. The soldiers needed the few horses we had, but a brother found that white one wandering among our sheep. Our remaining sheep. Is that the beast your Papa bought in Cecchino, Fiametta? He was robbed. Well . . . it saved my strength, I suppose.

"But when we all came up to the town gates, expecting a desperate battle, the Losimons were gone from them, pulled out by a mob of townsmen. So instead of leading the populace to the castle, we followed them. I had by then gained the idea that you were mounting some sort of magical attack, Fiametta, and I rode ahead as fast as I could, in great fear that Vitelli's demonic powers might indeed have grown so transcendent as to conquer death. And so it proved." Monreale vented a depressed sigh. "Not that this second-rate old man imagined himself a match for that dark power."

"Yet you came anyway," said Thur.

"Father, we would have been destroyed without you. In fact," Fiametta's brows drew down, puzzling this out, "none of us alone was a match for Vitelli. I could release Papa, but I could not hold Vitelli. Papa could hold Vitelli, but could not exorcise him. You could speed him to banishment, which thing neither Papa nor I were capable of . . . but only if he were held. And we could never have entered in here at all without Uri, who would not have been made without Thur. We may all of us be lesser folk, but we were a first-rate company together."

"Huh." Monreale smiled slowly, his eyes half-lidded. "Could that be the lesson God had been trying to teach me, all this time? From the mouths of babes."

"I am not a babe," said Fiametta with some determination.

"Child, from the vantage of my half-century, you *all* look like babes." Monreale pulled himself up by his crozier, straightening painfully. He gazed a moment more at the bronze statue. "No. You are not a babe. And so you stand in a grown woman's danger."

"Father," said Thur. "There's something you had better see, right away before it gets disturbed. I left one of your monks to guard the door."

Monreale nodded. "Lead me, boy. For there is much yet to do."

Thur beckoned him into the castle by the servant's entry and down the now-familiar corridors into the dungeon. At least they were out of the rain. A monk held a torch for his abbot. Thur was not sure how the stone-cut halls could be any darker at night than in the day, but they seemed so. The strength that relentless terror had lent him was passing off, and he bumped into the walls as he walked. Limped. Every muscle he owned seemed shot through with rust and grit, twinging when he moved, aching when he stood still.

The racks of iron bars that were the cell doors stood open; the prison was half-emptied of prisoners. The hale had already departed to join the fray. The injured were being helped out by Montefoglian townsmen, some of them relatives.

Thur's little procession wound down the stairway to the lower hall. A white-faced monk stood holding Thur's sledgehammer outside the shattered, splintered door to the necromancers' magic work chamber. They all entered after Monreale, and Thur took the one burning candle and lit the slagged remains of others from it.

Monreale's breath hissed out between his front teeth. The trestles were knocked over, and the salt crate dropped and split and spilled where Thur and a monk had snatched the lid in their haste to bring out Master Beneforte's body. Upon the floor spiraled a complex double diagram; one lobe was emptied— Thur had lifted up Master Beneforte's remains himself, when the frightened monk had refused to touch them—the other lobe framed yet another corpse. A naked young man, dreadfully mutilated, his throat slit.

"*That* was the power by which they finally forced Papa into the spirit ring," breathed Fiametta, peering fearfully around Monreale. "The new ghost. I *saw* him, inside Vitelli. Oh, Father." She turned, and closed her eyes, and swallowed hard.

That could have been himself, Thur thought, looking, but out of the corner of his eye. "Who is this poor wretch, Father?"

Monreale moistened his lips, and cautiously approached and knelt by the dead man's head. But whatever magic had been generated by this dark deed was apparently now consumed. "Yes. I know the boy. He's one of my brethren . . . his name was Luca. He is the monk I sent to spy two days before you, Thur, and heard no more of. Vitelli must have selected him for this from among the prisoners, after you escaped. He has a family in town, parents and brothers and sisters. . . . Murder, murder of the blackest." He bent his head in deep sorrow, and began the rites of blessing.

When he rose, Thur asked in worry, "Should we have this room boarded up, or something?"

Monreale sucked grimly on his lower lip, and walked around, muffling his shock, examining the evidence with the cool thoroughness of one who realizes he must soon write an official report upon it all. "Hm? No . . ." He gathered up the notes and papers on the worktable. "*These* should not be left about, however. No, Thur, quite the contrary. This room should be left open, and every guard and citizen who can should be brought to view it. Let the evidence of Vitelli and Ferrante's wrongdoing be made public before as many witnesses as can be gathered." He paused. "As many witnesses as saw a bronze statue get up and walk, and slay two men. At least that many witnesses."

He turned on his heel to face Thur and Fiametta. "You two know what you have done, and we will talk of it further. Later. The first reports to the Archdiocese, the Curia, and the general of my Order will be written by me. In the meantime . . . you may be certain that the most fantastical rumors will be flying among the people about tonight's events. I hope as many of those rumors as possible may attach to Vitelli, and not to yourself. Do you understand?"

Fiametta nodded rather doubtfully; Thur shook his head in honest bewilderment. Monreale motioned him over, and lowered his voice. "Look, boy. It is absolutely essential that Fiametta never come to be questioned by the Inquisition. They would burn her for her hot tongue alone at the end of the first day, the evidence go hang. Understand?"

"Oh . . ." Thur could see it, yes.

"If you love her, help her keep her head down and her mouth *shut*. Church politics are my department. If necessary, well, a man or two owes me a favor or two. But Fiametta must take care not to offend her neighbors, or to appear . . . too unusual. Or I might not be able to control all of the consequences."

"Uh . . . would getting married and setting up shop in her father's house be too . . . unusual?"

"No. That would be ideal. Her setting up shop *without* getting married, now *that* could be dangerous."

Thur brightened. "I'll help her all she'll let me, Father."

"You'd better be prepared to help her more than that, boy, if necessary," Monreale murmured dryly.

"With all my heart, sir."

Monreale gave Thur a short nod, and turned to go out. Thur paused for one last disturbed sidelong look at the sacrificed man lying in his pooled blood.

"He was . . . my scapegoat. Luca." He must remember that name, even as he hoped others would remember Uri's.

Monreale pursed his lips. "Yes, in a sense . . . though if you had died yesterday, it would not have saved him tonight. Still, I charge you to light a candle for him each Sunday in Montefoglia Cathedral, and pray for his soul."

"Yes, Father," said Thur, comforted.

Monreale nodded, and led them out.

While passing again through the now nearly deserted prison corridor, one level up, Thur heard a faint moan. "Wait . . ." He ducked back to the end cell. Sure enough, a bundled shape lay on the woven straw pallet. "Why has this door not been opened? Where is the key?" Thur called.

An elderly townsman appeared from the guard station, rattling the key ring. "They told us he was mad, sir. Is the proper sergeant coming, to take these?"

"I'll take them," said Monreale, unburdening the townsman of the ring. He passed it to Thur, who bent and opened the lock.

Lord Pia lay alone in the cell under a thin blanket. His face was very gray, and his glazed eyes seemed not to recognize Thur. The wound in his arm had never been bandaged, and was thickly clotted with blood. Judging by his mottled bruises, he had been badly beaten upon his final recapture. To satisfy his mind, Thur stuck his head out of the cell window. One bar remained at the side; around it were tied the points of a stretched-out silk hose leg, its foot in turn tied to another to make a rope of sorts, now hanging limp and wet against the cliff face. How very simple. Thur was both relieved and slightly disappointed. Lord

Pia had not flown down like a giant bat to Vitelli's dark chamber window last night after all. Thur imagined he would have liked to.

Monreale sent for help, and soon had the poor castellan laid on a plank and carried out of the dungeon before them by a sturdy monk and another townsman-parishioner. They all arrived back at the courtyard to find a swirl of shouting people coalescing around Duchess Letitia, who had been released from the tower. She had called Sandrino's surviving officers to her, and was organizing them to regain control of her castle, first from the remaining Losimons, and then from the Montefoglian townsmen. The Montefoglians, while scorning to steal from their late Duke directly, were not above relieving any captured or killed Losimon looters of their booty. Monreale was promptly drawn into the Duchess's whirlwind.

Lady Pia ran to her husband's side, looking distressed. Lord Pia seemed to recognize her, despite his debilitation and uncertain mental state. He smiled weakly up at her, and grasped her hand as she knelt by him. She immediately browbeat some passing men into carrying him upstairs to their apartments in the tower, once more a home and not a prison, and ruthlessly diverted a healer-monk in Monreale's train to her aid.

Somehow, the center of all this midnight chaos had shifted, from them to Monreale to the Duchess. Thur was just as glad. The rain was letting up, turning to a fine misting drizzle. Thur put his arm around Fiametta's shivering shoulders.

"I guess we can take your Papa's body home, now."

"If my house is still standing. What . . . what of Uri?"

"You mean the statue? Leave it, I suppose. It's only a statue, now. Nobody's going to steal him without the aid of a couple of yokes of oxen."

She nodded, her eyes wide in the wavering half-light. They picked their way to the crate lid resting on the cobbles with its shrouded burden. "Thur, I don't think I can carry my half," she worried.

"I don't think I could either, right now," Thur said honestly. "D'you want your horse back?"

The white horse was sniffing dolefully at the cobbles, where no grass grew. It had not wandered far, and for some reason no one had attempted to abscond with it while Monreale's back was turned. Thur captured it by walking up to it and scratching it behind the ears. It rubbed its head against him, scraping Thur's skin on the bridle studs and shedding wet white hairs.

Thur handed the reins to Fiametta, and went to look for a piece of rope. He found a coil hanging on a nail in the stables. No one disputed his claim of it. He tied one end of the rope to a stirrup, wound it around the headboard of the crate lid, and tied the other end to the other stirrup, converting the lid to a makeshift drag or sledge. The white horse flared its nostrils in worry at the scraping sound behind it, and sidled, giving Thur a mad vision of the beast bolting across the country with Master Beneforte thudding and bouncing along behind in one last wild ride. But after a moment the horse settled down to its usual tired plod, and Thur judged it safe to help Fiametta aboard. She wrapped her hands in the long mane, and drooped over the animal's thick neck. Thur led them out the ruined castle gate and down the hill.

The streets of Montefoglia were growing quieter as the night waned. They passed only two small groups of excited men with torches, who yet swung as wide as the narrow streets permitted around Thur's little cavalcade. Thur was too tired to do anything but ignore them. They arrived at the wrecked oak door to Fiametta's house without being accosted. The walls were still standing, nor had the tile roof fallen in. That was nice, if unexpected.

Thur helped Fiametta down; she stumbled inside. His fingers numb, Thur picked at the knots in the rope, and freed the crate lid. By that time Tich came out with a lantern and led the horse around to the high gate into the back garden.

Together, they tied it out of range of the spring onions and lettuces of the kitchen vegetable plot. Tich brought the beast a bucket of water, which it drank thirstily, with a grateful snuffle that blew slobber all over him. In the general filth and soot of Tich's tunic it was scarcely noticeable.

"We'll have to find it fodder in the morning," Tich said in a tone of judicious expertise. "This little bit of grass won't last."

"Not the way it eats. I'll help you go look for your mules tomorrow, too."

Tich nodded, satisfied, and they locked the garden gate. Tich helped Thur carry Master Beneforte's plank inside, to lay in the front room next to Uri's; someone had moved him to rest again in this quieter place.

"They should be buried soon," said Thur. "Properly."

"There's going to be a lot of funerals tomorrow in Montefoglia, from what we've heard," said Tich.

"They'll make room for these two," said Thur. "I'll make them make room."

"Ruberta has put bedrolls for us in the front hall," said Tich. "She says we can guard the door that way till it's fixed."

Thur half-smiled. "I don't think anyone is going to bother this house." *Bedroll.* What a beautiful word. Thur could have wept at the beautiful charity of someone making a bedroll for him.

Tich retired to his bedroll before it had entirely cooled, but Thur stumbled one last time into the courtyard. A light shone there, candle or lantern—both, he saw, entering. Fiametta had stuck a candle-stub upright in the dirt beside the empty casting pit, and was holding up a lantern for closer inspection of the damages.

The place looked like a midden. Abandoned furnace, empty casting pit, broken-up furniture, scattered tools. The center of one side of the gallery was gone, the whitewash above it was black with smoke stain, and charred timbers swung dangerously loose in the corners.

"They got the fire out," Thur noted brightly.

"Yes," said Fiametta. "Ruberta and Tich and the neighbors. I did not know . . . I had such friends." She sat down heavily upon the cinder-scattered flagstones in her sodden velvets. "Oh, Thur! My poor house is a shambles!"

"Now. Now." Gingerly, he eased himself down beside her and stroked her shaking shoulders. "Maybe it won't look that bad in the morning. I'll help you fix it up. That gallery's the easy part. I used to help build mine-timbering, you know. I can build you a gallery that won't *ever* come down."

Her breath puffed out between her quivering lips, whether in a laugh or a sob Thur could not tell. "Is there anything you can't do?"

"I don't know." Thur considered this. "I haven't tried everything."

Her brows rose quizzically. "Do you want to try everything?"

He took a breath, for courage. "I'd like to try being your husband."

She blinked, rapidly, and rubbed her eyes with a soot-smudged hand. "I'd be a bad wife. My tongue is too sharp. Everybody says so. You'd get henpecked."

Thur wrinkled his brows. "Was that yes, or no? Come. Where else will you find a fellow brave enough to marry a girl who can set him on fire with a word?"

"I'd never!" Her spine straightened. "But truly. I talk a lot—Papa said so—and I'm not very patient."

"I'm very patient," Thur offered. "I'm patient enough for us both."

"You weren't very patient with the caking bronze." Her lips curved up.

"Yes, well . . . it wasn't right. I needed it to be excellent." *He* needed to be eloquent. He shouldn't be trying to say these things when he was so damned tired he couldn't even see straight. He looked up, and was startled by an orange tinge outlined by the shadowy black square of the tile roof. Was the town afire? "Why is the sky that funny color?"

Fiametta looked up, too. "It's dawn," she said after a long moment. "The clouds are breaking up."

So it was. An apricot luminosity edged slate-blue masses. "Oh." His brains felt like porridge.

Fiametta giggled, and sniffled. *She* ought to be in a bedroll, and in a dry gown, too. He gathered her into his lap, and hugged her for warmth. She did not object. In fact, she twined her arms around his neck. And so they sat for a time, while the sky lightened.

"It looks worse," Fiametta observed in a dreamy voice.

"Huh?" Thur jerked awake.

"It looks worse. In the morning."

He stared over her rat's nest of hair at the wreck of a courtyard. "Well. Yes."

Fiametta's nose wrinkled. "Yes."

"Yes what?" Thur asked after a minute's pause decided him that he no longer had any idea what they were talking about.

"Yes. I want to marry you, too."

"Oh. Good." He blinked, and hugged her closer.

"I think it's because you understand excellence. What it takes."

"What is?"

"Why I love you."

A slow grin fought its way onto his exhaustion-numbed face. "Of course. That's why I love *you*."

Epilogue

By design, the high light of midsummer morning falling through the clerestory windows sent a beam directly down upon the altar of Montefoglia Cathedral. The light caught the garnet of the lion ring as Fiametta slipped it onto Thur's finger. The gem blazed like a ruby, like a star. The gold lion mask seemed to purr under Fiametta's hand, like the most satisfied and cream-stuffed of great cats. Thur felt it too, Fiametta thought, for he smiled like a great cream-stuffed cat himself. He caught her in an embrace that bent her ribs, till Bishop Monreale cleared his throat, and they took the hint and turned obediently, hand in hand, to receive his final benediction. Fiametta could not decide if Monreale looked more at home in his plain gray monk's habit, or as now, splendid in the flowing silk, red cloak, and high mitered hat of the bishophric. Equally easy, perhaps. Monreale was not made by his garments, and so his clothes always conformed to him.

Thur's clothes did not make him, she mused, so much as reveal him. She kept sipping little contented glimpses from the corner of her eye even while bowing her head. He had not let her see his wedding garments till this morning, a conspiracy between himself, Ruberta, and the tailor. Fiametta and Thur had frugally divided the purchase of a length of silk between them, so his green tunic matched her overgown. Still, the clever tailor had squeezed enough material for proper pleats. Thur's upright bearing made the modest decorative braid on the sleeves and hem look restrained rather than plain. And many a spindle-shanked rich lord might envy the calves that most perfectly filled those white silk hose. New polished shoes, and no one needed to know he only had one other pair of boots. His bright blond hair was topped by a fine big dark green cloth hat with a copper-gilt badge of Fiametta's own design. *Eat your hearts out, ladies of Montefoglia. He's mine.*

Fiametta had cast her own wedding ring—without ensorcellments, this time—in the mask of a lioness. Its tiny gold teeth closed on a green-faceted chip borrowed from the eye of her silver snake-belt; the gems upon testing had proved to be real emeralds. That chaste snake must just wink a while, till she could afford a replacement stone. She turned her hand a little to make the green flash, and smirked into her lap.

They turned from the altar to collect kisses and hugs and hearty congratulations from the witnesses, each according to their style; Lorenzetti the notary shook hands, Tich pecked her cheek, Ruberta embraced everyone, and dabbed at her eyes. Thur's mother grasped Fiametta's hands, and gave her a warm smile, though her swimming eyes were still tinged with a searching doubt. Time would put those doubts to rest,

Monreale had assured Fiametta privately. Fiametta smiled back in earnest hope thereof.

Tich had escorted Mistress Ochs personally from Bruinwald, on his first round-trip with his pack mules. He had finally managed to recover all but two of the lost beasts. His eager personal persuasion and good offices had much to do with prying the aging woman from her familiar cottage and carrying her on this mixed adventure, fraught with both sorrow and joy, to visit one son's grave and the other's wedding. Thur and Fiametta had awaited her arrival anxiously, as the date of their wedding had been agreed between them to be the day after her arrival. She seemed a quiet woman, obviously devoted to Thur; perhaps that was enough mutual interest upon which to start building her acquaintance with her new daughter-in-law. She had clearly been thrilled by his new clothes.

Before leaving the cathedral they stopped into one of the side chapels. This holy chamber had been the recipient, over a year ago, of a noble gift from Master Beneforte's hand: a fine carved marble crucifix with a white Christ upon a black marble cross, now affixed to the wall with its iron clamps. In exchange, the building committee had permitted his humble request: space for a stone sarcophagus beneath Our Lord's feet. Fiametta did not think this represented morbid premonition, exactly, because he had not then ordered the sarcophagus. The stonecutters she'd hired had placed the tomb only a week ago, but at least it was in time for her to kneel and lay her wedding flowers upon it. "Peace, Papa," she whispered.

To her gnawing regret, she had not found her mother's death mask again. It had been nowhere in the patiently sorted shambles of her house, nor had her inquiries among neighbors who had recovered portions of their looted possessions borne fruit. Even Thur's peculiar talent proved no help this time, though he had walked for hours, absent-faced with concentration, quartering Montefoglia. The bronze mask must have been carried out of the city.

I am a sorceress. If I truly seek, I must find you at last, Mama, Fiametta made silent oath. *Someday. Someday.*

When she rose she found Monreale standing back looking at the Christ, meditating artistically rather than theologically, for he said, "It's very fine. The proportions are strange, yet they hold the eye and the mind."

"He did not use a model. It was from a vision, Papa told me, that he had when he was in prison in Rome once upon . . . uh . . . what he said were false charges."

"Yes, I heard that tale from him. The vision, at least, was true," Monreale mused. "Well, he rests now under better eyes than mine. It is good for him to have such a guardian.

"Speaking of guardians," he turned to her, "I have a wedding present for you." From his robe he drew a folded piece of parchment, and handed it to her.

She crackled it open eagerly, read, and bounced twice into the air. "*Wonderful!* My Guild permit! Now I can make and sell spells, as well as metal bagatelles!"

"Only such as are inspected and approved for your level of license," he cautioned. "You are officially listed as my apprentice, so I am in part responsible for the consequences of your actions. I will not be able to watch you daily as an ordinary master would, but you may be sure I will inspect your shop frequently." He mustered a stern frown for emphasis. "I'll have no more such Beneforte tricks as your Papa played upon me, now!"

"No, sir!" Fiametta danced, and hugged Thur. "Now we're truly in business!" He grinned, reflecting back her shining delight.

Monreale lowered his voice to her ear alone. "I mean that most seriously, Fiametta. I had to use the utmost care, in dealing with the committee from the Inquisition over the matter of the late and damned Vitelli, to keep you out of it. As far as any official report states, Uri's spirit got into that casting by itself, as an accidental result of Vitelli's machinations. I do not recommend that you draw their attention twice."

"It *was* by itself," Fiametta argued *sotto voce*. "I did not compel, I only channeled him."

"I tried not to trouble their minds with that subtle distinction. Consider the matter sealed under my authority as your master, and do not discuss it without my permission. Eh?"

Fiametta smiled. "Yes—Master."

Monreale nodded, grimly satisfied. With blessings all round he excused himself to attend to the Diocese, and the chancellory business that had come upon him as he found himself chief advisor to Duchess Letitia in her unaccustomed role as Regent for little Duke Ascanio.

The wedding party spilled out into the beautiful morning light on the cathedral steps. Ruberta and Lorenzetti headed back on foot to the house, to supervise the laying of the tables and the tapping of the wine cask, respectively, before all the neighbors who had helped put out the house fire arrived for the fete. "I don't trust that hired girl with my pastries," Ruberta sniffed. The kobolds had not been invited; in fact, Fiametta had not even seen one of the shy gnomes since that wild night of spell and metal casting. But the bowl of goat's milk she laid out nightly on the floor of the root cellar was always empty the next morning.

Thur helped his mother up onto a white mule, borrowed from Tich, and Fiametta up onto their white horse. Fiametta herself had spent yesterday afternoon shampooing both beasts and scrubbing them clean of every manure stain. She'd pinned old sheets around them overnight to protect her labors. Both animals' hooves were blacked with polish and their manes and tails braided with colored ribbons. The white horse's swayed back was built up with enough pads and flowers to look almost normal, and Fiametta happily arranged her green brocade outer skirt and cream-white inner skirt over the rugs. As if in response to all this attention the old horse arched its neck and stepped out finely. Thur walked between the two mounted women. They wound through the streets and headed up the hill toward Montefoglia castle.

The battlements seemed to glow, sunny and open, not the midnight-sinister pile of stone they had been in the rain-swept dark of that terrifying night six weeks ago. Only six weeks ago? It seemed a world past. When the word of the deaths of their leader and his dark advisor had arrived, the Losimon army had turned away at the border fords and marched back to their own capital. A Ferrante cousin appointed heir by the Curia was presently scrambling for political control there, and in no mood to seek extra trouble from his new neighbors.

The animals' hooves clopped, echoing off the stone walls, as the women rode through the tower-flanked gate into a busy and noisy castle courtyard. Blacksmiths were at work repairing the portcullis, and their laborers stoked a portable forge. Lord Pia, dressed in summer linens and an Egyptian cotton shirt, leaned on a cane supervising. Under his wife's devoted care he'd made a good recovery, though appearing more frail, as his hair was grayer and he'd lost some of his robust girth. Except for a certain uncharacteristic hesitancy, his tone of mind was much improved from the over-stressed dementia of those days of madness, magic, and murder. He recognized Fiametta, and favored her with a friendly wave of his hand. Fiametta waved back while trying to look very busy, lest he come over and corner Thur again for more talk of his proposed bat-wing experiments.

The bronze Perseus/Uri had been raised to its stone plinth, square in front of the marble staircase. And so Duke Sandrino's captain guarded his house for all time. Fiametta still bit her lip in frustration that the Duchess had chosen to entrust the finishing details to di Rimini, and not to Fiametta. She trusted Papa was truly sped far from this world of woe; even his ghost would have been livid at the thought of his greatest work fallen into the hands of his rival, though he would probably have been almost equally horrified at the thought of it in the hands of his daughter. Well . . . di Rimini appeared to have done a competent job, so far. At least the thing hadn't fallen over yet.

One could only carry on. The Duchess, frugal in the uncertain days of her new widowhood, had elected not to have the body of the Medusa cast to lie at the Perseus's feet and complete the tableau, but to mount the statue as it was. This saved that work from going to di Rimini, but also gave her the excuse to knock a full half off the payment Papa had thought to get from Duke Sandrino.

Thur read these tense thoughts from Fiametta's face; she'd expressed them often and vigorously enough to his ear. Lifting her down from the horse before the bronze, he kissed her forehead and whispered, "Daily bread, love."

She nodded, and sighed in resignation. The half-payment, plus the residue of monies still owed on the saltcellar, had at least settled all of Papa's debts. After buying new tools for the shop and setting aside enough to live on until business was established, Thur had stretched it further by doing repairs on the wrecked house himself. His new gallery looked sturdy enough for the Sultan's elephants to dance upon.

New furniture and fine clothes could wait. Thur had

cooled her tongue by pointing out that God only promised daily bread, not a bakery. And indeed, the Duchess had soon given her a commission for some silver and pearl jewelry for Julia. And where the Duchess shopped, all the great ladies of Montefoglia must soon follow.

They laid the armload of flowers they'd brought at the bronze Uri's feet, and Fiametta stood back respectfully to let Thur's mother gaze, one last unexpected time, upon the features of her lost son. Would she appreciate the beautiful flowing form, the dramatic pose, the perfection of the casting? Would she be moved at this monument to his memory and his courage?

"Thur," the aging lady said in a choked voice, "he's *naked.*" Her hand touched her lips in dismay.

"Well, yes, Mama," said Thur, placatingly phlegmatic. "That's the way the Italians make their statues. Maybe it's because of the hot climate."

"Oh, dear."

Thur scratched his head, looking as if he was wondering if he ought to jump up on the plinth and affix a bouquet in a strategic spot, to console her.

But she overcame her horror enough to quaver politely, "It's . . . it's very fine. I'm sure." *But he's naked!* Fiametta could almost hear her wail in her thoughts.

Fiametta, uncertain whether to smile or snarl, bit her fingers and said nothing. She raised her eyes to the bronze face under the winged helmet, those metal lips curled faintly at the corners, and knew.

Uri would have laughed.

Author's Note

For the curious book lover, I'd like to add a word on the principal historical sources for *The Spirit Ring*.

This novel started with a book—three books, to be precise, all with family connections, which sat side by side on my bookshelf for years. The first seed from my family tree, and surely the rarest book among my inspirations, was a scholarly monograph published in 1907 titled *The Grateful Dead, The History of a Folk Story*, written by my great uncle Gordon Hall Gerould, B. Litt. (Oxon.), Preceptor in English in Princeton University. It came down through my mother's side of the family. In 174 densely written pages Uncle Gordon traced the history, through about twenty countries and twenty centuries, of a very old folk tale of that name. The fast-forward version goes: Young man goes out to seek his fortune, and comes across an altercation where the body of a debtor lies unburied until his debts are paid. Our hero forks over his grubstake (varying wildly depending on the version, but always the whole of his resources) and gets the debtor planted. He goes on down the road to further adventures, in the course in which he finds himself supernaturally aided by the grateful ghost of the dead man, in reward for his pious deed.

It was quite clear from the wide range of versions, studding the monograph like little dried raisins and crying out to have the life pumped back into them, that here was a universal theme of great power.

Enter two more books, inherited from my engineer-father's extensive and eclectic bookshelf. *De Re Metallica* by Agricola is a 16th century Latin treatise on mining and metallurgy, translated into English by Herbert and Lou Henry Hoover. (Yes, the President. He was a mining engineer before he was a politician. His wife was also a Latin scholar.) Agricola inspired *The Spirit Ring*'s hero, the self-effacing Swiss miner's son Thur Ochs. The kobolds came from a footnote therein. And *The Autobiography of Benvenuto Cellini* of course yielded up Prospero Beneforte, and a great deal more besides. Agricola is not light reading, but I highly recommend Cellini to all comers. In it you will discover the golden saltcellar, the bronze Perseus, the mad castellan, the vision in the dungeon of the Castel Sain' Angelo, and a thousand other delightful or horrifying details of the times, as well as that wonderful egotistical monster, Cellini himself.

A couple dozen more research books followed in my reading (you will find Lorenzo d'Medici's spirit ring in the gorgeously illustrated *Europe 1492* by Franco Cardini), but these three were the generative seeds.

Cellini leaves no record of ever having had a daughter. Fiametta is my own creation.

PRAISE FOR
LOIS MCMASTER BUJOLD

What the critics say:

The Warrior's Apprentice: "Now here's a fun romp through the spaceways—not so much a space opera as space ballet.... it has all the 'right stuff.' A lot of thought and thoughtfulness stand behind the all-too-human characters. Enjoy this one, and look forward to the next." —Dean Lambe, *SF Reviews*

"The pace is breathless, the characterization thoughtful and emotionally powerful, and the author's narrative technique and command of language compelling. Highly recommended."
—*Booklist*

Brothers in Arms: " ... she gives it a genuine depth of character, while reveling in the wild turnings of her tale.... Bujold is as audacious as her favorite hero, and as brilliantly (if sneakily) successful." —*Locus*

"Miles Vorkosigan is such a great character that I'll read anything Lois wants to write about him. ... a book to re-read on cold rainy days." —Robert Coulson, *Comic Buyer's Guide*

Borders of Infinity: "Bujold's series hero Miles Vorkosigan may be a lord by birth and an admiral by rank, but a bone disease that has left him hobbled and in frequent pain has sensitized him to the suffering of outcasts in his very hierarchical era. ... Playing off Miles's reserve and cleverness, Bujold draws outrageous and outlandish foils to color her high-minded adventures." —*Publishers Weekly*

Falling Free: "In *Falling Free* Lois McMaster Bujold has written her fourth straight superb novel.... How to break down a talent like Bujold's into analyzable components? Best not to try. Best to say: 'Read, or you will be missing something extraordinary.' " —Roland Green, *Chicago Sun-Times*

The Vor Game: "The chronicles of Miles Vorkosigan are far too witty to be literary junk food, but they rouse the kind of craving that makes popcorn magically vanish during a double feature." —Faren Miller, *Locus*

MORE PRAISE FOR
LOIS MCMASTER BUJOLD

What the readers say:

"My copy of *Shards of Honor* is falling apart I've reread it so often. . . . I'll read whatever you write. You've certainly proved yourself a grand storyteller."

—Lisa Kolbe, Colorado Springs, CO

"I experience the stories of Miles Vorkosigan as almost viscerally uplifting. . . . But certainly, even the weightiest theme would have less impact than a cinder on snow were it not for a rousing good story, and good story-telling with it. This is the second thing I want to thank you for. . . . I suppose if you boiled down all I've said to its simplest expression, it would be that I immensely enjoy and admire your work. I submit that, as literature, your work raises the overall level of the science fiction genre, and spiritually, your work cannot avoid positively influencing all who read it."

—Glen Stonebraker, Gaithersburg, MD

" 'The Mountains of Mourning' [in *Borders of Infinity*] was one of the best-crafted, and simply best, works I'd ever read. When I finished it, I immediately turned back to the beginning and read it again, and I can't remember the last time I did that."

—Betsy Bizot, Lisle, IL

"I can only hope that you will continue to write, so that I can continue to read (and of course buy) your books, for they make me laugh and cry and think . . . rare indeed."

—Steven Knott, Major, USAF

THE SHIP WHO SANG IS NOT ALONE!

Anne McCaffrey, with Mercedes Lackey, S.M. Stirling, and Jody Lynn Nye, explores the universe she created with her groundbreaking novel, The Ship Who Sang.

THE SHIP WHO SEARCHED
by Anne McCaffrey & Mercedes Lackey

Tia, a bright and spunky seven-year-old accompanying her exo-archaeologist parents on a dig, is afflicted by a paralyzing alien virus. Tia won't be satisfied to glide through life like a ghost in a machine. Like her predecessor Helva, *The Ship Who Sang*, she would rather strap on a spaceship!

THE CITY WHO FOUGHT
by Anne McCaffrey & S.M. Stirling

Simeon was the "brain" running a peaceful space station—but when the invaders arrived, his only hope of protecting his crew and himself was to become *The City Who Fought*.

THE SHIP WHO WON
by Anne McCaffrey & Jody Lynn Nye

"The brainship Carialle and her brawn, Keff, find a habitable planet inhabited by an apparent mix of races and cultures and dominated by an elite of apparent magicians. Appearances are deceiving, however . . . a brisk, well-told often amusing tale. . . . Fans of either author, or both, will have fun with this book."   —*Booklist*